✓ P9-BBQ-165

Praise for *The Vacation*

One of the *New York Post*'s "30 Best Summer Books to Help You Escape 2020"

"The tantalizing twists, enjoyably written from various characters' viewpoints, culminate in an unexpected ending . . . Logan specializes in portraying the lasting effects of split-second decisions; his fans will enjoy another take on that theme here."   —*Booklist*

"The twists come fast and furious . . . fans of plot-driven domestic thrillers won't be disappointed."
                                        —*Publishers Weekly*

"A summer page-turner . . . Logan advances this irresistible story with intelligent pacing."
                                        —*Fredericksburg Free Lance-Star*

"Irresistible."   —*Minnesota Star Tribune*

Praise for *29 Seconds*

"Logan spins out suspense to the final pages in this timely #MeToo thriller."   —*Booklist*

Praise for *Lies*

"Positively riveting."

—Sandra Brown, #1 *New York Times*
bestselling author

"Assured, compelling, and hypnotically readable."
—Lee Child, *New York Times* bestselling author

"A tense and gripping thriller."

—B.A. Paris, bestselling author of
Behind Closed Doors

"This jaw-dropping psychological thriller is a twisted
page-turner that will keep you guessing!"

—*InTouch Weekly*

"A whodunit of the best kind."   —*Shelf Awareness*

"A fast-moving joyride of nerve-wracking suspense and
intrigue."   —*Library Journal*

"Gripping . . . full of unexpected twists and turns."
—*Publishers Weekly*

"An adrenaline-fueled page-turner."

—*Kirkus Reviews*

ALSO BY T. M. LOGAN

Lies
29 Seconds

THE VACATION

T. M. LOGAN

GLOUCESTER COUNTY LIBRARY
389 WOLFERT STATION ROAD
MULLICA HILL, NJ 08062

St. Martin's Paperbacks

NOTE: If you purchased this book without a cover you should be aware that this book is stolen property. It was reported as "unsold and destroyed" to the publisher, and neither the author nor the publisher has received any payment for this "stripped book."

This is a work of fiction. All of the characters, organizations, and events portrayed in this novel are either products of the author's imagination or are used fictitiously.

Originally published in Great Britain under the title *The Holiday* by Zaffre, Bonnier Books UK.

Published in the United States by St. Martin's Paperbacks, an imprint of St. Martin's Publishing Group.

THE VACATION

Copyright © 2019 by Logan Communications Ltd.

All rights reserved.

For information, address St. Martin's Publishing Group, 120 Broadway, New York, NY 10271.

www.stmartins.com

Library of Congress Catalog Card Number: 2019059157

ISBN: 978-1-250-79718-6

Our books may be purchased in bulk for promotional, educational, or business use. Please contact your local bookseller or the Macmillan Corporate and Premium Sales Department at 1-800-221-7945, ext. 5442, or by email at MacmillanSpecialMarkets@macmillan.com.

Printed in the United States of America

St. Martin's Press hardcover edition published 2020
St. Martin's Paperbacks edition published 2021

10 9 8 7 6 5 4 3 2 1

For my brothers,
Ralph and Ollie

It is easier to forgive an enemy than to forgive a friend.

—William Blake

The fly circles, and lands.

Crawls undisturbed on cooling skin.

An outstretched finger.

An open palm, smeared red.

An arm bent backward, bone broken against the rock.

More flies circle around the head, drawn by the scent of death.

Drawn by blood pooling darkly around the shattered skull.

Below, blood drips steadily into the clear mountain stream.

Above, a cliff edge sharp against the perfect blue sky.

SATURDAY

I

We drove north, away from the coast.

Through the outskirts of Béziers and deeper into the Languedoc. Vineyards heavy with fruit lined the road on both sides, ranks of low green vines marching off into the distance under a deep blue Mediterranean sky. Sean driving, his eyes hidden behind aviator shades, the kids in the back with hand luggage wedged between them, Lucy dozing while Daniel plays on his phone, me staring out the window as the scenery rolls by, the rental car's AC just about keeping the sticky midafternoon heat at bay.

If I'd known what was coming, what we were driving toward, I would have made Sean stop the car and take us straight back to the airport. I would have grabbed the steering wheel myself, forced the car off the road, and made him do a U-turn right there.

But I didn't know.

My instincts had been telling me for a couple of weeks, as we wound down toward the summer holidays, that *something* was up. Something was wrong. Sean had always been the one to look on the bright side, to make the kids laugh, to bring me a gin and tonic when I needed cheering up. In the unconscious allocation of roles in our marriage, I was the organizer, the rule-setter, the guardian of boundaries. Sean was the light to my shade—always open, funny, patient, the optimist of the family.

Now he was defensive, secretive, serious. Distracted, constantly staring at his phone. Perhaps work was getting on top of him—hassle from his new boss? He'd half suggested that maybe he should stay at home this week, because of work. Or perhaps it was his fear of reaching forty, which seemed to grow stronger as his birthday drew nearer. Some kind of midlife crisis? I'd asked him if he thought he might be depressed—if I knew what was wrong, we could tackle it together. But he had brushed my questions aside, insisting he was fine.

I flinched as he touched my thigh.

"Kate?"

"Sorry," I said, forcing a smile. "Miles away."

"How long until we turn off this road?"

I checked my phone.

"About another ten minutes."

He took his hand off my thigh and moved it back to the steering wheel. The warmth of his fingertips lingered for a moment and I tried to remember the last time I'd felt his touch, the last time he had reached out to me. Weeks? A month?

The fact that you're even thinking it means something isn't right. That's what Rowan would have said. The holiday had been her idea, two years in the planning. Rowan, Jennifer, Izzy, and me—best friends marking our fortieth birthdays with a week together in the south of France, husbands and children included.

"Grand," Sean said. "You OK?"

"Fine. Just want to get there, get unpacked."

"Have you heard from Jennifer and Alistair?" He glanced up at the rearview mirror. "Since they lost us?"

"No, but I'm sure they're not far behind."

"I *told* them I'd lead the way and they could follow."

I turned to look at my husband. It wasn't like him to worry about Jennifer and her husband—he got along with them OK but had little in common with them, apart from me.

"You know what Alistair's like," I said. "He could get lost in his own back garden."

"Sure, I suppose you're right."

I went back to staring out the window at the lush green vineyards rolling past, dark grapes ripening in the summer heat. Off in the distance, the conical black towers of an ancient château stood out against the skyline.

After ten miles or so, Google Maps directed us off the main road and up through one tiny hamlet after another. Puimisson, Saint-Geniès, Cabrerolles—sleepy villages of narrow streets and ancient stone, old men sitting impassively in the shade watching us pass by. We peeled off onto an even smaller road that climbed

higher, winding back and forth up a hill where the vineyards gave way to dark pine trees, finally emerging
onto the crest of a hill above the village of Autignac,
a tall, whitewashed wall flanking the road. The wall
ended in black metal gates tipped with faux spear-
points, and my phone informed us that we had arrived
at our destination.

Sean slowed the car to turn in and the black metal
gates swung noiselessly open. Gravel crunched softly
beneath the wheels as we turned onto the estate and
headed for the villa, tall cypress trees, slim and straight
and perfectly pruned, lining the long driveway like a
guard of honor. On both sides were lush lawns of thick
green grass, watered by sprinklers circling lazily in
the midafternoon heat.

Sean pulled up next to Rowan's Land Rover Discovery, already parked in front of the villa's sweeping
stone staircase.

I turned in my seat. Lucy was still asleep in the
back, head tucked into her balled-up sweatshirt, long
blond hair falling across her face. Since hitting her
teens she seemed able to sleep anywhere, at any time
of the day, if she sat down for more than ten minutes:
she had slept on the way to the airport, and on the plane,
and was fast asleep now. I had always loved watching
her sleep, right from when she was a baby. She would
always be *my* baby, even though she was sixteen now—
and taller than me.

"Lucy, love," I said, softly. "We're here."

She didn't stir.

Her younger brother, Daniel, sat next to her, head-phones on, absorbed in a game of something on his phone. He was her opposite in many respects—a little ball of energy who had never been keen on sleep, either as a newborn or now, an excitable nine-year-old. He un-covered one ear and took his first look out the window.

"Are we there?"

"Give your sister a nudge," I said. *"Gently."*

He grinned mischievously and poked her arm.

"We're here, Sleeping Beauty. At the vacation house."

When she gave no response, Sean unclipped his seat belt.

"Might as well let her have another five minutes while we take the bags in. Come on."

I opened my door and stepped out, stretching my arms after the journey, the air-conditioned chill vanish-ing instantly as the late-July heat enveloped me like a blanket. The air smelled of olives and pine and summer heat baked into the dark earth. There was no sound—no traffic, no people—except for the gentle swishing of the breeze high up in the cypress trees, the car engine tick-ing quietly as it cooled.

We stood there, stretching and blinking in the dazzling sun, taking in the villa. Rowan hadn't ex-aggerated: three wide stories of whitewashed stone and terracotta tiles, the parking circle shaded by olive trees, broad stone steps leading up to a double front door in dark, studded oak.

"Wow," Sean said beside me, and for a moment he looked happy, like his usual self—his old self.

I slipped my arm around his waist, needing for a moment to feel his physical presence as we stood side by side, admiring the villa. I needed to feel his warmth, the touch of his skin, the solidity of muscles beneath his shirt. To anchor him to me.

But after a few seconds he moved away, out of my grasp.

2

Rowan appeared at the top of the stone staircase, holding her hands out in greeting.

"Welcome to Villa Corbières!" she said with a grin. "Isn't it *marvelous*?"

She made her way down toward us, the heels of her expensive-looking sandals clicking on the stone. Since starting her own business she always looked immaculate, and today she was wearing a pale cream cami dress with Cartier sunglasses pushed up into her straight auburn hair. How far my slightly awkward student friend—who'd had braces on her teeth and New Kids on the Block posters on her wall—had come since we'd first met. I guess we all had come a long way, but Rowan definitely felt the furthest from her past self. She hugged me and I closed my eyes for a second, letting the smell of her expensive perfume surround me.

"This place is even bigger than it looked in the pictures!" I said, forcing myself to smile, watching Sean out of the corner of my eye as he ducked his tall frame into the car and checked his phone.

"Wait until you see the interior," she said. "Come on, I'll give you the tour."

Inside, it was all white marble and smooth stone walls, one exquisitely furnished room after another, full of light and beautifully decorated with discreet abstract paintings here and there. It was also deliciously cool, thanks to the air conditioning.

"It belongs to a client." Rowan flashed me a conspiratorial smile. "We've been getting on particularly well, recently."

"It's amazing," I said, and it really was: like something out of a coffee-table magazine. "Have you heard from the others?"

"Jennifer's crowd are still en route—they went the wrong way on the A9, apparently. And Izzy's flight from Bangkok gets in tomorrow morning. I'm going to pick her up."

We had met on the first day of university in Bristol, the four of us neighbors in the same hall of residence, then went on to a shared house until we all graduated. For a moment, I wished myself back to our shared house so powerfully that I could almost smell Izzy's weird and wonderful vegetarian cooking from those days, the perennial post-tennis Bengay smell of Jennifer's room, the heady cocktail of perfume and nail varnish and rosé as we got ready in Rowan's room for a Friday night out. Back then, it seemed like all four of us were essentially the same—same starting point, same university, same hopes and dreams for the future, just waiting for life to happen to us. We all wanted the same things. Then we had graduated and left our younger selves behind, like snakes shedding their skin.

For more than ten years after finishing university we had made a point of going away for a long weekend every summer, each year somewhere different: Dublin or Prague, Edinburgh or Barcelona. We'd kept the tradition going despite everything—despite babies and work and other commitments—but then one year, when Rowan was heavily pregnant with Odette in the summer, we didn't get organized, and we just . . . stopped going after that, until we'd missed five years' worth of trips. I didn't really know why.

This vacation was supposed to kick-start the tradition again, doing something together to mark the year we all turned forty. *The big four-oh.* It felt as if, if we didn't do this all together now, we never would, so for the first time ever we were going to break with tradition by bringing all the children too, plus husbands, for a whole week rather than just a weekend. Spend some proper time together.

And so here we were, half a lifetime after we'd first met.

A little girl appeared at Rowan's side, holding both hands up to her. Her wavy red hair was tied in pigtails, her chubby cheeks lively with freckles.

"Pick me up, Mummy!"

Rowan scooped the little girl up and balanced her on a hip.

"You're getting a bit big to be carried now, Odette."

"I'm *not* too big."

"Hello, Odette," I said to the little girl. "You *are* getting big. How old are you now?"

She studied me with big hazel eyes, fingers gripping the strap of her mother's sundress. I realized that mother and daughter were wearing virtually identical outfits.

"Five."

"Daniel's around here somewhere. I'm sure he'd love to play with you."

"Don't like *boys,*" she said firmly.

As if on cue, Daniel raced into the room and skidded to a stop in front of us, his pale skin flushed.

"Have you seen the TV?" he said in an awestruck voice. "It's *massive.*"

Rowan gave him a wide smile.

"There's a gym, a games room, a sauna and pool, too."

"Mum, can I borrow the camcorder later to make a house video?"

"Yes, but ask your dad first."

"Cool. I'm going to find the pool!" he shouted, haring off again.

"Be careful," I said to his retreating back.

Rowan opened the sliding French windows and led the way out onto a wide stone balcony. There was a long table and twelve chairs, all shaded by sun umbrellas, a view over a large vineyard on a hill sloping gently away from us. Fields and woods and low, rolling hills stretched out beyond.

"People have lived here since the first century," Rowan said. "There was a Roman villa on this site originally, then a medieval château which fell into disrepair, and now this. It's west facing so you get the most amazing sunsets."

I stood on the balcony, drinking in the French landscape. A rainbow of greens dotted with light brown terracotta roofs, villas and farmhouses spaced far apart, vineyards and olive groves, wheat fields lined with fruit trees. I felt a little ache inside, a feeling of *how the other half lives*: we could never normally afford to stay in a place like this. Not even close. Was that why Sean was acting so strange? Self-conscious because this place was so far out of our reach, so far beyond his salary—both our salaries combined?

"It's absolutely breathtaking, Rowan. Thank you so much for arranging it and having us all here—I dread to think how much it would cost for a week."

She squeezed my arm and followed my gaze across the perfect scene.

"Probably about twenty thousand in high season," she said. "But they don't hire it out to the public—it's just used for corporate events, jollies, schmoozing. You know the kind of thing."

I nodded, but in truth I didn't know: *jollies* and *schmoozing* didn't really ever come into my working life, and standing there with Rowan, the reality of how far apart our worlds had grown stung a little. I loved my job; I'd been a crime analyst with the Metropolitan Police for thirteen years now, collecting data and tracking patterns in crime, but maybe I only noticed everyone else changing because I felt rooted to the same spot—same job, same house, same path—as I had been for years. Maybe it was all about perspective.

Or maybe it was all about Sean.

"With the vineyard, the gardens, and the wall, we've got total privacy," Rowan continued. "All the vineyards inside the wall are part of the property, sloping down toward those trees." She put Odette down on the tiled floor and ignored her complaints, pointing instead to a thick line of trees about two hundred yards away. "We should all go down there later to have a look: apparently there's the most spectacular gorge beyond the trees, with a little path cut into the rock face so you can get down to the pools below. Purest water you'll ever bathe in—comes straight down off the mountains."

"Sounds a bit cold for me." As soon as the words were out of my mouth I knew they sounded ungrateful, although Rowan didn't seem to notice. *What is wrong with me?* I needed to be happy here, in this remarkable villa, with all the people I loved together for a week.

"Over there," Rowan said, pointing at a church steeple, "is Autignac, ten minutes' walk away. There's a bakery, a little *supermarché,* and a lovely little restaurant in the square. On Wednesday mornings they have the most wonderful street market—lots of local produce, food and drink and crafts. You'll love it."

She pointed down at a tall, dark-haired man in a white linen shirt and chinos, talking on his phone, pacing by the side of the pool.

"Look, Odette, there's Daddy."

"Daddy!" the little girl shouted, her hands pressed against the stone balustrade of the balcony.

The tall man continued pacing and talking, raising a cigarette to his lips.

"Daddy!" Odette shouted again, louder. "Daddy! Daddy!"

He still appeared not to have heard, even as the echo of Odette's call rolled away down the hillside.

"DADDY!" she shouted again, her voice so piercing that I had to lean away.

Finally he acknowledged her with a half-smile and a distracted wave of his cigarette before going back to his phone call.

I instinctively reached out to touch Odette's arm, trying to calm her growing anger, but she batted my hand away and started pulling again at her mother's dress.

"Does Russ always have to be contactable for work?" I rested my elbows on the parapet, the smooth stone warm against my skin.

"Pretty much twenty-four seven," Rowan said. "Money never sleeps—or whatever Gordon Gekko bullshit his boss comes out with."

I was only aware of Russ's job in the vaguest terms: something high powered to do with hedge funds and currencies and city trading. I assumed it involved lots of money, but I knew none of the details.

Rowan's phone beeped with a message and she checked the display.

"Mummy! Pick me up again!" Odette was still pulling at her mother's dress, leaving little sweaty hand marks on the beautiful fabric.

Rowan began typing a rapid reply on the phone's screen with her thumbs.

"Why don't you . . . go and see what Daddy's doing?"

"No!" Odette stamped a pink-sandaled foot on the stone floor, her cherubic little face screwing up. "Pick me up!"

"Just a minute, darling," Rowan said, moving back into the house and the vast living area.

Odette shouted one last time and then ran into the house after her mother, her long ginger bunches bouncing with an angry rhythm.

I had to suppress a smile at her display of temper. Odette had thrown the most incredible tantrums from before she could walk, and she didn't show any sign of stopping. If anything, it seemed her outbursts were getting worse the older she got.

My own daughter wandered out onto the balcony, phone in hand, yawning and stretching.

"You're awake!" I said. "Oh, Lucy, come here and look at this amazing view. Isn't it incredible?"

She came to stand next to me, glancing at the landscape for perhaps a second.

"Cool," she said, turning to me. "Have you got the Wi-Fi password?"

3

There were ten bedrooms, split between the ground and first floors. Ours was off the first-floor landing, with a creamy marble floor and antique wooden furniture, gauzy mosquito nets tied at each corner of the four-poster bed. Sean heaved our suitcases up onto the bed and we began to unpack.

Daniel appeared in his swimming shorts, all skinny legs and arms and pale English skin. "I'm ready!" He put his goggles over his eyes and gave us a double thumbs-up. "Are you ready for the pool, Dad?"

Sean broke into a smile, shaking his head.

"Not quite."

"I want to be the first in!"

"J'ai presque fini," Sean said, putting a stack of T-shirts into the chest of drawers.

"Eh?"

"It's French for 'I'm nearly ready.'"

"Hang on, they speak French here?"

Lucy leaned on the doorframe, arms crossed. *"Duh,"* she said. "That's why it's called France?"

Daniel pulled a face. "I can't really do French. Can you, Dad?"

"Sure and us Irish have always had a lot in common with our French brothers and sisters."

"Like what?"

"Neither of us can stand the English."

In spite of myself, I threw a towel at him, smiling.

"Just kidding," he said, catching it against his chest.

"Daddy's just being silly, Daniel," I said. "We get along very well with the French, that's why you're learning it at school."

"Can't really remember anything we've learned, apart from bonjour and pommes frites."

Sean found his swimming shorts in the suitcase, plucking them out from under a pile of shirts.

"That'll actually get you a long way, big lad," he said. "Hey, do you know why the French only eat one egg for breakfast?"

"I don't know, Dad."

"Because one egg is *un oeuf*!"

Daniel laughed for a hysterical moment, then stopped. "I don't get it."

"Un oeuf? Enough? An egg in French is—"

"Jesus, Dad." Lucy rolled her eyes. "That's literally like the worst joke I've ever heard."

Sean retreated into the en suite to get changed as Lucy turned and went back to her own room.

Daniel wrinkled his nose.

"Tell me it again."

Sean repeated the joke as he emerged in his swimming shorts, bare chested, tossing his jeans, shirt, wallet, and keys into a pile on the bed. He had started going to the gym and exercising regularly in the last few months and it was easy to tell—his chest and shoulders were broader and more defined, his waist slimmer. He hadn't been in bad shape before, but he'd definitely been putting the work in recently. I felt a strange pang of insecurity and something else—jealousy?—as if he'd been working out to try to impress someone else. Someone other than me.

Daniel was laughing again as he skipped out of our bedroom and into the hallway.

With our son gone for a moment, the smile on Sean's face faltered and died, and for a moment he looked grim faced and serious. Deadly serious.

I froze, a pair of shoes in each hand, not sure how to react. His expression was so unexpected, such a change from a moment ago, that it took me completely off guard.

He caught me looking and plastered his smile back on. "Just going to the pool with Aquaboy, then."

"Sure. You OK, love?"

"Grand. Never better."

"I'll finish here. Quick shower, then I'll come and join you."

"Right you are."

I watched him as he walked out of our bedroom. He started in with the jokes again as they headed for the stairs, his deep Irish brogue echoing down the hallway.

I turned and went back to unpacking clothes into the wardrobe, a feeling of fear and sickness building so fast inside I had to sit down on the bed. I knew Sean better than I knew anyone else. I knew when he was unhappy, when he was telling jokes to hide nerves, when he was lying. And the look on his face as he'd said he was grand? I couldn't remember the last time I'd seen him like that. At his father's funeral, perhaps.

My phone beeped with a muffled singsong Messenger tone and I stood up, digging it out of my shorts pocket, unlocking it with my thumbprint.

No new messages.

I frowned and put it back in my pocket.

The beep came again, still muffled. Across the room.

I went to the clothes Sean had left on the bed, a short-sleeved shirt and jeans. Without thinking too much about what I was doing, I picked up the jeans and felt the pockets. A few coins, but no phone. I dropped his jeans back on the bed and listened to the silence of the villa around me. From downstairs, outside, came the faintest sounds from the pool. Splashing, laughing, Daniel's excited voice.

The muffled Messenger tone sounded for a third time.

Sean's bedside drawer.

From where I stood, it was close enough to touch. I put my hand out and snatched it back. Sat for a long moment, without moving. Then reached out again and pulled the drawer open slowly.

It was empty apart from his phone, facedown. He'd started going everywhere with it, as if man and phone were connected by an invisible umbilical cord. So much so that I'd started watching him these last few weeks, only half-deliberately, looking out of the corner of my eye whenever he picked up his phone, trying to see what was absorbing so much of his time and attention. Trying to see the unlock pattern he traced on the screen. Trying to see if I really was going mad, or if this was the start of something unimaginable.

I watched my hand reach in, pick his phone up. Watched my thumb press the power button. Watched the screen light up with a picture of the kids from our last vacation together.

Just a quick look, I told myself. *To put my mind at rest.*

Before I could talk myself out of it, I drew his unlock pattern, my heart racing.

I know I shouldn't have looked. I *know*.

But I did.

And that was when everything started to come apart at the seams.

4

This is what it feels like: it's as if you're falling.

As if a trapdoor has opened beneath your feet and you're falling through it. One minute everything's fine, you're coasting along just as you have done for years. The next minute you're dropping, plunging, plummeting into the dark. You can't see the ground, can't break your fall. Everything around you is falling, too. Everything you've built.

And this is where it starts: with a little blue numeral indicating three unread items in Messenger.

I clicked on it. At the top of the screen were new messages from someone called CoralGirl. Three new messages, just received.

—Message me later when you can x
—Need to be careful this week like we discussed
—Remember to delete messages as soon as you've read

I scrolled down to yesterday's string of back-and-forth messages, reading up from the bottom. The first one was a seven-word message from Sean that stopped my heart.

> Can't stop thinking about what you said x
>   —I meant every word
> Need to talk to you again
>   —Does K suspect anything?
> She has no idea. But I can't go on like this
>   —We'll decide when we're in France. Figure out what to do
> I need to tell her. Soon
>   —We talked about this. Better a secret.
> I know but I feel so bad for lying to K

I couldn't bear to read the messages but I couldn't stop, either, couldn't take my eyes off the little words on the screen, each one another bomb exploding under my marriage.

I scrolled back up and read them again.

> —Does K suspect anything?
> She has no idea. But I can't go on like this

Something splashed onto the phone's screen and I realized that I was crying.

In that moment, it was as if I didn't know my own history anymore, my own story. We'd had one life, our life together, and within a second it felt like fiction. I hadn't even realized I was playing a role. With my hand shaking, I clicked "View Profile" on CoralGirl's account. A generic silhouette instead of a picture. *Lives in London. Female.* That was it.

I hastily marked the latest messages as unread, then locked his phone and shut it back in the drawer. Sitting on an unfamiliar bed, in a strange house, in a foreign country, staring blankly at the wall in front of me.

Cold and hot. Angry and tearful and sick with betrayal.

Falling backward into the dark.

A dozen questions, then a dozen more.

Was it serious?

Why had Sean done this?

How could I have misjudged him so badly?

But the biggest question—*who is she?*—was already half answered, the clue right there in tiny black letters on a screen.

We'll decide when we're in France

France.

One word. But as soon as I saw it, I knew immediately what it meant. Because this week was about the four of us: Rowan, Jennifer, Izzy, and me.

Which meant my husband, my soul mate, my *rock,* was having an affair with one of my three oldest and dearest friends.

5

He wasn't the type to have an affair, I told myself.

Not my Sean. Not my kind, loving, funny husband who told stupid jokes and gave the kids piggybacks and had sung them to sleep when they were babies.

And yet all the signs had been there these last few weeks: he had been increasingly secretive and preoccupied. Serious, even defensive at times. Constantly on his phone, going to the gym, taking more care of his appearance.

How could I have been so blind when it was happening right in front of me?

Who was she? Which one of my friends had betrayed me?

My heart was thudding in my chest, as if my life were at risk from some unseen danger. I took my phone into the en suite and locked the door behind me, sat down on the closed toilet seat, and opened up the picture gallery, selecting an album from the last time we had all been together, a party at Rowan and Russ's house in Chiswick.

There. A candid picture of all four of us, one of a few that Daniel had taken. Rowan, talking and frowning into her iPhone, gesticulating with her free hand. Jennifer, fussing around her two teenage boys with suntan lotion. Izzy, leaning back against a wall, taking it all in with a wry smile on her face.

And me on the edge of the picture, looking distractedly at the camera.

Had it already begun then?

We knew each other's secrets, I thought. Those secret things that bound you together for all time, a common language of memories. We had talked about things with one another that we hadn't shared with boyfriends or husbands. Things we hadn't shared with *anyone* else. I thought I knew them—and it turned out I didn't know one of them at all.

But I knew this: I had wronged all of them in one way or another. That was all I could think about. Over the years of our friendship, I had said and done things that—deliberately or not—had caused anguish and pain and grief to all three of my friends.

Maybe I deserved this.

It felt like I was fifteen again, crippled with anxiety and self-doubt, as if the last twenty-five years had been a dream. Taking off my clothes as if on autopilot, I dropped them in a pile on the floor and stepped into the shower.

I turned the water on and let the tears come, the rushing water stifling the sound of my sobs.

I knew, of course, what I *should* have done. I should have marched down to the pool and asked him about the messages, what they meant, who they were from. Who she was.

But I didn't.

As the shower water pounded the back of my neck, it started to feel that it wasn't enough, in the scales of our relationship: one flippant question weighed against twenty years together. There wasn't enough weight to it, enough heft, to justify hurling this slender missile at him without knowing more. It would have been . . . irresponsible, somehow. Our marriage wasn't perfect by any means, but who has a perfect marriage? I was happy enough, and I thought he was, too. Maybe if I could find out more, I could fix it, rather than destroying it with one reckless question.

And of course I was scared, too. Scared that he would leave me and the kids, discard us for something new. I didn't want it to be real. Didn't want to *make* it real, any more than it already was. I was scared that saying it out loud would make it real.

So I didn't. I couldn't. How do you even start that conversation?

So, Sean, I memorized the unlock code for your phone and waited for you to leave it unguarded. So who's the other woman? Who is she? What the hell is going on?

How could you do this to me? To our family?

I rehearsed it in my head, practiced forming the words in my mouth. Imagined hearing myself saying them. But it all sounded crazy, even to me.

There was another option, of course: to pretend I never saw the messages. Pretend I had never looked. Just let myself float along with the current, as if everything were still the way it was. Why rock the boat? Maybe it would be better to just imagine he was the good husband and I was the good wife who didn't snoop on his phone. Didn't see what could not now be unseen.

But I hated the not-knowing, the gray area between the truth and everything else. Black and white suited me best; I didn't deal well with gray. Never had. I wanted to know—for sure—one way or the other, before deciding what to do next.

It would be torture to play happy families for a week with the knowledge that Sean had betrayed me with one of my best friends, that my marriage was a car crash happening in slow motion. But I had to know. Observing him, *seeing* him, I felt sure I would know which one he had picked over me. I spent every working day with evidence, one way or another. Collecting, recording, examining, putting all the pieces together: it was what I did for a living. All I had to do was find the evidence of my husband's infidelity and follow it to the source.

I'm going to smoke you out, find out which one of

you has betrayed me, which one of you is trying to break my family apart. If I could find out exactly what was going on, maybe I could stop it before it was too late. I had a week to find out the truth, to find out what was going on with my marriage and whether it could be saved—with a string of messages between us like an invisible fault line just beneath the surface, waiting to crack wide open and leave me on one side, Sean on the other. Deep within me was a sick, self-destructive urge to know, to know *everything,* every last sordid detail. To see for myself, with my own eyes. Until then, I was going to have to act as if nothing were wrong. Try to act normal—or as close to normal as I could get.

I turned the shower off, feeling more alone than I ever had before, as if I were standing on a ledge, about to step out onto a tightrope into the darkness—a tightrope between my old life, the life I thought I knew, and what came next. What was at the other end? Grief and heartbreak, most likely. But it was a journey I had to take, for my own sanity, for my own self-respect. I would get dressed, paint on a smile, and get ready for our week together. And I would find out the truth.

A knock on the bathroom door. Then another.

"Mummy?" Daniel's voice, high and excitable. "Are you in there?"

"Yes. Just getting ready."

"Rowan said to tell you that she's had a text. Jennifer's nearly here."

6

I dressed quickly in a simple floral print dress and sandals. Listening to Jennifer's arrival downstairs—Rowan's greeting typically loud and exuberant—I sat down at the dressing table to rapidly reapply my makeup in an effort to disguise eyes puffy from crying. Tried to marshal my thoughts.

Act normal.

And then Jennifer was standing in the bedroom doorway, in cutoff jeans and a pink strapless tube top, sunglasses pushed up into her long blond hair, phone in hand. She wore no makeup—she rarely needed it—and little jewelry apart from a small silver crucifix around her neck. Even in bare feet she was at least half a head taller than me, and only a couple of inches shorter than Sean's six feet. She was Amazonian tall, as he had once put it, and straightforwardly pretty in the way that athletic people usually were.

"Knock, knock," she said, holding her arms out.

I got up and we hugged, exchanging observations

about the weather, the car journey, and her husband's inability to follow Google Maps.

"So, what do you think?" Jennifer said. "Amazing villa, isn't it—have you had the guided tour yet?"

"Rowan showed me around. The view from the balcony is incredible."

"I know, right?" She spoke quietly, as if the owner might be listening. "It's like one of the judges' houses on *The X Factor*."

Jennifer had grown up in California and whenever she got excited or stressed her accent pushed out stronger, stretching the vowels and reminding us that, although she'd lived in the UK more than half her life, the Valley Girl was still in there somewhere. Her family had come to the UK when she was fourteen, relocating from Los Angeles to follow her father's job as CEO of a multinational, and she had never left, retaining a transatlantic twang to her accent that Americans confused for British and vice versa.

I studied her a moment. She seemed a bit flustered.

"Are the boys settling in all right?" I said.

"They're exploring, I think." She checked down the corridor and leaned nearer, lowering her voice. "They've still not quite forgiven me."

"Forgiven you for what?"

"We had a bit of a falling-out last night when they were packing. They wanted to bring the Xbox—Ethan had already packed it in his suitcase. I made him take it out, told them they weren't to waste this week sitting in a darkened room playing stupid *Call of Duty* or

Fortnite or whatever—not when we have the Mediterranean on our doorstep."

"I take it that didn't go down very well?"

She waved a hand. "Not especially. But hopefully they'll be fine once they've seen how much there is to do here."

She was trying to hide it, but I could tell she was bothered that they had argued. She made it a point never to raise her voice to her boys, never to shout, never to be sarcastic and never, ever, to raise a hand to them. Not even when Jake, aged seven, had been playing with matches and come perilously close to burning their house down.

The boys were her project, her mission in life. Born only eleven months apart, Jake and Ethan had become all-consuming in the way that small children could be, and Jennifer had quit her job and never gone back. She'd thrown herself into the role of full-time mum with a gusto verging on mania, and was both hugely proud and fiercely protective of her boys. Even when Ethan had joined his older brother at primary school, she had resisted a return to her physiotherapy career and had got a part-time admin job in the school office instead.

Sean walked into the bedroom, a towel around his waist, hair wet from the pool. I felt my face flush instantly with a burning sense of anger and heartache. And a million questions. The discovery of the messages on his phone was so raw, and there had been so little time to process what I was feeling—I needed to arrange my expression, my emotions, in a way that didn't instantly give away the toxic secret I now carried inside me.

I couldn't bear to look at my husband, but I couldn't look away, either.

He greeted Jennifer with a peck on the cheek—*curiously chaste in the circumstances? Perhaps not?*—and returned to his suitcase to continue unpacking.

"There's a games room downstairs," I said, hearing the weirdly forced tone of my own words. "A pool table, table football, and all sorts. I'm sure the children will find something to do."

Jennifer nodded, not seeming to notice the tension in my voice.

"I'm really hoping they'll spend lots of time outside," she said. "The air is so much cleaner here than in London. And they spend *so* much time playing on that damn Xbox."

Jennifer's husband, Alistair, appeared at her side in full summer vacation mode: belly-hugging vest top and Speedos, hairy shoulders and bare thighs. I'd always thought they were a bit of a mismatch—physically at least—and they'd turned into one of those couples that didn't seem to have aged at the same rate. She still had the tall, long-limbed Californian grace that had beguiled a succession of university boyfriends all those years ago, while Alistair seemed chunkier and more disheveled than ever with his full, bushy beard and tortoiseshell glasses.

"Aha!" Alistair said. "I knew you would still be talking about Xbox-gate."

Jennifer sighed. "Don't keep calling it that. It was a storm in a teacup."

"I said she should have just let them bring it," Alistair told me. "One has to start making one's own decisions sooner or later, making one's own mistakes. Why not now? The boys are at that stage in their lives when they're pushing boundaries, testing themselves and others, and we should encourage it as a move away from childhood into early adulthood. They're not little boys anymore."

"They're still *my* little boys," Jennifer said, crossing her arms. "And it would be nice if you backed me up once in a while, instead of always making me be the bad cop."

"But you're equally as good at being the good cop, *ma chérie*." He gave me a conspiratorial wink. "You've got that covered as well."

"All the same, it would be nice if you could treat Jake and Ethan as our *children*, rather than just a couple more patients to be studied and advised."

Daniel burst in, out of breath, hair wet, his Crocs slapping on the floor.

"Can I borrow your camcorder, Dad? I'm going to do a house tour like a proper YouTuber!"

Sean went to a drawer and handed over the little camera.

"Be careful with it."

"Careful is my middle name!" He ran out of the room.

Alistair gestured toward the expensively decorated surroundings.

"The villa is absolutely sensational, isn't it? Anyone coming for a dip?"

"Maybe later," I said. "If the water's still warm enough."

"Eighty-four degrees, apparently—just like a warm bath. You coming, Jennifer?"

"Have you seen Jake?"

"Not since they went to their rooms."

"Could you check down by the pool for him?"

"I'm sure the boys are fine, darling."

"Please?"

"Righty-ho." He padded off, flip-flops clicking on the tile floor.

"See you down at the pool?" Jennifer said to me.

"Sure."

Sean, who had said nothing so far during this exchange, was taking the last few things from his suitcase.

"Might go for another dip," he said, "when I've got this finished. Amazing pool."

Jennifer either didn't hear him, or acted as if she hadn't.

Something was not quite right here, like a bad smell in the room that no one wanted to acknowledge. *She's acting like Sean's not there. Why would she do that?*

"Catch you later, then," Jennifer said. "I'd better go and see about my boys." She walked off toward the stairs.

I glanced at Sean as he hung shirts in the wardrobe.

Are you just going down to the pool because she's going? So you can have a few minutes together? Why was she ignoring you? Why can't she even meet your eye?

Perhaps the answer was obvious.

She can't meet your eye because she doesn't want to give herself away. It's that simple. Is it?

Is it Jennifer, then?

I was reminded, more forcefully than ever before, that Jennifer and Sean had been a couple for close to two months when we were students.

And after their split he had got together with me.

There had been no crossover. At least, that was the story we'd always maintained. It was best to keep the story simple, best for all concerned.

It came back to me then: the worst thing that Sean had ever said to me, the most hurtful words he had ever uttered—buried in my memory for so long I thought I had forgotten. The game of Truth or Dare we had played after a few months together, Sean almost too drunk to stand. *Best sex I ever had? That would have to be Jennifer, ha ha, first love and all that . . .*

A furious row had followed, as I tearfully explained to him that you weren't necessarily supposed to tell the *truth* in Truth or Dare, especially if it was as hurtful and horrible as what he had said. Especially if it was about his tall, athletic, American ex-girlfriend who was also one of *my* best friends. Him blinking drunkenly at me, saying *sorry sorry sorry,* over and over again, pleading, swaying on his feet, telling me it was just a joke, just a stupid joke and he didn't mean it.

We had split up for a fortnight before I relented to his begging and took him back. It had never been mentioned since and it was so long ago that I hoped it would never surface again. I had never told Jennifer, or the other two.

How about it, Jennifer? Is it you and Sean? Is it a second go-around for the two of you? Best sex he ever had, after all.

Rekindling a first love, something like that?

Is it long-overdue revenge for stealing your boyfriend all those years ago?

No. That was mad.

Or was it?

7

Crickets filled the evening air with their soft burr as we meandered slowly down the hill to the restaurant in the village. In front of us, Lucy was talking to Rowan, Jennifer, and Alistair, while Russ carried Odette on his back. The three boys were somewhere farther ahead, Daniel scampering after the two lanky teenagers like a puppy desperate for attention.

I had reapplied my makeup and knocked back a glass of champagne to calm my nerves. Sean and I were bringing up the rear of our little group, him walking beside me in a not entirely straight line.

"So, are you going to tell me what's wrong?" he said. "Or do I have to guess?"

He put his hands in his pockets and extended the crook of his arm. Reluctantly, I linked arms with him.

"Nothing's wrong," I said.

"I thought you'd be happy to be here."

"I am," I said without looking at him. "Busy day."

"Are you feeling all right? Was it that questionable sandwich you had on the plane?"

"I'm fine."

He considered this for a moment. "Seriously, what's up, Kate?"

Apart from you putting a bomb under our marriage?

"Nothing's up," I said.

"I've hardly seen you all afternoon."

"Just a bit tired, that's all."

"That's probably the heat getting to you." His voice was light, but he was choosing his words carefully. "It was like a blast furnace today."

"Probably."

For a moment, I thought about asking him right then and there—just coming out with it. Get it over with, like ripping a Band-Aid off in one quick pull.

Who is it? Which one? Rowan, Jennifer, or Izzy?

But I knew it wasn't the time. I had no concrete evidence—not yet. The messages on his phone would be long gone by now.

Not until you have proof. He will simply deny it otherwise.

Sean tried another tack to get me talking.

"Wonderful spot for a vacation," he said.

"Perfect."

"Do you ever wonder," he said wistfully, "what it would be like to come somewhere like this every year? Every summer? How amazing would that be?"

"Sean, we couldn't even afford to come here once, let alone every year."

"That's what I mean. Doesn't it make you feel like . . ." He trailed off, gesticulating with his free hand. "Oh, I dunno."

"Feel like what?"

"Like we should be able to afford it by now. That we should be able to do nice things for the kids, be able to splash out on a summer vacation like this."

"Maybe a bit."

"Y'know, I was in the pool earlier and I looked at the villa, and the balcony, and the vineyard, and I just thought, Christ, I'm about to turn forty, and there's literally no way I could ever stay somewhere like this without Rowan making it possible." His Irish accent always got stronger when he'd had a few drinks, and it was in full flow now. "I mean, is this going to be out of my reach *forever*? There are a million places in the world that I want to see, but I feel as though I've barely even started—and my time's already half over. What the hell have I been doing with my life?"

"How many beers have you had?"

"Not enough," he said with a sigh.

We walked on in silence for a moment.

I said quietly, "I think it's just nice that we're even able to come here once." Could he really be that unhappy with the life we'd built? Was that why his eye had wandered in the first place, another middle-aged man looking for validation of his place in the world?

"Of course," he said. "I get that; it's just knowing

how far out of reach it is to us in our normal lives. Makes me feel like a bit of a failure."

"You're not a failure."

"I'm not exactly a success. A network security manager for a medium-sized IT business." His voice took on a sarcastic edge. "It's every young lad's dream, isn't it? Not."

I felt the familiar instinct to reassure him, comfort him, to support my closest teammate—despite my worst fears of betrayal.

"You protect people and the things that are important to them."

"I protect *data*. Not really the same thing."

"Yes, but what's that saying? Life's a journey, isn't it? Not a destination."

"Christ." He laughed. "You must be pissed, too, if you're quoting Aerosmith lyrics at me."

"I think it was Ralph Waldo Emerson, actually. But you know what I mean."

"Feel like I've spent the whole of my thirties doing, I don't know . . ." He held his hands up in the air. "I don't *know* what I've been doing. And now they're gone forever and before we know it, in another couple of years Lucy will be out of the door to university. Even though—"

"Do you think she's all right?"

"Who?"

"Lucy."

He hesitated, and I felt his arm stiffen slightly against mine.

"Sure," he said. "What makes you say that?"

I paused and slowed our pace, to let the others get a little farther ahead. Glad to talk about something that would always put me and my husband on the same page: our daughter.

"She just seems . . . not really herself recently. Quieter than usual, but more snappy."

"I don't think she can be quieter *and* more snappy at the same time, love."

"You know what I mean. She seems more distracted than normal, on her phone all the time."

"She's *always* on her phone. It's compulsory for Generation Z, or whatever they're called."

"She's worried about her GCSE exams, I suppose."

He paused, seeming to consider this for a moment. "Makes sense."

"Even though she's predicted stellar grades in everything?"

"She's always been a bit highly strung—and you know what teenagers can be like." He shook his head suddenly and picked up the thread of our earlier conversation. "Christ, it only feels like five minutes ago that I was bringing her home from the hospital in her car seat and changing my first diaper. Now I'm knocking on forty and I'm losing my bloody hair and it feels like, *What the hell just happened?*"

"I don't care about your hair, Sean."

"Every day I look in the mirror and it's creeping further and further up my bloody head. You know, the other week I was in town and I caught sight of this old feller's reflection in a shop window and I thought, *Who's that old bastard? He's definitely trying too hard.* Then I realized it was me. Jesus."

"What are you trying to say?"

"I . . . I don't know. Too many beers, that's all."

Maybe it was the champagne, but just walking with him, talking to him the way we'd always done, feeling his skin on mine, reminded me again of everything we'd had together. All the good things, now and in the past.

Everything we stood to lose.

I knew our situation was bad, but he was still *my* husband. And maybe he was still worth fighting for.

8

The village square in Autignac was strung with fairy lights that crisscrossed the space above our heads, a warm glow against the long shadows of approaching dusk. The village church, its restored Romanesque steeple rising into the darkening night sky, formed one side of the square while the little trio of boulangerie, boucherie, and charcuterie were shuttered and dark on the other side. A skinny tabby cat sat on a first-floor window ledge, blinking down at us with luminous yellow eyes.

The restaurant was bright and busy. We sat at one of a dozen wooden tables arranged in the square, catering to tourists staying in the villas and apartments in and around the village. It was almost eight o'clock, but the air was still warm, thick with the smells of rib eye steak and roast duck, rich sauces and local red wine. Candles and glasses and half-empty bottles lined our table. I sipped my wine and tried to relax. But I couldn't help it. I'd spent the evening examining everything—every conversation, every look, every silence, minutely—holding each moment in my hand and studying it from every angle, trying to pry the truth from it like a pearl from a clam.

Like now, for example.

Sean was chatting amiably to Rowan about her business, genuinely interested, smiling and engaged, giving her lots of eye contact. He was a people pleaser, always had been, always seemed to know the right thing to say to get on someone's good side, always wanted to find the good in *them*. Was that what his affair was, how it had started? One of my friends coming to him for help, and things progressed to the point where he just couldn't bring himself to say no? Couldn't bring himself to upset her?

Sean was already a glass of red wine ahead of me, on top of the beers he'd had back at the house before coming out. Russ had been constantly refilling everyone's glasses every time he filled his own—which was often—the crimson flush of alcohol already blotting his cheeks. I couldn't decide whether Rowan's husband didn't like our company, or just liked his booze. A bit of both, probably. His chair was empty for the moment as he stood beneath the carved stone portico of the church, taking long slow drags on a cigarette.

Odette, in a bright yellow dress, ran around and around the long wooden table, chasing the cats that occasionally appeared from the shadows to pick up tidbits dropped by diners. She narrowly avoided colliding with a waiter and skipped away again into the gap between two tables, a defiant grin on her face.

"Odette," Rowan said for the third or fourth time, "please come and sit down, your dinner is about to arrive."

The little girl shook her head, long ginger bunches jiggling from side to side. She ran off again, giggling and dodging around the tables of other diners.

Farther down the table, Daniel was reading his Harry Potter book while Lucy was slumped silently in her chair, absorbed by her phone.

Jennifer's boys were also transfixed by their phones. They had never looked particularly alike, but they seemed to grow further apart in looks as they grew into their midteens. Jake, the older of the two and in the same year as Lucy at school, was his mother's son with fair hair and gray-blue eyes, beautiful long eyelashes and Cupid's bow lips. Tall and slim, long-limbed like her—he was going to be a heartbreaker. His younger brother, Ethan, on the other hand, had all his father's genes: dark hair and olive skin, eyes so deep brown they were almost black. Just fifteen, he was already stockier through the shoulders and waist, his legs thick with hair.

Russ returned to the table as the food arrived, steaming plates of creamy chicken in mushroom sauce, entrecôte with Camembert, turkey escalope, panfried potatoes, pasta salads, and mountains of pommes frites, along with two more bottles of La Deuxieme Chance.

Odette finally came and sat down, her little face wrinkled in disgust.

"Don't like that," she said, pointing a small finger at her plate. "Or that."

Rowan leaned over and began cutting it up for her.

"Of course you do, darling. It's just chicken like you have at home."

"Smells funny." She pointed at Rowan's bowl of pasta salad. "I want yours, Mummy."

"You have yours, darling. Look, it's chicken, do you see? You always have chicken."

"Want *yours*." Her high voice was suddenly strident and sharp, cutting through the rest of our conversations. "Don't want chicken."

"Sit at the table, please," Rowan said calmly.

"No!"

Watching their argument unfold, I realized that everyone else at the table was doing the same, looking at the confrontation but trying to pretend that they weren't. Rubbernecking at the scene of a domestic incident like drivers gawking at a highway pileup.

Odette tossed her head and started walking away.

Keeping her voice even, Rowan said, "Odette, darling, if you eat some of your chicken you can have pudding afterward."

"Don't *want* pudding."

"How about you just have some of the fries instead of—"

Russ turned suddenly in his chair, his face an angry shade of red.

"ODETTE! COME BACK HERE AND SIT

DOWN!" he bellowed, his deep voice echoing off the old stone walls. "NOW!"

A hush fell over the little village square as all the other diners turned to look—a dozen conversations halted midsentence, forks frozen midair, wine midpour—eyes flicking between the tiny child and the tall man. Every customer and every waiter staring at the standoff.

Russ was sitting next to me and I could feel the anger crackling around him like static electricity. I didn't know where to look. I certainly couldn't look at Rowan. I caught Jennifer's eye, opposite me at the table, and saw my own expression mirrored there.

Odette slowly returned to the table, slumping back in her chair and folding her arms.

Rowan squirted ketchup onto the side of her daughter's plate. "Thanks, Russ," she said quietly, her voice dripping with sarcasm. "But I don't think that was completely necessary, was it?"

Russ ignored her, pulling his daughter's chair as close to the table as it would go.

"Now *eat*," he said to her, his voice low and hard.

Slowly, the murmur of conversation returned to the tables around us as people went back to their meals.

With a tear running down her face, Odette picked up a single fry, dipped it carefully in the ketchup, and began to eat it with tiny bites.

9

An awkward silence descended on our table, broken only by the clink and tap of cutlery on plates, Odette sniffing back her tears, and the bustle of the waiters around us. Russ picked up his own cutlery and began furiously sawing at his steak, the rest of us mutely resuming our meals. The atmosphere was as thick as soup, but no one wanted to be the first to break the impasse.

Eventually, Alistair and Jennifer both spoke up at the same moment.

"Hey, boys—"

"Have you—"

Jennifer gave an embarrassed smile and gestured to her husband to continue.

"Hey, boys?" Alistair said to his sons, leaning forward over his turkey escalope. "Do you know why this square is called Place du Quatorze Juillet?"

"Nope," Jake said, not looking up from his plate.

"To mark the fourteenth of July. It's a big day in France—do you know why?"

"Nope."

"Can you guess?"

Jake studiously avoided eye contact with his dad as he shoveled pommes frites into his mouth.

"Nah."

"From the French Revolution," Alistair said, holding his hands up. "Bastille Day."

"*Bastard* day?" Jake said, grinning.

Ethan snickered through a mouthful of food.

"Jake!" Jennifer said sharply. "You know what I've told you about swearing."

"Dad started it."

"Bas*tille* Day," Alistair repeated. "When the revolutionaries stormed the biggest fortress in Paris. It was a great victory for the—"

Jake gave an exaggerated yawn and turned back to his plate. "—common man," Alistair finished.

Jennifer picked up the baton and the conversation drifted to a couple I knew vaguely through the PTA, Laura and David something, who had been the subject of a maelstrom of school-gate gossip in the last week of term.

"Apparently," Jennifer said conspiratorially, "he was only doing thirty-six in a thirty zone when he was clocked by the camera. Not exactly *dangerous*. But he already had nine points, and he'd done that tedious speed awareness course already, so he was going to lose his license. Only problem is, he's a sales director for some big food company, drives every day for work."

"So he asked his wife to take his points?" Rowan said. "Say she was driving, not him?"

"That's what I heard. She agreed, but somehow it came out that she was in Brighton that day—something she put on Facebook—and the police got to know about it, and the you-know-what really hit the fan."

"That's awful," Rowan said. "So she's taking the rap for it?"

"They're *both* taking the rap—he's lost his license, anyway, and she's in hot water for lying to the police. They both blamed each other."

"Awful," Rowan said again.

"Isn't it? I heard they'd separated and he's moved out."

Alistair said, "It was probably the straw that broke the camel's back. There must have been other . . . *concerns* in their marriage, things we don't know about."

"The gossip is," Jennifer said, leaning forward, "they're now talking about lawyers, divorce, custody—all of that."

Lawyers, divorce, custody. Each word felt like a slap across my face. What did Jennifer know about it, anyway? What right did she have to be gossiping about people she barely knew? Sticking her nose into someone else's marriage? With considerable effort, I managed to stay silent.

Rowan was shaking her head, genuine sadness on her face.

"All that over a dumb speeding ticket; it seems so unfair. Their poor kids."

"I know, right? She was only trying to help him out of a tricky situation. I'd have done the same."

"Me too," Rowan said. She looked over at Sean and Alistair. "How about you, boys?"

"Perhaps," Alistair said with a theatrical flourish.

"Probably," Sean said, refilling his wineglass.

Jennifer looked over at me. "What do you think, Kate?"

"Me?"

"About the Laura and David thing?"

I shrugged. "I heard some of the rumors. Didn't realize they'd separated."

"But what would you have done? Do you think she was right to take his points?"

"Right?" I shook my head. "Of course not."

"Even though she was trying to protect him, help him keep his job? Wasn't she trying to do the best thing for all of them?"

"Doesn't make it right. She broke the law, made herself into a liar."

"For the right reason, though."

"It's either right or it isn't, Jen. It's not complicated. There isn't a third answer."

I felt myself getting wound up, the simmering heat of my anger over Sean's betrayal threatening to boil over. *Not here, not now!* I needed to be calm. Do what Sean sometimes gently suggested: let things go more often, bend a little, smile and shake my head and just move on. He would joke about it sometimes, asking me, *What's the view like up there on your high horse,*

Kate? The irony of that seemed particularly dark, in light of what I'd discovered.

"The truth," Sean muttered into his wine, "the whole truth, and nothing but the truth."

There was another awkward silence.

Jennifer grabbed her fork and *tinged* it loudly against the side of her glass. "How about we have a toast?" she said brightly, filling the glasses nearest to her with more of the smooth local red wine. "As it's our first night here."

There was a general murmur of agreement, glasses being raised. I held my own glass up, forcing my mouth into a smile.

"To Rowan," Jennifer said. "For making it possible for all of us to stay in this wonderful place, and bringing us all together."

All the adults clinked glasses and drank.

"So, Rowan," Jennifer said briskly, "I hear great news could be on the way for your company?"

"Fingers crossed," Rowan said.

"Is it happening, then? It's really going to go ahead?"

Rowan nodded slowly, smiling like a proud parent. "All the signs are looking good at the moment."

Her company specialized in ethical PR—total transparency and commitment to the very highest ethical standards, both in her own operation and the people she worked for. It set her apart from some of the competition and had won her an impressive roster of clients over the last ten years, principally tech and social media companies keen to avoid the stigma of privacy breaches and fake news that had afflicted Facebook and others. So much so that she had caught the attention of a global leader in the ethical field, a US-based company, which was proposing a buyout. As founding partner and CEO, Rowan stood to become very wealthy from the move.

"Hopefully it should go through in the next month or so," she added.

Russ returned from another cigarette break. Even though the cigarette was out, a fug of stale smoke came with him as he sat down next to me at the table, opposite his wife, folding his long frame into the wicker chair.

"As long as you can convince them you're absolutely squeaky clean, right, darling?"

It was virtually the first time I'd heard him speak since his outburst at Odette. His voice was loud, with a tone of forced joviality that was impossible to miss. I watched as Rowan turned her gaze on her husband, something in her eyes I couldn't place, a slight narrowing of the eyes. As if they'd had this conversation before.

"The due diligence has been very thorough," she said. "No stone unturned."

Russ took a long drink of wine, emptying half the glass in one gulp.

"*Squeaky* clean," he said again.

10

I couldn't sleep.

Sean's soft snores had taken on the slow regularity of deep sleep perhaps an hour ago. He'd always had the annoying ability to drop off as soon as his head hit the pillow, not bothered in the slightest by the low hum of the air conditioning. But it wasn't the barely perceptible noise of chilled air circulating that was keeping me awake.

Every time I closed my eyes, I started to feel sick. So instead, I stared up at the darkness, crisp cotton sheets cool against my skin, my mind sifting through an endless carousel of possibilities: round and round, and then round and round again. With every circuit, my inadequacies became clearer. Inadequacies as a woman, wife, mother. How come I'd never seen this before? It seemed so obvious now.

My friends.

Rowan, who was cleverer than me, always had been.

Jennifer, prettier than me, then and now.

Izzy, who was funnier than me, always able to make Sean laugh.

How could I compete against that? What was I good at? What did I contribute? Where did I fit in, compared to them? Somewhere in the middle, I supposed. Somewhere in the background.

Round and round, went the carousel.

My friends.

Rowan. On the verge of becoming wealthy enough to afford the lifestyle Sean had always yearned for and never had.

Jennifer. His university sweetheart, his first love. And he had told me in a moment of either a) drunken candor or b) misjudged humor, the best sex he'd ever had.

Izzy. Sean's oldest female friend, who had suddenly reappeared in our lives, apparently with a plan to settle down. What was she to him? Freedom, lack of commitment, no kids, no ties. Another chance at youth, another chance to start again.

Rowan. Jennifer. Izzy. We were all intertwined, had been for years. I had worried that we'd been drifting apart as our lives took us in different directions, but in reality it was the opposite—at least for one of them. One of them had got closer to my family than I would ever have wanted.

But which one of them was it? Which one was playing this elaborate game? The more I thought about it, the more sleep eluded me, and at one o'clock I gave up.

Pulling on my thin summer dressing gown, I padded out of our bedroom, marble tiles cool against the soles of my bare feet. I went to Daniel's room first, opening the door as quietly as I could and waiting for a moment as my eyes adjusted to the darkness. He had turned the air-conditioning unit off, insisting the low, blowing noise would keep him awake. He often didn't sleep well on the first few nights in a new place anyway—away from his own bed, his own pillow, his own *things*—but tonight he was fast asleep, curled into the sheet. I moved closer, leaning in until I was above him, close enough to see the rise and fall of his chest in the shadows of his room. My little miracle boy, who had arrived unexpectedly after three miscarriages—at a time when I was starting to resign myself to never having a second child.

I held my breath and stood very still, turning my ear toward him until I could hear slow, steady breathing, hear the breaths in and out . . . in and out.

It was a habit I'd developed when Lucy was a baby, standing over her Moses basket in the middle of one broken night, unable to sleep until I was sure she was OK, listening in the silence, punch-drunk with fatigue, until I was sure I could hear her breaths coming and going. And here I was now, sixteen years later, still doing it with her brother. Still listening. Still checking, even though I knew it was not entirely rational. Daniel was fine—he had been fine when he went to bed, and he would be fine in the morning.

But it was a hard habit to break.

He was still in his pajamas, despite the heat. I touched my fingertips lightly to his forehead. Satisfied he wasn't too hot, I closed his door quietly behind me and went across the hall to his sister's room.

Lucy was awake, her face illuminated by the light from her phone screen. I opened the door a little wider.

"Lucy," I whispered, "it's one o'clock in the morning. You should turn that off and get some sleep now."

"Not yet."

I took a step into the room and saw that there were tears on her face, shining in the iPhone's cold glow. "What's the matter, Luce?"

She turned onto her side, away from me, the phone still inches from her face.

I sat down on the edge of her bed and put a hand on her shoulder. Her skin felt hot, despite the air-conditioned chill of the room. I made a mental note to check she was using enough suntan lotion tomorrow.

"What's happened, Luce?"

"Nothing, Mum. It's fine."

"Doesn't *look* fine. Is something bothering you?"

"No."

"You know you can talk to me about anything, don't you?"

She nodded and sniffed, wiping tears away with the heel of her hand. "I know, Mum."

"Anything at all. Doesn't matter what it is."

She half turned toward me but wouldn't look me in the eye. "Even if it's something . . . bad?"

"Especially if it's something bad."

"Something awful?"

I took a tissue from the box on the bedside table and handed it to her. There was a lot about her that I didn't know—more and more each day, it seemed. "I can help you, Lucy. Whatever it is."

She wiped her eyes with the tissue. I waited, letting the silence stretch out between us.

"Sometimes I hate myself," she said quietly.

I felt an ache, deep in my chest. Fingers squeezing my heart. "Why?"

"Because I'm . . . worthless. I'm a horrible person."

"Of course you're not, Lucy! What's happened?"

"Doesn't matter. Can't do anything about it now, anyway."

"About what?" I said gently. "Is it a boy?"

She said nothing.

"Is it one of your friends? Being mean?" I was constantly amazed by the capacity of teenage girls to be horrible to one another. Girls who were supposed to be friends but who seemed to delight in making one another miserable. Was I like that, too, as a teenager? Did we still carry it with us now, this capacity to spite and sting and wound those closest to us, hidden under a thin veneer of adult civility?

Lucy gave a tiny shake of her head, fresh tears welling in her eyes.

Without another word, she sat up suddenly and hugged me, close and fierce, clinging on tight like she used to when she was a little girl. She used to love hugs, especially when she was upset. But now, as a sixteen-year-old, she was so blasé and standoffish that it took me by surprise when she hugged me. It was one of those things she wouldn't do anymore in front of her friends, wouldn't do in public. A few years ago—I wasn't sure exactly when it had happened—she had suddenly become embarrassed by me, the closeness we had had seeming to fall away as she grew taller and more beautiful with every day. Sometimes, when she looked at me, I thought I saw open contempt in her eyes.

But not now, not in this moment. This hug was real. The real Lucy.

We sat like that for a minute, me stroking her hair and shushing her, my heart brimming. Her hot tears on my shoulder.

I mentally berated myself for being so caught up in my own self-pity, in the revelations about my marriage, that I'd not picked up Lucy's signals sooner. I thought she would say more, tell me what was bothering her, but she simply hugged me in silence.

So quietly it was almost a whisper, she said, "It's just Alex, that's all."

Alex?

There was a girl in her friend group called Alex who had been inseparable best friends with Lucy: sharing anything and everything with her—and then ignored her completely for a week straight. Had they fallen out again? She'd not mentioned it to me, but it wouldn't be the first time.

"What about Alex? Has she been leaving you out of things again?"

"No," she said, resting her cheek on my shoulder. "Not that."

"Just rise above it, sweetheart. Don't get drawn in."

"Hmm . . ."

Before I could ask her anything else, she lay back down, switching her phone off and pushing it under the pillow.

"Night, Mum."

I kissed her on the forehead and crept out of her bedroom. She would tell me when she was ready; forcing the issue would make her clam up even more. I knew enough to know that. Downstairs, the huge open living room was eerily quiet apart from the ever-present hum of the air conditioning, the full moon casting long shadows across the tiled floor. The room had an ethereal glow in the moonlight, the grand piano lit across its dark surface. I fetched myself a glass of water from the kitchen and was about to go back up when I stopped. There *was* another sound: the crickets in the garden. Someone had left the sliding glass doors to the balcony slightly open.

I stepped outside, drawn by the smells of olive trees, pine, and rich red earth cooling in the darkness. The chirping of crickets was a continuous soft background tone beneath everything else, the sky ink black, a perfect blanket of stars stretching from one horizon to the other. More stars than I could ever remember seeing at home.

My eye was drawn down again, and from deep within the shadows I saw a tiny flicker of movement. An orange glow.

I wasn't alone on the balcony.

11

I flinched as something flew out of the darkness, fluttering close to my head.

"The bats are out in force tonight," a deep voice said.

I turned toward it, the orange glow of a cigarette end like a firefly in the dark.

"They come out for the insects," the voice continued.

"Russ?" I said, gathering the dressing gown more tightly around my body.

"Evening." His voice was low and slow. "Couldn't you sleep?"

"I needed some water." As my eyes adjusted to the darkness, I made out Rowan's husband slumped in one of the big wicker chairs at the edge of the balcony, long legs splayed out in front of him, a bottle on the small table next to him, a brandy glass next to it with an inch of amber liquid in it.

"Fancy a drink?"

"I'm OK with water, thanks."

He held up the bottle. "This will help you sleep. Twenty-year-old cognac, the finest sedative money can buy."

"Really, I'm fine."

"Works every time, guaranteed." He sloshed more brandy into his own glass.

Another bat flittered overhead, a tiny black shape against the dark sky. Arms crossed over my chest, I looked behind me at the villa. All the windows were dark; everyone else was asleep. It was just the two of us still awake. I couldn't remember the last time I'd had a chat one-to-one with Russ, a conversation that hadn't been an awkward few minutes at a barbecue or New Year's Eve party. In fact, I'd seen Odette's live-in nanny, Inés, far more often than I'd seen him at the family home.

I wanted to get away, go back to bed, but part of me was also intrigued.

"Have you been out here long?" I asked.

He plucked a new cigarette out of the packet and lit it straight off the old one before flicking the butt away with a practiced *snap* of thumb and forefinger. The glowing orange butt spun in a high arc, end over end, and there was a hiss from the darkness below as it hit the swimming pool.

"Not long enough for my darling wife."

I didn't know how to respond to that. A row, I guessed, although I'd not heard anything.

"Can't believe how warm it still is," I said. "Will

you close the sliding door when you come in?" I turned to go and was almost at the door when he spoke again.

"You probably think," he said abruptly, "that I was too harsh with Odette this evening, don't you?"

I stopped, turning back to him. "I know how difficult it can be sometimes with small children."

"The bloody nanny lets her get away with anything. No discipline. Nothing. And she's so bloody stubborn, just like her mother. Always has to get what she wants, never does what she's told."

"It's just a stage, all kids go through it."

He grunted and took another swallow of brandy. "I bet you think I'm one of those blokes who can't stand his wife to earn more than him."

"No," I said, not entirely truthfully.

"Not like you and your other half."

"How do you mean?"

"Well, you're like the perfect couple, aren't you?"

"I don't know about that."

He pointed a long finger at me. "That's what Rowan says to me. 'Why can't you be more like Sean?' It's her favorite line. And I say to her, 'What, be more Irish?'" He gave a mirthless, gravelly laugh.

A chill ran through me. "Really?"

He poured another inch of brandy into his glass. "Oh yes, your husband is quite the role model, apparently." He held the bottle out to me. "You sure you won't change your mind about that drink?"

Cognac was the last thing on my mind, but I wanted to keep him talking.

Why can't you be more like Sean?

"Go on then. A small one."

I drank my water down in a swift gulp and handed him the empty glass, accepting it back a moment later with a hefty measure of the amber liquid in the bottom. At least a triple, I guessed. I perched on the edge of the chair next to him and we stared out into the darkness, the distant hills bathed in silvery moonlight. Somewhere below us, down in the village, a dog barked once then fell silent.

I sipped the cognac, the fiery liquid burning as it went down. It reminded me of teenage parties, raiding my parents' booze cabinet and grimacing through shots of dessert liqueur and Greek ouzo and long-forgotten cherry brandy.

"So," I said, "what do you think she means when she says she wants you to be more like Sean?"

"God knows. Better with Odette. Better at home. Just . . . better."

For one mad moment I thought about telling him what I knew. About the messages. To share this burden with someone, get another point of view. A *neutral* point of view. Russ was so drunk that he probably wouldn't remember it in the morning, anyway, but I couldn't take the risk. I had to keep this secret to myself, at least for now.

"Sean's far from perfect," I said. "I can tell you that for a fact."

"Oh well, I've a feeling it might be too late anyway."

"What makes you say that?"

He let his head roll back onto the headrest of the chair, blinking blearily up at the stars, his chest rising and falling in a slow rhythm.

When he spoke again, his voice was clearer, softer, stripped of all its hard edges. All the swagger, all his alpha-male toughness, had gone.

"I think Rowan is having an affair," he said.

12

A wave of dizziness, as if I had stood up too fast.

"An affair?"

"Yup."

"I'm sure she wouldn't do that, Russ."

"Are you?"

Are you? Are you really sure?

"Yes."

He pointed a finger at me, a lopsided grin on his face. "But you hesitated before you said yes. You hesitated."

"I'm still half asleep."

"You hesitated, Kate. Admit it."

The urge to match his revelation with my own, to share what I knew about Sean's betrayal, was so strong I could feel it tugging at me like a centrifugal force, pulling me away from my husband.

Tell him what you know about Sean.

Tell him what you've found.

Tell him.

I took a deep breath and plunged in with a question instead, before I could change my mind.

"Who is it?" I said quietly. "Who do you think she's seeing?"

Please don't say Sean, please don't say Sean. Please, not him.

Russ shrugged.

"Reckon it's someone she's known for a while. Not someone new."

"What makes you say that?"

"Gut feeling. You're her friend, you've known her since you were both"—he waved his glass vaguely in front of him, more of the brandy spilling over the lip— "like eighteen, or whatever. Has she talked to you about it?"

"No."

"Not even a hint?"

"Nothing."

He snorted. "You wouldn't even tell me if she had, though, would you?"

"She's not said anything to me. She'd be more likely to confide in Jennifer, to be honest. They were always more of a pair when we were younger."

I was torn between defending my friend and getting Russ to open up, tell me about his suspicions. Wanting to carry on in blissful ignorance versus wanting to know everything.

"Something's going on," he said. "I just know it."

"Doesn't sound like she's doing a very good job of keeping it secret, if you suspect something is going on."

"She thinks I haven't twigged. You think I should ask her, point-blank?"

Confronted with what might give the answer to my question, I was suddenly cautious. If Russ blundered in now, accusing his wife of an affair, I'd lose my chance of finding out the truth for myself. She would be on her guard for the rest of the week.

"I think you should be . . . careful, Russ."

He snorted and took another slug of brandy, some of it dribbling down his chin.

"Why should *I* be careful? She hasn't been."

"Because once you ask her, once it's out there, it'll always be between you. The genie can't be put back in the bottle."

And because you don't know how much damage a single accusation can cause.

But I do. I know. So does Rowan.

I took another sip of my drink, wondering whether to tell him the truth. Whether he already *knew* the truth. An ugly, unpleasant truth that I had locked away years ago.

Did you ever wonder why Rowan was single when you met her, Russ? Why she'd split with her first husband? Why a perfectly good relationship ended in anger and tears and bitterness?

Because of an accusation.

Because of me.

Russ leaned back in his chair and exhaled heavily.

"I knew you'd say something like that."

"Why?"

"Sensible Kate. Always got your scientific head on, haven't you?"

"I don't know about that."

"You're probably right, all the same. I'm supposed to be playing the 'good husband.'" He emphasized the last two words with air quotes. "Make sure there's no impediment to her big deal going through."

I frowned in the darkness, feeling as though I'd missed something.

"How would any of that affect her deal?"

He took a drag on his cigarette, the tip glowing cherry red in the darkness.

"How much has she told you about the potential buyers? Not the division she'll be absorbed into, but the actual owners at the top of the tree?"

I searched my memory. Rowan had not said much to me at all about this deal, even though it was potentially huge for her career. Why was that? It felt like another example of how far apart we had drifted in recent years. She had talked in generalities about her clients, her business, rather than who she was getting into bed with as part of this deal.

I flinched inwardly. *Getting into bed with* seemed about right.

"They're a US-based multinational, I think?"

"Correct. Garrison Incorporated is a family-based company, three generations and still going. They've run it since the 1950s, market cap somewhere north of eighteen billion dollars, headquartered in Oklahoma City for the last seventy years. And those three generations of Garrisons have something else in common."

"What's that?"

"God."

I leaned forward a little, waiting for him to elaborate, but instead he drew heavily on his cigarette again and blew out two thick streams of smoke from his nostrils.

"God?" I repeated.

"The big man himself." He flicked the ash from his cigarette and pointed with the glowing tip, to emphasize each word. "They're superevangelical, fundamentalist Christians and they run their businesses accordingly. Massively conservative, Bible-thumping types who have certain *expectations* of their top people."

"In terms of personal life?"

"In terms of *everything*. They're doing the presignature due diligence checks now, and those bastards are thorough. They're going through everything in forensic detail, not just the business and the company projections, but past history going back twenty years, potential staff issues, black sheep in the family, client connections, potential negative headlines, any skeletons in the closet. Needless to say, any hint of a potential new partner shagging around will send all the red flags up in Oklahoma City, that's for sure."

"Would they pull out?"

"If they find out she's been playing away from

home? Oh, they'll cut their losses, no question. The slightest sniff of a scandal and it will be goodbye buy-out, goodbye payoff. Goodbye eight million quid."

I took another small sip of the brandy. "And Rowan knows this?"

He drained his own glass and reached for the bottle again "Yeah, but she thinks she's smarter than them."

"Then she's taking an astronomical risk."

"That's my wife for you. Always gung ho, always the risk-taker."

"*If* it's true."

He gave me an exasperated look, as if I'd not been paying attention. "Something's going on. I'm bloody certain of it."

TEN MONTHS EARLIER

"This is the year that school gets real."

Her mum had been saying it all summer. She ignored it: hard work had never been a problem for her. Top 5 percent since primary school, ever the competitive one. Just like she ignored the seniors who said the GCSE exams didn't really count for anything, that getting the top grades didn't matter, were just a stepping-stone to A levels at 18. That might be true for most people, but not if you wanted to be a doctor. The medical schools did look at your GCSE grades—they looked at everything, to decide who got a place and who didn't. To make sure you'd not just got lucky with your A levels after making a mess of your GCSEs.

And anyway, when her mum said the thing about school "getting real" in Year 11, what she actually meant was This is not the time to get distracted.

In her mum's eyes, distracted equaled boys. Boys will get you sidetracked.

Boys will get you focusing on the wrong things.

Boys don't do as well as girls at school, and there are good reasons for that.

Blah, blah, blah, blah.

She understands all this. She gets it. She knows she'll have to work hard to get the grades, and she's more than prepared to put the hours in.

But. But. There's a new boy in her year.

And he's not like the rest.

He's tall—at least six feet—that's the first thing she noticed about him. Wide shoulders and a square jaw, proper stubble, not just silly peach fuzz like some of the other boys in her year. His sleeves are rolled up, forearms broad with muscle. And he has this way of standing, of looking around, as if he knows everyone is looking at him and he's perfectly OK with that, he's used to it. Chestnut-brown hair in this gorgeous fade cut, long at the front, and she loves the way he brushes it away from his eyes. Eyes a bright, shining blue, serious and funny and dangerous and deep.

They draw you in.

He doesn't even know she exists, not yet. He's not the sort of guy you can just go up to, start talking to, without having an intro, a link, a mutual acquaintance.

That's where her friend Jake comes in.

Jake is going to introduce her—as soon as he stops making excuses, stops putting it off until the next day and the next.

She knows she can persuade him. It's just a matter of time.

SUNDAY

13

The smell of fresh coffee woke me up. Sean put the cup down carefully on the bedside table beside me and I propped myself up on my elbows, mumbling a thank-you without meeting his eye. How much sleep had I managed? A few hours? I felt shattered, hollowed out with fatigue, and took the coffee with me as I shuffled into the en suite.

By the time I was dressed and had made my way downstairs, Rowan had fetched Izzy from the airport and they were chatting in the air-conditioned cool of the kitchen. We hugged our hellos and I asked about the journey from Bangkok.

"It's so lovely to see you," Izzy said. "To see *every-one* again."

"You too," I said, sipping a second coffee.

It was months since I'd last seen her, but she didn't look any different. She never seemed to age. She was dressed in a simple short-sleeved blouse and loose-fitting three-quarters from Vietnam or somewhere similar, and looked thoroughly at home in the heat. Her black hair was tied back in a loose ponytail, a green crystal on leather twine around her neck, plus her usual collection of bracelets and bangles for positive energy. She was the only one of us without kids, and single, and it seemed to me that she looked ten years younger than us as a result—no wear and tear, no stretch marks, no wrinkles and lines from all the sleepless nights. She was the smallest of the four of us, an elfin five feet two, slight and petite, and somehow that made her look younger, too. Small, delicate features, catlike eyes behind red-framed glasses and a mouth that was almost always smiling.

"How are you, Kate?"

"Great. Lovely."

Izzy grinned playfully.

"Big first night last night, was it?"

"Not really."

"You look exhausted, woman."

I shook my head, smiling in spite of myself. Izzy had always been one to call a spade a spade.

"Thanks," I said. "You always know how to lift my spirits."

"Just saying, that's all. Concerned for you."

"I do feel exhausted, actually, didn't sleep that well." I reached for a convincing lie—one with a kernel of truth. "I'm actually a bit worried about Lucy."

In broad brushstrokes, I told them how my daughter had been more withdrawn recently, her mood swings more pronounced with the pressure of the looming

GCSE results. And how I had failed to notice the signs until last night.

Jennifer had joined us and was nodding along in sympathy.

"It's understandable," she said. "It's a tough gig that you've set for yourself."

I shrugged. "No tougher than anyone else has got it."

"But it can't be easy for you, keeping on top of everything with all of your . . . commitments."

"How do you mean?"

"You know," she said. "Your career."

I felt my hackles rising. "What about it?"

"It must be hard, doing the mom thing and working full time as well."

"No," I said, trying to keep my voice calm. "That's not it. Not at all."

"I mean, it's great and everything, but it can't be easy fitting it all in. I don't know how you guys do it."

Maybe it was lack of sleep, but I sensed a certain tone in her voice that I didn't like. Rowan seemed to sense it, too, jumping in before we slid into a full-blown argument.

"Hey, Jennifer?" Rowan said. "I promised Odette I'd bring you down to the pool this morning to watch her doggy paddle—do you want to come now?"

"Sure," Jennifer said, following her out of the kitchen.

Izzy and I exchanged glances after they'd left the room, both smiling and shaking our heads as if to say: *a classic Jennifer comment.* We went out onto the balcony and sat down at the end of the table, in the shade of a large umbrella.

"How are you finding it," I said, "being back in Europe?"

"Like I never bloody left," she said with a small smile. "Same as it ever was. So how are you *really,* Kate? Honestly? Now it's just the two of us, you can tell me."

"Me? I'm fine." I shrugged, smiled back. "Same as I ever was."

"You sure?"

"Absolutely. It's just Lucy, like I said."

She took a sip of coffee and studied me for a moment. She had always been the most perceptive one of us, the most likely to see what was hidden. And she never held back, never left things unsaid—even if it meant a difficult conversation.

"You just look a little bit . . . I don't know. Not quite yourself."

"Busy day yesterday, you know. Travel day's always a bit of a slog, isn't it?"

"That just means you're not traveling enough, woman. You need more practice."

Izzy had spent much of her late twenties and thirties traveling and working overseas, teaching English as a foreign language, first in sub-Saharan Africa, then in Thailand, Vietnam, and Cambodia and other parts of Southeast Asia. Some years ago, on one of her extended stays in Tibet, she had become a Buddhist and it seemed to have made her calmer, happier, less bothered about all the things that most people spent so long worrying about.

She was from the same part of Limerick as Sean, and had been indirectly responsible for us getting together at university. As soon as she introduced him to our little group, I was instantly smitten by this broad-shouldered Irishman who was always smiling, who could talk to anyone, who danced like a fool, and whose heart beat so hard the first time we kissed that I thought it would burst out of his chest. He looked at me the way boys had never done before. *Really* looked at me. I had been amazed when he'd first asked me out. I'd always felt like he was out of my league—he could have had the pick of the girls.

My Sean.

He and Izzy had never been an item, but he *had* once told me—after a considerable amount of Guinness and red wine—that they had made a pact at the age of sixteen. That if they were both still single at forty—and Sean had not yet "made his first million"—they would get married. One of those jokey, teenage agreements that was done tongue in cheek—but maybe meant more to one of them than they were willing to admit.

They had always kept in touch—even while she was working abroad. They would exchange jokey texts about shared interests, about sports, films, and hometown reminiscences, that I was only ever on the periphery of, never really involved in.

Izzy had ended up getting engaged to Sean's best friend, Mark. But the marriage had never happened—and I didn't want to think about that, about what had happened to him. Not now.

I sipped my coffee.

"So," I said, "what made you come back?"

Izzy shrugged, gave me a smile.

"I think maybe it's time I finally put down some roots."

"You seeing anyone?"

"It's still the early stages."

"You're being very cryptic about it."

She waved a hand, colored bangles jangling and clinking together on her wrist.

"Don't want to curse it."

"When do we get to meet him, this new chap?"

"Not for a bit." She gave me a wink, her eyes twinkling. "It's complicated."

"There you go, being cryptic again."

She fingered her necklace, a cloudy green stone surrounded by a crescent moon, rolling the slim leather cord between her fingers.

"It's just going to need some careful handling, that's all."

"Is he the shy, retiring type?"

"Not exactly. There aren't many of them from my hometown."

"From Limerick?"

She nodded. "Spooky, isn't it? How things turn out?

Spend half your life abroad and end up seeing some-one who grew up a mile from your house."

I suddenly realized what she meant, my heart drop-ping into my shoes. Surely she couldn't possibly be so brazen about it, could she? In front of me, talking to *me*? But that was Izzy all over—it always had been. She had always been a straight talker, never sugar-coated anything, never compromised, never took the easy path. *There are only two mistakes one can make along the road to truth: not going all the way, and not starting.* That was her way, her Buddhist faith.

And that's why she can't keep a man, Russ had once said in an unkind moment.

I tried to smile along. Just keep smiling. "Oh my God, Izzy."

"What?"

Keeping my voice level, I said, "He's married, isn't he?"

Izzy raised an eyebrow, fixing me with a weird look. "I couldn't *possibly* comment."

"But is he?"

"What makes you think it's even a he?"

"Well, your previous boyfriends, for one thing."

"This is true."

"So: married?"

"Are you asking that question as an officer of the law?"

"Of course not. And us analysts are civilians, any-way. I'm asking as your friend."

"Can't tell you yet. Soon."

The question that she had never really answered came back to me, pushing its way to the front of my mind.

Why did you come back to the UK, Izzy? Why now?

All of a sudden I was seeing that question in a whole new light.

Before I could decide what to think about Izzy's revelation, Odette marched up to us with a look of utter determination on her face. She was in a pink sparkly swimsuit, with pink armbands, pink goggles on her head, a pink inflatable ring around her midriff, and a blow-up dolphin under her arm. Also pink.

She planted her feet apart, fists on her hips.

"Right," she said, her high voice cutting across our conversation, "who wants to go to the beach?"

14

The beach at Cap d'Agde was crowded.

The Mediterranean was a brilliant, sparkling blue, small waves whipped up by a gentle onshore breeze that brought a note of coolness to the merciless midday sunshine. Our little group was subdued after last night, our towels grouped around a pair of large parasols, bags and books and a big blue cooler piled at the center of our encampment. The smell of suntan lotion mingled with a salty breeze off the sea and cigarette smoke drifting over us from a French couple nearby. I rubbed suntan lotion into Lucy's back and shoulders as she held her long blond hair out of the way with one hand, thumb-typing on her phone with her other. I was glad to be here, glad to be distracted—in the thick of things—rather than back at the villa, letting my mind wander to dark places. I felt as though I were living in some TV drama, and everywhere I looked a camera was zooming on each of my best friends' faces, shouted accusations coming one after another.

Is it you? Or you, or you?

Sean had been more attentive than usual, carrying bags, setting up umbrellas, fetching chilled water and snacks for me and the kids. Was he trying extra hard because of what he'd done? What he was *still* doing?

Jennifer was beside me on a large straw mat, propped up on her elbows, surveying the packed beach around us. A serious-looking paperback—*The Optimistic Child: A Revolutionary Approach to Raising Resilient Children*—lay untouched on the sand next to her. She had been a star athlete when we met, playing tennis and hockey in the national university leagues. At five feet ten, she was the tallest of the four of us and had managed to maintain a lean, strong physique with a weekly routine of tennis, Pilates, and jogging. There had been a time when I didn't particularly enjoy being next to her on the beach, or at the pool, or *anywhere* in a swimsuit. I was the pale Englishwoman, always trying—and never quite succeeding—to get back to my wedding-day weight, next to this toned, tanned Californian who never appeared to put on a pound.

I thought I had got over that particular insecurity. Maybe not. It seemed to have returned with a vengeance today.

"We seem to have chosen the wrong day to come to the beach," I said. "It's like half of Béziers is here."

"Isn't Cap d'Agde supposed to be a nudist beach?"

I pointed up the coast, where the sandy beach

curved into the distance. "That's around the headland, a bit further up. Why, do you fancy it?"

Jennifer laughed. "Are you kidding me? Lots of old guys with their junk hanging out? Ee-yew."

"Better a busy beach than a naked beach, then?"

"For sure. The boys like it, too." She indicated a small inlet where Jake and Ethan were busy digging in the sand. "It's so lovely to see them playing for once, properly *playing,* like they used to. Like children should play. Rather than sitting in a dark room staring at a screen."

I finished rubbing lotion into Lucy's back. She smiled a thank-you and lay facedown on her towel, her skin glistening in the sun. Neither of us had mentioned our conversation last night, but she seemed a bit better today, a bit calmer. She was getting on well with Jake and Ethan, which I was pleased about. Something to take her mind off things, keep her from brooding so much.

"Sometimes I forget that your boys are only just in their teens," I said. "Since they got so tall."

"Jake's already bigger than Alistair, you know," Jennifer said. "Won't be long until Ethan gets there, too. It feels so strange to suddenly become the smallest one in the family."

Sean had taken Daniel to the beach café for an ice cream. Russ lay flat on his back in the shade of a big beach umbrella, straw hat over his face, pure brandy sweating out of his pores. I'd never thought you could actually smell the alcohol coming off someone's sweat, but today I could. It was coming off him in waves, a sickly sweet odor that hung around him and snatched at your nostrils when you got too close.

Jennifer sat up, resting her chin on her knees. "I'm sorry about earlier," she said to me. "Sometimes I just . . . I don't know, open my mouth without thinking, I guess."

"It's OK," I said. "I know what you were trying to say."

She smiled, staring across the sand toward her boys. "Can you imagine life without them?" she said quietly.

"Who?"

"Your children."

"Not really."

"Seems impossible, doesn't it, that once upon a time we were just us? Alone, I mean. Flying solo, no kids, no husbands."

Izzy spoke up without opening her eyes. "Some of us still are."

Jennifer gave a little start of surprise. "Oh! I thought you were asleep. Sorry, Izzy, I didn't mean anything by it."

Izzy smiled and turned over onto her front. "It's fine. Flying solo has its advantages."

Jennifer smiled, embarrassed. "When we first met," she said, "it seems like another life, a different lifetime. Do you think it's changed us?"

I shrugged. "Of course. It's inevitable, isn't it? If we

were still the same now as we were twenty years ago, that would be . . . weird. Life shapes us, doesn't it?"

In good ways and bad, I thought, trying to work out where Jennifer was heading with this.

"I mean it changes *everything*."

"I don't know about that," I said. "Still feel like who I was back then. Just a bit more skeptical."

"I remember when Jakey was tiny, probably six months or something, and I was already just pregnant with Ethan. The three of us went to Cromer for a week, to be by the sea. And while we were there we went out on a boat trip along the coastline, just for an hour or so. I was holding Jakey in my arms, and I looked at Alistair and knew, with absolute certainty in that moment, that if the boat went down and there weren't enough life jackets—and I could only save one of them—I would save Jake without even a second's hesitation. Not even a *second*. I would watch my husband drown if it meant saving my baby. It was like a scientific fact, like gravity; you couldn't argue with it or deny it. And before I knew what I was doing, I could hear myself telling him this—I just came straight out and said it, without really realizing I was saying it. I felt awful. But it was true."

She fell silent for a moment, the breeze coming off the sea ruffling her blond hair.

I said, "That's natural, I suppose. A mother's instinct."

"Yes, but do you know what Alistair said? He said he was just thinking the same thing. That he would save

Jake if he could only save one of us." She was smiling a little now, shaking her head. "At that moment, sitting on that boat and feeling a bit seasick in Cromer harbor, it felt that something changed between me and Alistair. Changed from it being about me and him, into something else. Like it was the end of one chapter in my life and the start of another."

I didn't know what to say in response. Since seeing the messages on Sean's phone, I'd felt that a chapter in my life was about to end, too. Rolling grains of sand between my thumb and forefinger, I wondered if Jennifer would be the cause. Tall, beautiful Jennifer, who'd turned Sean's head when we first met as teenagers. Tense, worried Jennifer, who'd given off an air of brittle unease since we arrived in France.

She asked, "Have you ever thought that, too? About Sean?"

I shrugged, staring out at the ruined fort that occupied a tiny island in the bay. "Not in so many words. But I suppose we'd all say the same thing, wouldn't we? We all put our kids first: it's what we're programmed to do."

"It's just that I worry about them so much," Jennifer said. "*All* the time. I can't switch it off. I've tried to, but I can't."

"Same here. But Lucy and your boys will be at a point soon where they're big enough to look after themselves."

"Can't imagine that. They'll always be my boys. Always."

I looked around briefly to see who might be listening in. Izzy seemed to be dozing again. Russ was dead to the world, face covered by his hat. Alistair had wandered off somewhere to take pictures. The others, including Lucy, had gone to get an ice cream and find out about renting a paddleboat.

A little way out to sea, flying low and slow, a small plane trailed a long banner advertising Luna Park fairground.

Leaning closer to Jennifer and lowering my voice, I said, "Is everything . . . all right?"

She looked up. "Of course. Everything's fine. What do you mean?"

"You just seemed a little, I don't know . . . What you said about life changing people. Sounded as if you had something on your mind."

Jennifer looked away then, her mouth set in a hard, straight line. She turned back and seemed about to answer when Ethan wandered up, his hairy legs covered in a layer of sand

"Is there anything to eat, Mum? I'm *starving.*"

Jennifer reached into the cooler and held out an apple to her younger son.

He frowned. "Is there anything else? Any cookies?"

"Just fruit and water." She leaned forward and put the apple in his hand.

Rowan returned from the café, holding three Popsicles in their wrappers. She looked around. "Where's Odette? Was she playing with you and your brother?"

"Nope. Not seen her."

"I thought she was with you."

"She was for a bit, but she kept kicking holes in our dam. Said it was boring." Ethan took a huge bite out of the apple. "Said she was coming back here."

"Well, where *is* she?" She looked at her sleeping husband, laid out on his towel. "Russ?"

Ethan took another bite from his apple, shading his eyes with one hand as he scanned the beach. "Is that her, over there by the water?"

15

It *was* Odette. Standing at the water's edge, sun glinting off the shiny panels on her pink swimsuit, ankle-deep in the lapping surf. The tide was out and it was a good fifty or sixty meters away from our spot on the beach. It made me uncomfortable, seeing her alone near the water.

Rowan put a hand to her chest. "Why is she on her own?" She raised her voice and waved both hands over her head. "Odette!"

As we watched, a tall figure walked up to her. Bent over to talk, before taking her hand. A man in a baseball cap and sunglasses, his shirt open. I only needed to see him for a split second to know who it was. His stride, his profile, the way his shoulders moved, the way he held her hand.

Sean.

Hand in hand, he walked Odette back to our little encampment of towels, Daniel trotting along beside him carrying two big bottles of water.

Rowan went down on one knee, taking her daughter gently by the shoulders.

"You gave me a fright, Odette," she chided. "You must promise that you'll never go into the sea again without someone to look after you, OK? Do you promise?"

"Wasn't in the sea," the little girl mumbled, stubbing at the sand with her toe. "Only in the tiny waves."

"Russ?" Rowan said, her face lined with worry. "Why weren't you with her?"

Russ sat up. "Eh?" He blinked in the bright sunlight. "She was supposed to be playing with the boys, making a dam. I told her not to go into the sea without me, but she doesn't bloody listen."

"Perhaps if you weren't sleeping off a hangover," Rowan said, her voice rising, "you would have noticed her in the water on her own! Christ, you're so irresponsible!"

"It's all down to me, is it? As usual."

Odette whispered something into her mother's ear.

Rowan frowned. "What do you mean, honey?"

In reply, Odette turned to look at Jake and Ethan, pointing her tiny index finger at them. "It was the boys," she said in a small voice.

"What was, honey?"

"Their fault."

Rowan frowned over at the two teenagers.

"Why?"

"Wanted to play with them but Jake said I couldn't, said I wasn't allowed." Her index finger prodded the air for emphasis. "He told me to go and play on my own, in the *water*."

Jake's face darkened. "That's not true," he said, his voice rising. "She was trying to tell us what to do all the time, she wanted to build a fairy castle instead of a dam. She was kicking holes in it, letting the water through. Then she said she wasn't playing and stormed off."

"Never!" Odette said.

"Did!" Jake said loudly. "She's just trying to get us in trouble!"

Sean held his hands up as more voices collided in disagreement.

"All right, all right, the main thing is she's safe now, right? So why don't we all have an ice cream or something."

Rowan stood up and went over to Sean, hugging him tightly, arms clasped around his broad back. "Thank you, Sean, thank you," she said, her voice cracking. "I don't know what to say. Thank you for keeping an eye out for her."

He hugged her in return, biceps flattened against her back.

"No worries," he said quietly. "It was nothing."

They stood there like that, not saying anything else, simply holding each other tight.

Two people, two parents, giving and receiving thanks for the safety of a young child.

Holding each other.

For just a little too long.

Just as they were about to part, half turning away

from me, Rowan lifted her head up and stood on tip-toes, her lips near his ear. Just for a moment. Sean tilted his head down so his ear was almost touching her lips. Her hands at the back of his neck. His expression softening into a smile. A few seconds, nothing more, then they moved apart into an awkward silence.

Had I imagined it?

Had she whispered something?

What did she say?

What *was* that?

Finally, they separated. Rowan smiling at my husband, the hero.

My husband, who seemed to be losing his way in life.

Whose midlife crisis had snowballed into an affair.

Who had been lying to me for weeks, maybe months.

Not for the first time, I wondered whether Rowan had brought us here to impress *him,* to impress my husband. If that was what was really going on. The free vacation and the villa and the champagne were all to impress Sean. An in-joke, of which only the two of them were aware. They had worked out a way to come away on vacation together—the rest of us just happened to have been invited along for the ride.

Stop it.

Stop. It.

Russ extended a hand and Sean shook it, both men nodding awkwardly.

Sean had strong hands. I loved his hands. They were

already starting to darken with exposure to the Mediterranean sun. I noticed something else about him as
he reached to drink from a bottle of water: a pale line
of skin around the fourth finger of his left hand.

Where his wedding ring should have been.

16

ETHAN

Ethan tore a bunch of dark grapes from the vine, picked the biggest one, and put it in his mouth. He bit into it, the juice sweet and sharp on his tongue, chewing slowly to savor the taste. Turning away from Jake and spitting the pips on the ground before plucking another from the bunch, savoring the *pop* as the grape burst between his teeth. *Pluck, chew, spit, repeat.* He'd never been in a vineyard before. He'd never eaten grapes straight off the vine before, either. Always from the supermarket packet, always washed and rinsed because Jen—calling her that instead of Mum wound her up every time—*insisted* they were washed, never eaten when they were even slightly soft or had been left out of the fridge or might have had flies buzzing around them.

There was no breeze at all and the afternoon heat was brutal. He and his brother were in the middle of the vineyard down the hill from the villa, stretched out in the shade of a row of vines bushy with green leaves and fat red grapes. It was more private here; they couldn't be seen from any of the balconies unless they stood up.

Ethan propped himself up on one elbow, plucking another bunch of grapes from the nearest stem.

"So," he said, "are you going to ask her then?"

"Ask her what?" Jake said.

"You know."

"Nope."

Ethan slid a grape between his lips.

"Whether she's with anyone."

"What the fuck do you know about it? About girls? About anything?"

Ethan shrugged. It was one of his brother's surefire windups: girls. *Wind him up and watch him go,* and if he stood close enough when Jake kicked off, maybe— just maybe—Mum would notice him, too. He ran through a few options: straight to the point; or maybe the rumor about Rosie's party; or the rich rugby boy; or go for the nuclear option? Nah. That was best kept for another time. Might as well get straight to the point.

"So do you fancy her?"

"Fuck off," Jake said.

"You do, don't you?"

"Fuck. *Off.*"

"That's a yes, then."

"You've got literally no idea what you're talking about. You haven't got the first clue what I do or don't think."

"Right."

"You're such a twat."

"Oh, *I'm* a twat? That's brilliant." Ethan reached for a lie with enough weight to do some damage. "I'm not the one making a twat of myself over some girl who's done every lad in Year Eleven."

Jake's head snapped around.

"Say that again."

Ethan shrugged again.

"Just saying what I've heard."

"You heard wrong," Jake said. "Way wrong. That's total bullshit, what you've heard about her."

"OK, fair enough." Ethan paused a beat. "So you *do* fancy her, then?"

Jake got to his feet, his hands tightening into fists. "You never know when to shut the fuck up, do you?" He threw the half-eaten bunch of grapes he was holding into the undergrowth. "You never know when to stop."

"That's funny, bro, that's a good one." *Watch him go.* "Especially coming from you."

Ethan braced himself for the first blow.

They used to fight a lot when they were younger. Ethan had figured out how to light the fuse at a young age: niggle—provocation—anger—confrontation—scrap. Dead arms, Chinese burns, barked shins, stinging ears, pulled hair, bent fingers and bruised balls on a daily basis. Then they had both started getting bigger, almost at the same time, and a few months ago things had got a whole lot more serious without either of them realizing before it was too late. They found themselves having a next-level scrap, a full-on, proper, adult-sized fistfight over—Christ, Ethan had no memory of what even caused it, over *something,* anyway—and it had ended with split lips and black eyes, bloodied noses and bruised knuckles, Mum screaming at them to stop and Dad running downstairs and physically pulling Jake away from him, pinning him to a wall, Jake's eyes crazy wide, the way they always looked when he *really* kicked off. Ethan had grinned at him with blood on his teeth, dizzy from punches but jubilant, ready for round two. Blood on both of them, on their clothes, on their knuckles, big fat drops of it on the cream carpet. Mum had an absolute *shitfit.* It was kind of hilarious.

That was the day Ethan discovered he liked the taste of blood in his mouth.

But since then there had been an unspoken truce. Each knew the kind of damage he could do to the other. Jake was taller and had a longer reach, but Ethan had strength and power on his side. Both knew that whenever they had a proper fight now, both would end up bloodied—whoever won.

"Stand up," Jake said.

"Why?"

"Just fucking stand up and you'll find—"

He stopped midsentence, staring back up the hill.

"What?" Ethan said, following his brother's stare.

Lucy was walking toward them between the parallel rows of vines. Ethan sat up to get a proper look at her. She was wearing a white vest top and short cotton skirt, a wide-brimmed straw hat over blond hair still damp from the beach. The white top was *very* white, almost dazzling in the bright sunlight, so that it was hard to look at her. She was all-right-looking, he supposed. Better than all right—she was hot. Tall, nice face, slim but with big tits, not much to fault her on, really. Way out of Jake's league, although he didn't seem to realize, which was pretty funny.

She walked slowly, unselfconsciously, taking her straw hat off when she reached them.

"What's going on?" she said.

"Not much," Jake said, trying for nonchalance. "You all right?"

"Bit bored. You?"

"God, yeah. This heat is savage, isn't it?"

"I kind of like it." He brushed a hand through his fair hair. "What do you reckon, then?"

"About what?"

"This place."

"Pretty amazing," she said. "The pool's great."

"Yeah."

Ethan had to agree: all in all this wasn't a bad place. Not bad at all. Much better than the crap rentals they usually had to put up with on summer vacations.

Lucy fanned herself with the straw hat, one hand brushing her long blond hair back away from her face, before setting it on her head with the brim tilted back.

She gave Jake a big smile. "It's just so hot out here and there's no shade at all, is there?"

"Fancy a drink?"

"What've you got?"

Jake produced a half-sized bottle of vodka from the pocket of his black cargo shorts, unscrewing the cap and handing it to her. She took a swig and grimaced as she swallowed, coughing as she gave it back to him.

"Prefer it with a bit of Coke," she gasped.

"I'll get some from the house, if you want."

"No, no." She laughed and held a hand up. "It's fine."

Jake took a swig from the bottle and set it down in between him and Lucy.

Ethan thought about asking for a go on the vodka but didn't want to give his brother the opportunity to say no, to embarrass him in front of her. He watched them chatting, his muggy older brother and this hot girl with her chest stretching her vest top. *The beautiful people.* Laughing together, having fun together, and she wasn't even pretending this time like she sometimes did. The three of them went to the same school and knew one another in that respect—even though they were in different years—as much as they did family friends. *Jake trying to be all cool and casual,* Ethan thought, spitting another pip into the dry earth. It was obvious that his older brother didn't want him to be here. *Well, tough shit. I'm not going anywhere.*

"So," Jake said, turning his back on Ethan to block his view. "You OK?"

Lucy nodded. "Yeah. Just want to get the GCSE results day out of the way."

"Me too. Bet you'll get all nines though."

She snorted. "Don't know about that."

"Everything else . . . all right?"

"Yeah." She took another swig of vodka. "Peachy."

Ethan's ears pricked up at her tone. There was a silence between the two older teenagers for a moment, something passing wordlessly between them. Ethan leaned around to look at them but he was too late. The moment had gone.

"Right." Lucy looked farther down the hill. "Who's coming down to the woods, then?"

17

My book lay unread in my lap. Every time I picked it up and read a few lines, my mind slid off in another direction as I wrestled with the painful truth of my husband's infidelity: the poison at the heart of our marriage.

Sean had been upstairs taking a nap since we returned from the beach. It seemed incredible to me that he could act perfectly normal, that he could appear normal, in the face of what he'd done and what he was *still* doing. How could he carry on this pretense so blatantly that he wasn't even wearing his wedding ring anymore? What had Rowan whispered to him at the beach? Was Russ right to suspect her of having an affair? It was exhausting thinking about it all the time.

I needed a plan.

I sat up on the sun lounger and looked around. Russ was pushing Odette around the pool on a pink floating mattress. Rowan was nowhere to be seen. Alistair was wandering around the gardens with his phone, snapping pictures of . . . I wasn't really sure what he was taking pictures of. He turned his back to me and held up the phone again, zooming in on something. A bird in the tree, maybe? He was a bit too far away. Tonight, the four of us were going out for dinner: Rowan, Jennifer, Izzy, and me. I was going to have to be careful, keep my emotions in check, because right now every time I opened my mouth I felt like I was going to cry or confess everything—especially if someone tried to be nice to me. I was coiled up so tightly with worry and fear and desperation that it felt as if an accusation might burst out of me at any moment. But I had to keep a lid on all of that long enough to make sense of what was happening. If I could get on the front foot, find out what Sean was doing, I could prepare myself for what was coming. And maybe that would mean a better chance of keeping my family together.

I had done enough watching, enough listening. It was time for *action*. Time to do something.

I crept along the first-floor hallway on the balls of my feet. No sound, no voices. Pushing the heavy oak door open, I peered inside Rowan and Russ's bedroom. Like ours, it was decorated in creamy marble and antique wood, with a four-poster bed and beautiful carved bookcases. The sliding glass door out to the balcony was open slightly, gauzy white curtains stirring gently in the breeze from outside.

What was I looking for? What was I even doing in here?

I didn't really know. But there had to be something, some clue that would help me find my way out of this maze. Where would I hide something, if it were me? If this were my room?

The wardrobe doors were open. I pushed a dozen dresses and tops aside and saw two matching red Samsonite suitcases stacked at the back of the space, one slightly smaller than the other. I selected the smaller of the two and unzipped it, poking through empty plastic bags, charger cables, and a gray cotton laundry sack, also empty. The pockets inside the lid of the case had a few papers in them that seemed to relate to Rowan's company, columns of figures and accounting terms that I couldn't make head nor tail of.

I crossed the room and pulled open a bedside drawer. An open carton of ten packets of Marlboros, with only six packs remaining. A spare lighter. Assorted pills, a penknife, a plastic envelope stuffed with a thick wedge of fifty-euro notes, a phone charging cable, an iPad, and a Google Pixel cell phone, both switched off. Russ's side of the bed. That was a bit weird, that his phone was here, switched off. He seemed to be on it all the time.

Creeping around the other side of the bed, I pulled open the drawer there.

Three passports, paperwork for the rental car, flight details in a plastic wallet, packets of pills, hair straighteners, scissors, a notebook, pens, lip balm, suntan lotion.

I moved the boxes of pills aside and reached farther

into the drawer, trying to leave the other contents as I found them.

But none of it was familiar, none of it meant anything. None of it *helped*.

Hold on.

Wait.

There.

Something I *did* recognize. Something I knew very well. Perhaps the last thing I actually expected to find in this room.

Without realizing I was doing it, without even making a conscious decision, I reached in and picked it up. Held it between thumb and forefinger, shaking my head. Hot tears pricking my eyes.

I felt dizzy, as though I'd been struck in the back of the head. Up until now I'd had suspicion, fear, and maybe a tiny bit of hope that this could all—somehow—be a misunderstanding.

Now that hope was extinguished. Now I knew.

But if I took it now, Rowan would notice it was gone and she'd know someone had been in here. She'd probably be able to work out who. The smart move would be to put it back where I found it, avoid the danger of being discovered.

I slipped it into my pocket instead.

For a moment I forgot where I was and what I was doing. The room seemed to spin around me, colors swimming in my vision as I fought to hold back the tears. The fact that I'd found this, *particularly* this, just made everything worse. More hopeless.

Lucy's voice floated up from outside, from the pool below, snapping me back into the moment. Our conversation on the first night had been revolving in my head all morning, bouncing from one thought to the next as I tried to work out how to help her. *My girl.* There was so much she kept from me now, so many things she kept out of my reach, that I sometimes felt like I was spying on her. But I only wanted to help. Moving the sheer curtains aside, I pulled the sliding glass door open a little farther and slipped out onto Russ and Rowan's balcony.

This side of the villa was in direct, dazzling sunlight, and I felt the skin of my arms and face instantly start to cook in the heat. From here, I had a good view over the infinity pool and across to the main balcony off the living room. Lucy was in the pool, doing lengths with her smooth, graceful breaststroke. Back and forth.

If she looked up, she'd see me straightaway. I crouched down on the corner of the balcony, peering through a gap between two towels hung from the railing.

I watched her for a moment, the smooth movement of her limbs hardly rippling the surface of the water.

She had switched to backstroke when my eye was drawn to a flicker of movement in a shady corner under the stone staircase that ran up to the balcony. At first I thought it was a little statue, a stone figure of a cat, but then the head swiveled slightly to look up in my direction. It was a small ginger-and-white cat, more of a big kitten really, yellow eyes blinking slowly at me as I stared back from my vantage point.

Alistair was directly below me, stretched out on a sun lounger in what seemed to be his standard poolside attire: Speedos and a vest top, black socks and sandals. Plus cell phone, of course. I squinted through the bars of the balcony again, straight down at him. As I watched, he shifted the position of the phone in his lap, angling it up slightly and zooming in on something.

What exactly was he *doing*?

18

ALISTAIR

Alistair had started the bogus social media accounts for a totally legitimate reason: so he could follow his sons' activity on Instagram and Snapchat, keep an eye on what they were doing from a respectful distance. Particularly after the tough time Jake had gone through recently, and Jennifer always worrying about what they were getting up to. Initially, Alistair had tried to follow them under his real name—rookie mistake—but they'd just ignored his friend requests.

A subtler approach was called for.

So he made up a couple of fake accounts—username SkyBlue-Lad99—using a generic teenage boy profile image downloaded from a picture-sharing website, started populating it with more generic images of cars, food, football players, and celebrity tittle-tattle, and sure enough they'd accepted his friend request and followed him back. Jake and Ethan had hundreds of friends on the sites, most of whom they barely knew in real life. It was pretty easy to blend into the background.

It wasn't long before he'd discovered that the bogus accounts allowed him to see the whole picture, the background of everything the boys were going through, the environment in which they lived and interacted and were judged, the ocean in which they swam. Things were said on social media that they would never in a million years say in front of him and now he followed lots of others on Instagram, Snapchat, and Twitter. As ever, the beauty of it was that he could be on his phone—looking at literally anything, taking pictures—and no one would be any the wiser. They'd think he was just checking his emails or scrolling through Facebook.

So what were the young folks posting on Instagram today? He started with his boys, scrolling through a series of pictures from the poolside, Jake standing on the edge, with his arms aloft. Always Jake doing the doing, always Ethan daring him. That was an interesting dynamic in itself. He came out of Jake's profile and went back to his own feed, made up of their schoolmates and friends. There were copious sun-drenched vacation pictures from various spots on the globe, lots of posts about a girl called Lexie, who was having a sixteenth birthday party over the weekend, a shaky video of some boys dancing in a club, posts about someone called B-Boy with sad face emojis and kisses, quizzes, the usual dogs, cats, food and drink pictures, funny memes, diets, and other random teenage things that Alistair didn't pretend to understand.

After a few more minutes of light stalking, satisfied there was not too much going on with his boys that he didn't know about, he typed *LucyLupin22* into the search box and selected the account. A selfie of Lucy on the balcony of the villa filled the screen, the landscape spread out behind her. Various other pictures of the beach, the vineyard, the gorge from this morning. He scrolled back further. A picture of Lucy and two other girls, all in animal onesies: a sheep, a giraffe, and a panda. It looked like they'd been at a sleepover a few days ago.

OK. That all looked OK.

He switched to his real account and pulled up the pictures he'd just taken a few minutes before: a beautiful sleek creature with perfect features and effortless poise—it made him smile just looking at it. He picked the best one and posted it to his own Instagram account with the caption *Extra guest at the villa #Cats_of_Instagram.*

Lucy climbed out of the pool. She lifted her face to the sun and smoothed her long hair down her back with both hands. He was pleased to see that in this company—among friends she had known all her short life—she could still be unselfconscious, unguarded. It was good to see. He knew that on her Instagram account she could pout and pose along with the rest of her friends, filtering the image and getting the angle just right to show herself off in the best light. But when she thought no one was watching, she could still be natural. That was a healthy sign from a mental health perspective; there was a lot that troubled him about the deliberate fakery of most social media content.

Lucy walked back over to the sun lounger and pulled on her dress, then grabbed her phone, checking it with a frown and walking off in the direction of the vineyard. Minutes later, Izzy came down the steps to the pool in a silk sarong, sitting down on the sun lounger Lucy had just vacated. Izzy was another interesting character. Very honest, no artifice to her at all. No pretense. Well traveled. No kids, none of the baggage, none of the stretch marks and excess weight that women took on board when they joined the motherhood mafia.

Alistair spotted the ginger-and-white kitten again, and went back to his phone.

19

I was hurrying down to see my daughter by the pool, the images I'd seen on Alistair's phone still flashing in my mind, when I ran straight into Jennifer.

"Have you seen Jake?" she said. "Or Ethan?"

"Not recently, no. Not since we—"

"I haven't seen them since we got back from the beach."

"Not at all?"

"No."

"Have you tried texting them?"

"Yes, but they've not replied."

"Maybe they're in their rooms, or the games room?"

She shook her head. "I've checked already. No sign of them anywhere."

There was no sign of Lucy, either—where had she gone?

Jennifer threw a look at Rowan on the far side of

the pool, then lowered her voice. "I think Jake was a bit upset."

"Why? What happened?"

"About what Odette said at the beach, that the boys had told her she couldn't play with them."

"I don't think she meant anything by it, did she? Maybe she was just a bit confused."

"Jake *hates* liars. He gets so wound up when people say things about him, when they try to get him in trouble."

"I don't think she was doing it on purpose, Jennifer. She's only five."

"That's *perfectly* old enough to know what a lie is."

"Look, do you want a hand looking for the boys?"

Her expression softened. "Would you?"

"Of course. I don't know where Lucy's gone to, either. Perhaps they're all hanging out together somewhere."

The late afternoon sun was still strong and my sleeveless top was starting to stick to my back with sweat. Jennifer and I walked on through the vineyard, looking for the three teenagers, green creepers high on either side of us, calling their names as we walked toward the woods.

Having checked the garden and the villa without success, I had pulled up the Find My iPhone app on my phone, logging in with Lucy's details. Short of implanting her with a GPS chip, it was the surest and fastest way of finding her: she was never parted from her phone.

Twenty-first-century parenting.

I watched as the map zoomed in on our location—there was the village, and the road out, and the junction. The image of her phone appeared in the center of the screen, about seventy-five meters to the west. I zoomed in further, then out, looking around me to get my bearings.

At the edge of the vineyard there was an unmarked dirt path leading on through the trees. The path wound around a pair of towering oaks, their bark gnarled with age, past pine and tall, slender cypresses and olive trees that crouched low to the ground. The trees thickened as the path dropped into a dip, curving away, then up and around again, past a big standing rock and a fallen tree, exposed roots twisted like intestines spilling from a wound. A waist-high sign, faded and peeling with age, bore the word ATTENTION! in large red letters, above some other French that I didn't quite understand. Below the text was an outline of a cliff face, rocks tumbling down the side.

It was cooler here, the occasional call of birds the only sound above the whispering leaves in the canopy of the trees high above. I checked the iPhone map again and we walked on, Jennifer quickening her pace and me hurrying to keep up. Ahead, the trees thinned out into a clearing, an open area where the sun was stronger, a dusty spur of open ground where the trees seemed to stop abruptly. A shaft of sunlight pierced the thinning tree cover and I was momentarily blinded. Blinking and raising a hand to the light, I looked up and caught a glimpse of red through the trees. A T-shirt?

Jennifer broke into a jog, calling her boys' names a bit louder.

We emerged into the small clearing and skidded to an abrupt halt.

To the right, there was a sign indicating a steep path winding down to the gorge below. Directly in front were two olive trees, perhaps fifteen feet apart, the tattered remains of an orange plastic mesh fence hanging limply from each trunk. Between the two olive trees was a dusty outcrop jutting into empty air, a shelf of rock that led to nothing but a vertical drop straight down into the gorge below.

Jake had his back to us.

He was standing right on the edge. "Jake!" Jennifer shouted. "Stay still!"

Her shrill voice sent birds scattering from the canopy of branches above us.

Ethan sat cross-legged a few feet from the edge, phone held up, snapping pictures of his older brother.

"Go on," he said to his older brother. "Right to the edge."

Jake shuffled forward another few inches, posing for another photograph.

I looked wildly about me for Lucy, heart leaping against my rib cage.

There. She was sitting on a large flat rock, barely seeming to notice Jake posing for the camera. I perched on the rock next to her.

"Everything all right?"

"Of course," she said, her voice toneless and flat. She wouldn't look at me. "Why wouldn't it be?"

I gestured wordlessly toward Jake, and we watched as Jennifer walked slowly toward him, hands out, as if she were approaching a skittish animal.

"Jake," she said, a wobble of panic in her voice, "just take a step back from the edge, darling."

In response, Jake struck a new pose, holding his arms out to each side, raising them to shoulder height like a diver getting ready to leap. He tilted his head back and looked at the sky.

"If you look up," he said to no one in particular, "it feels like you're flying."

"Nice one," said Ethan, taking more pictures on his phone.

"Jake, *please*." Jennifer's voice cracked. "Please come away from the edge."

The breeze ruffled Jake's red T-shirt, the tips of his flip-flops sticking out into open air.

"You know, I thought this place was going to be really dull but *this*"—he indicated the drop into the gorge at his feet—"is properly cool."

"Listen to me, Jake, I just need you to take two steps back, OK? Two steps toward me."

He turned slightly to look at his mother, seeming to lose his footing a little, arms flailing to keep his balance.

"Whoa!" he said with a laugh. "That was close."

Jennifer took another step toward him, her face a mask of terror. "Jake, I'm begging you. Just one step back."

He held out his hand and let a smooth, round stone fall from his palm. There was no sound, no impact, for what seemed like forever. Then a sharp echoing *crack* as it struck the rocks below.

"Sick," he said.

Jennifer moved another step closer to her son. "Didn't you hear me shouting for you, Jakey? I was looking for you."

He leaned forward slightly, peering down into the gorge.

"There are some rock pools down there, Ethan. We should check them out."

"Definitely," Ethan said, leaning over to look.

I took a step toward Jake, feeling a sick, lurching sensation in my stomach as I neared the edge: vertigo by proxy.

Jennifer held both hands up in silent alarm. I froze.

She turned back to her son. "Don't look down, Jake," she said, trying to keep her voice steady.

He turned back to look at her, blond fringe falling over one eye.

"Why not?"

"Because you might lose your balance. Better to keep your head up, look at the horizon."

"Nah."

"Please, Jake," Jennifer said, her voice taut, "just don't, OK?"

He gave Lucy a grin full of bravado, then turned and looked straight down into the gorge.

20

Jake leaned forward slightly to look down and then jerked straight again, knees wobbling, arms windmilling at his sides for balance.

Jennifer's hand flew to her mouth. "Jake!"

He stepped back from the edge abruptly, turning to give a little bow.

"Ta-da! You see? Safe."

Jennifer grabbed his arm and pulled him farther away from the bluff.

"Don't *ever* do that again, Jake! That is so dangerous. I was *so* scared."

"Don't overreact, *Jen,* it's just a bit of fun."

He shook her off and went to stand with Ethan, who was holding up his phone.

"Nice one," Jake said, scrolling through the pictures his brother had taken. "Might post a few of these. Send them to me, yeah?"

I put an arm on Lucy's shoulder.

"Luce, you must promise me never ever to go near

the edge here, do you hear me? In fact, you shouldn't come down here at all until the barrier is fixed."

She shrugged my hand off and stood up.

"You don't have to treat me like a five-year-old."

"I'm just worried about you, that's all."

She walked over to Ethan and Jake without a word.

Jennifer and I moved closer to Jake as if we might have to grab him back from the edge at any moment: mother tigers circling the errant cub. I touched her gently on the arm.

"Are you OK?" I asked.

"Yeah," Jennifer said in a monotone, her eyes not leaving her sons.

She didn't look OK. The deep flush in her face had spread down to her neck and chest, her whole body shaking with adrenaline.

"This drop-off is pretty scary," I said.

"It's *so* dangerous!" she said, her voice rising. "How could Rowan have not told us about this? How is it even *allowed*?"

"We're all fine," I said, giving her a quick hug. "We're all safe. *Jake's* safe."

I inched slowly and carefully to the drop-off, taking small steps in the dusty soil.

Where we stood was an overhang, projecting out into nothing but thin air. I put my left foot sideways onto the edge and peered carefully into the gorge below: it was a straight drop down onto smooth, bare rock, scrubby green bushes sticking out here and there from the rock face on the way down. At the bottom, there was a thin stream running from one rock pool to the next, clear blue water sparkling in the late afternoon sun.

I had another sudden, powerful wave of vertigo, my stomach turning over so hard I had to step back and crouch down on the dusty ground, touching the earth with my fingertips.

"Jesus," I breathed, "that's some drop. It's got to be a hundred feet."

"I can't believe Rowan didn't tell us about this." There was an accusatory tone in her voice. "We should make it off limits to all the kids, or can we fence it off with something?"

"I'll ask her to call the maintenance company in the morning, see if they can send someone out straightaway."

"Boys?" Jennifer said to her sons. "You're not to come down here on your own until the barrier is fixed up again. OK?"

Ethan gave her a quick nod and a smile.

Jake gave no sign of having heard her at all.

21

Jennifer paced up and down the big bedroom's marble floor, arms crossed tightly against her chest. She had taken one of her pills but it didn't seem to be having any effect—sometimes they were like that. Instead of *wrapping her in a favorite warm blanket* (which was the way Alistair had described the dosage to her), there was just a slight softening at the edges of her anxiety, a slight blurring, but that was all. Nothing more. It wasn't enough.

This vacation was a bad idea, she decided. It was as simple as that.

Maybe not a bad idea in itself—in *theory,* it was a lovely idea—just not right now. Not with how things were. In fact, it was pretty much the last thing she needed at the moment, with everything else going on, all the other complications that life with two teenage boys could throw her way.

Jake and Ethan were at the stage in their teenage

lives when they were pushing boundaries, testing themselves and others. Like the whole thing with them calling her Jen now, instead of Mum. She didn't like that, not one bit, but Alistair had positively encouraged it as a move away from childhood into early adulthood. "It's a measure of maturity," he'd told her. "It empowers them: when the child moves into adulthood it no longer sees the parents as 'parents,' but rather as equals." Sometimes she wished her husband could see the children as *theirs,* as different and special and unique, rather than as just two more patients to be scrutinized and counseled according to the textbooks. Their boys were not long into their teens, but it seemed they were already lifting themselves out of the nest and sniffing the air. It wouldn't be long until they spread their wings and took flight.

That didn't bear thinking about.

She stopped pacing.

"He was *this* close to the edge," she said, holding her thumb and forefinger a millimeter apart. "I only just got to him in time . . . he was so close."

"I know," Alistair said.

"Then how can you be so relaxed about it, Ali? Jake was standing on the edge as though he had no fear at all."

Alistair sat back in the armchair, crossing one leg over the other. "He has no fear because the teenage brain has an undeveloped appreciation of consequences. He is impulsive and intense—and sometimes spontaneous to the point of being reckless. We know this already about our son."

"Well, that's *really* helpful," she said, her voice loaded with sarcasm. "I feel so much better now."

"What I mean is, I'm not relaxed, Jen. I'm focused. I'm looking for a solution."

"The solution is simple: we ban them from going into the vineyard and the woods."

"Ban them? How would we make that work, exactly?"

"I don't know, Ali, but we need to do something! I'm worried about him, worried about all of the children. Daniel's only nine. He's very impressionable."

"Ethan's got a sensible old head on his young shoulders. He won't let anything happen. And besides, exploring is a natural part of growing up. Physically, mentally, spiritually. They have to find out who they are and where they fit in the world."

"Christ! You're bloody impossible sometimes. These are *our children* we're talking about—here, now, today—not some case study you're presenting at a conference in six months' time."

"Come and sit down for a minute, Jen."

She ignored him and resumed her pacing. She wished for a time when Jake had listened to her, *really* listened, his little face turned up to hers, absorbing every word she said. When she had been the only female in his life.

More and more often she found herself longing for the time when her boys were little. Full, golden days that had stretched out with endless promise, days of playing and stories and bath times and naps and going to the park with the double stroller. Long days that were pure and simple and planned out from start to finish. What in the world could compete with a beautiful, sleepy, contented baby dozing on your chest? Nothing. Nothing at all.

At the time, other mothers had complained of the routine, of the long hours, of the sleepless nights. But not Jennifer. She missed those days with an ache deep in her chest, a physical pain that sometimes kept her awake at night. Life before her boys was a blur, as if it belonged to someone else entirely—as if those years weren't really important enough to remember. Sometimes she would watch the home videos of when they were little, toddling and laughing and playing up to the camera, and she'd find herself with tears running down her face.

She longed for the days when they relied on her completely, when she was the center of their world. For the last few years, as her boys had grown bigger and taller and more distant, it felt as though a vacuum were growing inside her, a hollow space that Jake and Ethan no longer wanted to occupy.

She longed to feel whole again, for something to fill the void that was left behind.

Her phone *pinged* with a new message and she checked the screen, firing off a quick message in reply before stowing the phone in her pocket.

"I can't be passive about this, Ali," she said. "I can't just sit and watch like a spectator."

"Why do you feel that way?"

"You *know* why, after what happened."

"Let's talk about Jake, then. Let's break his behavior down and think about how we can best respond to—"

"Do you have to be so damn analytical all the time? Can you not just think like a father, rather than a therapist?"

"I can do a better job as a father if I use what I know. My professional knowledge."

Jennifer turned to look at her husband, who was sweating lightly in a maroon vest top and blue shorts.

"Sometimes I wish that you were a traffic warden, an estate agent—a damn bus driver."

"If I'd been a bus driver we would probably never have met, my dear."

It was true, she supposed: that was how their paths had collided in the autumn after graduation. At first she'd thought her black mood was some kind of post-university slump, the inevitable dip caused by the end of three intense years living with her three brilliant new best friends. They'd all returned to their respective hometowns—initially, at least—and Jennifer had felt a loss of something so fundamental, so important, that she didn't know if she would ever find it again. It wasn't that she missed her friends back in California; that was a long way behind her by then, and she'd already started to think of herself as more British than American. But it felt like an ending to the best three years of her life. Summer came and went without the black cloud lifting, and when a routine visit to the doctor ended with her breaking down in tears and sobbing her heart out, she was referred for counseling.

It wasn't love at first sight. That wasn't how Alistair affected her. But slowly, over the weeks and months, she began to look forward to seeing him more and more. She would feel a little lift, a little brightness, when her Wednesday sessions came around with this calm, kind man who seemed to have all the answers, who could relax her, who was the first man who actually *listened* to her. The first man who understood her. Almost ten years older, already married and divorced, he had a wisdom about him, a tranquility, that she found intoxicating. He was a scholar, a thinker, a lifelong student of the mind. He had answers for questions she'd not even realized she had.

And then, one February Wednesday, she had made a decision. She bundled herself up in her thickest coat, gloves, scarf, and boots and settled herself on a park bench across the street from his practice, after her session was over. When he came out to buy his lunchtime sandwich from the little deli on the high street, she followed him and just *happened* to bump into him as he sat at the window seat with his pastrami on rye.

That was how it started.

They had sailed pretty close to the wind in terms of his code of professional ethics because in the early days there were times when they *had* got a bit carried away. But he'd avoided trouble by having her assigned to another therapist, so that their burgeoning relationship could be aboveboard, out in the open. Everything had happened quickly after that. Moving into his apartment, then a little house together, a baby, then another, a bigger house, then a civil wedding with two of the cutest little pageboys you could ever wish for. Jake, her sweet, sensitive, complicated firstborn with a head of golden hair, and Ethan, who was just . . . Ethan. Her sensible second child.

She knew mothers weren't supposed to admit that they had favorites. Of course they *said* they didn't. But deep down they all knew; they were just prevented from saying it out loud because it was part of the carefully constructed fiction that parents maintained. Like how you were supposed to say that day care was just the same as parental care, as if somehow letting your babies be looked after by total strangers was just as good as looking after them yourself. Just as good for your baby's development, just as good for socialization and motor skills and language acquisition. How was that even logical? How could it even be half-true?

It was one of her biggest regrets—now, more than ever—that she'd decided not to do the logical thing ten years ago and homeschool Jake and Ethan. For once in his life, Alistair had put his foot down when it came to the boys and insisted that they go to a regular school, so Jennifer had done the next best thing and got herself a job there, in the office, so she could be near them. So she could look after them.

Because, of course, it was true that a mother's care was better than a stranger's.

And of course it was true that every mother had a favorite.

It wasn't Ethan's fault that his brother had stuff going on that needed his mother's attention. That was just how things were. She'd read somewhere that second children were more resilient than firstborns because they had never had the experience of being an only one. Ethan was pragmatic, like his father—he just got on with things, even as a baby he'd been the same. He didn't mind not being the center of attention; he was much more self-contained than Jake.

Jake was her special one.

At first, she'd thought Alistair was laid back in his parenting style just to balance her out. To create an equilibrium between them—her responsible parenting on one side of the scales, his *let them get on with it* approach on the other. But over time she'd realized it wasn't anything deliberate on his part, it was just the way he was. With everything. Which was fine when the boys were little, but now it seemed almost irresponsible.

Alistair sat forward in his seat, clasping his hands together.

"OK," he said. "How about this: we all go down there, all four of us. We walk down into the gorge, talk to the boys, find out what they're thinking, make sure they're aware of the dangers of the terrain and the consequences of a fall from that kind of height. We talk it through with them, articulate it clearly, ensure they're fully cognizant of all the facts, ask them to stay away from the danger. That's really all we can do."

"That's not enough, Ali."

"What do you suggest, Jen? They're bigger than me, bigger than both of us: we can't physically prevent them from leaving the villa. They're almost adults; we need to start treating them accordingly. We can't track them, follow them around twenty-four hours a day."

"Maybe not. But we can do a damn sight more than just *talk*."

She slammed the door on her way out.

22

Sunday night was our night, when we would leave the children and men at the villa and have a women-only meal. Just the four of us, a chance to catch up without interruption, to talk to one another properly, enjoying good food and wine for a few hours. Knowing what I did, there was nothing I wanted to do less—but there was no way to get out of it.

I put on my newest dress and sat at the dressing table, brushing the knots out of my hair on autopilot. Brushing, brushing, brushing. I didn't recognize the washed-out reflection that stared back at me: dark shadows beneath my eyes that I had done my best to disguise with concealer, pale skin that seemed untouched by a full day of Mediterranean sunshine.

I stood and went to the window, opening it wide into the air-conditioned bedroom and feeling the oven-like heat of the day wrap itself around me. The view was breathtaking: wide open skies, green fields ready for harvest, little ochre-roofed farmhouses dotted here and there. The leaves of the olive trees below me moved gently in a light breeze, tiny ripples ruffling the surface of the infinity pool.

Daniel was down in the garden below, Sean's camcorder in hand, skipping along, filming the pool area and the back of the villa.

For the first time since we'd been here I felt a moment of peace, a moment of pure tenderness: my bright, funny boy, so innocent in his love of funny videos and slapstick and silly jokes. So unaware of everything that was going on beneath the surface. He caught sight of me and stopped to wave, his high voice echoing across the quiet garden.

"Mummy! Hello!"

I waved back and gave him my best smile as he zoomed in on me. After a moment he waved again and then he was off, disappearing around the side of the villa with the camera held out in front of him, chattering as he went.

I felt my smile fade and checked my watch. It was nearly time to go.

The air had a golden quality, the evening light soft and honey warm as the sun sank toward the hills.

Rowan had driven us into the foothills of the Monts de l'Espinouse, to the little town of Olargues. Perched in the shadow of a ruined medieval castle, our table at Les Amis gave stunning views down into the Jaur valley as it softened into dusk. Below us was the curving stone arch of the Pont du Diable, the *Devil's Bridge*, which, according to local folklore, had been built by the Devil himself in exchange for the first soul that walked across it.

We had ordered food and were waiting for starters of mussels and scallops and tomato galettes. Normally the conversation flowed when we got together: work and children and schools, reminiscences about university life in Bristol, our shared house as an inseparable gang of four, parties and nights out.

But not tonight. Jennifer had barely said a word to Rowan all evening and I couldn't hold on to the thread of any conversation for more than a few minutes before my mind started wandering again, looking for clues in what each of them said and how they seemed. I couldn't stop thinking about what I'd discovered during my search of Rowan's room that afternoon. Izzy was valiantly keeping things going with one of our standing jokey tales about the first time we had gone for a meal in a restaurant as freshmen at university. That night, she and I had gone to the ladies and when we returned the other two were already on their way out the door, giggling drunkenly. It was only when we were halfway down the street that Rowan admitted they had run out without paying the bill—at which point I had marched them back to the restaurant and insisted that we pay up.

"Nice that Rowan has got us a table near the exit so she can try her usual trick," Izzy said with a smile. "Old habits die hard, eh, Mrs. James?"

Rowan held her hands up.

"I can assure you, that was the first and only time I've ever done that." She gestured at me. "Couldn't bear to be shamed again by Mrs. Goody Two-Shoes here."

I looked at her, trying to smile, trying to think of something to say, but all I could think of was her whispering in Sean's ear at the beach this afternoon. Hugging him for just a little *too* long.

"Shame you?" I said with a tight smile. "I wouldn't dare."

Rowan sipped her drink, giving me a quizzical look.

Izzy raised her glass suddenly. "We should have a toast," she said.

"To what?" Rowan said.

"Being forty?"

"Oh God, really? That's way too depressing."

"Forty is the new thirty, according to Oprah."

"How about a toast to all of us being together again?"

We clinked glasses and drank. Icy champagne bubbles bursting against the back of my throat usually reminded me of my wedding day, that first beautiful glass before dinner as Sean and I circulated among our guests, newly married, basking in the afterglow. But tonight it tasted bitter.

I put my nearly full glass down on the table.

Jennifer took the tiniest of sips and sat back with a frown.

"What is it, Jen?" Izzy said. "What's up?"

"I'm still a bit freaked out, that's all."

"Oh. Sure, right."

"After what happened with the boys this afternoon." She turned to Rowan. "Why didn't you tell us about the gorge?"

"I'm so—"

"Jake could have been killed," Jennifer interrupted. "*Any* of the children could have been killed, wandering down there in the woods. It's *so* dangerous."

Rowan put down her glass, nodding apologetically. "I know, I'm sorry," she said. "My client mentioned something about the French having a bit of a sketchy attitude to health and safety, but no specifics. I was going to go down there and check it out myself on our first day but everything got away from me with the unpacking and getting things set up."

"How is it even allowed? How can they rent it out to people?"

"It's private land," Rowan said. "There are signs up, but they're not legally obliged to fence it off because it's not actually rented out to the public. Sorry, guys."

"I can't imagine what might have happened if Jake had slipped." She put a hand over her mouth. "It's too awful to even think about."

"I understand that. We're all in the same boat here, Jen."

"But being a full-time mum, things are different for me—Jake and Ethan are my whole world. Everything is about keeping them safe."

Rowan leaned forward, elbows on the table.

"*I* feel the same way about Odette."

"I know you do," Jennifer said placatingly. "But it's not the *same,* you've got all this stuff going on with your company, all these distractions, and it seems so irresponsible that your client didn't tell you about the gorge, about the danger and—"

I put a hand over hers.

"It's OK, Jen. We'll keep an eye on all the kids, we'll look out for each other."

"Like we always have done," Rowan added forcefully.

Jennifer gave a little nod, but wouldn't look at any of us.

I drank another mouthful of champagne, swallowing back the bitterness.

"Hey, I almost forgot," Izzy said, breaking the silence. She reached into her handbag. "Look what I found. My brother was clearing out his garage. Boxes and boxes of my old stuff that he's been looking after while I was away and I haven't looked at in years."

She produced a slim paperback book, *Mrs. Dalloway* by Virginia Woolf, and from within its pages plucked a photograph, a color print that was creased and bent at the edges. "Nineteen years ago."

Rowan picked it up. "Oh my God! My *hair*. What on earth was I thinking?"

"I think it was your Jennifer Aniston phase. The graduation ball. Remember?"

She passed it on to Jennifer, who studied the picture in turn. Finally, she allowed herself a small smile.

"Izzy, you've hardly changed a bit. What's your se-cret?"

Izzy shrugged. "Not having kids?"

The picture came around to me and I held it up to the light of the candles flickering in the middle of the table. It showed us standing close together, shoulder to shoulder, arms around one another's waists. Ball gowns and big smiles and glasses of buck's fizz, balloons and streamers strewn at our feet while young men in tuxedos milled around in the background of the shot, a big white marquee set out in the central quad.

The picture had caught Rowan midlaugh, hair styled and tinted like the *Friends* actress, in a deep crimson ball gown; next to her was Jennifer in a sleeveless, pale green two-piece that showed off all her curves; Izzy, her chestnut-brown hair cut pixie short, stunning in a black cocktail dress—the only time I could remember her wearing a dress. And me at the end of the row, in royal blue.

God, we looked so *young*. But we looked happy. Like anything was possible.

Izzy leaned over to get another look at the picture in my hand. "Wasn't that the night Jen finally snogged Darren Burton?"

"That was *you,* if memory serves," Jennifer said indignantly. "I was still on the rebound."

"From who?"

Jennifer hesitated.

"You know who," she said quietly, giving me a quick glance.

"Oh," Izzy said. "Right. Forgot about that."

Jennifer had never talked about her relationship with Sean in those terms before. The ball had been in May but they had broken up the month before, as we came up to the Easter break. Had she still been on the rebound a month later, still hurting from the breakup?

And why mention it now?

Rowan pointed to a lad with a ponytail in the background of the picture.

"And after Darren Burton threw up," she said to Izzy, "you moved on to his housemate."

"God, yeah! I vaguely remember him—what was his name again? Kissed like he was trying to suck your face off."

"Nice," Rowan said, laughing.

Izzy clicked her fingers and pointed at me, as if she'd just remembered something else.

"I tell you what I *do* remember," she said. "That was the night, wasn't it? The night you and Sean first got together."

I nodded. It was true, in a way. That was the night we had first held hands, danced together, kissed, with other people around. The first time he'd held me so close I could feel his heart bumping in his chest, when we didn't care anymore who saw us.

The whole truth and nothing but the truth was a little more complicated than that.

The truth was, I'd been in love with Sean since the end of our first year at Bristol. I had admired him from afar while he went out with a string of girls who were prettier, cleverer, and more confident than me. I'd been in love with him for the one month, three weeks, and four days he was with Jennifer. I didn't *mean* for it to happen, but it just did. And slowly, Sean had become aware of my feelings. When he split up with Jennifer, he told her he was freaking out about his upcoming exams and worried about getting kicked out of uni, and he wanted a break to focus on his studies. It was at least partly true, but there was more to it than that. Much more.

There was me.

He broke up with her because of me, because of what had been growing between us.

Me, comforting a heartbroken Jennifer who couldn't understand why her first real boyfriend had ended their relationship. Who had convinced herself that she was too straight, too highly strung, too high maintenance for him. Me offering sympathy and wine and a shoulder to cry on, and all the while fighting the guilt that I was the cause of her misery.

Had I really been a good friend to Jennifer, back then? A true friend? I suppose I knew the answer to that.

"Yup." I smiled. "That was the night me and Sean finally got together."

"You know what?" Izzy said. "We should do a selfie, just like this picture."

"So we can see how haggard and crappy we look now compared to then?" Rowan said.

"Shush, Rowan, you look absolutely lovely. Stand

up now, everyone." Izzy took her phone out and began marshaling us into position, in the same order that we stood in the old photograph: Rowan on the left, then Jennifer, then Izzy and me on the end. We stood like that, backs to the low wall at the edge of the patio, arms around one another's waists, smiling for the camera just like we'd done nineteen years ago.

"Say cheese!" Izzy said, holding her arm out to get us all in the shot.

The camera clicked once, twice, and she held the phone's screen out to us so we could all see.

"Perfect."

I looked at the picture. The four of us, just like always. A beautiful meal on a fine warm evening, the lights of the valley below twinkling in the darkness. A wonderful time with my dearest friends, people I had known more than half my life. People close enough to be almost family.

It should have been perfect, but one of them had turned it into a lie.

And maybe that was no more than I deserved.

23

Sean

Sean used the stubby pencil to cross out another box on his score sheet. That was his big street, full house and Yahtzee all gone. He would be lucky not to finish last. He sighed and handed the dice and shaker to Russ, who was taking it all very seriously.

He studied the other men for a moment: Russ and Alistair, opposite him on one of the big sofas, an awkward pair if he'd ever seen one. Russ, all angles and elbows and alpha-dog cheekbones next to Alistair—soft edges and sloping shoulders, beer belly and bushy beard. Did either of them know? Did either of them have the slightest inkling of what was going on? Russ seemed to spend half the day on his cell phone and the other half drinking rather than paying close attention to what was happening around him. Alistair, on the other hand, appeared more observant, more tuned in most of the time.

Jake and Ethan were sprawled at each end of a sofa,

Lucy cross-legged between them. Each was splitting their attention between taking their turn in the game and their respective cell phones. Dinner was finished and the two younger children had been put to bed.

Russ rolled a full house straight off the bat.

"Get in!" He clenched a fist in triumph and wrote the score on his sheet.

Alistair took the dice from him and rolled three ones, a four, and a six.

"Here we go, boys. Your old dad's going to get a Yahtzee."

He picked up the dice and rolled them twice more, ending up with three ones, a two, and a three. A bust.

Jake shook his head, exchanging a glance with his younger brother.

"You really are crap at this, aren't you, Dad?"

"It's a game of luck, my boy. Now chess, on the other hand, that's more my thing."

"Isn't chess, like, the most boring game ever invented?"

"All skill, no luck, Jake. How a game *should* be. When I was your age I was—"

A high-pitched cry reached them from upstairs.

"Daddy! Daddy!"

Sean muted the music and looked over at Russ.

"Yours or mine?" he said.

Russ turned his head toward the sound, narrowing his eyes. A moment later, the cry came again.

"Daddy!"

"Mine, I think," Russ said, popping the cap off another bottle of beer and taking a long pull. "But she'll stop in a minute."

Jake and Ethan took their turns before the cry from upstairs came again.

"Daddy!"

Sean smiled at Russ, pointing toward the stairs.

"Definitely yours," he said.

Ethan gathered the dice back into the little plastic cup and handed it to Lucy, who took it from him as she scrolled one-handed on her phone.

Odette appeared at the bottom of the stairs in her Peppa Pig pajamas, her hair a nest of straggling bedhead curls around her head. Her face was flushed pink, a deep frown creasing her forehead.

"Dad-*ee*!" She stuck out her bottom lip in an exaggerated pout. "Why didn't you come when I shouted?"

"Couldn't hear you, darling."

"I shouted and shouted and you didn't come! I can't get to sleep."

"Have you tried lying very quietly and thinking about nice things?"

She folded her arms. "I want a Daddy story."

"You had a Daddy story already, sweetie. In fact, you had *two* stories."

"Want another one."

"No."

"Want a Mummy story, then."

"Mummy's out at dinner."

"Then *you* have to do it. And you have to wait with me while I fall asleep in case the baddies try to get me."

"The baddies aren't going to get you, Odette."

She stamped her little foot on the white-tiled floor. "Want a *story*! And you have to *wait* with me!"

Russ stood up with a sigh, grabbing his beer from the table and scooping up his daughter with his other arm. He headed back up the stairs for the second time that evening. "Are we carrying on, or what?" Jake said impatiently.

"We should probably wait for Russ to come back," Sean said, "since he's in the lead."

"How long's he going to be, then?"

"Not long."

Jake went back to looking at his phone.

Sean looked at the three teenagers on the sofa across from him. His daughter was only a year older than Jake, and close to two years older than Ethan, but there was a world of difference between them. His daughter looked like a young woman—with a full face of makeup, he knew she could pass for eighteen at least—while Jake had the size of a man but the face of a boy, as if he'd grown too fast for his features to keep up. No, that wasn't quite right: not a boy, exactly, but a curious teenage hybrid that was neither one nor the other.

Jake stood up and stretched, yawning hugely. "*So* bored. Who's up for some pool downstairs?"

Ethan unfolded himself from the sofa and stood, too. "I'll give you a thrashing if you want, bro."

To Sean's surprise, Lucy stood up, too.

"I'll play the winner."

"That," Ethan said with a lopsided grin, "will be me."

The three of them trooped off down the hall, the *slap-slap* of their flip-flops echoing on the stairs as they went down to the basement.

Alistair sat back in his armchair, lacing his fingers behind his head.

"And then there were two."

"Game abandoned, then."

"I guess so."

"Oh well," Sean said. "I was going to lose, anyway."

Russ's iPhone started ringing quietly on the low tabletop, the display showing an unrecognized number.

Sean ignored it and began collecting up the Yahtzee score sheets and dice scattered across the low table.

"Must have been something we said." He looked at his watch. "When are the ladies due back, anyway?"

"Not for at least another hour, I shouldn't think. I expect they'll just be getting into the *aren't-men-awful* stage of the evening."

"No doubt."

There was an awkward silence as Sean finished clearing up the game and drained the last of his beer.

"Fancy another drink?"

"Oh, go on then," Alistair said. "If you're going to twist my arm."

Sean went into the kitchen to grab another couple Kronenbourgs from the giant fridge, pausing on his way back to listen at the bottom of the staircase. The muffled *crack* of a pool ball came up from the basement, but all seemed quiet upstairs. That was good.

He sat back down opposite Alistair and handed him one of the beers. They clinked bottles and Alistair leaned over the iPod dock, scrolling through the playlists. The kids' chart mix was abruptly replaced by Pink Floyd's "Comfortably Numb."

"So, Sean," Alistair said, settling back into his chair, "tell me about our newest arrival."

"Izzy?"

"You two grew up together, didn't you? What was she like back then?"

"Ah, she was great, a live wire. Funny, too, you know? We laughed a lot back then."

"Never married?"

Sean hesitated and took another gulp of beer, the glass of the bottle ice cold against the palm of his hand. Didn't Alistair know the history? Maybe he'd forgotten, or filed it away somewhere in his mcmory. He could never tell what the other man was thinking.

Engaged, but not married.

"No. Never."

Alistair steepled his fingers together.

"I find her quite fascinating."

"Yeah, she's an amazing woman, really." He added quickly, "So strong, despite everything that life's thrown at her. I'm really glad she was able to make it out here this week."

Stop talking. You are rambling. Just stop.

He was suddenly aware of the way the older man was looking at him, fists beneath his chin, as if Sean were one of his clients. He felt as if he were being scrutinized by Alistair the counselor, the accredited professional who spent his days listening to other people's problems. As if Alistair were mentally taking notes on what he said, how he said it, what he left out, to create a profile and make a diagnosis of his shortcomings. To put them on show for the world to see.

And how about you then, Alistair? Have you ever turned that penetrating gaze on yourself? Ever done anything that you knew was wrong? Have you ever looked in the mirror, ever taken a close look at your own flaws and failings as a man, a father, a husband?

Sean felt the sweet sting of guilt, his constant companion.

Have any of us, for that matter?

NINE MONTHS EARLIER

It's not until Daisy Marshall's sixteenth birthday party that she talks to him properly.

She's sitting with Fran and Emma and Megan in the garden, everyone doing vodka shots. She knows he's been invited, she's checked, but it's anyone's guess as to whether he'll turn up. He trains a lot on evenings and weekends with the Saracens rugby academy, where they bring through all their best young players. Saracens is one of the biggest teams in the country and he mostly plays fly half, in the No. 10 shirt.

She's done her research.

Then, halfway through the evening, he's there with his mates, looking hotter than ever, crisp white shirt taut across his shoulders, hair still looking wet from the shower, one of the other lads pressing a bottle of beer into his hand. He's like a younger version of Chris Hemsworth, but even better in her humble opinion. He's ridiculously hot. He's so hot it's kind of unfair for all the other boys in the year, who look like little kids standing next to him.

She wonders if he thinks the same way about her.

Jake finally beckons her over, that weird look on his face like when he's pissed off about something but trying not to show it. He introduces them, just like she asked him to, and she has to tell herself not to smile too much, not to be too keen, too soon. Brushing her blond hair away from her face.

She raises a hand in a little wave and she's like, "Hi, I'm—"

But he cuts her off with a smile.

"I know who you are."

"Do you? You do?"

Missing cool by about a million miles.

"Me and Jake are both in the first team for rugby. He's told me all about you." His bright blue eyes on hers, long lashes blinking once, twice. "He was right, too."

"Right about what?"

"You are the hottest girl in Year Eleven."

And there's a little starburst of joy, a deep glow in the center of her chest.

A little sun inside her, burning hot.

MONDAY

24

The water was icy, a brutal, paralyzing cold that felt like frozen fire, a million tiny needles piercing my skin at once. Rushing down from the mountains, it was pure and beautifully clear but I couldn't imagine paddling in it, let alone getting my shoulders under. I lifted my feet out of the stream and sat back on the rock, full of delicious relief as the July sun warmed my feet back into life.

I felt like the captain of a sinking ship, standing on the deck, waiting for the water to take me.

We had driven north into the hills to the Gorges d'Héric, a deep gully of sparkling red granite. Hiking a mile up the path, we found ourselves the perfect sunny spot—a steep-sided valley carpeted with oak trees, jagged peaks of rock above us on both sides jutting against the blue sky. Just upstream, a mini waterfall emptied into a deep pool of clear mountain water, rocks rising vertically above it on both sides.

We were arrayed around the edges of a smaller rock

pool, complete with tiny sandy beach, our towels laid out on broad, flat rocks, slabs of granite speckled with tiny flecks of quartz that sparkled in the sunlight. I watched as Sean played with Daniel and Odette in the shallow water of the rock pool, the two children squealing and splashing with delight as Sean dared them to wade deeper into the cold mountain water. Lucy, in a black bikini and Jackie O sunglasses, lay back on a rock tilted toward the sun.

Jennifer had gone farther up the gorge in search of her boys, while Rowan had climbed higher off the path, looking for an elusive single bar of cell phone reception.

Izzy walked over and set out her towel on the rock next to mine. She lay down, propping herself on her elbows, face to the sun. When she spoke, her voice was quiet, gentle.

"So, Kate. Are you going to tell me?"

"Tell you what?"

"I've hardly seen you crack a smile once since I got here. What's up?"

"Nothing," I said. "Just a bit preoccupied, that's all."

"You can't fool me, woman. Half the time it's like you're not even there, you're away with the fairies somewhere." She paused. "It's Lucy, is it?"

"I feel like she's having a tough time of it at the moment."

Izzy shrugged. "She's at a difficult age. Boys and hormones and exams and bitchy friends—can't be easy."

"What were you like at sixteen?"

"Me?" She smiled. "I was awful. A nightmare. Me and my dad used to fall out on a daily basis. He'd threaten to take my bedroom door off if I didn't do as I was told, but I still wouldn't. One day I came home from school and it was gone, hinges and all. Weeks and weeks I went, with my brother peering in every time he walked past my bedroom, helping himself to my stuff if I wasn't there."

"You'd calmed down a bit by the time you went to uni, then?"

"Mark used to say I had the temper of an Italian housewife. In a good way." Her smile faded and I could see echoes of the pain that was normally hidden, but which had never really left. Not completely. "It's fifteen years ago this year, you know?"

Despite the heat of the morning, I felt a cold wave wash over me, a chill of grief and guilt. Sudden memories of a life cut short. Mention of the name was a sudden gearchange I was not prepared for, a lurch into the past that I had built a wall around in the years since.

"Since the accident?" I said.

The accident. Not *since it happened,* or *since he died.* Definitely not *since your fiancé was killed.*

The accident.

"I still think about him sometimes, you know," Izzy said. "Weird things, like how he'd have three sugars in his tea, or his weird obsession with Al Pacino. The silly catchphrases he'd come out with. He'd have loved it here. This place."

Words bubbled up in my throat, words that would always be inadequate. If it hadn't been for me, Izzy might well have been sitting here with Mark by her side, maybe a couple of kids, too. Maybe a girl and a boy, like mine, splashing in the rock pool. Her life could have taken a very different course.

Their wedding had been just a week away. Plans made for the future. An apartment together.

If it hadn't been for me.

That night, fifteen years ago. The night Mark was killed. A funeral instead of a wedding.

Justice never done.

In the days and weeks that followed, I would try to remember that night, Izzy's bachelorette party, the sequence of events that led up to what happened. I could remember the meal, having a few drinks and being happily merry—but not out of control, not falling-down drunk. I could remember walking into the nightclub, some random guy insisting on buying me a glass of champagne at the bar. And after that, nothing. A blank. A dark hole in my memory. It was only much later that I learned that champagne was a popular choice for spiked drinks because the bubbles helped to disguise any aftertaste.

I didn't remember the other three walking me out of the club, or being so calamitously sick that no taxi driver would take me.

I didn't remember Izzy texting her fiancé, Mark, asking him to drive into town to pick the four of us up instead.

I didn't see Mark arriving, parking across the street, waving and smiling as he crossed the road.

I didn't see the car hit him and leave him dying on the tarmac.

But I vividly remembered Izzy's withdrawal from everything afterward, locking herself away from friends and family. Selling the apartment, quitting her job, a flight to the other side of the world. A life of traveling and teaching that she'd been leading ever since. Over the years she had grown tougher and more resilient than ever, more self-sufficient than any of us.

The emotions I had been holding at bay for the last few weeks surged to the surface and suddenly I was on the point of crying. Which was ridiculous, considering Mark had been her fiancé, not mine. But I couldn't stop them.

"I'm sorry, Izzy." I swallowed, my voice cracking. "For everything, for making Mark come into town that night to—"

"Shush yourself," she said, putting her hand over mine. "That's in the past. Everything that needs to be said has been said, a long time ago. You don't have to apologize anymore."

Oh, but I do. I do.

And maybe losing Sean is my penance.

Maybe it's revenge. Karma. Some kind of payback for what happened fifteen years ago.

25

"We're not talking about that night," Izzy said, forcing a smile, "we're talking about you and Lucy."

I used a napkin to wipe a tear from the corner of my eye.

"Lucy's . . . oh, I don't know. She doesn't talk to me like she used to."

"She's growing up."

"Too fast."

She took a drink from a bottle of water. "It's more than that though, isn't it?"

"What makes you say that?"

The urge to confide in her was rising, pulling at me like a riptide.

But what if it's Izzy? What if she's the one? She's already admitted there's a new mystery man in her life.

She looked at me for a long moment, seeming to weigh up her next words. Finally she gave me a sad little smile. "It's not my place to say anything, and please tell me to shut up and mind my own business if you want to, but I'm a bit worried about you."

"Me?"

"Is something going on with Sean?"

My stomach dropped.

"What?"

"The thing that's bothering you. Is it about him?"

"Why do you say that?"

"Seems like it's a bit tense between the two of you. There's kind of a weird atmosphere thing going on."

Is she just trying to get inside my head? Probing to find out how much I know? Or does she really want to help?

I picked up a flask of coffee and poured myself half a cup. It was intensely strong but I was glad of the caffeine hit after two sleepless nights.

She had known Sean longer than me, longer than any of us. Maybe she could help.

"Not sure if I ever told you this," I said. "But there was a woman, Zoe, I met at birthing classes when I was pregnant with Daniel. We stayed in touch after the kids were born and her husband was really lovely, charming, funny—he doted on them both. Absolutely no sign that anything was wrong, and then last year— *boom*—he left her for someone he'd met through work, totally out of the blue. She came home one day and he'd taken a car trunk full of his stuff and just left her a note. That was it."

"Did he come back?"

"No. And it was only after it happened that she looked back over everything, *properly* looked, and saw that the signs had been there all along, for months. That he was preoccupied and secretive and making more effort with his appearance, going to the gym four times a week. All the usual giveaways. Zoe had just chosen to ignore them, pretend everything was OK. But it wasn't." I paused, shaking my head. "It feels as if the same thing is happening to me with Sean. And, just like her, maybe I've seen the signs too late."

Izzy looked me straight in the eyes. "I don't think Sean would do something like that. Not him."

But I've seen the evidence. I've seen the messages. I know what he's doing.

"That's what I thought," I said in a small voice. "That's what Zoe thought, too."

"I've known Sean since primary school, Kate, since we were five years old, and I can honestly tell you he's the most straight-up-and-down bloke I've ever known." She smiled and put her small hand over mine. "He's so honest it's funny, sometimes. When we were in the same class at St. Jude's, he used to admit to things he hadn't even done, things he *couldn't* have done. It's one of the strange and wonderful things about your husband."

Tell her what you saw.
But what if she's the one?
Just tell her.
What have you got to lose?

"There were messages, too," I said.

Izzy looked up sharply.

"What? Where?"

"On his phone."

She studied me for a moment, her smile fading.

"You saw them?"

"Yes."

"What *exactly* did you see?"

"I was only on his phone for a few seconds but there was a back and forth about how he couldn't stop thinking about her, that he couldn't go on lying to me, whether or not I suspected anything . . ."

"What else?"

"That they were going to figure out the next step together, in France. This week."

"And you don't know who was sending the messages?"

"No."

She sat back in her chair, steepling her fingers.

"But, logically, it must be one of us?"

"Yes."

"Either Rowan or Jennifer?"

"Yes." *Or you.*

"Right. OK."

I wanted to tell her what I'd found in Rowan's bedside drawer, but sneaking around my friend's bedroom sounded too crazy, even to me. I decided to hold it back for now.

"Have you seen anything weird, with Sean and one of them?" I said instead. "Overheard anything? Picked up any vibes at all?"

"Nope. Nothing." She looked up the valley for a moment, gray peaks rising ragged and bare into the blue sky. "Although I suppose there is another possibility."

"Is there?"

"That it's neither of them."

I turned, slowly, to look at her. What was this? Was she about to confess, to come clean? Right here, now? Was this what everything had been leading up to?

Working to keep my voice neutral, I said, "If not them, then who?"

"Rowan and Jennifer aren't the only ones," she said carefully. "What about the boys?"

"The boys?"

"Russ and Alistair are here, too."

I blinked in surprise, my mouth opening slightly.

What?

"Russ and Alistair? But they're not . . . Sean's not . . . I mean they're married. They're not gay."

"The human heart is a strange old thing, Kate."

"The messages are from someone called CoralGirl, so I assumed that the sender was a woman."

"I'm playing devil's advocate," she said. "Trying to see it from every angle."

"Do you know what, Izz, that had actually never occurred to me."

She shrugged.

"Just saying it's a possibility, that's all."

"Christ, I don't think I've got the headspace for that just at the moment."

"Have you got anything else to go on, any other evidence?"

I thought again about the multimillion-pound deal that depended on Rowan keeping the relationship a closely guarded secret. What I'd found in her bedside drawer. Russ's drunken revelation on the balcony.

I think Rowan is having an affair. Something's going on. I'm bloody certain of it.

"Nothing . . . conclusive."

"And did you ask him about it?"

"I couldn't, I didn't want to. It was such a shock at the time and I've just been trying to work out what to do for the best."

"Oh, Kate." She pulled me into a hug, rubbing my back. "You poor thing. You must be so upset."

I nodded, a painful lump in my throat. Willing myself not to cry again. Not again. "I've had better weeks. What do you think I should do?"

"To put your mind at rest?"

"So I'll know one way or the other."

"I honestly don't know, love. If it were me, I think I'd talk to Sean directly, face-to-face."

Daniel called up to me from the rock pool. "Mummy?"

"Just a minute, love."

I turned back to Izzy, keeping my voice low. "But you still don't think he did it?"

"Sean's not got it in him to lie like that."

"How can you know that, though? How can any of us really know?"

She shrugged. "I just do."

I wanted to believe her, I really did. But one thought was bouncing around inside my head like a crazy firework.

You would say that, wouldn't you, Izzy? If you're the other woman?

26

Russ

Russ sneaked a look at his phone while his daughter counted up their scores, scanning a handful of work emails and taking a quick peek at the FTSE 100 and the Dow: nothing too startling in the markets today.

Someone—some massive sadist—had included Hungry Hungry Hippos in the collection of board games at the villa. As every adult knew, Hungry Hungry Hippos was the loudest game ever invented, every round a frantic earsplitting forty seconds of *BANG-BANG-BANG-BANG,* with plastic smashing against plastic as the players tried to get their hippos to gobble up more balls than the opposition. The noise was like a machine gun, a pneumatic drill—it was like putting your head inside a steel bucket and having people hurl golf balls at it, especially the frantically competitive way that Odette played. Russ still had painful memories of games against his daughter at five thirty last Christmas morning, a truly catastrophic hangover making the noise sound as if someone had set off a string of firecrackers inside his skull.

Still, Odette loved it, and that was the main thing.

"I have nine balls and you have twelve," she said sadly. "You win again, Daddy."

Russ didn't believe in letting his daughter win at games. Rowan let her win. Rowan's parents let her win. The bloody nanny always lets her win, at everything. But it wasn't good for her, not at five years old: it took away her competitive edge, her drive to succeed. There was no real pleasure in being handed success on a plate; on the other hand, nothing tasted better than a hard-fought victory that you fully deserved.

The downside of that, of course, was that she always wanted to carry on playing every game until she *did* win.

"Play again?" she said.

Stretched out full-length on the tiled floor of the games room, Russ sat up with a groan as his joints protested. He crossed his long legs underneath him.

"Do you want Hippos again, or shall we look for something else?"

"Hippos! Want Mummy to play as well." She looked around the room. "Where is Mummy, anyway?"

He looked at his watch. Where *was* Rowan? They were supposed to be doing things together on this vacation, the three of them. But she was missing in action, *again,* even though she'd promised to put her phone up in the bedroom and leave it switched off for a couple

of hours. His suspicions had hardened since he'd con-
fided in Kate the other night and it was even tougher
to keep track of his wife here than it was at home.
Something was definitely going on with her. She'd
been increasingly secretive and elusive these past few
weeks, and yes, the business deal with the Americans
was massive, with a life-changing amount of money
involved, but there was more than that. There was
something else, he was sure of it.

"Good question, Odette. I don't know where she's
got to." He leaned forward. "Hey, I've got an idea: how
about we play some hide-and-seek?"

Odette's little face lit up. "Yay! Let me hide! Let me
hide!"

"Not yet, sweetie."

"But I want to go first!"

"You can be next. Let's say Mummy's gone first and
we have to find her. But we have to be superquiet so
we can sneak up on her without her knowing."

Odette jumped up and down. "Yes!" she shouted.
"Superquiet!"

Russ put a finger to his smiling lips.

"Shh," Odette agreed.

"Do you want a piggy?"

"Yes," she whispered, holding her arms up.

He turned and knelt down, lifting her up to give her
a piggyback. She put her little arms over his shoulders
and kissed the back of his neck. Russ felt a little rush
of love, of pride, of paternal joy, and couldn't stop the

grin spreading across his face. Odette was so small, so light, she weighed almost nothing clamped onto his broad back.

"I'm as tall as you now, Daddy," she whispered.

"You are, sweetie. Tall as a tree."

He walked up the stairs to the main living area, then the next flight up to their bedroom. No sign of Rowan. Back down to the kitchen, the balcony, the pool, and the garden. Still no joy. One of Jennifer's lads—the surly, blond pretty boy—pointed him around the side of the villa and he followed the path through a gate into the front garden, looking across to the parking area and the tree-lined drive up to the main gate.

There she was, leaning up against the rental car with her back to him. On her phone.

Found you.

"Shh," Odette said, her breath hot in Russ's ear.

Russ nodded and moved off the gravel path, onto the grass. Quieter. He walked slowly and noiselessly across the lawn toward his wife.

She still hadn't heard him.

Russ turned and winked at his daughter as he carried her on his back. She was grinning hugely, excited to take her mother by surprise: this was a good game. He crept a bit nearer, slowing down now, until he could just about make out her side of the conversation.

"That's what I'm telling you," Rowan said. "I'm asking you, I mean. I want to know what all the options are, when everything is supposed to happen."

He took another step toward her, straining to hear every word.

"No," she said forcefully, her back still to them. "No. Of course I haven't told him."

She switched the phone from one hand to the other, tucking her dark auburn hair behind her ear.

"I know that. I know! How do you think it makes *me* feel?" She paused for a moment, listening. "When the time's right, I'll tell him. When I've had enough time to make a decision that's based on what I—"

Odette giggled, unable to contain herself any longer.

Rowan whirled around to face them, her eyes wide.

"What the—"

"Boo!" shouted Odette. "We found you, Mummy!"

Rowan stared at them both for a moment.

"I'll call you back," she said, ending the call.

She slipped the phone into the pocket of her shorts and crossed her arms.

"What's going on?"

"Who was that?" Russ said.

Odette shouted over both of them.

"We're playing hide-and-seek, Mummy!"

"Work stuff."

Russ pulled a skeptical face.

"Didn't sound like work."

"I'm not having this conversation with you. Not now."

"Why not? Worried it might ruin the wonderful vacation atmosphere we've got going on?"

Odette jigged up and down excitedly on her father's back. "Mummy—"

"Because there's nothing to talk about."

"Don't try to pull your usual bull on me. I see how you are with him."

"With *who*?"

"Sean. Yesterday at the beach you were all over him."

"He was looking out for our daughter while you were sleeping off a hangover. Again."

"Why do you have to do this? Why do you have to embarrass me?"

"I think you're managing that very well on your own."

"What's that supposed to mean?"

"Do you have to drink at every single meal?"

"I'm on vacation! Supposed to be bloody enjoying myself—but I didn't choose the company, did I? They're your friends, not mine."

"All the same, it would be nice if you played with our daughter instead of passing out in the sun every afternoon."

"We're playing *now*. You're the one skulking out here on your phone."

Odette clapped her hands.

"My turn to hide, Mummy!"

Rowan reached for her daughter, giving her a smile. "Come on then, baby." She plucked Odette off Russ's back, settled the little girl on her hip the way she had carried her when she was a toddler. "Let's find a place."

"And then we can both hide?"

"Yes. We'll both hide from Daddy, somewhere really clever." She turned and headed off down the path around to the back of the house, Odette bouncing on her hip. "Somewhere he'll never find us."

27

I found Sean in our en suite, fresh from the shower. He was shirtless, his broad chest and back already darkening from three days of sun.

Izzy was right. If I really wanted to put my mind at rest, it was time to talk to Sean. Besides, between the drama of finding the teenagers at the gorge and last night's tension-filled dinner with the girls, I still hadn't had a chance to tell him about what I'd seen Alistair doing by the pool.

The conversation was going to be beyond awkward considering how long we had known each other, but it would be a lot easier than what was to come after. The children's well-being had to take priority—we were parents first, partners second—and a part of me hoped, selfishly, that a concern for his children might bring him to his senses. Bring him back to me.

If not, it was time to confront him with the truth.

I'd thought I could ride things out for a week as I built the picture, piece by piece.

But all of the evidence I had collected pointed in one direction. I couldn't wait.

It was time to force the truth out of him, one way or another: I had to know. Not here, not where everyone could hear us, where one of the kids might walk in on us at any moment. And not where *she* might interrupt. She knew the estate and all of its secret places.

Not here, in the villa. But I knew the perfect place.

"Hey," I said, leaning against the doorframe.

"Hey yourself," he said, spraying aftershave.

"Do you want to go for a walk before dinner?"

He looked at me a little uncertainly. "A walk?"

"Down through the vineyard. It's a lovely spot at this time of day—you get a wonderful view of the sun going down."

"What about the kids?"

"Daniel's going out in a minute to play with the bigger boys and I've asked Izzy to keep an eye on Lucy."

"OK. Sure." He gave me a wary look. "I'll be right with you."

I sat down on the end of the bed and watched him buttoning a pale blue shirt, thinking back to my talk with our daughter the other night.

"Has Lucy talked to you about her friend Alex?"

"The crazy one?"

"Tall, skinny girl, plays the clarinet. In Lucy's friend group."

"No. Have they had another argument?"

"Lucy mentioned her the other night; she was upset about something but wouldn't say what."

Sean shrugged, turning away to close the wardrobe.

"She's not talked to me about it."

Across the corridor I heard Daniel's door shut with a click. Our son hurried past as if he were late for something.

"Daniel?" I called to him.

His face appeared in the doorway.

"What? I'm just going to meet up with Jake and Ethan."

"That's nice." I forced a smile. "Hey, has Lucy said anything to you?"

"About what?"

"Alex. From school."

"She doesn't talk to *me,* Mummy. Not about girls' stuff." He looked at his watch. "Or do you mean big Alex from Year Eleven?"

"I don't know. Who's she?"

"*He.* The one who had that thing."

"What thing?"

I frowned. Conversations about school sometimes went like this, when I hadn't been paying close enough attention to the comings and goings of friendship groups, gossip, the falling-out and making up that seemed to happen on a weekly or daily basis.

"Is Lucy friends with him?"

Daniel shrugged.

"Dunno."

"He had a *thing,* do you mean a party?"

One of the older boys—I wasn't sure which—

shouted his name from downstairs. Daniel's head snapped around: he was being summoned.

"Got to go. Bye!" He scampered off.

We followed him downstairs and out onto the balcony. It was still blisteringly hot, the air thick with humidity. Sean took my hand as we walked through the garden and I didn't pull away.

"Where are we going?" he asked.

"I'll show you."

"Very mysterious."

We walked through the vineyard, the soft chirp of birds high overhead.

"I need to tell you something," I said, "away from everyone else."

"OK," he said. "From mysterious to ominous inside a minute. This can't be good."

"Something . . . something happened yesterday and you need to be aware of it."

I described what I had seen Alistair doing by the pool, looking at the pictures on Lucy's Instagram feed, glossing over the details of where I'd been standing when I saw it. Sean's frown deepened as I related the images of our daughter on the screen of Alistair's phone. He didn't speak at all until we reached the trees and the clearing by the gorge.

"That's pretty weird," he said finally. "Did you confront him about it?"

"I was going to, but by the time I'd got down to the pool he'd disappeared and I couldn't find him."

"Right. I'll have a word with him."

I knew this was how he would react. It was another of the reasons I had brought him down here, away from the villa.

"Don't," I said. "Not yet."

"Are you kidding?"

"I don't want to cause a big thing, and Lucy will be mortified. I can keep an eye on her, talk to her if necessary, suggest she change her privacy settings, but I'd rather she didn't find out—it's just too creepy."

"She needs to know."

"It'll scar her for life. Trust me."

"I'll just have a quiet word with Alistair."

"Sean," I said. "Please don't, not now. I just wanted you to be aware, that's all. It's probably nothing."

"He was looking at her Instagram account!"

"He was looking at lots of accounts, from what I could see."

"All right. But if I see him doing it I'm going to take his phone off him and shove it up his—"

"*Sean.*"

He held a hand up.

"OK, OK. I always knew there was something a bit odd about him, though. I *knew* it. Christ, maybe this vacation wasn't such a good idea after all."

"Maybe," I said.

That was the easy bit. Now for the hard part.

I crossed my arms over my chest, trying to summon all my remaining strength. Fear was boiling up inside me, as if I were about to take a leap into the dark with no idea where the ground was. I reminded myself that—sometimes, at least—to find the answer to a question you simply had to ask it out loud.

"Sean, I've said what I needed to say." I swallowed hard against the painful lump in my throat. "Now, is there anything you want to tell me?"

28

He stared at me for a moment, a frown creasing his forehead.

"Tell you what, love?"

"You *know* what."

He shook his head. "No. You're going to have to give me a clue."

He was giving almost nothing away. If he was acting, he was doing an amazing job. But I had seen him acting in front of people before, laying on the Irish charm so thickly you could slice it with a knife.

He'd charmed me, too, once upon a time.

I gestured back up toward the villa. "I could just ask her instead, if you like."

"Ask who?"

"You know damn well who!"

"What are you talking about?"

"Russ told me on our first night here. He thinks Rowan is having an affair."

"What?"

"An affair."

"With who?"

"I think you know the answer to that question."

Sean's frown deepened. "What? Why are you telling me this?"

I changed tack. "What did Rowan say to you at the beach, after you brought Odette back from the sea?"

"I don't . . . I don't remember. Thank you?"

"She whispered something to you."

He looked momentarily embarrassed, before his mask of composure dropped back into place like shutters being pulled down.

"No, she didn't."

"She damn well did, Sean, don't lie!"

"She thought her daughter was lost and she was grateful that I found her, that's all."

"She was hugging you."

"So? She was upset. She was grateful. You'd have been the same if Lucy had been missing and Russ had found her."

"It was more than that. It was . . . She said something to you, I *saw* it."

He sighed and shook his head. "What is this all about, Kate?"

"What about your wedding ring?"

"What about it?"

"Do you take it off when you're with her? Is that what you do?"

He rubbed absently at the bare fourth finger of his left hand.

"No."

"So where is it?"

He stood and moved nearer to the cliff edge until he was only a few feet away from the drop.

"There's a little gym downstairs next to the games room—have you been down there? I was doing some weights the other day and I didn't want to scratch the gold. So I took it off and put it on the side, on one of the speakers. Must have slipped my mind when I finished my workout. I'm sure it'll turn up."

It was a long and convoluted answer to a question I had only obliquely asked.

The truth is simple, I thought. *Lies are complicated.*

"When did you use the gym?"

"I don't know . . . yesterday, before we went to the beach?"

"You don't know, or yesterday? Which is it?"

"Yesterday." He nodded. "Definitely."

"And where is it now?"

"Somebody must have picked it up."

"Somebody?" I couldn't keep the sarcasm out of my voice.

"There's only a few places it could be, it can't have gone far."

I took his wedding ring from my pocket and held it out to him, the gold shining in the late afternoon sun.

"Can you guess where I found this?"

"In the gym, probably."

I waited a beat, winding up for what I hoped would be a knockout blow.

"In Rowan's bedroom, in her bedside drawer."

He stared at me for a moment.

"Why were you looking through your friend's bedside drawer?"

"Because I was looking for something!" I said, my voice rising. "And I found it!"

Without thinking, I threw the ring at him, hard. It bounced off his chest and fell to the ground, rolling toward the edge of the cliff.

He crouched to pick it up, rubbing the dust and dirt off before slipping it onto his finger. "Rowan must have found it in the gym; she was probably just holding on to it for safekeeping."

"Is that the best you can do?"

"This is getting ridiculous, Kate."

"Is it?"

"You've got the wrong end of the stick."

"Why are you lying, Sean?"

He looked down.

"It's not a lie," he said softly.

I was getting nowhere—he was giving nothing away. It was time to play my trump card.

"I saw the messages on your phone."

There was a change in his posture then, a slowing of his movements. The muscles of his forearms bunched, as if for a fight, his chin lowered like a prizefighter expecting a blow.

"What messages?" he said.

"On Messenger, to CoralGirl. Saying you couldn't stop thinking about her. Saying you felt bad about lying to me and didn't know how much longer you could keep on doing it."

He twisted the wedding ring on his finger. Round and round.

"When?"

"Does it matter?" I felt the heat of tears behind my eyes. "A few days ago. The day we arrived."

I moved a little nearer to him, to the edge of the gorge, willing him to tell the truth.

Please don't lie. Please. Not now. Please show me that I'm wrong, that I've got this all totally wrong, that there's an explanation for all of it.

He looked away, his jaw tight.

"I don't know what you're talking about."

"Messages on your phone. You said you were going to sort things out when we were in France. This week."

"So you unlocked my phone?"

"Yes."

A muscle twitched under his eye.

"You looked at my phone. My personal stuff."

"It's Rowan, isn't it?" I felt my heart breaking, even as I said it. "The one you're . . . seeing?"

He looked at me with a mixture of shame and regret and anger, and for a moment I thought he was going to tell me. To come out with everything, right here, in this unfamiliar place with our oblivious children nearby. To tell me he was sorry, that it didn't mean anything, that he would finish it, and all those other things that men are supposed to say when they're caught in a lie. There was something in his eyes that told me he wanted to tell it all, he *wanted* to confess, but couldn't quite bring himself to do it.

I looked up at him, the sun behind him creating a halo of light around his head.

"Well? Tell me."

"You shouldn't have looked at my phone."

"Swear it to me."

He took his hands out of his pockets and moved a step closer to me. "What?"

"Swear that you're not having an affair with Rowan."

"This is bloody crazy."

"Why?" I said, my voice rising in pitch. "Why is it crazy? Why can't you just say it?"

He sighed and looked at me, *right* at me, holding my eyes with his. No tremor, no flicker, no shadow of dishonesty.

"All right," he said. "I swear I'm not involved with Rowan. There, I said it. Are you happy now?"

"So who are you sending messages to? Who's CoralGirl?"

He blinked once, twice, then looked away.

"I don't know what you're talking about."

"Is that really the best you can do?"

"It's the truth."

"The truth? I don't think you know what that is."

If I had been paying more attention, if I had been a bit more careful—if I had been a little less upset and angry and bewildered—I might have noticed how close we were to the edge. Just a few feet away.

He took another step toward me.

29

DANIEL

Play with the bigger boys, his mum had said.

But she didn't know them, not really. Jake and Ethan were OK when grown-ups were around but when they were on their own they were a little bit . . . crazy. Like, *scary* crazy, like Mason Reese at his school who'd been permanently expelled for setting a firework off in assembly. And grown-ups didn't really understand the age gap. They said *oh you're nearly ten and Ethan's just turned fifteen, that's only a few years, not much really.* But it was a *lot.* It was loads. It was almost half a lifetime. And Jake was almost a year older than his brother.

The two brothers were dressed in shorts and T-shirts, black and khaki, flip-flops kicked off their feet. He'd not really spoken to them much since they'd all arrived at the vacation house. They'd both got *massive*—at least compared to Daniel—lanky and spotty, size 11 feet and funny deep voices like a dog barking.

He was slightly scared of them, if he was honest.

They'd been wandering around the big field behind the villa—a *vinn-yard* his mum had called it—but it turned out to be a bit boring. Just rows and rows of grape plants, all running in the same direction. Maybe he would go and find his sister—she was always good for some sport, in one way or another. She was usually by the pool: all she was interested in was getting a suntan. Sometimes he made funny videos of her with Dad's camcorder, without her realizing it—that usually got a reaction. Although she was even grumpier and crosser and more boring recently than normal.

Daniel watched the brothers as they tried to get the big outdoor gas heaters lit. They were in the stone gazebo at the edge of the garden, which had two big shiny metal heaters, bigger and taller than he was, and Daniel didn't really know why they wanted to light them because it was still *boiling* hot. But he didn't want them to think he was a goody-goody, so he was content to sit back on his reclining chair and just leave them to it, watching as they pressed and prodded and turned the controls, swearing at each other as they tried to make the flames start.

Odette said a lot of bad words, too. She'd called Daniel a *bloody bastard* yesterday when none of the grown-ups could hear, when he wouldn't let her play with the beach ball. He wasn't exactly sure what a *bastard* meant, what it really meant, but he knew it wasn't good. It was the sort of word that would get him in trouble with his mum and dad. He tried to avoid getting into trouble if he possibly could.

As he watched, a figure emerged from the woods, walking quickly.

It was his dad. He thought maybe his mum might be there, too. He'd seen them go down there together not long ago, holding hands. He liked it when they held hands.

He watched as his dad walked up the hill toward the house, coming in their direction. He was striding along, doing the fast walk that he did when he was cross. He didn't get cross very often, but when he did, he would do what Mum called his *angry walking*. Daniel had to jog to keep up with him then. And he could be quite scary and loud. He certainly looked angry, a deep frown furrowing his forehead, his mouth set into a hard, flat line.

He didn't look behind him.

Daniel looked back to the woods, hoping his mum might be there, following his dad.

But she wasn't coming.

He wondered where she was.

"Daniel." Jake's voice.

Daniel's head snapped round.

"Eh?" He sat up in his recliner. "What?"

The older boys had given up on the gas heaters and were now scrutinizing him.

"So what's it like?" Ethan said with a sly smile.

"What's what like?"

"Having a sister?"

Daniel hurried to put his glasses back on.

"Rubbish," he said. "She's always moody and mean

and never wants to play anything anymore. She'd rather talk about makeup or boys or stupid stuff at school."

"Has she got a boyfriend?"

"Dunno."

"What about that rugby lad, Alex? She liked him, didn't she?"

Daniel nodded.

"He came to the house a few times, before Mum and Dad were back from work."

"She likes boys, yeah?" Ethan flashed him an unpleasant smile. "Very popular with the Year Eleven lads, that's what everyone—"

Jake punched his brother on the shoulder, hard.

"Shut the fuck up, Ethan! You have literally *no* idea what you're talking about."

"Just telling you what I've heard."

"You heard wrong. Way wrong. That's total bullshit, what you just said."

Ethan held his hands up in mock surrender.

"All right, all right. Calm down, bro." He paused a beat. "So you still fancy her then?"

Jake ignored his brother, turning to Daniel instead.

He produced a packet of cigarettes from the pocket of his shorts. On the front was a picture of a lady dancing in smoke, and in big blue letters the word *Gitanes*. He opened the pack and offered one to Daniel. "Smoke?"

But I don't want to get cancer, Daniel thought, staring at the picture on the front of the packet.

"A whole one?"

"Yeah. Are you up for it?"

"I don't really know how to smoke," Daniel said in a small voice.

"We'll show you."

Ethan held his hand out to his brother.

"Let's have one, then."

Jake checked over his shoulder and quickly shoved the cigarettes back into his shorts pocket.

"Put it away," he hissed.

Ethan followed suit immediately.

Daniel looked up as Jake and Ethan's mum appeared in a wide-brimmed straw hat, holding two small bottles of water. He liked her. She had a bit of a funny accent that sometimes sounded like she was American and just pretending to do a British voice.

"Hey there, boys," Jennifer said. "Are you having a cool time playing?"

Jake gave a grunt in reply.

Jennifer held the bottles out to them. "I brought you some water to take with you when you go exploring."

"Not thirsty," Jake said.

"But you will be soon, in this heat."

"No thanks."

Jennifer turned to her younger son. "You need some water, Ethan, otherwise you'll get sunstroke."

"I'm all right," Ethan mumbled.

She turned to Daniel, as if noticing him for the first time. She held one of the plastic bottles out to him. "Would you like a water, Daniel?"

Daniel really did. He'd not had a drink since his apple juice at lunch and his throat was really dry with all the running about and exploring they'd been doing. His mum had said not to drink the water out of the tap here because it might give him an upset tummy and the French orange squash tasted funny so he'd not drunk anything for *hours*. He sneaked another look at Jake, who looked back out of the corner of his eye.

"No thank you, Mrs. Marsh," Daniel said. "I'm fine."

"Well, all right, then," she said. "So what are you boys up to today?"

"Stuff," Jake said.

"Exploring, are you? Super. Remember what I said about the gorge though, Jakey, won't you?"

"Uh-huh."

"You can play wherever you want to in the grounds, but not in the woods down by the gorge, where the drop-off is, all right? There's a man coming this week to fix the fence at the cliff, but until he does you're to stay away from there. And away from the woods."

"Sure," Jake grunted.

"I'll leave you to it, then. Have fun."

She turned and headed back across the garden to the villa compound, the older boys snickering as their mother walked away.

"She's *so* embarrassing."

"She's, *well,* clingy," Ethan added.

Jennifer turned and waved when she reached the

gate. Daniel gave her a little wave back, but dropped his hand when he saw that neither of the bigger boys was acknowledging their mother.

As soon as she was out of sight, Jake stood up. "Come on," he said. He set off down the hill, his brother following him.

Daniel fell in behind them. "Where are we going?"

Jake turned and grinned over his shoulder. "Down to the woods, of course."

30

Sean

K suspects

   —Shit. What has she said to you?

She knows something is going on

   —Specifics?

Not yet. Need to see you

   —Yes but not today

When?

   —Will come back to you

I can't stand lying to her. She knows something

   —You need to calm down. Remember what is at stake

I know what's at stake. That's why I can't be calm

   —Meet tomorrow?

When?

   —Will message you

OK, sooner is better x

   —Remember to delete all messages as soon as you've read x

31

ROWAN

Rowan didn't have long.

She locked the door behind her and looked quickly around an en suite bathroom that was bigger than her entire bedroom back home. Perched on the edge of a marble bathtub, she checked her messages in silence, scrolling quickly through her in-box. Deal with, delegate, or delete. Rowan was the queen of the six-word email. She cleared what needed to be done urgently before switching to a couple messaging apps and listening to a voice mail that had dropped in while she was in the pool. Sent a nine-word email in response. Done.

The way things had worked out, it was pretty awkward that the vacation had fallen on this week, of all weeks, considering everything that was going on in her life. It was fabulous to see the girls again—putting the gang back together; seeing Kate, Jennifer, and Izzy always reminded her of all the good times they'd shared, but the timing was rather . . . unfortunate.

Who was she kidding? She'd been looking forward

to this for months. It wasn't great timing, but—*fuck it*—that couldn't be helped.

And besides, when was anything ever the perfect time? Was there ever a perfect time to take a break from the office, to step away from the business? No. Was there a perfect age to get married, or divorced? Depended which of your marriages you were talking about. Was there ever a perfect time to have a baby? No, not really. Especially not when you were trying to get a new company off the ground and you were both working stupid hours to keep the mortgage rolling, the exorbitant school fees covered, and the nanny paid in full.

If you waited for the perfect time, you'd wait forever, so when you saw something you wanted, you had to go out there and take it. Sometimes you just had to trust your instincts and jump right in.

Rowan had always had good instincts—aside from that one time with her first husband—and she was a great believer in the *move fast and break things* mode of doing business. Who was it who said that? Mark Zuckerberg, she thought, or one of those other Facebook guys. She'd met Zuckerberg once at a client's event in New York, couldn't remember much about him apart from how ridiculously young he looked. And short. But she liked his mantra, because he was right—when you were running your own company you had to keep moving, like a shark. If the shark stayed still for too long, it was dead. If you let yourself get slower, you got into a rut, you got into bad habits, and soon enough you found yourself eaten alive by the competition. *Better to be the one doing the eating,* had always been Rowan's philosophy.

You could never stand still. Not in business, not in relationships, not in life. Not in anything. Especially now, when there was so much at stake.

Move fast and break things.

For all his faults—and he had a few, bless him— Russ would understand that better than most. At almost eight years together, their relationship was already the longest she'd had by quite some margin. But sometimes life threw things at you, complications that you couldn't plan for, and you had to just roll with them rather than fighting them all the time. Especially if they were *nice* complications. With that thought in mind, leaning against the lip of the bathtub, she quickly thumb-typed a final message and pressed Send.

She had always been good at keeping secrets.

But she would tell Russ, sooner or later.

At a time of *her* choosing. No one else's.

Small footsteps reached her through the door.

"Mummy?"

"What is it, Odette?"

"Are you coming out now?"

"I'll come out in a minute, darling."

A pause.

"*Are* you coming, Mummy?"

"Yes, I'll be right there."

Rowan locked her phone, flushed the pristine toilet—just for effect—and ran both taps noisily into the Italian marble sink for good measure.

She unlocked the door of the en suite and reached for the handle.

32

I don't know how long I stayed there at the edge of the gorge. Long enough to watch as the sun sank slowly toward the horizon, turning from blinding white to blistering gold and then a deep, burning orange as the dark hills rose up to meet it.

Did it stack up, Sean's denial?

I don't know what you're talking about.

I swear I'm not involved with Rowan.

It's the truth.

How could I still believe in him? Because I may not have seen the fire, but I could certainly smell the smoke. I could almost *taste* it, harsh in my throat. His refusal to explain, his silence, was deafening and incriminating, all at the same time.

Eventually I looked at my watch. It was getting late and the kids would be wanting their tea soon. I stood up and began the walk back up the hill.

By the time I reached the villa, the kitchen was a hive of activity, Alistair in an apron making a big bowl of paella while Russ poured drinks and Izzy set the dining table. Rowan put a glass of white wine in my hand, informing me it was one of the local varieties and was chilled to absolute *perfection*. I studied her as I took a sip, the chilled Faugères like ice on my tongue, trying to discern any sign of deceit in her eyes, any sign of treachery. But there was nothing. I reminded myself that she worked in PR, that presenting a story—an image—to the world, was what she did every day, and that she was very good at her job.

"You all right, honey?" she said. "You look as if you could use a bigger glass."

I pushed down the anger, forcing a smile to the surface.

"Just a bit hot. You're right about this wine, though, it's exactly what—"

Daniel ran up the steps to the balcony, squealing past me, with Lucy in hot pursuit.

"Mum! Dad! Help, she's gone mad!"

Lucy stalked after him, her face flushed with anger.

"Give it to me!" she shouted. "Now!"

I stepped in between them, holding my hands up like a referee stopping a boxing match.

"Whoa!" I said. "What's going on?"

"He's filming me!" Lucy shouted, jabbing a finger at her brother. She swiped at him, trying to grab the camcorder from him as I held them apart.

Daniel dodged away from his sister's grasp, still squealing with nervous laughter.

"She's crazy!"

"Tell him to stop filming me!"

"Daniel," I said, "you shouldn't film people unless they're OK with it. Give me the camera, please."

"She's just being moody. No one else minds when I do it."

"Well, your sister minds. Did you ask her permission?"

"Yes. Sort of."

"Liar!" Lucy said. "You never even said you were filming! I was just sunbathing and then you were there with the camera!"

"Daniel, you've been told not to film her, but you did it anyway. Why did you do that?"

"I was just doing a funny video. It's only for fun."

"It's not fun for Lucy, is it?"

There was a tremor in Lucy's voice. She was on the verge of tears.

"Tell him to delete it, Mum."

I took the camera from my son's hand. "Go and help Izzy lay the table for dinner, Daniel. I'll come and talk to you in a minute."

He skipped off toward the kitchen with a quick backward glance to make sure he was no longer being pursued. But Lucy had collapsed onto a chair, all the fight gone out of her. She put her head in her hands and started to cry.

I sat down on the arm of the chair and put an arm around her. "What's up, Lucy? It's just your brother being silly."

"Don't like people having pictures of me, ones I don't know about."

"Look. We'll tape over what he's just done, OK? I'll delete it, no one will see it."

"No one?"

"I promise."

Her voice was so low it was almost a whisper. "Thanks, Mum."

"Is it just that, Lucy? Is there something else going on?"

She shook her head but said nothing.

"Are you sure?"

She disengaged from our embrace and wiped a tear away with the heel of her hand. "I'm going to my room for a bit."

I watched her go, still wondering about her reaction. There was regular friction between Lucy and Daniel, who were no different from siblings the world over, and Daniel seemed to get a kick out of winding his sister up, but her reaction this time seemed to be on a different level.

I went upstairs and sat down on my bed with the video camera, opened out the little viewing screen on its side, and pressed Play, then Rewind. The screen came to life as the tape ran backward showing the pool, the loungers, then Lucy in her lemon-yellow bikini. I let the tape run back for a few more seconds, then pressed Play again. Daniel had filmed his sister as she sunbathed, going in for extreme close-ups of her belly button, the big toe of her right foot, and then a shot up her nose that zoomed in right up one nostril. The crash zoom was so fast it made me dizzy just watching it. Finally, she seemed to realize he was there, jumped up, and began chasing him. The picture zigzagged crazily as he ran away, his squeals of panic loud on the soundtrack.

It wasn't very flattering but it did seem a bit of an overreaction on Lucy's part.

I pressed Stop and then Rewind to take it back. The tape whirred as it spun backward, the digital counter on the screen running down. I glanced out the window. From our bedroom you could see out to the poolside, where Sean had sat Daniel down on a sun lounger and was talking to him at length, the boy nodding solemnly every so often.

It hadn't always been like this. When we had first brought Daniel home from the hospital, six-year-old Lucy had been absolutely ecstatic to have a sibling—a real baby of her own to go along with the assortment of toy babies she lined up in her bed every day for feeding, stories, and bath time. But by the time he had learned to talk—and answer back—the sibling novelty had worn off and they had settled into a relationship that veered between grudging tolerance and open warfare on a daily basis. Daniel delighted in winding her up and Lucy delighted in taking offense—even more so now she was a teenager. It was an exhausting combination.

But I didn't want them to grow up apart, to be

separated, to have to be ferried from one parent to the other and back again every weekend, or however custody arrangements worked. And however much they fought, they would want to be together, too. They belonged together.

The camera gave a click as the tape reached the beginning. I pressed Play and Daniel's grinning face appeared as he introduced the house tour.

"Welcome to the big white villa on the hill. Our vacation house, in France," he added in the mock-serious tone of a TV presenter. "And welcome to Daniel's video diary. We start today in my bedroom."

In spite of myself and how low I was feeling, I couldn't help but smile at his commentary as he chattered on, panning the camera around his room, his books stacked neatly next to his little digital clock, his Lego superheroes on the bedside table. I knew, from his previous vacation videos, that he could go on like this for quite some time. I hit Fast Forward, watching as the images flashed past: our bedroom, Lucy's room, and the others along the corridor, the games room and what looked like a wine cellar, then out onto the balcony, images of Rowan and me on the first day here with the inevitable extreme close-up. Back into the living room, jerking crazily up the stairs to the first floor, a shot of the hills in the distance, another zooming close-up down by the double garage, and there was someone half hidden behind a low white wall, then the shot swinging away and over to the infinity pool—

Wait. I jabbed the Pause button, a strange tingling sensation at the back of my neck, then rewound the tape a minute or so and hit Play.

Daniel's commentary started up again as the camera panned over distant hills, shimmering in the heat haze.

"And here we have some more boring countryside," his high little voice announced, "just loads of trees and hills and more boring trees really. Not very interesting. Not even a McDonald's or a KFC anywhere."

The camera zoomed out again, pulling right back to the grounds, an outbuilding, a sweep across the roof of the double garage at the top of the driveway.

There. On the other side of a low wall.

The image caught Sean's top half, from the chest upward. He had sunglasses on and was talking to someone, smiling, holding his hands out to them. Whoever he was talking to was hidden behind the garage wall.

"It's Daddy," Daniel's voice-over said on the tape. "Hello, Daddy!"

Sean seemed not to hear his son's voice. He carried on talking earnestly to the person behind the garage, who was still hidden.

Come out, take a step forward so I can see you.

Come out.

"Daddy's gone deaf," Daniel grumbled to himself on the tape. *"Typical."*

Just as the camera swung away again, Sean moved to embrace the mystery person and I saw a flash of something that made my breath catch in my throat.

I rewound the tape and pressed Play again, my finger poised over the Pause button.

On the camera's little screen, Sean moved in for the embrace again.

I hit Pause. There. There it was. A flash of long blond hair, a face caught in profile for a fraction of a second. A face I knew only too well.

Jennifer.

33

It didn't make sense. I had been fully expecting to see Rowan caught in the video with Sean. It was *Rowan* who was having an affair—according to her husband—and she was the one who'd had Sean's wedding ring, who'd whispered to him at the beach. It should have been Rowan in the video, but it wasn't.

I took out my phone, zoomed the camera in on the little video screen, and snapped a picture of the freeze-framed image. Then I ejected the tape and tucked it into the back of my bedside drawer.

I had a feeling I might need it, sooner rather than later.

The sky was fading to a heavy blue black, the brightest stars already pinpricks of light against the darkness. With dinner out of the way, I sat down next to my daughter on a bench in the garden, the white stone still holding a ghost of warmth from the day.

"I took care of that video, Lucy."

She nodded. "Thanks."

"And your brother says sorry. He won't do it again."

"Yeah, right." She sniffed. "Until the next time."

"I made him promise."

She nodded again, but said nothing.

I turned on the bench slightly, so I was facing toward her. "What was it about it that really upset you, Luce? Daniel's done it before, you know what he's like. He does it to me, too, and your dad. But you've never reacted like this before."

She shrugged, once. "I just don't like being filmed."

"Is that all? Seems like there's a bit more to it than that."

She was silent, fingers twisting a long strand of her golden-blond hair round and around, just like she had done since she was very small.

I rested my fingertips on her arm. "You're not going to tell me, are you?"

She looked at me for a moment, then looked away. "It doesn't matter."

"You know I won't tell anyone, don't you? Not your dad, not Izzy or the others, not your teacher. No one."

"You wouldn't understand."

"Maybe not. But I'll try to."

She leaned forward, her face hidden by her curtain of long blond hair. There was a long pause. When she finally spoke, she wouldn't look at me.

"When you film something, people think it's just a laugh," she said. "They think it's just something to do in that minute, on that day. They don't think about what happens to it after that, do they?"

"And what does happen to it after that?"

"Well, it's out there, isn't it? Forever. Out there on the internet, somewhere. Even after you die, it will still be out there, floating about somewhere. Something you did when you were a teenager, whatever stupid thing you did or said—forever and ever."

I started to get an uncomfortable feeling deep in my stomach.

"The internet never forgets," I said, remembering something a detective colleague was fond of saying.

"Yeah. That's what I mean."

I hesitated, not sure how to phrase the next question.

"Is there something out there, that you did? Something that you wished wasn't out there?"

She stared out across the manicured lawn and the darkening vineyard beyond. When she looked back at me, there were tears in her eyes.

"Yes," she said quietly.

"Do you want to talk about it? A little bit?"

She shook her head. "No."

"Why not?"

"I can't."

"Who says you can't?"

"You wouldn't understand."

"I'll do my best, love."

She shook her head again. "I've told you. I can't."

"I'm not going to force it out of you, Lucy. But it

makes me feel so useless, the idea that I can't help you. Dad and I have always done everything for you, but now it feels like there are things that are beyond our reach. And I hate not being able to be there for you."

She stared out toward the hills, another tear running down her cheek.

"You can't help. No one can."

I put my arm around her shoulders, my heart breaking over the gap that had grown between us. My wonderful girl, my firstborn, my smart, funny, sweet child, was drifting further away from me with each passing day. And it seemed as if there were nothing I could do to bring her back.

"This—this thing that's out there on the internet. Is it a video?"

She closed her eyes and nodded, once. A single, tiny movement.

A watery feeling of helpless anxiety began to spread outward from my stomach.

"A video with you in it? The sort of thing you—you wouldn't want me to see?"

A pause. Then another tiny nod.

"There must be *something* we can do to get it taken down, removed from whatever site it's on. Dad works in computer security, he might know a way to do it."

She stood up and swiped angrily at her tears.

"I've *told* you. You can't help! No one can!"

She walked off toward the house without another word.

I gave her a minute, then followed her in. This was

something that should be shared with Sean, so we could discuss it, work out what to do—on any normal day that's what I would have done. But normal was now a distant memory.

I could hardly look at him after today, let alone speak to him.

Daniel's iPad lay discarded on the low coffee table in the living room. I took it into the dining room and shut the door behind me, propping the iPad on its stand at the end of the long table. There was a rolling, sick feeling in my stomach.

My little girl is somewhere out there on the internet. Naked. Vulnerable. Naive.

I sat down and unlocked the tablet before realizing that I had no real idea where to start. This video of my child—or whatever it was of—was out there somewhere other people could see it. Somewhere that other people could find it. Knowing that made me feel more helpless than ever.

It was one of those teenage things; I knew it went on, but I was pretty hazy on the details. Did they get posted on YouTube? Did they allow that kind of thing? It didn't seem likely. Weren't there moderators to remove nudity and sex? I had colleagues back home in the Computer Crimes Unit who could probably advise, but it was the kind of thing that needed to be done face-to-face. Discreetly.

After an hour of fruitless Googling and scrolling through lists of results, I turned the iPad off and headed upstairs. The truth was, I had very little idea about what she might have posted, or where it was, or how to get it taken down. And if she couldn't do it, what chance did I have? We were friends on Facebook for a short time, before Lucy deleted her account, declaring that Facebook was *full of adults and weirdos.* I couldn't really argue with her on that.

By the time I climbed into bed and switched my light out, I knew I had another sleepless night ahead of me.

Too many questions without answers.

I thought Sean was asleep and jumped when his deep voice reached across the darkness between us.

"Night," he said quietly. "Love you."

He always said it, last thing at night.

I didn't say it back.

Six Months Earlier

It's stupid, really. She knows it's stupid. It isn't how things work.

But she can't stop thinking about it a hundred times a day. Can't stop imagining it when she's with him, visualizing it when they are together and he has his arm around her and pulls her into him. When he holds her close against his chest. When he kisses her and it feels like a crackle of electricity going up and down her spine.

If her mum saw him, she'd understand. She'd get it. But it's better that she doesn't know anything, not now, not after all the lectures on staying focused and school getting real as the GCSE exams get closer and closer. And she doesn't mind keeping a secret. It's kind of cool, actually, to have a proper secret, like a secret room in your house full of secret stuff that no one else knows about. It's not like she's actually banned from having a boyfriend, just that her mum and dad have quite specific ideas about boys.

But he's not like most boys; he's much more mature. She can talk to him about anything. School, exams, family, brothers and sisters and mates and the real reason they call him B-Boy at school. About how she's going to be a doctor and how he got talent-spotted by Saracens

at the age of eleven and wants to go professional when he's eighteen and play rugby for
England one day. Win trophies.

There's one thing she doesn't talk to him
about.

The stupid thing.

It is *stupid*. On one level, she knows that.

But she still can't stop thinking it: she's
going to marry this boy.

TUESDAY

34

The bedroom was still dark when I woke, the black-out curtains keeping all but a tiny sliver of light out. I turned over and stretched out a leg onto Sean's side of the bed, but there was nothing there. I reached an arm out, but the sheets were cold. The other side of the bed was empty.

The digital clock on the bedside table read 8:14. I sat up, rubbing my eyes. Our en suite was empty, too, and out in the living room the day was already dazzling bright, morning sunlight streaming through the big windows at the front of the villa. I shielded my eyes and closed the blinds a little to reduce the glare.

Daniel was perched on the big leather sofa in his pajamas, eating a bowl of cereal and watching a film on the giant TV. Two Transformers were having a fist-fight in the rubble of New York City. I sat down next to him, kissing the side of his head.

"Morning, Daniel. Sleep all right, love?"

"Mmm."

"Where's your dad?"

"He went out."

"Where?"

"Shopping for bread or something. In the village."

"When did he go?"

Daniel shrugged.

"Dunno. Half an hour ago? They were going to get bread and I asked if they could get Chocolate Weetos, too, but they said they probably wouldn't be able to find that because they have all different—"

"They?"

"What?"

"He didn't go on his own? He went with someone else?"

"Oh, yeah. Jake and Ethan's mum." He slurped milk off his spoon and pulled a face. "I don't really like French milk, Mummy. Can we get normal milk?"

"That is normal for France, love. It just tastes a bit different because it's ultra-pasteurized to kill any bugs." I stood up and peered into the empty kitchen. "So just the two of them went? Just your dad and Jennifer?"

"Yeah. I wanted to go, too, but they said they were only going for a few bits and anyway, I still had my PJs on." He carried on munching his cereal. "What are we doing today?"

"Don't know yet," I said absently. "Something nice."

Izzy appeared at the foot of the stairs, yawning hugely in her pajamas. She raised a hand in silent greeting and padded into the kitchen.

I nodded back and decided to call Sean's phone. As

it rang, I walked around the villa, out onto the balcony, popping my head into the dining room. No one else seemed to be up and about yet.

Sean's phone went to voice mail. I hung up and tried again, leaving a brief message the second time, asking them to get some pastries and cakes for lunch.

I went to the front window and looked out onto the drive. All three cars were there, so they must have walked into the village. Ten minutes there, ten minutes in the boulangerie—assuming there was a line—and ten minutes walking back. About half an hour, all told, which meant they should be on their way back. Strolling back hand in hand, perhaps? Sitting in the little café in the village square, sharing a coffee? Enjoying the privacy of a few quiet moments together, somewhere they wouldn't be seen?

Maybe. Maybe not. But I could catch them out if I was quick.

I went to the bedroom and hurriedly put on my running gear.

"Stay here with Izzy," I said to Daniel. "I'm going for a run."

My son nodded without taking his eyes from the TV screen.

"Get some proper milk if you see any."

I grabbed a key and headed out.

Running had been Sean's idea, in the beginning.

It was part of his midlife crisis, he said. He'd greeted

the arrival of his thirty-ninth birthday with a rash of new hobbies, new goals, and plans for life-changing self-improvement.

It had come along with joining a gym, buying a new road bike, trying to lose weight, and cutting out midweek drinking. Along with taking bin bags full of old shirts and jeans to the charity shop and buying new clothes, ditching the stubble, getting his hair cut shorter, and generally making more of an effort with his appearance.

Along with having an affair.

They were all signs, I supposed. Big, flashing neon that said something was going on in his life, his head, his heart. A change was happening. The indications were there, but I had misread them. I'd seen them as positives, when they were anything but. Although he'd already ditched the running, a few weeks ago. Just stopped. Needed all of his energy for other things, presumably.

At the end of the villa's tree-lined gravel drive, I turned right and headed along the narrow road toward Autignac. It was still early, but the sun was already high in the cloudless sky, beating down with a relentless heat that half blinded me as I ran. In my rush, I'd forgotten to bring my sunglasses and had to squint as I jogged along the road that ran along the boundary of the estate, trying to get a rhythm going in limbs still stiff and heavy with sleep. The air was thick with humidity and I'd barely made it past the end of the tall white stone wall when I felt the first sweat under my arms and at the back of my neck.

Sometimes Sean and I ran together—in the beginning, anyway, after we had caught the running bug and had opportunities when the kids wouldn't be home alone. But then he'd started training for half marathons, running late into the evening after Daniel had gone to bed, when all I wanted to do was put my dressing gown on and wind down with a bit of TV. In any case, he was too quick for me, and I usually felt like I was holding him back.

Was that what I was doing now? Holding him back? And what was I supposed to do if I ran around a bend in the road here and found them strolling arm in arm, hip to hip? Or sitting on a bench, sharing a stolen kiss? I knew what I had to do—force it out of them right there by the roadside, get them to admit what was going on, confess.

I ran on.

By the time I reached the village, my T-shirt was stuck to my back with sweat and I was breathing hard in the clammy heat. The square was quiet, just a couple of elderly women gossiping outside the boulangerie, a handful of others enjoying an early coffee in the shade of the town hall. No sign of Sean and Jennifer. I looped around the far side of the village, beyond the main square, coming back around and rejoining the little road that led up to the villa.

Halfway up the little hill at the back of the house,

my legs got so heavy I had to stop for a minute, stand-ing at the side of the road, hands on my hips. The trees were thick here, oak and pine and olive trees, with the white of the villa walls just visible above me at the prow of the hill. I walked the rest of the way.

Sean was in the kitchen when I got back, unload-ing bags of baguettes, croissants, macaroons, and pas-tries from three bulging shopping bags. Jennifer stood next to him, busying herself with the coffee machine. She looked cool and composed in white culottes and a pale pink vest top, straw hat still on her head.

I was acutely aware that I was soaked in sweat and red faced from the heat.

"Oh," I said. "You're here. How did you get back?"

They were the first words I'd spoken to him since our confrontation at the gorge yesterday afternoon. It seemed like an age ago.

Sean shrugged.

"We walked back from the village."

I shook my head.

"I just ran that way. Didn't see you."

"There's a little path up the hill, a shortcut. Quite steep, though."

"I tried calling your phone."

"Left it here. Sorry."

"You were gone a long time."

He jerked a thumb over his shoulder in the direc-tion of the village.

"There was a street market and Jen wanted to have a look. They had some lovely arts-and-crafty stuff."

"I ran through the square. I didn't see a market."

He didn't reply and wouldn't meet my eye, using the excuse of unloading the shopping to keep his back to me.

I opened a paper bag of pastries, the smell of freshly baked croissants filling my nose. It should have made me hungry, but my appetite had almost completely disappeared these last few days.

"I'll heat some croissants up for the kids. Do you want one?"

"In a bit. Just going to grab a quick shower."

"Oh."

A shower, I thought. *To wash her smell off him.*

He gave me his best grin.

"Absolutely scorching out there already."

Daniel wandered into the kitchen and looked me up and down.

"Did you find any proper milk, Mummy?"

35

Izzy

Izzy followed the sound of the grand piano, the notes swelling and sweeping in perfect rhythm through the villa's ground floor and out onto the balcony. The music rose and fell, heavy with emotion, a flawless rendition of a complicated piece. She climbed the staircase up from the pool, crossed the balcony into the living room, and perched on the arm of a sofa to watch Lucy as she played.

Perhaps when she settled down, bought a place of her own, she'd have a piano again. She had played as a girl, though not to Lucy's level, but a decent standard nonetheless. It was one of the things she missed the most about not having a home to come back to. While her three friends had spent the past couple of decades accumulating more and more belongings, Izzy had gone in the opposite direction and probably had fewer possessions now—fewer clothes, fewer books, fewer gadgets, less *stuff,* full stop—than she had when she was twenty-one. The furniture from her late parents' house had mostly been sold off or given to charity, apart from a few items put into storage for their sentimental value. Most of what she owned she could carry on her back, in the same tattered seventy-liter rucksack she'd had since leaving Ireland fifteen years before. But maybe the time had come now to retire her beloved Berghaus.

It was only supposed to have been for a year or two in the beginning. But the longer she was away, the weaker the ties became. She'd honestly thought the opposite would be the case, that the desire for home would grow with each month, homesickness accumulating like interest on a debt as the years passed. But in fact, the longer she was away, the easier it became. A year became two, and then five, then ten. And now here she was.

Mostly when she was home she spent the time thinking about when she would be able to leave again. The ties that bound her to her homeland, her hometown, the streets where she'd grown up, became weaker as each November 2nd came and went.

Each time the anniversary of Mark's death approached, she dreaded it, hoping that the pain would retreat a little, at the same time hating herself for wanting to forget.

Because that felt like selfishness: it was up to her to keep the memory alive, to keep *his* memory alive. It was the right thing to do, simple as that. But the memory meant pain—and she'd been carrying the pain for so long now that perhaps it was finally time to ease it off her shoulders and set it down by the side of the road. It didn't mean she would forget—she would never forget—just that it was time to move on.

She'd not wanted to come back before, because there'd been no reason to. Both her parents were gone and her brother had moved to Canada. Was it strange that they had both moved so far away from home, left Ireland behind them? That they had wanted to get away from Limerick in search of something better? Maybe it was a natural instinct.

But now she had a reason to come back.

Izzy took her phone from her pocket, looking at the string of messages again, scrolling down to the most recent. It made her smile when she thought of their time together—and then she'd catch herself and look around quickly to see if anyone was watching, wondering why she was grinning like a fool. She typed a quick reply and pressed Send.

She was glad that her traveling days were over. It was time to return to the fold. Not quite *home,* but close enough to it. Because now she had a reason, the best one of all. The *only* reason that ever made sense, when all was said and done.

It was time to settle down. For good.

She would swap her rucksack for a piano, in her new place. She would learn to play again, as part of her new start, and maybe one day she might be as good as Lucy.

She moved nearer to watch the teenager's delicate hands flying over the keys.

Lucy turned, startled, brushing tears from her cheeks.

"Sorry, don't stop," Izzy said. "Didn't mean to interrupt. I could listen to you play all day."

"No, it's fine, I was almost finished anyway. Really."

Izzy smiled, but she knew straightaway that something was off. One of the many lovely things about Lucy was that she didn't lie well. She didn't hide her emotions well, either.

Just like her father.

Izzy lowered her voice.

"Are you all right, Lucy?"

"Yes, of course." Lucy took a deep, shuddering breath, using the sleeve of her top to wipe hastily at her cheeks until all traces of the tears were gone. "I just get a bit emotional sometimes, playing that piece."

"You have a wonderful talent."

"Thanks. I'm supposed to practice every day."

"It sounds familiar but I can't quite place it."

"*Kinderszenen,* by Schumann. It means—"

"*Scenes from Childhood.*"

Lucy smiled. "How many languages do you speak, exactly?"

"My fiancé used to play. He wasn't quite as good as you, though."

Izzy thought she saw a shadow flit momentarily across Lucy's face, then it was gone.

"I did this piece for my last exam," the teenager said. "Some of it, anyway."

"So what's next for you? A-levels, right?"

Lucy nodded. "Assuming I get the GCSE grades I need."

"Still got your heart set on medical school?"

"Yes."

"If anyone can do it, you can. You'll make a brilliant doctor."

Lucy smiled, shyly. "Long way to go, yet."

Izzy pulled a chair over and sat down next to Lucy at the grand piano, leaning in close. She had known this child since she was born, first held her when she was a week old, a perfect tiny new person with a full head of startlingly white-blond hair. She had seen her grow up and every time she had returned from working abroad Lucy had been a little bit smarter, a little bit taller. She had reached Izzy's height—five feet two in her bare feet—at the age of twelve and had grown much taller since then. She'd known this girl all her life, and she felt a strong urge to reconnect with her properly now she was back. To reestablish their relationship.

She wanted to be close to her and Daniel again, to be part of their inner circle.

"Are you *really* all right, Lucy?"

"Hmm."

"You know you can talk to me about anything, right? I'm a neutral." Izzy smiled. "I'm like Switzerland, not on anyone's side. If you can't talk to your mum or dad about it, you can talk to me instead. I can just listen and it doesn't have to go any further."

Lucy tucked a strand of her long blond hair behind her ear.

"It's just . . . I don't know, it's probably nothing."

"If it's getting you down, it's not nothing. Not if it's ruining your vacation, bothering you that much. Don't you think?"

"I suppose so."

"I don't like seeing you unhappy, Lucy."

She let this hang there for a moment, knowing that the teenager would fill the silence. And a moment later, she did.

"Mum and Dad are . . . Something weird is going on between them."

Izzy sat up straighter, frowning.

"Weird *how,* exactly?"

It was a disturbing echo of Kate's comments at the Gorges d'Héric the day before, her concerns about Sean. *There were messages.*

"I don't know," Lucy said quietly. "They're being strange around each other. I've never seen them like this before. Dad reckons I don't notice anything, but I do. I pick up on a lot of stuff. You must have noticed it, too?"

"Yes." Izzy nodded. "I have."

"So what do you think's going on?"

Izzy considered her options, searching for the one that was least painful. Tell Lucy about her father messaging another woman? About her mother's suspicions? Her doubts about Sean? Tell her the truth?

But is it really my place to do that?

"Honestly? I've no idea, Lucy." She patted the teenager's arm. "But whatever it is, I'm sure they'll work it out soon. One way or another."

36

Sean and I spent a wordless morning, circling each other like wounded animals, the memory of yesterday's confrontation still raw. The silence between us stretched out, broken by Izzy announcing that lunch was ready.

Outside on the balcony, the long table was laid with enough to feed a small army, every inch of the checked tablecloth covered with food and drink. A wooden board filled with a dozen cheeses took pride of place in the center of the table, next to bowls of tomatoes and olives, apples and grapes, and the cutting board was piled high with sliced baguette and fresh pastries. There was honey and dark jam from the village market, a slab of golden butter, thick cuts of pink ham and roasted chicken breast. Jugs of apple juice, stubby green bottles of beer, and two bottles of white wine were out, too.

"Twelve of us," said Alistair, standing at the head of the table looking pleased with himself. "We've got the wine and the bread: all we need is a bag with thirty pieces of silver."

"And a Judas," Russ added, uncorking a bottle of Saint-Chinian with a soft *pop*.

"How's that?" Jennifer said.

"You know," Alistair said, spreading his hands expansively, "da Vinci's *Last Supper*."

Everyone busied themselves filling their plates. All except Odette, who wrinkled her nose and began pointing out all the things she didn't like.

"Don't like them, or them, or that. Definitely not that. Have we got any normal proper slicey bread?"

Rowan put some baguette and ham onto her daughter's plate, and began slicing an apple into small wedges.

I looked up to see Sean and Jennifer, on opposite sides of the long wooden table, reach for one of the bottles of wine at the same moment.

Sean's hand brushed against hers—seeming to linger for a second as their eyes met—but she reacted as if she'd touched a live wire, almost dropping the bottle in her haste. As if they were mirror images of each other, they both smiled and looked embarrassed, gestured to the other to go first.

"Go on," Sean said.

"No," Jennifer said. "You go ahead."

He smiled and filled her glass first, then Russ's, before his own.

Jennifer shot a furtive glance at me, a half turn of her head before her eyes dropped back to the table.

Checking to see whether I noticed that?

Yes. I did notice. What was it?

What, precisely, was it?

I willed her to make eye contact again, for a chance to read her expression, find out what was written there.

Does it feel awkward to touch my husband's hand in front of everyone? Is that it?

She took a sip of wine but wouldn't meet my eye again.

My mind jumping and sparking with fresh accusations, I looked away in time to see Alistair filling Lucy's wineglass from the other bottle of Saint-Chinian.

"Actually," I said to Alistair, "if you don't mind, I'd prefer it if Lucy didn't have wine at lunch."

Lucy looked as if I'd just slapped her. Alistair just smiled and moved on to Jake's glass.

"Oh? Thought you'd be all right with it."

"What with the children going in the pool, and the heat and dehydration it's better if they stick to Orangina." *And the fact that you're checking out her Instagram account.* "Isn't that right, Sean?"

"Yeah," he said halfheartedly.

Lucy crossed her arms, her cheeks reddening.

"Daisy Marshall has had wine at home since she was like thirteen. Her parents don't make a massive deal out of it."

"That's their choice. But until you're a little bit older, *we* decide what's best for you."

"What about *my* choice?"

I paused long enough to take a breath, biting back my instinctive reply.

"You get a choice when you're an adult. Then you can do as you please."

"Can't believe you sometimes." She scowled at me with murder in her eyes. "The white is barely even ten percent, not even strong."

"Une gorgée de vin pour les enfants," Alistair said, gesturing with his free hand. "A sip of wine for the children. It's very much the done thing here in France, you know."

"So is eating sheep's bollocks," Russ muttered.

Alistair seemed not to have heard him.

"What *we* do, Kate, is we always try to encourage our children to test boundaries. Exploring boundaries can be a really powerful way to reduce conflict, improve communication, and build trust in the relationship with your—"

Lucy cut him off.

"When did you first have a drink, Mum?"

"In my teens." I shrugged. "But that was different."

"How?"

"It wasn't with my parents."

"You're *such* a hypocrite!" she said and pointed at me. "So it's OK for me to have a bit of wine as long as you don't find out?"

"That's not what I'm saying."

"We're on vacation! In the middle of a bloody vineyard! And you're drinking every day!"

"Stop shouting, Lucy."

She stood up and grabbed her glass. "Stop treating me like a kid!"

She pushed her chair back and stalked off, the angry *slap, slap* of her flip-flops receding as she descended the stone stairs to the pool.

I stood up to follow.

"Leave her," Sean said quietly. "Let her calm down a bit first."

"She needs to eat something."

"Just give her a minute."

He was right, of course. Lucy and I were too much alike, in too many ways, and once we got entrenched in an argument I rarely knew how to dig my way out. I was too judgmental, too black and white, too quick to switch into analytical mode—my *work brain,* as Sean called it—for parenting issues that required a softer approach.

I sat back down and noticed for the first time that all eyes at the table were on me. Except Jennifer's— she was studiously buttering slices of baguette, eyes on her task.

"Is it me," Alistair said breezily, spearing a large slice of ham with his fork, "or is it getting hotter every day?"

37

LUCY

Lucy marched over to the shaded stone bench at the far corner of the garden and sat down heavily, the heat of anger burning her cheeks. She liked this bench: it was away from the house but still just about in range of the Wi-Fi. She unlocked her phone and began scrolling furiously through her Instagram feed.

It was so un*fair*. All she wanted was a bit of wine to take her mind off things, to take the edge off her feelings, but *no*, it always had to be some big drama with her mum, some load of crap about the legal drinking age and doing what she was told. Her bloody mum was always the same: *this is the law, this is the way it is.* She claimed to be all supportive when Lucy got upset about stuff, but wouldn't let her have a *tiny* bit of wine to help her relax. It was infuriating, being treated like a little kid all the time.

She jumped as Jake sat down next to her on the bench and held out two Solero icc creams.

"Orange or strawberry?" he said.

She took the strawberry Popsicle from him with a sigh. "Thanks, Jake."

"No worries."

"Where's your brother, your little shadow?"

"Dunno. Shaken him off, I guess."

Lucy unwrapped her ice cream and took a bite, the chill delicious on her tongue. "God, she's such a bloody *hypocrite*."

"What's up?"

She looked out across the pristine garden with its infinity pool and palm trees and brightly colored flowers.

"It doesn't matter."

"Sounds like it does."

"Oh, let's talk about something else."

Jake bit into his ice cream. "Have you heard anything? From back home?"

"About what?"

He stole a sideways glance at her. "You know."

She held up her phone. "Only what's been posted."

"You haven't heard anything else? Like from family or something?"

"Why should I have?"

"Just thought that because you were . . ."

"Because I was what?"

He shrugged, feeling the blush rising in his cheeks. "Dunno," he said quietly, staring at the ground. "I was going to ask you the other day, but Ethan was there and he's always talking shit about everybody, so I didn't want to do it in front of him. Wanted to check that you were all right, that's all."

"All right?" She snorted. "No, not really. I'm about as far from all right as it's possible to be."

The silence stretched out between them until Lucy raised a hand in apology.

"Sorry, Jake. Not having a go at you, but I don't know more than anyone else, OK?"

"I sort of feel bad because I was the one who introduced you."

"It's not your fault. None of it is your fault."

Jake cleared his throat, glancing at her quickly before looking away. "Have you ever been in love?"

She turned to stare at him. It was pretty much the last thing she was expecting him to say. "Love?"

"Yeah."

"I don't know. Maybe."

"You're not sure?"

"I thought I was, once," she said slowly. "But I was wrong, I don't know what that word even means anymore. Do you?"

"It means you'll do anything for the person you love. Anything and everything. Even if you have to—"

He stopped, watching as his mother strode across the lawn toward them, a linen tote bag over her shoulder.

"*There* you are, Jake," Jennifer said. "I've been looking everywhere for you."

"And?"

"So what are you two chattering about?"

"Nothing."

She smiled, but there was little warmth in it. "Looks like one of those deep and meaningful conversations to me."

"What, are you spying on us?"

"We're going down to the gorge, Jake. All four of us, your dad and me and your brother. Come on."

"No, I'll see you later."

"You're coming with us, Jake. I want us to go exploring together. Come on, it'll be lovely."

"I'm not going. I'm talking to Lucy."

"Come on, they're waiting." Her voice was brittle. "We've hardly done anything together since we've been here and I want to get a nice family photograph of the four of us."

Mother and son stared at each other, neither willing to back down.

Finally, Lucy stood up to break the impasse.

"It's OK, Jake, you go on. I was going to go in the pool for a bit anyway. Catch up later, yeah?"

Jake sighed and tossed his Popsicle stick into the bush. Reluctantly, he got to his feet.

"Yeah, later."

With one last look at Lucy, he turned and followed his mother out of the garden.

38

I lay on a lounger watching the scene unfold on the far side of the garden.

Jennifer seemed determined to keep Lucy and Jake apart, or at least limit the amount of time they spent with each other—she couldn't even stand to watch them sharing an ice cream. What was that about? Some kind of mother-son issue? Maybe she couldn't stand to be replaced by another woman, couldn't cope with not being the number-one female in his life anymore? Was that even a thing? Would I be the same with Daniel in a few years' time? No. Or perhaps just a little.

A book unread in my lap, the midafternoon heat prickling my skin with sweat, I kept one eye on my daughter and one on my son. Daniel was splashing in the shallow end of the pool with Odette, an assortment of inflatables floating around them. Rowan and Russ sat across from us on the opposite side of the pool, looking at their phones; the others had gone to explore the rock pools down in the gorge.

Sean was laid out on the lounger next to me—an uneasy truce between us for the sake of the children. I had been running through everything he had said when I confronted him twenty-four hours ago, feeling the ground still shifting beneath my feet.

I swear I'm not involved with Rowan.

It's the truth.

He had denied it point-blank, without a flicker.

And maybe now I knew why—because it *was* the truth?

Not Rowan, but Jennifer.

Not for the first time, I kicked myself for not confronting him on Saturday when I'd discovered the messages on his phone. If I'd had the guts to do it right then and there, I could have got to the truth. Avoided this agony of suspicion and doubt. If I'd walked up to him and just showed him those messages straight-away, there would have been no way he could deny the affair.

The messages were proof. They were the key.

I'd wanted to unlock his phone again the following day, and the day after that, but he'd not left it out of his sight for more than a second—it was with him now, inches from his outstretched hand on the sun lounger. He lay flat on his back in the full glare of the sun, sun-glasses on, skin glistening with factor 30. He burned every summer, with his pale Irish complexion, but it never seemed to put him off.

I turned my head slightly so that I could get a better look at him without attracting his attention. He was quite still, his broad chest rising and falling with a slow rhythm that I knew well from the thousands of nights we had shared a bed.

He was asleep.

And his phone was right there within reach.

Russ and Rowan, across the pool, were still absorbed in their own phones.

Slowly, I shifted my weight, trying not to make a sound that might disturb him. Sitting up, I put my book on the floor and swung my legs off the lounger, leaning toward him so I could get a better look at his phone. It lay faceup on the edge of the lounger, not quite touching his hand.

I leaned in closer and pushed the Power button. The phone's lock screen appeared, asking for the unlock pattern.

Sean didn't stir.

I held my breath. With the lightest of touches, I used my index finger to trace his unlock pattern: a *J*.

J for Jennifer, maybe?

The display shook from side to side, the words *NO MATCH* appearing. I tried again. *NO MATCH.*

Shit.

He had changed it, probably after our row yesterday. Telling him about the messages had been stupid, I realized—I had tipped him off and now there was no way I could guess the new pattern. No way. There would be thousands of different combinations—or he could have changed it to a four-digit PIN.

Unless . . . unless it wasn't either of those. Perhaps

he'd changed it to something quick and altogether more personal than a pattern or a number. Something unique that I couldn't get past again. Why not? It was worth a try. I picked his phone up off the sun lounger, heart thudding in my chest.

His right hand was hanging over the edge of the lounger. Gently, oh so gently, I touched the phone's home button to his thumb.

The phone recognized his thumbprint instantly and came to life.

39

With the phone unlocked, I quickly selected the little blue-and-white Messenger icon. The menu screen came up, with a list of conversations.

There she was. Right there at the top, the most recent conversation: CoralGirl.

With a quick glance at Sean—who still seemed to be asleep—I selected the conversation with CoralGirl, where I had found the string of messages five days ago.

The conversation history was empty: all the previous messages had been deleted.

Bile burned in my throat, as if I might be sick.

What do I do now? You weren't imagining it before. His affair is still going on and he's trying to hide the evidence. It's been Jennifer all along: she's CoralGirl.

But how could I be sure?

Sean's head turned slightly toward me but his chest continued to rise and fall, rise and fall, in its steady rhythm. He was still dozing.

How do you explain it, Sean? What does she give you that I can't?

I had an idea.

In the text box I typed a new message:

Need to talk to you URGENTLY. Meet me in clearing at top of gorge in 15 minutes

Out of the corner of my eye, I caught a flash of movement as Daniel launched himself into the pool, cannonball style. A splash of water landed on Sean's foot.

He stirred on the lounger, turning his head toward me.

I hit the phone's Power button and hurriedly laid it back down next to his hand, reaching for the suntan lotion.

"You're going to get burned if you're not careful," I said.

He pushed his sunglasses up his forehead, blinking in the glare of the sun.

"Eh? What were you doing, love?"

A flush of guilt rose to my cheeks: caught redhanded.

"Just getting you the lotion." I passed it to him. "You should get some shade. Can you watch the kids? I'm going inside to cool down a bit and put my swimsuit on. Think I fancy a dip after all."

He squirted suntan lotion into the palm of his hand and began rubbing it onto his shoulder.

"OK. I'm about ready to go in myself."

I grabbed my sandals and sarong, walking slowly, as casually as I could, to the stairs that led up to the balcony, checking my watch as I did so. It was only as I reached the top and glanced back that I saw Russ was now alone on his side of the pool.

Rowan was gone.

In the house, I went straight through to the kitchen, grabbed the key from the hook on the wall, and went out into the main living room area. The air conditioning was set high in here and the cool air against my skin was a blessed relief after the scorching heat of the sun outside. I wrapped the sarong around me and went to the bottom of the wide marble staircase.

I stood very still and listened.

Just the faint sound of squeals from the pool outside. Nothing nearer.

"Rowan?" I said into the silence.

No response. The estate and the villa were both huge, but there were a limited number of places where she could have got to in the last couple of minutes. I ran up the stairs to the master bedroom to find the big oak door ajar. I knocked, once.

"Rowan?"

I pushed the door open and took a step inside.

Neat, orderly, exquisitely furnished. A faint smell of Rowan's expensive perfume lingering in the air.

But empty. She wasn't here.

Perhaps it wasn't Jennifer, after all.

Where are you, Rowan? On your way to meet my husband, summoned by text?

How about I give you both a surprise, instead?

I ran back downstairs and into the bedroom Sean and I shared. I kicked off my flip-flops and grabbed some strappy sandals from the bottom of the wardrobe, sitting down on the bed to pull them onto my feet. Flip-flops were fine around the villa but I needed better shoes if I was going to be skulking about down in the woods. Standing up, I caught sight of myself in the mirror by the door. I looked flustered and flushed, lines of worry creasing my forehead. There was fear, too, in the eyes that stared back at me. Not just fear. Terror. The anticipation of what I was about to find out, and what it would do to me, to my family. To my life.

To all our lives.

You could have left this alone, but you chose not to. You chose to set this in motion, you laid this trap, and now it's time to find out who gets caught: time to find out who's left standing when the music stops.

I pulled the bedroom door closed behind me and checked my watch. Twelve minutes to get down to the meeting place. Plenty of time, if I didn't delay.

"Mummy?"

I jumped at the sound of my son's voice behind me in the corridor.

"Daniel?" I said, a hand on my chest. "You startled me."

"You were scared." He grinned. "What were you doing?"

"Didn't hear you coming, that's all. What is it?"

"Can you help me find Daddy's goggles?"

"Now?"

"Mine broke," he said sadly, holding up the snapped elastic strap of his own pair. "And now the pool water is making my eyes all red."

"Can we find them later?"

"That's what he said."

"I'm just a bit busy now, that's all."

He looked at me, standing there with nothing in my hands except my phone. "Busy doing what?"

"Things."

"*Please,* Mummy." He put his little hand in mine and looked up with a hopeful grin. "I can never find things on my own."

"That's because you're like your dad, you never look properly." I checked my watch: eleven minutes until the meeting time. "I'll help you in a little while, I just have to do something first."

I made to move past him but he grabbed my leg with both arms, pressing his face against my side like a limpet.

"*Pleeeeeeeease!* You're the best at looking."

"Daniel, let go of my leg."

He gripped a little tighter. "You're the best mummy in the world."

"Hardly," I muttered.

"The absolute *best.*"

I sighed. He wasn't going to let go. "Come on then, let's be quick."

"Yes!" he said.

"Where did Daddy put his goggles?"

"Dunno. Somewhere in his stuff?"

He detached himself from my leg and followed me into the big bedroom. He sat in the armchair while I did a quick search of the wardrobe, bedside drawers, and under the bed.

"He didn't say where he'd put them?"

Daniel shook his head.

The suitcases were in the walk-in wardrobe. I hauled Sean's down, feeling that it was light and empty even as I did so. I laid it flat on the floor anyway.

Kneeling and unzipping the case, I flipped the top open. Empty. I was about to move on to our hand luggage when I remembered there were a couple of zip pockets in the top lining. The first was flat and empty but in the other—the smaller of the two—there was something small. Hardly noticeable.

"Aha," I said.

"Have you found them?" Daniel said excitedly from behind me.

I put my hand into the little pocket, fingers brushing smooth plastic, flexible, yielding—

Condoms.

40

There was a fluttery, weak feeling in my stomach, as if I were going to be sick.

Six condoms, loose, a brand I'd never seen before. I held them in the palm of one shaking hand, a small bundle of square plastic wrappers, trying to think of a reason why they were there, a legitimate reason, an explanation that made sense—instead of being one more nail in the coffin of our marriage.

But there was nothing. No explanation other than the obvious one—because I had been on the pill since our son was born.

Daniel came up behind me and I quickly shoved one of the condoms into my pocket, the rest back into the case before closing it again.

"Have you got the goggles?" he said.

"False alarm," I said, heaving the suitcase back onto the shelf. "Let's keep looking."

I found them in Sean's hand luggage, under a

bundle of charger cables. Daniel put them on straight-away, tightening the strap and giving me a frog-eyed thumbs-up.

"I *knew* you'd find them, Mummy."

I walked him out onto the balcony so I could be sure he was going back to Sean. He started down the steps to the pool, then turned back to me.

"Last one in the pool's a doughnut!" He gave me a grin. "Come on then, Mummy!"

I stayed where I was. "I'll be down in a bit."

He ran down the rest of the steps and leaped into the pool with a splash, narrowly missing his sister in the deep end. I lingered a moment longer, watching as he ducked below the surface and swam to the edge. Sean was there, and Russ. He would be safe.

Go.

I hurried back through the villa and headed out the front door, closing it quietly behind me. Down the big curving staircase, past the parked cars, branching onto a gravel path that took me out to the manicured lawn. An arched iron gate threaded with purple blos-soms led into the vineyard, out of sight of the pool.

Shielding my eyes against the sun, I squinted toward the stand of trees that bordered the bottom of the vineyard. There was no one around. I scanned the breadth of the slope on both sides of me but saw no movement. There were probably other ways down there, other ways of reaching the woods, but I didn't know what they were. Certainly you could come up from the gorge side—Rowan had showed us the path cut into the rock—and maybe there were also ways around the far side of the estate. But there was no time to check now.

I looked at my watch again—barely six minutes left—and broke into a half run. The bare path between the rows of vines was rutted and uneven, threatening to trip me as the *slap-slap-slap* of my sandals took me downhill. The sun seemed hotter out here than by the pool, high in a cloudless sky, its blistering heat beating down on my head and shoulders like a physical force. There was no shade out here on the hillside— the vines were only about four feet tall and provided no protection from the heat of the afternoon. Neither did they give any concealment unless I bent double and stooped over as I ran. But there was no time for that.

I felt totally exposed for every yard that I hurried away from the villa.

Perhaps she's watching me right now. Watching me coming.

At the tree line I stopped running, panting for breath, hands on my hips, trying to make my breathing as quiet as possible, still dazzled from the bright sun on the hillside. There was sweat at the small of my back and under my arms, but at least there was some shade here. The worn dirt path wound around the big oak and sycamore trees, the bark of their trees rutted with age. Here was the dip, the hollow, then up and around again, past the big rock and the fallen tree. The sign stuck lopsidedly into the ground: ATTENTION! in faded red lettering. Here was the clearing that led out to the bluff. This was the spot. I stepped off the path and into the trees. The cover wasn't great here, but there were some low bushes and the thick canopy of leaves above threw much of the woods into a warm, earthy shade.

Edging farther into the undergrowth, branches scratched at my arms and a mulch of old leaves rustled at my feet. I knelt down behind a fallen tree, getting as low as I could, gathering the fabric of the sarong around my thighs. It was as good a spot as any. From here, I could see right across the clearing to where the trees thinned out and gave way to the cliff edge. I would also get a good view of whoever came along in a few minutes' time, well before they could see me. My phone was warm in my hand and already slippery with sweat. I opened the camera mode and selected the Burst option, which would shoot a dozen images in rapid succession, in case there were only a few seconds to get the picture.

I settled back to wait, one hand unconsciously tapping the outline of the condom in the pocket of my shorts.

Who would respond to the message? How would I feel when I knew? Was it better to know?

Or did I still have time to walk away?

No. This had to be played out, all the way. It was better to—

Out of the corner of my eye, I caught a small movement to my right, deeper into the woods. A rustling, the snap of a twig. An animal? Or someone whispering in the trees?

I shifted position slightly to get a better look.

Another rustle from my right, closer now, another flash of movement at the edge of my vision. I squinted into the trees. A bird, maybe? Cat?

More silence. Sweat prickled the back of my neck.

I checked my watch again. The fifteen minutes were up.

Maybe she wasn't coming. Maybe Sean found the message and warned her off.

A sound. Steps, hurrying up the path from the gorge below.

A figure appeared. A petite woman in a wide-brimmed straw hat, black hair pulled back into a loose ponytail, phone in hand.

It was Izzy.

41

Izzy stopped in the clearing and turned around as if looking for someone, staring through the trees to left and right. She was breathing heavily.

She looked out at the view, hands on her hips, shoulders rising and falling with every breath. Her head moved in a little semicircle, taking in the rock formations on the far side of the gorge, the fields and forests and hills rising into the distance beyond.

For a few seconds I was too stunned to do anything.

CoralGirl was not supposed to be Izzy. It was supposed to be Jennifer. Or Rowan.

But now I thought about it, the pseudonym was a clue in itself. CoralGirl. Coral Island was a place in Thailand—I couldn't remember its real name—but Izzy had spent a year there, teaching, not long ago.

With my phone raised, I zoomed in and pressed the button to take a picture. The camera clicked with its shutter sound. *Shit*. I ducked down but she didn't seem to have heard it.

I studied her for a moment. Anger boiled in my stomach, my chest, my throat.

Izzy! Not Rowan. Not Jennifer. Does this make sense? Of course it does. You had your suspicions about her coming back to the UK. This *is why she came back. She's known Sean longer than me, longer than any of us. They grew up together, went to school together, they've always had that shared history, in-jokes and mutual friends from Ireland and their stupid teenage pact that they would get together at forty if they were both still single.*

Well, guess what, Izzy? He isn't *single.*

I stepped onto the path in front of her.

Izzy took a step back in surprise.

"Jesus!" she said, her hand flying to her chest. "Oh, Kate, you startled me."

"Sorry."

She gave a nervous laugh. "What are you doing, jumping out on people?"

"Fancied a walk."

I looked into her eyes, willing her to give up, to give in, to admit what she was doing there. To concede defeat, make it easier on both of us. I didn't want to force it out of her, but I would if I had to. I stood across the middle of the path, blocking her way.

"You looked as if you were waiting for someone?"

"Me? No, just getting my breath back after that climb up from the gorge."

"I know what you were doing," I said tonelessly. "You were looking for Sean."

She looked nonplussed, her brow furrowing.

"Sean? No. I thought he was up at the villa?"

"He was," I said, crossing my arms. "He is, I mean."

"So I wouldn't be seeing him down here then, would I?"

"Apparently not."

She was giving absolutely nothing away. Not a flicker. Not even the tiniest hint that I had caught her in a lie.

"Are you all right, Kate?" she said.

"I saw you stop in the clearing and assumed you were looking for someone."

"Looking for my lost youth, maybe." She took her hat off and fanned herself with it. "Twenty years ago I could have skipped up that cliff path without breaking a sweat. But now I feel like I might need CPR—the path's a *killer* on the way back up. Absolutely beautiful rock pools at the bottom of the gorge, though. Have you been exploring yet?"

"Not yet. I thought you were with Jennifer and Alistair and the boys?"

She nodded, gesturing down into the gorge with a thumb.

"I was. Volunteered to come back early to make a start on getting tea ready." She checked her watch. "You can help me if you like."

I held her gaze.

You're not going to admit it, are you? Not even now?

"Of course."

We made our way back up toward the villa, through the vineyard, the ground hard and uneven under my sandals. Izzy was chatting, talking about everything and nothing in a constant nervous stream, but I couldn't concentrate on what she was saying.

Izzy was there. Izzy came to the rendezvous. She responded to a message she thought Sean had sent. Or was it just coincidence? Had she really left the gorge early to make tea? It was the kind of thing she would volunteer to do. And where had Rowan disappeared to?

We were halfway back to the villa when Izzy put a hand gently on my arm and gave me an inquisitive look.

"Don't you think, Kate?"

"Think what? Sorry, I was miles away."

"That Jennifer's eldest is a bit of a strange one?"

"Jake?"

"He just seems a bit . . . out there. Like he's operating on a different plane to everyone else."

"That's teenage boys for you."

"Do you think he realizes that Lucy is out of his league?"

I turned to her in surprise, not sure if this was just another way for her to divert attention away from her secret meeting with my husband.

"Lucy?"

"Yes."

"I didn't think . . . I've always thought of them more like siblings."

"Kate, haven't you seen the way he looks at her?"

"How does he look at her?"

She laughed.

"With his tongue hanging out, mostly."

"Really?"

"Believe me, he's crushing hard on her." She picked a bunch of grapes from a vine as we passed, putting one in her mouth. "He's been showing off to try and impress her since we got here. That whole standing on the edge of the cliff thing, the day after we arrived? He was trying to impress her. Why else would he do something like that?"

"He's always been a little bit strange, I suppose."

"And letting Daniel tag along with their little gang?"

"I thought that was quite sweet of them, allowing him to join in."

"But you know they're only doing it to get in Lucy's good books, right?"

"Oh." I felt a protective pang for my son, always the last to be picked for every team. "I thought they were just being nice."

"Afraid not." She popped another grape into her mouth. "It's all about hormones—there's always an ulterior motive, right?"

All of a sudden I couldn't wait to get away from her. It felt as if she were taunting me, goading me, trying to provoke a reaction based on what I had just discovered.

You're right, Izzy.

And I've figured out your *ulterior motive.*

42

We separated when we got to the arched gateway that led from the vineyard into the gardens, Izzy heading straight up to the villa and the kitchen. I took the white gravel pathway to the right, toward the pool, glad to put some distance between us.

Sean was in the pool, splashing around with Daniel, Lucy, and Odette plus an assortment of inflatables, the kids squealing and laughing as they played a game of piggy in the middle. I took the long way around the infinity pool, to pass by where Russ was stretched out on a lounger with a John Grisham novel and a small green bottle of French beer.

"Nice to see the kids playing so well together," I said.

"Hmm," he said, taking a swig from his bottle.

"Oh, where's Rowan? I was going to ask her something."

"She went to make some calls, I think." He gestured vaguely in the direction of the house. "Work stuff."

I went back to my sun lounger on the other side of the pool. Sean surfaced from the deep end, brushing his hair back off his forehead.

"You were gone a long time, Kate," he said, batting a beach ball back toward the children.

"Had a bit of a lie down in the bedroom. To cool off."

He eyed me for a long moment, neck-deep in water.

"You still look a bit hot, love."

I put a hand to my cheek, feeling the heat radiating from my skin. I *was* still hot from hurrying back up the hill.

As calmly as I could, I said, "Where's your phone, Sean?"

Daniel clambered onto his back, hanging on with one hand and slapping the water with the other.

Sean said, "My what?"

"Your phone."

"Why?"

"Thought I heard it ringing."

He looked at me again, with something in his eyes I couldn't quite work out.

"Dunno. It's there somewhere. Underneath the lounger?"

I looked.

"Nope."

"Is it under my book, on the table?"

I moved his book, hat, and T-shirt from the table.

"It's not here, Sean."

"Uh-oh," he said, an undertone of regret in his voice. "Oh no. What an *eejit*."

"Who's an idiot?" Daniel said indignantly.

"I am. You're never going to guess what I've gone and done."

Still standing in the deep end of the pool, my husband reached down into the water, into the side pocket of his swimming shorts, and pulled out his phone.

"It says here," Daniel said, studying his iPad, "that if you put it in a bowl of rice for eighteen hours, then it will come back to life. The rice takes all the water out of it, or something."

Sean's cell phone lay, lifeless, on the kitchen table next to him. It had refused to switch on since being submerged in the pool, refused to power up, refused to do anything. He picked it up and pressed the Power button again. Nothing.

"I think it's a bit beyond that, Daniel."

"But you need a phone, Daddy. You can't *not* have a phone."

"I didn't have a phone when I was your age. I survived."

"Yeah, but that was like the olden days."

"The eighties."

"Was that before or after the Vikings?"

"The New Romantics, you young whippersnapper."

"Oscar in my class dropped his phone in the toilet once and he made it work again with rice."

"But I bet it was only in the water for a few seconds. That's a bit different to me being underwater and swimming around with the phone in my pocket for like ten minutes."

"Can't believe you jumped into the pool with it." Our son turned to me, smiling. "Can you believe it, Mummy?"

I knew why Sean had done it. He knew, too. But it didn't matter. This charade of ours was all for the kids' benefit.

"It *is* a bit of a Daddy thing to do," I said, as cheerfully as I could manage.

We both knew it wasn't an accident—I couldn't ask him about the messages now, and that was that. Now that his phone was broken, I couldn't access them unless I could get his login and password for Messenger online, and that was never going to happen. My guess was that after I left the poolside he'd checked his phone and seen the message. It seemed that he'd not been in time to warn Izzy off, though.

But I didn't want Daniel to be exposed to the corrosion that was eating away at his parents' marriage. Not yet. He needed to be protected for as long as possible.

43

Sean

"How long have you got?" Sean said, looking over his shoulder.

"Not long. Keep your voice down."

"I wanted to—"

"Not here," she said softly. "Where's Kate?"

"Busy with the kids."

"We can talk downstairs in the wine cellar. Follow me."

She led him across the kitchen to an alcove lined with jars and tins of food, with a door at the end. She went to it and pulled the door open, switching on the light and gesturing to him to follow.

A flight of concrete steps led downward into the bowels of the villa, the air cool and earthy away from the fierce heat of the evening. They walked side by side, hands almost touching, down a long passage carved out of the rock, lined from floor to ceiling on onc side with rack after rack of dusty wine bottles.

She stepped back into a shadow, beckoning to him.

"So how are you doing?"

He moved toward her, closing the distance between them. He put a hand on her arm, the skin warm and smooth beneath his fingers.

"Kate knows," he said.

She shook her head.

"No. She doesn't."

"How can you be so sure?"

"I just know."

"She's convinced herself that something is up."

She moved closer, lowering her voice.

"That's not the same thing as *knowing*. Not by a long way. What has she said to you?"

"It's just getting more and more complicated. I constantly feel like I'm going to fuck up and it's all going to come crashing down."

"That isn't going to happen."

"I don't know how much longer I can do this for. I feel so guilty about it."

"You think she's never kept secrets from you?"

"No. Not like this."

"Really?" She took his hands between hers. "This is not your fault, Sean."

"That's not strictly true, is it?"

"We're human, you and me. Just like they are, just like everyone else. Humans make mistakes. We just have to decide how we're going to deal with this one."

"You think this is a mistake? What we're doing?"

She smiled up at him. "This? No."

"I think we should come clean. Work out a way

forward that involves the least pain for everyone involved."

"We've talked about this already. This is the best way."

"Keeping her in the dark like this," he protested, shaking his head. "It's not fair. It's not right."

"Fair? Who said life was fair?"

"We can't keep it secret forever."

"Why not? Why shouldn't we?"

"Because sooner or later she's going to find out. *Someone's* going to find out, and when that happens it will only be a matter of time."

"She can't ever find out. And she won't if we're careful."

"I've told you, I'm no good at lying. Especially not to her."

"It's all about practice, Sean." She smiled. "The more you do it, the better you'll get."

"I'm just not sure how long I can keep going on as if everything's normal. I've never done this before."

"I don't exactly make a habit of it, either."

"Glad to hear it."

She moved closer, placing a hand on his chest, feeling the muscle hard and flat under her fingertips.

"Let's just keep on doing what we're doing," she said. "There's too much at stake to do anything else. Surely you must see that, Sean?"

"I do," he said quietly. "Absolutely."

TWO MONTHS EARLIER

Her mum's banging on the bedroom door.

"You're going to be late for school."

"I don't care," she shouts through her tears. "I'm not going."

"Don't be ridiculous, of course you're going." Her mum's incredulity is clear, despite the locked door between them. "You've got exams to prep for."

"Leave me alone!"

She doesn't want to go to stupid school anyway. She doesn't want to do anything. Doesn't want to leave the house, or leave her room, or even get out of bed. Not now. Not ever. Not after what he's done.

Her phone is on the pillow beside her, its screen black. She can't bring herself to unlock it, to look at anything, because she knows what she'll see.

She wants to stay in this room and never come out.

She closes her eyes and pulls her knees up under her chin, the pain in her head like a black hole swallowing every thought. How could she have been such an idiot? How could she have got him so wrong? How could he be such a bastard? Why did he do it? What had she done to deserve it?

She buries her face in the duvet.

Her mum is knocking on the door again.

WEDNESDAY

44

DANIEL

Mum was right, Daniel thought. It *was* good to play with the bigger boys.

Even if he was still slightly terrified of them, Jake and Ethan didn't send him away, like his sister and his parents did. Jake was tall—nearly as tall as Daniel's dad, who was more than six feet—and his brother, Ethan, wasn't far behind. They seemed like miniadults to Daniel, huge boy-men as big as teachers or parents.

And they were *cool*. Like the cool boys at school, the ones everyone wanted to hang with but everyone was a bit scared of, too, the ones who were good at football and funny and wanted to talk to girls.

Daniel wasn't into football. He liked *Minecraft,* and *Lego Star Wars,* and funny videos on YouTube.

But Jake and Ethan still didn't mind him tagging along while they went exploring the grounds of the vacation house. They had been everywhere, down to the games room, and the gym, out to the garage, the sauna, the woods, and the little gazebo. They were

good at exploring. They had found a secret room under the pool with loads of pipes and barrels of stuff,
and they had eaten grapes off the grape plants (even
though Daniel said they shouldn't) and then Ethan had
almost caught a lizard but its tail had come off in
his hand and it was dis*gusting* but also funny. He ran
around with it, waggling it in their faces like it was still
alive. Daniel laughed along, but he didn't really want
the lizard tail to touch him.

Awe and fear. It was a dangerous combination.

The three of them were sprawled in the shade of
a tall oak at the bottom of the vineyard. The sun was
intense, a baking, nonstop heat that stuck the T-shirt
to Daniel's back and made his glasses slide down the
bridge of his nose.

Jake leaned forward, his long fringe falling over his
eyes. "Do you want to see something cool?"

"Yeah," Daniel said automatically.

"Not here. Come on."

The older boy stood up and led them deeper into
the woods, Ethan following Jake and Daniel bringing
up the rear.

When they had gone farther in and the view from
the villa was fully obscured by trees, Jake reached into
his back pocket.

"Hey, I got something for you."

He held it out for Daniel to see. Bright yellow see-
through plastic with a silver top, see-through liquid
sloshing around inside the plastic. Daniel had never
held one before but he knew what it was.

"It's yours," the older boy said. "I got a three-pack from that cigarette shop in the village."

He and his brother held identical lighters, in red and green.

"You got one for me?" Daniel smiled broadly.

"Do you want it?"

"Yeah," he said. It would be *so* cool if they had one each, like they were equals, almost. Like he was fully one of the gang.

"You roll the metal thing to make a spark," Jake said, "then push down with your thumb to make the flame come out."

He demonstrated, sparking the lighter into a tall flame.

"You try."

Daniel took it from him and instantly burned his thumb on the hot metal where the flame had come out.

"Ow!" He dropped the lighter with a clatter. Ethan snorted with laughter.

Jake picked it up and held it out to him.

"If you want it, to keep for good, all you have to do is pass the test."

"What test?" Daniel said, sucking his singed thumb.

Jake studied him for a moment, his face blank. "We have an actual gang, me and Ethan."

Daniel looked from one teenager to the other. "A gang with two people?"

"It'll be three if you get in, if you want to be a proper full member."

"So how do I get in?"

"You have to do the initiation."

"The what?"

"Initiation," Ethan said. "A test." He put a hand on Daniel's shoulder. "We've both done it already," he said.

"What do I have to do?"

"Come on. We'll show you."

45

DANIEL

The edge of the cliff was jagged and uneven, with some bits that stuck out and some that looked like they'd sort of crumbled away. In the middle of it, where the trees gave way to the clearing and the clearing gave way to the edge, there was a crescent-shaped gap in between two scraggly low-down trees, a semicircular space that looked as though it had just kind of sheared off and fallen into the gorge, maybe like a million years ago, Daniel thought.

The crescent-shaped gap was about five feet across—about as wide as Daniel was tall, he reckoned.

"Here," Ethan said, standing right on the edge, in the gap between two spits of rock. "It's just like doing long jump in PE."

PE was Daniel's least favorite class at school. He always got picked last for football and when they had to play tag rugby—ugh, he *hated* tag rugby—he made a point of running in the opposite direction to where the ball was. He was OK at running and jumping, though.

Running and jumping he could do. Well, everyone could do them, really. They weren't really *sports,* were they?

"Long jump?" he said, trying to stop his voice from going high.

He would never have jumped this gap on his own. Not in a million years. But he wasn't on his own, he was with his friends, his *crew,* even if they were a lot taller and bigger and better at jumping than him.

"You have to jump from here," Jake indicated his side of the gap, "over to there. We did a jump like this in Army Cadets. 'Cept it was wider."

"Cool," Daniel said, playing for time. "How old do you have to be for Cadets?"

"Dunno. Not in it anymore."

"Why?"

He shrugged. "Didn't like being shouted at and ordered about."

"They kicked him out," Ethan said with a smirk.

"No, they never!" Jake punched his brother on the arm. "It got boring, all the marching and that shit. There was hardly any shooting."

Daniel checked over his shoulder in case a grown-up was there. He couldn't help it. He always did, when someone swore.

"It's easy," Jake said. "I'll show you."

He took a short run-up and jumped across the gap, landing hard on the other side in a cloud of dust kicked up by his trainers.

Ethan followed suit, only just making it, sprawling

to his knees when he hit the far side. He stood up quickly, brushing himself down and coming to stand next to his brother. They both stared at Daniel.

"Your turn," Ethan said.

Daniel inched a bit closer to the edge and looked down into the gorge. Blue water sparkled in the stream at the bottom, sunlight glinting like diamonds in the sun.

"It's a long way down, isn't it?"

"Kill you for sure, a drop like that," Ethan said.

"Are you chicken?"

"No."

"You are, you're a chicken-man," Ethan said, adding suddenly a cruel smile, "Chicken-man Dan!"

He began to make *buck-buck-buck* chicken noises, flapping his arms at his sides. Jake looked on, frowning.

"Shut up, Ethan. He doesn't have to do it if he doesn't want to."

But his younger brother ignored him.

"Chicken-man Dan! Chicken-man Dan!" Ethan capered in circles, arms flapping. "Buck-buck-buck!"

Daniel felt the heat rising to his cheeks. Suddenly he needed a wee, really badly. It was like the worst bits of school all rolled into one, PE and bullies and high-up things and always getting picked last for the football team.

He might have been scared, but he *wasn't* a chicken. He *wasn't*.

He would show them.

"I'm not chicken."

Ethan stopped flapping his arms, his smile turning cold.

"I think you are, little man."

"Not!"

"Prove it then."

Daniel stepped back six paces and took a couple deep breaths.

He *wasn't* a chicken.

He ran toward the gap, fists pumping, feet slapping the dusty earth, eyes fixed on the far side—

And jumped.

46

The three of us ordered coffees and found a table in a shady part of the village square. The only other customers were a couple whiskery old men, sitting on a wooden bench with their walking sticks propped beside them. The French tricolor hung listlessly from the town hall next to the restaurant, no breeze at all to stir it in the early afternoon heat.

"I have a confession to make," I said.

Rowan and Jennifer both looked up from their drinks.

"That sounds a bit dramatic," Rowan said.

"Is everything all right?" Jennifer said.

I shook my head.

"No, not really." I looked down. "It's a very long way from all right."

"What's up, honey?" Jennifer said, her voice soft with concern. "What's happened?"

I watched as an elderly lady in a stretched black dress emerged from the little church across the square, walking stick in her hand. Very slowly, she began to make her way toward the café.

"It's a confession with an apology thrown in."

Quickly, without going into too much detail, I told them what had been happening over the last five days, my suspicions about Sean—suspicions that had hardened into the cold, hard knowledge that he was having an affair. How I had suspected first Rowan, then Jennifer, of being the other woman. And how confirmation had arrived yesterday that I had been wrong on both counts.

"That ring," Rowan said. "I found it in the gym. I didn't know it belonged to Sean—I thought it might have been a previous guest, so I just picked it up and put it in my drawer for safekeeping. Was going to ask everyone but it slipped my mind."

"I know," I said. "And apologies for thinking bad thoughts about you both. I'm really sorry. I just haven't been able to see the wood for the trees. And the worst thing is, I bloody talked to Izzy about this earlier in the week and she assured me that Sean would never go behind my back. Which of course is exactly what you *would* say if you were the other woman. I was so stupid."

They greeted my revelation with a moment of silence.

"This is mad, I can't believe it," Rowan said eventually, shaking her head. "I thought you'd been a bit weird these last few days. Couldn't put my finger on what it was. You poor thing."

"Me too," Jennifer said. "I sensed something wasn't right, was going to ask you. It must have been terrible for you, having to find out like that."

Rowan stirred her coffee.

"How certain are you? How sure?"

"Pretty certain. He's denied it point-blank but I know he's hiding something. I just don't know what to do next."

"Do you want us to talk to her?" Jennifer said, pushing her sunglasses up into her hair. "The two of us?"

And say what? Tell her to back off, find her own man? Why would that have any effect?

"I don't know," I said. "Maybe. Not yet. She told me the other day that she was seeing someone, but she didn't want to tell us yet because he's still married. He's in the process of getting a divorce, apparently, but she didn't think we'd approve."

"What's his name?"

"She wouldn't say."

"Or we could talk to Sean," Rowan said.

"No. Not that. I've tried already, anyway."

"Maybe he'll come to his senses. Give him a little bit of time."

I shook my head. "It's too late for that. I'll go mad if I don't do something; I just don't want to make the wrong call." I looked pointedly at Rowan. "Not again."

She gave me a little nod of understanding; she knew who I was referring to.

"But that was different," she said softly. "With Henry."

"Was it?"

Henry, Rowan's first husband. My mind drifted back to a time when the shoe had been on the other foot, the part I had played in the end of her first marriage. Would I have wanted to know, too, if I had been in her shoes?

The question brought me up short. I *was* in her shoes. It was my turn now.

I stirred my coffee slowly.

Ten years ago—almost to the day—Rowan and I had sat drinking coffee in the sitting room of my small end-of-terrace house in north London. The Sunday roast finished, dishes washed, Sean and Henry dispatched to the park with Lucy wobbling along on the new bike she'd received for her sixth birthday, shiny pink streamers trailing from the handgrips. Talking about school catchment areas and nurseries, Rowan announcing that she had come off the pill and was taking folic acid instead. And I had hesitated, and changed my mind, changed it again, put down my coffee and come out with seven words that would end up changing the course of her life.

I think Henry might be playing around.

I had heard it on very good authority that he was cheating on Rowan and had grappled with that knowledge for weeks as I tried to decide whether to tell her. Trying to work out what to do for the best, to do what was right—however hard that might be. Rowan, oblivious, talking about trying for their first child. What was

I supposed to do with the information that I had? Stay quiet while everyone talked about it behind her back? Let her find out for herself? Watch her being taken for a ride by the man she'd married? Sean had counseled caution, but in the end I went against his advice and told Rowan what I'd heard. Told her, in good faith, the stories that were doing the rounds about Henry.

Stories that turned out to be untrue. Malicious lies, circulated by an old flame with an agenda of her own, someone I'd never even met.

But malicious or not, the effect had been catastrophic. When Rowan confronted him with her explosive accusation, their marriage had unraveled in spectacular fashion.

They separated three months later.

"I wanted to say sorry again, Rowan," I said. "For what happened with Henry, the way it happened. I shouldn't have done what I did."

"Nonsense. You did what you thought was right at the time."

"I should have known, should have found out before I told you."

She leaned forward, put a hand on my arm. "It was up to me what I did with that information, and up to him how he reacted. It wasn't your fault, you were just the messenger. Anyway, it was probably for the best."

"How's that?"

"Henry didn't actually want children, not really. So if I was still with him today, I wouldn't have Odette."

"That's one way of looking at it, I suppose."

"You're worried about history repeating itself, aren't you?"

"Yes," I said. "Terrified."

I had been wrong before. I couldn't afford to be wrong again.

47

The house was eerily quiet when we returned from the village. Sean, Russ, and Izzy had taken the girls to a craft market in the nearby village of Murviel-lès-Béziers, while Alistair had volunteered to stay behind at the villa and look after the boys. But there was no sign of them when we got back. I checked the garden and the pool area, the gazebo and the games room. All deserted.

Eventually, I found Daniel alone in his bedroom. He was on his bed, lying with his back to me as I came in.

"Daniel?"

"Hi," he said, without turning around.

"What have you been up to? You OK?"

"Hmm."

I went around to the bed and sat down. "Wow, looks like you've nearly finished your book, we'll have to—"

I stopped, putting a hand to my mouth. There were cuts and grazes up his forearms, dirt and blood on his knees and shins. More dirt caked under his fingernails and on the front of his shorts. A smear of blood on his chin, his eyes red from crying. His favorite Harry Potter T-shirt was ripped at the neckline and under the arm was a long tear that went almost to his waist.

He looked as if he had been in a fight.

"What on earth happened to you, Daniel? Are you all right?"

"Fine."

"You look as if you've been dragged through a hedge backward. How did you get these cuts?"

"Fell down."

"Where?"

"Outside."

"Oh dear, you really are in a bit of a state. Sit up a minute and let me get a proper look at you."

He did as he was told and I gave him a quick check to see if anything was sprained or broken.

"Come on," I said. "Let's get you sorted out."

I took him into our bathroom and washed some of the dirt off with a washcloth, cleaning his cuts and scratches and dabbing on antiseptic with my fingertips. His T-shirt was beyond saving.

He stood, blank faced and silent, while I worked.

"Are you going to tell me how you got these cuts?"

"Told you," he said, eyes downcast. "Fell over."

"Were you with Jake and Ethan?"

He hesitated. Then, "They made me promise not to tell."

"Who?"

His voice so quiet it was almost inaudible, he said, "The boys."

"And where are they now?"

"Dunno."

"Aren't you all friends?"

"They said I couldn't play with them anymore, and they went off somewhere."

"They left you here on your own?"

He nodded miserably, the sharp tang of antiseptic cream making him wrinkle his nose.

I sat him down on the edge of the bathtub.

"What happened, Daniel?"

"When I fell down I was a bit upset, so Ethan got cross and then he said him and Jake were going out somewhere and I thought they meant they were just going outside, like hide-and-seek or something, so I went out to look for them in the garden but I couldn't find them. I looked for *ages* but I couldn't find them and I thought maybe they'd gone out in one of the cars. Their mum's rental car was gone. I looked everywhere." His voice dropped. "But I couldn't find anyone."

"What about Alistair?"

"Didn't know where he was."

My worry turned to anger.

"You couldn't find him either?"

"No. I ran around everywhere but it was like everyone had just left without me and I was all on my own and everyone had forgotten about me."

"Alistair was supposed to be here, looking after you."

He gave a little nod but still wouldn't look at me.

"I thought . . ." He trailed off, his voice growing quieter still.

"What did you think, darling?"

"I thought everyone had gone home without me. Back to England. Just left me here on my own in the vacation house and I didn't know what I was supposed to do. Like what happens to Kevin in *Home Alone,* but kind of the other way around."

I smiled and shook my head. *Home Alone* was one of his favorite films.

"You silly sausage! We'd never leave you all alone. *I* would never leave you."

"Are you cross, Mummy?"

"A bit," I said, giving him a hug. "But not with you."

"Will Jake and Ethan be in trouble?"

"It's not fair to go off and play without you so I need to find out why they left you on your own, and where Alistair was."

He stiffened.

"Mum! Please don't! Jake'll know that I told you even though I promised not to tell."

"Then I'll talk to Jennifer."

"*Please,* Mum." His voice cracked and I could tell he was on the verge of tears. "I just want to go home. I don't like it here anymore. I don't like the vacation house. It started off being really cool but now it's just horrible."

"We're going home on Saturday, Daniel. It's only a few days. In the meantime, perhaps steer clear of the bigger boys and stay near the villa." I looked away. "Play with your dad, OK?"

"What if something else bad happens?"

"Nothing else bad is going to happen, Daniel. I promise."

He sat, twisting his hands in his lap. He wouldn't look at me.

"Just want to go home," he said in a small voice. "Back to our normal house, with our normal things."

I gave him another hug and kissed the top of his head.

"Soon."

"Promise you won't tell Jake and Ethan?"

"I promise."

I handed him a clean T-shirt to wear.

"Where's my Harry Potter T-shirt, Mum?"

"It's ruined, Daniel, I had to throw it away."

His face crumpled again. "Please can you try to mend it?"

"It's all ripped up the side. I'll get you another one."

"Please?" He looked up at me with his big blue eyes. "It's my favorite."

"Well . . ."

"Please?"

I stood up.

"All right. If Jennifer has brought a sewing kit, I'll see what I can do."

I went to the pedal bin in the corner to fish out his

T-shirt and was about to let the lid fall again when something caught my eye beneath it. It was one of those things that you recognize instantly—even if you haven't held one in your hands for a decade or more.

I lifted it out of the bin, turning it over in my hand. Dizziness clouded my vision for a moment. This was . . . No, I didn't have the headspace to think about this right now, to even consider the implications of it. There was too much going on already, too many plates spinning. Too much worry and suspicion and fear. I slipped it into the back pocket of my jeans.

Just a piece of generic white plastic with a singular purpose.

But what on earth was it doing *here*?

I needed to ask Lucy as soon as she got back.

48

I found Jennifer out on the balcony, looking down into the vineyard.

"Jennifer, can I talk to you?"

She turned and gave me a sympathetic smile.

"Sure. Is everything all right?"

"Perhaps we could go somewhere a bit more private?"

"Of course."

She followed me down the outdoor steps and into the garden, the grass soft beneath my feet. We sat at either end of a bench made of clean white stone.

"I don't want to make a big deal out of this, Jen, but apparently the three boys had a big falling-out this afternoon. All a bit of a shame, really. Daniel said they left him alone in the house, and he also thinks . . ." I hesitated, knowing I was on shakier ground now. "He said something else as well."

"What?"

"He couldn't be sure, but he thinks they might have gone off in your rental car. For a drive."

Jennifer frowned.

"A *drive*?"

"He couldn't find them anywhere, and he said your car was missing."

"Hmm," Jennifer said. "Well, that doesn't sound like the sort of thing that Jake and Ethan would do. Jake's far too young to drive, for a start. It doesn't sound like my boys at all."

Yes it does, I thought, wondering how she could be so unaware of what her sons were like. *It sounds* exactly *like your boys.*

"Can you raise it with him? With Jake?"

"That's not a good idea."

"Why not? You can't have him driving around the French countryside. Who knows what might have happened."

"The truth is, he gets very upset sometimes when he feels he's in trouble. *Very* upset. Especially when he's accused of something he hasn't done."

"I understand that."

"And he didn't do what Daniel's saying." Her voice was quite firm, no room for maneuvering. "He didn't do those things."

"Daniel was quite specific—"

"He's mistaken. I'm sure Daniel was upset, and I'm very sorry about that, but I'm absolutely certain that my boy didn't do what he's saying. This estate is a very big place, there must be a hundred hiding places here. It sounds like a game of hide-and-seek that just got a bit out of hand."

"All the same, could you ask him? See what he says? Daniel was really very upset when he thought he'd been abandoned—he couldn't find Alistair, either."

"Like I said," she replied, her voice taking on a harder tone, "Jake doesn't take it well when he gets accused of things."

"And like *I* said, Daniel was quite specific."

She hesitated, looking around to make sure no one was eavesdropping.

"I need to tell you something. So you understand."

"OK."

"You have to promise it won't go any further. Not even Sean. Especially not your children."

"Of course."

"I'm only going to tell you this because you're my dear friend, and I want you to understand. Do you remember last year, when Jake had encephalitis?"

I nodded. "He's fine now, though, isn't he?"

She smiled a sad little smile and looked at the ground. "Most of the time, yes."

"And he's got so tall this past year, I can't believe he's already overtaken—"

"It wasn't encephalitis."

I waited for a moment, thinking I'd not heard her right. "He was misdiagnosed, you mean?"

"No."

"I don't understand, Jennifer."

"That was just what we told people. We didn't want him to be stigmatized."

She looked away, across the garden, tears in her eyes. I waited for her to continue, but she seemed to have lost her words.

I put a hand on her arm. "It's OK."

She looked back at me, then over to the villa, checking again that no one else was within earshot.

"The real reason was that he had to go away from us for a little while, for some treatment." A tear spilled down her cheek. "He was going to hurt himself, Kate. You can't understand if it's never happened to you, but we had an argument one day, seemed like nothing out of the ordinary, just something silly about tidying his room, which he never seemed to want to do. But he reacted like—like I'd accused him of a terrible crime. He went *nuclear.* And then I found him sitting on his window ledge, and you know his bedroom is two stories up, right?"

I nodded, put my hand over hers. "The attic room."

"Took me two hours to persuade him not to jump, and every single second my heart was in my throat. I didn't sleep for three nights after that. The next week he did it again, and the week after that we found him wandering up the railway track behind our house. It was awful, just the most awful thing imaginable. Every day worrying about what he would do next. Worrying about a phone call, or a visit from the police—or worse. We grounded him, but he just went out anyway, so we tried locking him in but he always found a way out. You can't keep your child prisoner in his own home, especially when he's bigger than either of us." Her voice dropped again, until it was barely above a whisper. "Eventually we got so scared that . . ." Her voice trailed off.

I waited for her to continue, giving her hand a little squeeze.

"What happened, Jen?"

She wiped a tear away. "We had him—we had him committed. So he could be treated."

"My God, Jen, I had no idea this was all going on!" I hugged her, rubbing her back. "I'm so sorry."

"We didn't tell anyone. The doctors spent a lot of time with him and eventually he was diagnosed with a borderline personality disorder—prone to impulsive behavior, risk-taking, emotional outbursts. Although I believe that's mostly garbage," she added hastily. "We knew he'd been getting in trouble at school, too— fighting and stealing and skipping classes. That's why we moved him and his brother to Lucy's school. We thought that if he had a fresh start, a clean break from all the bad influences at his old school, it would be easier for him to move on. That's what Alistair said, anyway. He's supposed to know about these things."

"Oh Jennifer, you poor thing. I had no idea you were dealing with all this."

"So you see, I have to be really careful. It's like he's on a knife-edge most of the time. Some days he can be superexcitable and into everything, trying everything, but other days he gets so low. He has these black moods and he's just knocked down by everything, especially when he's accused of doing things he hasn't done. And he's my baby, my firstborn. I have to protect him."

"I know that, Jen, I understand."

"You'd do the same for Lucy."

"You're right. I would, absolutely."

I paused, not sure how to ask the next question.

"Was there any . . . any treatment for him? To help him get through it?"

"He has pills, but he doesn't like taking them. Says they make him feel like a zombie." She turned her wedding ring on her finger, rolling it between thumb and forefinger. "I found a stash of them under his bed; he'd been pretending to take them but he'd just been hiding them instead. And I was so frightened. I didn't want to confront him in case it set him off again, so I just left them there. Pathetic, aren't I?"

"No, you're not. Not at all."

"Will you promise me you won't tell anyone about this?"

"Of course. I won't tell anyone."

"Not even Sean?"

"Not even him."

She got up off the bench and wiped her eyes, taking a deep breath and letting it out dramatically. "Let me talk to Ethan about—about whatever happened this afternoon with Daniel. I'll ask him to be nicer to him from now on."

"Thanks, Jennifer. Are you OK?"

"Fine." She summoned a shaky smile. "I'm always fine."

I watched her walking back across the lawn, toward the villa, and thought about what she'd said. It was a terrible thing to fear for your children, to fear they might come to harm. It was the unthinkable dread of every parent that their own flesh and blood could somehow end up being the cause of that harm. Anxiety, depression, isolation, self-harm; drugs to blot out the pain, blades to slice flesh where the scars couldn't be seen. The thought of your own child suffering in secret was unbearable.

I knew all of that. I felt it myself, for my own children.

49

Lucy was slumped in the big armchair with her phone when I knocked on her bedroom door.

I pushed the door shut behind me and sat down on the edge of her bed.

"How was shopping?"

"Good," she said, not looking up from her phone. "Hot."

"Get any bargains?"

"A few bits, a new hat and some sandals."

"Great, you must show me them later."

"Sure."

"Lucy?"

"Yeah?"

"Put your phone down a minute, I want to ask you something."

She sighed and put her phone in her lap. "What?"

"Have the boys—I mean Jake and Ethan—ever talked to you about taking one of the rental cars out for a drive, without the adults knowing?"

She gave me an exaggerated shrug. "Don't know. Don't think so."

"You sure?"

"They're both too young to drive, aren't they? Jake's not even sixteen yet."

We looked at each other, both aware that this was a dodge rather than an answer.

"So they've never mentioned it to you?"

She looked up and over my shoulder. "They talk about a lot of stuff, all kinds of things, boasting with each other. Why are you asking me this?"

"Just something I was wondering about."

She picked her phone up again and began scrolling. "Right."

"There's something else as well."

She sighed. "Is it about drinking wine again, because I haven't—"

"I found something in the bathroom next door, in the bin. The bathroom that you and your brother use."

"In the bin?"

"Yes."

She looked up from her phone again, frowning. "Because *that's* not weird at all, going through our bin—perfectly normal behavior."

I reached into my pocket and took out what I'd found. "Do you know what this is?"

She glanced at the short stick of white plastic that I was holding. Blinked once, twice. Looked away again.

"Yeah. We did it in biology."

"And?"

"It's one of those test things. A pregnancy test."

"Correct. Do you know how they work?"

"Not exactly." She shifted uncomfortably in her chair. "You have to wee on it or something?"

"Right again." I turned it over to show her the two parallel blue lines behind the clear plastic window. "Two lines means pregnant."

"I know that."

I thought for a moment about how to phrase the next question.

"And do you know," I said slowly, "how it got there? Into your bathroom?"

"Not a clue. Someone else must have put it there."

I leaned forward, smiling at her. Trying to soften my expression. "Is there something you want to tell me? It's OK if you are, we can talk about—"

"I'm not!" she said forcefully, crossing her arms.

"You're not what?"

"Pregnant. The test isn't mine. And if it had been mine, I wouldn't have been stupid enough to dump it in my own bathroom bin where anyone might find it and start asking questions. Where *Daniel* might find it."

I felt a little of the weight lift from my shoulders. "You're sure?"

"Trust me, Mum—I'd be way more sneaky about it than that. You'd never know."

50

JENNIFER

Behind a locked door in the downstairs bathroom, Jennifer wiped her eyes and blew her nose before taking another tissue to repair the damage to her eyeliner. She stared at the face in the mirror for a moment, hands grasping the granite countertop, taking ten deep breaths as she'd been taught to do. *In through the nose, out through the mouth.*

Calm. Clear. Do what needs to be done.

She went into the kitchen and found a cloth under the sink, took a small bottle of water from the fridge. She checked through the entrance hall window for anyone out on the front driveway, then, satisfied it was deserted, she took the keys from a hook by the front door and walked down the sweeping stone staircase that curved out onto the drive. Their rental car, a Ford Fiesta, was the cheapest one they could get that would still fit two lanky teenage boys in the back—just about—and all of their luggage.

Jennifer walked a slow circle around the car, running her eye over the paintwork, the bumpers, the trim. There were a couple new scrapes on the paintwork, low down near the offside rear tire. They'd not been there when they'd picked the car up from the airport four days previously. She squatted down, examining them more closely and touching an index finger to the metal. Parallel scratches in the bodywork, probably from a low wall or a boulder by the side of the road. But not deep. Not too hard to hide.

She poured water from the bottle into a patch of earth in the flower bed, dabbed the cloth in the wet mud, and smeared some dirt over the scratches—just enough to disguise the new marks. It had to be carefully done, so it just looked like the regular dirt you might get from driving around the French countryside.

Superficial stuff could be covered like that, well enough to fool the rental company inspection when they returned the car in three days' time. *We don't want to get hit with a hefty repair bill, do we?* Such a rip-off, anyway. They tried to charge you hundreds of euros for even the tiniest dent. Anything deeper would need a trip to a garage before they returned the car on Saturday.

She stood up and admired her handiwork, looking at the smudges of dirt and adding some more near the front wheel, so the marks were more consistent. When it dried, it would disguise the marks well enough.

With that done, she took the key fob from her

pocket and unlocked the doors. Opening the driver's side door, she pulled the seat forward, back to where she usually had it. Then she locked the Fiesta again and went back inside.

51

It was my turn to do the dishes after dinner. I was glad of the distraction, the chance to be away from the others for a little while, away from making polite conversation, away from having to pretend that everything was normal.

Away from Sean.

I filled the sink and began scrubbing at pots and pans, the water so hot it almost scalded my hands and arms. My emotions were a mess of hurt and confusion and despair that things could ever be put right again. As hard as I tried, I couldn't get the image of Izzy out of my mind—the image of her as she walked up into the clearing in the woods, summoned by a message from my husband's phone. The more I thought about it, the clearer it became that Izzy was the one—it had been her all along. She was the only single one among us. Her hometown connection with Sean had finally turned into something more intimate, more dangerous. More destructive.

Our conversation on her first day here came back with a sick, deadening realization that she had virtually admitted it to me.

"He's married, isn't he?"

"I couldn't possibly *comment."*

How could I have been so blind?

I had vowed to find answers, to find the source of Sean's betrayal. And now I knew. I knew more than I had ever wanted to know.

Only one question remained.

What am I going to do about it?

But I finally knew the answer to that one.

Sean appeared beside me at the sink, tea towel in hand. I could smell beer on his breath, on him, surrounding him like an invisible cloud. Something else, too, something stronger. Tequila. I felt myself stiffen.

"Need a hand?" he said.

I didn't look at him.

"If you want."

He picked up one of the frying pans dripping on the rack and began to dry it. His movements were slow, exaggerated, like he was concentrating hard on not dropping anything.

"Daniel's tucked up in bed reading his book," he said. "Going to turn out his light in ten minutes."

"Good."

There was a lengthy silence while I scrubbed violently at fragments of pasta stuck to the bottom of a pan. I wanted to throw my anger at him, wind it up and hurl it at him with all the strength I could muster.

Why her? What does she have that I don't? What the hell are you thinking?

How could you do this to me? To the kids? With one of my best friends?

He put the frying pan away and carefully picked up another from the rack.

"Are you OK, Kate?"

"Do you care?"

A pause.

"Yes," he said softly. "Of course I care."

"I'm fine."

He looked away.

"I'm sorry," he said quietly.

I stopped scrubbing.

"For what?"

"That we argued."

I stared into the soapy water in the sink.

Tell him. Tell him you know.

"What else are you sorry for?"

"Well now, let me see." The joviality was forced. "How long have you got?"

I turned to glare at him in time to see a halfhearted smile die on his lips.

"Seriously? You're trying to make jokes?"

His smile vanished completely.

"Sorry, Kate. Sorry."

I plunged the last of the pots into the sink, water splashing over the side and onto my feet, and resumed scrubbing even more vigorously than before.

"How's your phone, by the way?"

He shifted beside me, as if sensing a trap.

"Absolutely knackered. Won't even switch on."

"That's a shame, isn't it? How are you managing without it?"

His eyes flicked up to mine in the dark reflection of the window, then away again.

"All right."

"Still keeping up with your messages?" My voice was heavy with sarcasm. "Keeping on top of things?"

"It's no bother," he said quietly. "I'll sort it when we get back to England."

I finished the pots, drained the water, and dried my hands.

He took half a step toward me, hands out as if to hug me, but I shook my head.

"Don't," I said, a note of warning in my voice. "Don't even try."

"Kate, I'm—"

"You're what?"

He hesitated, seeming to weigh his words. "You know I've always been a rubbish liar."

"You seem to have got a lot better at it recently."

"Not really."

I crossed my arms tightly over my chest. "Why don't you just tell me?"

He seemed about to say something, then thought better of it, his eyes dropping to the floor.

"There's nothing to tell."

"Why can't you just tell me? I hate this! *Hate* it."

I fled from the kitchen before he could see my tears,

before he could say anything else. It was painful just to be near him, to have to talk to him. Instead I went upstairs to our bedroom, sitting on the bed in the air-conditioned cool until my heart had slowed to something near normal, wiping my eyes with a tissue.

This was a special kind of torture. Why wouldn't he just come out with it, put me out of my misery? Was I going mad? Was I losing it? *No.* I had evidence. I had seen things, heard things, that could not be denied or explained away, however hard he tried. My head was pounding. I opened my bedside drawer to find some Tylenol, shifting books and chargers and passports to one side, reaching to the back.

There, a box of Tylenol. But something was wrong. Out of place. Or, more accurately, absent. I had put it here two days ago, for safekeeping, and now it had disappeared.

The camcorder tape of Sean and Jennifer.

52

I checked again, shifting the drawer's contents around. No tape. Someone had moved it, taken it. *Sean?* Pushing the bedroom door shut, I went around to his side of the bed and quickly looked through his drawer, then the lining of his suitcase and the chest of drawers where T-shirts and shorts were neatly stacked, but no miniDV tape. It was gone.

The sounds of laughter from the pool below floated up to me in the bedroom. I couldn't hide up here forever. Checking my face quickly in the mirror, I took a deep breath and opened the door to the hall. Daniel's bedroom door was slightly ajar. I gave it the lightest of taps and pushed it open.

My son lay curled on his side, engrossed in Harry Potter.

"Was about to turn my light out," he said, putting the book down and taking his glasses off.

I sat down on the edge of his bed and brushed the hair off his forehead.

"Are you OK after what happened earlier?" I said. "Are those scratches and scrapes hurting?"

I held my arms out and enveloped him in a hug, feeling the warmth of his small chest against me, his sweet little-boy smell, his thin arms tight around me. Wondering how much longer he would let me hug him before he became too embarrassed, too self-conscious to do it anymore. Wondering whether he would blame me for what had happened between Sean and me, feeling the heat of tears behind my eyes.

Don't cry. Don't upset him.

"Are you all right, Mummy?"

"Of course," I said, swallowing hard and trying to keep my voice level. "Why wouldn't I be?"

"And is Daddy all right?"

"Yes."

"Oh."

"What makes you say that, Daniel?"

"Dunno," he said, his little chin resting on my shoulder. "He seems a bit funny this week."

"Funny how?"

"Just a bit weird."

I released him from the hug and looked at him properly in the light of the bedside lamp. "Funny with Izzy?"

"Maybe." He shrugged. "I don't think he likes Jake."

"Why not?"

"He keeps asking what we've been doing when we go out adventuring, says I don't have to play with them if I don't want to."

"Daddy just wants you to be safe, that's all. Jake's a bit of a daredevil, isn't he?"

"Hmm." He yawned. "What are we doing tomorrow?"

"Something nice." I kissed him on the forehead. "Night, Daniel. Love you."

Lucy wasn't in her room. Only her phone was there, plugged in to charge, winking and flashing in the darkness with more of the constant stream of updates from friends at home. The battery had died completely during our evening meal and I had been secretly glad to see her untethered from it for a little while, to have a conversation with her and not constantly feel I was trying—and failing—to compete for attention with the iPhone in her hand.

Back in the kitchen I refilled my wineglass and made my way down the stone steps to the pool, the evening air still hot and almost unbearably humid. Russ lay sprawled on a lounger, two inches of ash on the cigarette smoldering between his drooping fingers. Sean sat next to him, beer in hand, by a table clustered with glasses and bowls of snacks, empty bottles of wine and beer and a half-empty bottle of tequila. I could tell, in my peripheral vision, that he was turned toward me, trying to look at me. Trying to catch my eye.

I sipped my wine and kept my eyes on the swimming pool, where Lucy and Rowan plus Alistair, Jake, and Ethan were throwing a volleyball between them, shooting for little goal nets perched at each end. Underwater lights set deep in the walls gave the water an ethereal, shimmering glow against the darkness of the night, mosaic tiles portraying three dolphins standing out bright and colorful on the floor of the pool, the water above them perfectly clear.

"Are you coming in, Kate?" Alistair gestured at me, his beard glistening with droplets of water. "We need a sixth for water polo."

"Not tonight," I said, as cheerfully as I could manage. "Maybe another time."

"That *is* a shame," he said with an exaggerated grin. "How about you, Sean?"

My husband shook his head.

"Think I've had one too many beers. I'd probably sink."

"Nonsense," Alistair shouted, his voice bright with alcohol. "An invigorating, restorative dip is exactly what the doctor ordered at this stage of the evening's proceedings."

"Reckon I'll just watch, thanks."

"It's also the perfect cooling therapy for the Mediterranean heat."

Sean shook his head and sat back on the lounger.

"I'll take your word for it, pal."

Lucy slapped the pool's surface with her palm, splashing water toward him.

"Come on, Dad," she said. "I need you to be on my team."

"Well . . ."

"Pleeeease?" she said. "You've already got your swimming shorts on."

Sean sighed, took a long slug of his beer, and put it down by the side of the pool. Pulling his shirt over his head, he kicked off his flip-flops and stepped unsteadily into the pool with a heavy splash.

"Excellent," Alistair said, raising the ball above his head. "Let the game commence!"

53

I sat back on the lounger, watching them splash and play and laugh in the sparkling water of the infinity pool, the ball thrown back and forth as if none of them had a care in the world. Just an evening swim, an escape from the cloying heat, a refreshing dip in between drinks, Sean standing in the deep end, trying to catch my eye, trying to give me his smile, *that* smile, the one that had made my stomach do somersaults back when we first met. His charming, twinkling smile that felt as though we were sharing a private joke just between the two of us. A secret club that no one else could join.

Not anymore, though. Now his smile just made me feel a plunging heartbreak so deep, so dark, that I couldn't see the bottom. I knew, as surely as I'd ever known anything, that he had been on the point of confessing in the kitchen half an hour ago. He was about to tell me everything but had pulled back at the last moment. Why? Why waste time? Why not just get it over with? Perhaps he didn't want to do it while we were away, in front of all our friends. That was it; he wanted to be on home turf, on familiar ground.

His words rang in my head.

I'm sorry.

At least the fact that he was here in front of me, in the pool with our daughter, meant that he couldn't be with *her*. With Izzy. I wondered what their plan was, how they would do it. Was I supposed to just wait until he decided to tell me, until I found more of their secret messages, until they were caught in the act? Was I supposed to just sit and wait until I was told my marriage was over?

No. That wasn't going to happen. If Sean didn't have the guts to tell me, then I would force the issue—confront Izzy and make her admit it, get it out there in the open. Tonight. When she returned from whatever it was she was doing.

The game of water polo carried on regardless, Sean, Lucy, and Rowan versus Alistair and his boys. Sean and Alistair manned the goals at each end of the pool, while Rowan and the three teenagers blocked and dodged and took shots in the space in between. Sean was distracted, his eyes still wandering toward me, but I refused to give him the eye contact he was looking for. My eyes were firmly on Lucy, her golden hair fanned out behind her in the water, swimming and diving and turning like a beautiful mermaid. *My little girl.* Jake and Ethan had left their phones on a side table and they were pinging and bleeping almost constantly with notifications, a continuous stream of updates on social media that seemed ferociously frequent even by teenage standards. But it was nice to see Lucy—to see all three teenagers—doing something that didn't involve their phones, that didn't involve the endless picture posting and status sharing, the comparison with friends and the unspoken fear of missing out that drove the constant need to be connected all day, every day.

It was subtle, at first.

So subtle I almost didn't register it.

But as the ball was thrown back and forth and the players splashed and laughed, a sense of unease began creeping up my arms. With every goal scored, every shot blocked, the distance between certain players in the middle—Lucy, Jake, and Ethan, to be precise—got smaller. And then a little smaller still, until only a few feet separated them. The brothers moved farther and farther into the deep end, into Lucy's half of the pool.

As I watched, the prickle of concern climbing up to the back of my neck, Lucy got the ball and raised it high to throw at the goal. Ethan waded toward her and hurled himself forward with his arms raised high to take the ball from her, lunging into her, pushing his body into hers, no space between them at all, faces inches apart, arms touching, hands touching, his chest against hers, skin to skin, nose to nose, him pushing and reaching and grabbing in a full-contact tackle, his shoulders and arms overpowering her slender frame, his hands snatching the ball away from her and holding it up, and I knew, I just *knew,* that what he wanted more than anything was for her to come back at him and try to take it away as he had just done.

Instead, Jake lunged at his brother and took the ball from him, hurling it aside and shoving his brother in the chest. Pushing him away from Lucy.

"What the hell, Ethan?" he shouted angrily. "It's not a bloody rugby line-out, all right? It's not supposed to be full contact."

"Chill out, bro." Ethan splashed water into his brother's face. "Just a game, isn't it?"

Alistair started to wade forward to separate his boys, before seeming to think better of the idea. He moved back into his goal, reaching for the ball.

I sat forward in my seat, a hot bloom of anger unfurling in my chest, torn between a mother's instinct to protect her daughter and a parent's instinct to avoid embarrassing a teenager. But Lucy dived beneath the surface and came up a few feet away with her back to me, smoothing her hair off her face, holding her hands up to continue the game.

Perhaps I had imagined it—she seemed OK. The shout died in my throat.

Don't embarrass her. Don't make another scene. You've done that enough already this week.

Sean was taking a long pull from a bottle of beer at the side of the pool and appeared not to have noticed.

The game continued. Lucy intercepted the ball on its way to the goal and drew her arm back to throw, but Ethan was on her immediately. He waded forward and lunged again, hardly even seeming to go for the ball. Both hands held up, he launched himself toward her even more forcefully than the last time. Pushing and reaching, hands grabbing and pulling, his face in hers. Lucy wasn't giving in so easily this time and she turned to dodge away from him, but then he was all over her, grappling with her for the ball, laughing, both hands on her shoulders as he almost climbed up her back, spinning her around to face him. A thrashing melee of bodies and arms and water splashing everywhere, and then Jake was pulling Ethan away and squaring up to him, fist cocked back, Alistair diving forward, arms out, trying to separate his boys, Ethan dodging away—

Hands landing on Lucy's chest. Her shriek of alarm.

Sean's shout of anger.

Lucy dived under the surface again, kicking hard and surfacing next to Sean in the deep end, gasping for breath, one bikini strap hanging loose on her shoulder, a dark line of fingermarks showing red on her upper arm. Her face seemed to be frozen in shock, chest heaving for breath as she gripped the side.

Sean spoke to her briefly, quietly, a gentle hand on her elbow. She put her bikini strap back into place and said something back to him, her head down, then climbed out and wrapped a towel around her shoulders, pulling it tightly across her chest.

I hurried over to her, putting both hands on her shoulders. She was shaking and wouldn't look at me. We were both shaking.

"Lucy, are you OK?"

"Fine."

"Why don't you head up to your room? I'll come up in a minute."

She nodded and walked quickly to the stairs up to the balcony, head still down. Sean was wading into the middle of the pool, his face dark with anger.

He had evidently seen things differently from me.

"What the bloody hell do you think you're doing?" he said to Alistair.

Alistair retrieved the ball and threw it past him into the empty net.

"I'm sorry, what?"

"Grabbing my daughter? What the hell is that about?"

"It was an accident, Sean," he said, his voice neutral. "Nobody grabbed anyone. Water polo always includes a bit of rough-and-tumble."

"Rough-and-tumble?" Sean repeated. His voice had taken on an edge I had only heard once or twice before, his Limerick accent hard and loud. "Are you having a laugh?"

"You're drunk, Sean."

"And you're a bloody pervert."

Alistair turned and began to wade toward the steps

in the shallow end. "I'm not listening to this." He turned to Jake and Ethan. "Come on, boys, game over. Time to get out."

"Hey!" Sean shouted, going after him. "I'm talking to you!"

Alistair ignored him, water flowing off him as he climbed the steps out of the pool and picked up his towel. Sean caught up with him, grabbed his shoulder, and spun him around.

"I *said,* I'm talking to you. You know she's only sixteen, right? And you know what that makes you?"

Veins were standing out in Sean's neck and arms, his face a mask of rage, his hands clenched into fists. He was taller, broader than Alistair, and in much better shape. I hurried toward them along the side of the pool, dreading what was about to happen.

"Sean," I said, "I don't think that was how it—"

"I saw what he did," Sean said. "Grabbing at her."

Alistair, drying himself with the towel, cocked his head slightly to one side and gave Sean a concerned smile. His *counseling face,* Jennifer had called it once.

"I don't think that's quite how it happened, Sean."

"Fuck off! I saw you do it."

Ethan climbed out of the pool and Jake followed him, both keeping an eye on their dad in case punches started being thrown for real.

I could see that Alistair was in an impossible situation. What was he supposed to say? *It wasn't me who grabbed your daughter's breasts, Sean, it was my son.*

And I was trying to stop my other son from punching his lights out, OK?

I put a hand on my husband's arm.

"Sean?"

He seemed not to notice, jabbing the smaller man in the chest with his forefinger. Once. Twice.

"You're full of shit."

Alistair looked down at the finger.

"You know," he said, his voice shaking slightly, "technically that's assault."

"I tell you what, you put your hands on my daughter again and I'll show you what assault is. I'll *technically* take your fucking head off, how about that?"

Russ stood up and put both arms between them, shifting the two men apart slightly.

"Lads, lads," he said, his voice slow with alcohol. "Let's all step back and take a minute, shall we?"

Sean was immovable, a solid six-foot wall of anger.

"I'm warning you," he said, jabbing his finger at Alistair. "You stay away from her."

Russ put a hand on each man's shoulder.

"Lads, we're supposed to be on vacation, having a lovely jolly old time. Not challenging each other to fist-fights." Almost to himself, he added, "However entertaining that might be to watch."

Alistair turned away, slipping his glasses on.

"Come on, boys, into the villa now I think."

Jake and Ethan, heads down and absorbed in their phones, had already begun walking away toward the villa. Towels over their shoulders, faces lit by the glow of phone screens. Abruptly they both stopped, frozen in place.

Looking at each other, then back at their phones.

54

Russ

Russ held the book in his hands, but he didn't really need to: he had read *The Tiger Who Came to Tea* so many times he knew the words by heart. He thought Odette probably did, too, but she was finally drifting off now. It was her third Daddy story of the night and she was just about surrendering to sleep, her blinks getting longer and longer as he sat on the floor by her bed and turned the pages.

At the end of the story he sat with his daughter a moment, watching her breathe, feeling himself sobering up a little. Feeling the familiar pang of guilt because he *liked* this part of the day, he *liked* it when she went to sleep—but shouldn't he prefer it when she was awake? Why couldn't he be better with her during the day, more patient? Why couldn't he make the most of spending quality time with his only child?

He resolved, as he always did, to do better tomorrow.

Kissing her gently on the forehead, he backed slowly out of the room and dimmed the light.

He went downstairs and grabbed a fresh bottle of Kronenbourg from the kitchen, dumped a large bag of tortilla chips into a bowl, and carried them both out toward the balcony.

"Russ?"

He turned toward the voice, squinting into the shadows at the far end of the living room. Alistair was there, sitting on his own, hunched in one of the big armchairs.

"Hey, Alistair."

"Have you got a second?"

"Sure." Russ walked over to him. "What's up?"

"About . . . what happened earlier. I just wanted to say thank you for stepping in."

"Oh, that?" He shrugged. "No worries, it was nothing."

Alistair circled a fingertip around the rim of his almost-empty wineglass.

"All the same, I appreciate what you did." Speaking more softly, he added, "I'm not sure it would have ended well for me if you hadn't got involved."

Russ studied him for a moment, hearing the slight tremor in the older man's voice.

"Much ado about nothing," Russ said with a grin, checking over his shoulder to make sure no one was listening in. "Are you . . . all right, Alistair?"

"Oh yes, of course. Right as rain. Never better."

Russ picked up the wine bottle from the table and topped off Alistair's glass without asking.

"Thanks," Alistair said. "It wasn't what it looked like, you know. In the pool, I mean. I didn't do what Sean—"

"I know, buddy. I saw what happened. Ethan just needs to . . ." Russ struggled for the right words. "You know, learn, mature, whatever. You can talk to him about this stuff, he's still a young lad, isn't he?"

Alistair took a large sip of red wine.

"He has a lot of violence in him."

"Ethan?"

"Sean."

"You think?"

"We all saw it earlier, didn't we? There's a great deal of tension there, unresolved anxiety seeking a violent outlet."

"More like the booze and the heat making everyone snappy," Russ said.

"Aggravating factors, perhaps."

"I mean, there's violence in all of us, isn't there? If someone pushes the right buttons."

Alistair shook his head. "It shouldn't be that close to the surface. Sean is on a perilously short fuse this week, from what I've observed."

Russ drank half his beer in one long pull, wiping his mouth with the back of his hand.

"Tell me something," he said. "Do you analyze everybody you meet?"

"Occupational hazard. Sorry."

"So what's your analysis of me?"

"Well, if you really—"

"Actually, you know what?" Russ held a hand up, cutting him off. "Forget I said that; don't think I want to know. Let's just have a few more drinks and enjoy the evening, shall we?"

"That sounds like a good plan."

"Are you coming out onto the balcony? We'd better rejoin the ladies."

Alistair nodded reluctantly.

"Yes," he said, standing up. "I suppose we should."

55

Thankfully, Sean didn't react when the other two men reappeared on the far side of the balcony. I sensed him looking over, his eyes following Alistair and Russ as they sat down with drinks and snacks from the kitchen. Sean tensed, but didn't make a move, didn't say anything that might reignite their confrontation from a couple hours earlier. After a moment he went back to the cards he was shuffling, mechanically dealing out another hand of trumps to Rowan, Jennifer, and me.

A voice cut across us, coming from the vineyard gate.

"Guys? Can I get a little help, please?"

All eyes turned toward the sound. A couple had appeared at the edge of the garden, arm in arm, but deep in shadow. One much taller than the other, making painfully slow progress up the hill toward us.

Jennifer moved first, stumbling toward them.

"Jake?" she said, her voice rising. "Jake, is that you?"

The couple stepped into a pool of light at the edge of the garden. Izzy, her arm slung awkwardly around Jake's skinny waist. A third figure—Ethan, I realized—trailed after them before lying down flat in the grass.

Jennifer broke into a run, with me close behind.

"Jake?" she shouted. "Oh my God, Jakey, are you all right?"

He groaned in reply, his head lolling from side to side. Jennifer and I reached him and took an arm each, as Izzy disentangled herself.

"They were down in the gorge," she said.

"Jakey?" Jennifer said again. "Talk to me. Are you ill?"

Jake groaned again, put his hands on his knees and vomited noisily into the grass at his feet.

He was in a bad way. Jennifer and I led him to a lounger where he sat heavily and retched again, the stench of spilled wine and fresh vomit surrounding him like an overpowering cologne. Alistair wandered over, surveying his elder son with a rueful smile.

"Oh dear," he said. "Bit of overindulgence, Jake? Still, a useful lesson learned for you and your brother, eh? I'll get some water from the kitchen."

He headed off back toward the villa.

Jennifer knelt down, putting her hands on Jake's knees. "Talk to me, honey, what happened? Are you hurt? Did you fall down, did you bang your head?"

Rowan and I exchanged a confused glance. It

seemed painfully obvious to me why her son was as sick as a dog.

Jake groaned, a deep guttural sound like an animal in a trap. Jennifer didn't flinch.

"Oh dear, Jakey, what are we going to do with you? Was it something you ate at dinner?" She turned to the rest of us. "What did we have for dinner, the pasta and chicken? Maybe the chicken wasn't fully cooked through?"

Izzy sighed and spoke up. "It's not the chicken, Jennifer. It's the Saint-Chinian. Two empty bottles of wine down there with them in the gorge, and Jake had the lion's share, apparently."

Jennifer scowled up at her. "We don't know that for sure, do we?" More quietly, she said, "Have you been taking your medication, Jakey?"

He gave another noncommittal grunt.

"Oh, you poor boy," Jennifer said, rubbing his back. "You poor, poor boy."

I went to check on Ethan, lying a few yards away. He was stretched out on the coarse grass, flat on his back, eyes open to the night sky. I knelt down next to him.

"Are you OK, Ethan? Your dad's gone for some water. Do you want to be sick?"

He turned his head, looking at me coolly.

"M'all right."

"You sure?"

"Just going to have a little sleep."

"How much did you have?"

"Only a bit. Maybe half a bottle."

"Really?"

"Jake had a lot more than me." He blinked slowly. "The wine."

"He's brought most of it back up again, apparently."

"Hmm." He snorted, looking back up at the canopy of stars overhead. "He was on a mission."

"Looks like you both were." I thought back to my teenage years, booze smuggled out of my parents' house to drink in the park; laughing at anything, everything, laughing until it hurt, until tears came. Jake and Ethan didn't look like they'd been laughing. "What was the mission?"

A long, slow blink. Then another. He mumbled something I couldn't make out.

I leaned closer. "What, Ethan?"

He closed his eyes. "What's that word again? That Bastille song?"

He wasn't making sense.

"What song, Ethan?"

The word came out slowly, one syllable at a time.

"Oblivion."

I looked across to Jake, motionless on the grass. *Mission accomplished,* it seemed to me. Whatever Jennifer had said to him about the incident earlier today—with Daniel being left on his own in the villa while the brothers went for a joyride—I guessed that Jake had had an extreme reaction to being told off. Or maybe it was something to do with the water polo incident.

"Just stay here, your dad'll be back in a minute."

Ethan gave the slightest of nods. "No hurry."

I headed back up the hill, where Jennifer, Izzy, Russ, and Sean now made a semicircle of concerned adults around the stricken Jake, lying on his side in the recovery position.

"I don't think Ethan's as bad as . . ." I indicated his older brother. "Nothing a good sleep and a couple of Tylenol won't sort out."

No one spoke. I was suddenly aware of a strange, charged atmosphere, a weird tension between the two women.

Jennifer nodded at me and gave a tight smile before returning her attention to Izzy.

"It just seems to have taken an awfully long time for you to get back here, that's all I'm saying."

The note of accusation in her voice was unmistakable. Izzy put her hands on her hips, frowned.

"A simple 'thank you' would suffice, you know."

"Thank you," Jennifer said grudgingly. "But what were you doing all that time?"

"What do you think we were doing?" Izzy said. "We were walking back up from the gorge, the three of us. I tried calling to let you know but the phone signal kept dropping out."

"It's not a half-hour walk, though."

"Have you seen the state of him? He's absolutely plastered. And every time we stopped for him to be sick, he wanted to have a chat."

Jennifer looked up sharply. "A chat? With you?"

"Yes. With me."

"About what?"

"All kinds of stuff. Drunken stream of consciousness, mostly."

"Lots of garbage, most likely."

"Some."

"Probably best ignored."

Izzy gave her a strange look—something like pity, or concern, or disappointment—just for a second. And then it was gone.

"Probably," she said.

Sean put his hand on Izzy's arm. "The most important thing is, Izzy found them and we've got them back now, right? That's the main thing. How about we get these boys inside now?"

Seeing Sean touch her so casually, so easily, I felt a sharp pang of jealousy.

How quick you are to defend her, to be on her side, to touch her skin. Even in front of me. Even when I'm standing right here next to you both. How can you be so brazen about it, so obvious? How did you think I wouldn't find out, sooner or later?

Alistair reappeared, with two pint glasses full of water.

"Here we go," he said breezily, handing the glasses to Jennifer. "Now, who's going to help me carry the patient indoors?"

Russ held a hand up, lighting another cigarette.

"Not me, pal, I've only just got past shitty diapers. I don't do puke-stained teenagers, not yet."

Alistair turned to my husband, as if nothing untoward had happened between them this evening.

"Sean? Could you lend a hand?"

Sean glared at him, the anger still etched on his face.

"Aye," he grunted. "Come on, then."

With each of the men taking an arm, they propped Jake gently on his feet and began walking him back to the villa.

56

DANIEL

Daniel couldn't get off to sleep. He'd tried all the things his dad suggested—counting backward from a thousand, making his Christmas list, imagining the highway journey to Grandad's house in Reading—but none of them worked. There had been too much noise, for one thing. Voices that sounded like they were laughing or having one of those really loud and long and boring conversations that grown-ups seemed to do a lot when they drank wine. Then there had been the shouting.

He swung his legs out of bed, took the package from his bedside drawer, and padded across to the door, the tiled floor cool against the soles of his bare feet.

The corridor was dark, just the little night-light glowing near the stairs. He walked across and two doors along, hoping that her door would be open a little bit. But it was shut. He stopped and listened, pressing his ear to the smooth wood. Nothing.

Please don't be locked.

When he was small he would sometimes do this when he had a bad dream, when Mum and Dad weren't in bed yet. He would creep across the landing and climb into his sister's bed, and she would make up silly stories that made him forget the bad dream so he would be able to go back to sleep again. He always woke up in his own bed again the next morning, which was kind of a bit like magic. She hadn't done it for a long time, though, not since she started getting tall. That was when she'd started locking her bedroom door. He wasn't even allowed *in* her bedroom at home anymore—it made her go properly mad. But they weren't at home, so maybe she wouldn't mind.

He pushed down on her door handle and it opened with a soft *click*.

Daniel stood in the doorway, one hand behind his back. It was quieter on this side of the villa, away from the swimming pool. The room was dark, the only light from the soft glow of a phone screen.

"Lucy?" he whispered.

There was no reply. As his eyes began to adjust to the light, he made out the line of her back, turned to him as she lay in the big double bed. She was glued to her phone. As usual.

"Lucy?" he said again.

She shifted slightly, so he could see the left side of her face illuminated by the phone's pale glow.

"What?" she said sharply.

"Are you asleep?"

"Obviously not."

"I couldn't sleep with the grown-ups all shouting downstairs."

"What do you want, Daniel?"

He started toward her bed. "It's a surprise."

"Did I say you could come into my room?"

He stopped. "I've got something for you."

She sighed. "What?"

He came over to stand by her bed.

"I'm sorry about doing the film of you the other day, with Dad's camera. I didn't mean for you to be so upset." He brought his hand out from behind his back with a flourish, holding out a bag of strawberry bonbons. "I got you these. To apologize."

"Oh."

He stood there, holding out the bag for what seemed like a long time before she reached up a hand and took it from him. He smiled and put his hands in the pockets of his pajama trousers, feeling glad that he had made the effort, even if it had cost him half of his vacation pocket money.

A funny thing happened then.

Very softly, very quietly, his big sister started to cry.

Daniel frowned in the dark. That wasn't what he had meant to happen; she was supposed to be happy.

"Don't you like them?" he said. "I thought you liked those ones. They've always been your favorites."

She studied the bag as if she'd never seen one before.

"I do," she said quietly, a tear rolling down her cheek. "They are."

Daniel sat on the edge of the bed, regarding his sister with worried eyes. In a small voice, he said finally, "Why are you crying, Luce? What happened?"

She wiped her eyes angrily on the bedsheet. "It doesn't matter."

"I don't like it when you cry."

"Me neither." She sniffed. "Thank you for the sweets, though."

"Your hair is wet."

"From the pool."

"Are you going to open your sweets, then?"

She smiled. Just a tiny bit. "Do you want one, little bro?"

He smiled back. He liked it when she called him that.

"I've cleaned my teeth already."

She shook her head. "Seriously?"

"*You* should have some, though, so you're not sad anymore."

She took one from the packet and put it in her mouth. "When you're a bit older, you'll wish for the days when all you had to worry about was eating sweets after you've cleaned your teeth."

"Hmm," Daniel said, willing to take her word for it. "So what do *you* worry about?"

"Bad stuff happening. Bad things that can't be put right again." She shook her head. "You wouldn't understand."

He popped one of the sweets into his mouth.

"Nothing else bad is going to happen. Mum said."

"What if it already did?"

"What do you mean?"

"A bad thing already did happen."

"When?"

"Does it matter?"

"You can tell me, you know. I won't tell Mum."

She smiled. "Yes you will, you're such a goody-goody."

"Not."

"Are."

She handed him another sweet.

"Something happened and I sort of feel like it was my fault. Like I wanted it to happen."

They chewed in silence for a moment.

"*Did* you want it to happen?" Daniel said.

"No. Not at all."

Daniel pulled at a loose thread on his pajama top. "I thought it would be really nice being at the vacation house but it's like everything's going wrong, isn't it? I wish we could go home tomorrow. Do you want to go home?"

She looked down. "No. I'd rather be here."

"Do you think Mummy and Daddy are going to get a divorce?"

Lucy stopped chewing. "What?"

"A divorce. Like my friend, Isaac."

"No. What makes you say that?"

"They're being really weird with each other. They're not going to get divorced, are they? Isaac in my class, his parents are divorced, and he says it's all OK, but I can tell he's sad about it."

Lucy was silent for a moment, her face lit from below by the glow of the phone's screen.

"You shouldn't worry about stuff like that, little bro. I'm sure they'll figure it out."

"Really?"

"Really."

Daniel stood up and took a few steps toward the door but then stopped, turning back to his sister.

"Please don't tell Mum and Dad what I said about them having a divorce."

"OK. As long as you don't tell them I was upset."

"Deal."

She put the bag of sweets on her bedside table and lay back down on the pillow. "And thanks for the present."

"I'm glad you liked them." He smiled in the dark. "Night, then."

"Night, Daniel."

He pulled the door closed and crept back across the corridor to his own bed, pulling the covers up to his neck and tucking his body into the sheet the way he always did, so no spiders or bugs could crawl underneath in the night. The noise from the grown-ups outside by the pool seemed to have died down, and all he could hear through his open window was the chirping of crickets, a wall of sound in the night outside with no edges, no beginning, no end.

One Month Earlier

Shame boils away, leaving only a crust of anger behind.

She has more anger than she knows what to do with, feels it crowding out everything else.

She wants many things that she can't have.

She wants to blot it all out. To blot him out, and everything he meant to her. Everything he's done to her.

She wants to forget, to scrub the last nine months of her life and start again.

She wants things to go back to how they were, before it all went sour.

She wants to be able to walk into school without feeling the eyes on her back, seeing the pointing fingers, hearing the snickers.

She wants him to feel—just for a day, an hour, even a minute—as wretched as she feels now. As used and humiliated and panic-stricken and furious as she feels, every single minute that she's awake.

But she knows she can't have these things.

Because that's not how the world works.

THURSDAY

57

I woke with a ball of dread lodged deep in my stomach, in anticipation of what I had to do. I had put it off for a while now and the dramas of last night had shifted my attention elsewhere, but there was no avoiding it. No getting around it.

I left Sean still asleep in our bed, showering and dressing quickly as I mentally ticked off what I had found out in the last few days. Izzy had admitted she was seeing someone who was already married, but had refused to tell me his name. She'd admitted he came from Limerick, just like Sean. She had already tried to throw me off the scent by insisting that Sean would never betray my trust. Most damning of all, Izzy was the one who had appeared when I sent the message to CoralGirl from Sean's phone. I had set the trap and she had walked right into it. She had come when summoned.

But what about the other evidence? His lingering embrace on the beach with Rowan, his wedding ring in her drawer, Russ's insistence that she was having an affair? Sean had denied point-blank that anything was going on with her—he had looked me straight in the eye and sworn it, and he'd never been a good liar. It was one of the things I loved about him.

Had loved about him, I thought, with an ache deep in my chest. Then there was Jennifer and Sean being caught together unawares in Daniel's video, her weird reaction when their hands brushed at lunch, their early morning "walk" to the village together, supposedly delayed by a visit to the weekly market—the market that took place on a different day.

But it was all circumstantial. And all of it paled by comparison to seeing Izzy walk into that clearing by the gorge: a stone-cold piece of evidence that could not be disputed or misinterpreted. It was time to get this over with, right away, this morning, before I could spend too long thinking about it. Before I could change my mind or lose my nerve again.

The truth was, I had wronged them all. Each of them in different ways.

I had fallen in love with Jennifer's boyfriend at university.

I had helped bring Izzy's fiancé to the place where he met his death.

I had passed on the malicious accusation that destroyed Rowan's first marriage.

What kind of friend was I? Perhaps I deserved everything that was coming my way.

Lucy was on my mind, too. I wanted to talk to

her again about what had happened in the pool last night, but she was still fast asleep, her room dark thanks to the blackout curtains. There was no sound at Daniel's door, either. In fact, the whole villa was unnaturally quiet and empty as I made my way down to the kitchen to make coffee; there were no voices, no clatter of crockery from the dining area, no flip-flops on the polished tile floor. Daniel wasn't in the living room, where I'd usually found him at this time of the morning—perhaps he'd finally started sleeping in at last. Two days before we were due to go home, but better late than never.

There was a note on the kitchen countertop next to the kettle.

Gone for lunch in Béziers, back this afternoon. J+I x

Béziers was the nearest big town, half an hour south by car, on the way to the beach. It seemed that Jennifer and family had opted for a change of scenery today and Izzy had gone along for the ride. I checked my watch—it was only just nine o'clock—feeling simultaneously disappointed and relieved that the showdown with Izzy would have to wait until she got back. It would give me time to prepare what I was go-ing to say.

It wasn't a huge surprise that Jennifer, Alistair, and their boys had left the house early. After last night's row between Alistair and Sean, and the state the boys were in when they'd returned to the villa, it made sense that they'd want to skip the Awkward Morning After. That was Jennifer's usual tactic: avoid, ignore, look the other way, hold the problem at arm's length until it faded and was forgotten. Izzy, by contrast, had a tendency for straight-talking honesty that some people mistook for rudeness. I was somewhere in the middle, I supposed.

I sliced and buttered a croissant and took it out onto the balcony with my coffee. The sun was already fierce, the air heavy with humidity and the damp, claustrophobic heat of impending thunder. And yet the sky was still a perfect azure blue, no clouds in sight and not a breath of wind. The only sound was a pair of swallows whirling high above me, calling to each other as they turned and chased in an endless dance.

If truth be told, it was probably a good idea for everyone to have a few hours apart and do their own thing. Moments from last night kept coming back to me: Daniel pleading to go home; my husband's half apology in the kitchen; the look of horror on Lucy's face when she fled the game of water polo; Sean squaring up to Alistair, veins standing out in his neck, telling him what would happen if he didn't keep his hands to himself. The word on Ethan's lips as he lay, drunk, in the grass. *Oblivion.*

This vacation had gone wrong in so many ways, I had lost count.

Odette came out onto the balcony in her pink sparkly swimsuit, munching on a brioche. Rowan followed, espresso in one hand and car keys in the other.

"We're going to try the beach again for a couple of hours. Fancy it?"

"My lot are still asleep."

"How's Lucy doing?" She gave me a concerned look. "After what happened last night, I mean?"

"She was pretty upset."

"I thought Sean was going to punch Alistair's lights out."

"Watch this space," I said, "it might still happen."

"Give her a hug from me."

Russ emerged from the kitchen carrying a canvas beach bag, and they roared off in the Land Rover, leaving just the four of us at the villa.

Just me, my cheating husband, and my traumatized children.

Now would be the time to check Izzy's room, I realized. See what she had hidden in there that could confirm my suspicions beyond any possible doubt. Even though I wasn't totally sure what that might be. Something that belonged to him, perhaps, a note, a photo, a cell phone—evidence, of whatever kind. I hurried upstairs and was about to let myself into her room when Daniel's door opened across the corridor and he emerged, fully dressed, book in hand.

"Morning, Mummy," he said. "What are you doing?"

"Oh . . . just going to check whether Izzy had that book I wanted to read. Never mind."

Lucy and Sean seemed determined to sleep in, so Daniel and I walked into the village, his little hand tight in mine as we weaved our way through ancient streets too narrow for cars, house walls of weather-beaten stone pressing in high on both sides. We found a playground behind the church, with benches in the shade of tall plane trees, and I sat and watched as he played on the swings and slides, the climbing frame and merry-go-round, wondering how I would explain to him what his father had done, and what it meant for our family. How could my boy possibly understand a betrayal so large, so far reaching? Would he forgive his dad? Would he end up blaming me?

Eventually he tired of the playground so we walked into the village square for croque monsieurs and Oranginas in the shadow of the little town hall, watching a couple old men playing endless games of *pétanque* on a long rectangle of sand beside the bar.

Daniel asked to go to the shop after lunch, so we took a detour past the village's crumbling medieval ramparts and into the air-conditioned cool of the small *supermarché,* crammed between an estate agent and a tiny antiques shop, both closed for lunch. The supermarket catered mostly to visiting tourists, its shelves lined with wine and beer, fresh fruit and vegetables, suntan lotion, beach toys and barbecue charcoal. I picked up a few bits and found Daniel in the sweets aisle, weighing two big bags of sweets in each hand.

"Surely you can't still be hungry after that big lunch," I said.

"They're not for me. They're for Lucy."

"Well, aren't you a lovely brother?" I said, giving his fine dark hair a rub. "She'll be very pleased."

I remembered that we needed more bug spray and went around the other side of the aisle to look in the display. The local stuff was far more potent than anything you could get in the UK, which seemed to have almost no effect on the mosquitos here—I had already counted more than a dozen bites on my legs alone.

Through a gap in the shelves, Daniel said, "I'm trying to cheer her up."

"That's nice of you."

"She's been really sad about things."

I found a can of serious-looking mosquito repellent and tucked it under my arm.

"Uh-huh."

"I made that film of her and she was really cross. She's waiting for her exams and stuff, and her friends at school are being mean *and* thingamabob Bayley." He hesitated. "I saw her last night at bedtime and she was really upset."

"What thingamabob?"

"You know, that boy Alex Bayley, who was in the hospital—there's a tribute page on Facebook."

"Aren't you too young to be going on Facebook?"

"They don't check, not really. You just tick the box that says you're old enough."

Over the top of the shelf, he held up the two packets of sweets. "Shall I get her Starmix or Tangfastics?"

I offered to pay for the sweets but he insisted on using the last of his vacation pocket money, carrying them proudly out of the shop in a striped plastic bag.

We bought soft ice creams from the *tabac* and wound our way slowly back up the hill, Daniel excitedly telling me that Ethan had made friends with him again.

It was early afternoon by the time we got back, the villa's interior an oasis of cool after the noon heat. Lucy was still nowhere to be seen.

I gave her door a cautious knock.

"Lucy?"

Her room was in virtual darkness, shielded by the blackout curtains and chilled to the midteens by the air conditioning.

"Lucy?" I said softly. "Are you OK?"

No response.

Slowly my eyes made out her form on the bed, her back to me, curled into a fetal position.

"It's past one o'clock, love. Are you going to get up soon?"

Still there was no response. I was about to give her a gentle shake when Daniel's voice reached me from the bottom of the stairs.

"Mum!" he shouted. "I'm going in the pool, are you coming?"

I backed out of Lucy's room, pulling the door gently shut behind me.

58

I was aware of someone above me as I dozed in the shade of one of the big poolside umbrellas, a soft cushion behind my head, my phone in my lap. Voices, and footsteps, and activity up on the balcony, and then the presence next to me. A smell. Male.

I opened my eyes to find Ethan looking down at me.

"Tea's ready," he said. "Sleepyhead."

I looked for my watch, but my wrist was bare.

"What time is it?"

"Almost five."

Yawning and swinging my legs off the lounger, my phone clattered to the ground. I checked the screen for scratches, unlocked it, and saw it was still open on Facebook, the tribute page Daniel had mentioned earlier. I closed the app and followed Ethan slowly up the steps to the balcony. Out of the shade it was still fiercely hot and almost unbearably humid—the air as thick as soup—but the wind was picking up at last. For the first time in days I saw clouds on the horizon, a thick, gray wall to the south, coming in off the sea. The forecast had been predicting a thunderstorm for the last few days. Maybe it was finally here.

I dropped my eyes to the garden and found myself looking at my husband, sitting on an ornate white stone bench at the far corner of the lawn, partially hidden in the shade of an olive tree. Sitting next to him, so close their heads were almost touching, was Izzy.

They were both leaning forward with their heads down, talking fast, back and forth. I was too far away to hear what was being said but it was an animated conversation, Sean shaking his head repeatedly and Izzy nodding, emphatic, hands clasped together in front of her.

Look at them, thick as thieves. What are you two talking about? How you're going to break the news? How you're going to tell me?

There was a painful lump in my throat.

Or is it just a matter of when?

It looked as if Sean were disagreeing with her. Perhaps he wanted to wait until we were back home, but she didn't want to wait anymore? As I stared in fascinated horror, he looked up and spotted me. For a second our eyes locked and he stiffened, abruptly looking away as if he'd been seen somewhere he didn't want to be. He jumped up from the bench and walked away from Izzy toward the stone staircase and the balcony where dinner had been laid out.

I went and took my place at the table next to Daniel.

Lucy appeared in a long-sleeved T-shirt, whey faced, her hair unbrushed, and sat down without a word on the other side of me. She helped herself to a tall glass of lemonade from the jug in the middle of the table and then sat, sipping it, seemingly uninterested in any of the food. The big table was laid out with a huge array of cold meats, cheeses, fruit, pastries, freshly sliced baguettes, and three pizzas as big as hubcaps, cheese still bubbling from the oven. Everyone—except Lucy—began to fill their plates in near silence, punctuated only by Odette's excited babble of postbeach chatter with Rowan.

Jennifer and Izzy were the last to arrive, both of them blank faced and silent. Jennifer took her place to the end of the table, next to Alistair and her boys, while Izzy edged past the chairbacks to the last empty spot at the other end. As she passed me she paused, touching me lightly on the shoulder.

"Kate?" she said gently, almost apologetically. "We need to talk."

I felt a jolt, as if I'd just grabbed a live wire.

"OK." My voice almost cracked. "What about?"

She held my eyes for a moment, then dropped her gaze.

"Tell you in a bit. After we've eaten." She went to the empty chair at the head of the table and sat down.

At the other end of the table, Jennifer stared at her with a look that I couldn't quite define. Anger?

Disappointment? Her blue eyes darted quickly in my direction before settling back on Izzy.

Alistair's voice broke the silence.

"We'd best eat up before *that* arrives," he said, gesturing toward the mass of dark clouds to the south. "There's a storm coming."

59

My appetite had disappeared. I put a couple pieces of bread on my plate anyway, just to give my hands something to do, reaching for a sharp knife and cutting thin slices of Roquefort cheese that I had no intention of eating.

We need to talk.

So this was it, the moment of truth, the confession. The moment when she finally came out with it, finally put me out of my misery. I felt as if I had been waiting for it for months, for years, but in reality it had been less than a week since discovering the messages on Sean's phone. I had sworn to find the evidence, to smoke her out. And this was what it came down to.

I felt sick, scared, angry. Numb.

Conversation around the table was muted. A muttered exchange between Jake and Ethan, Daniel asking me about the pizza toppings. Odette's voice piercingly loud as she pointed out—yet again—all the things on the table that she didn't like and wouldn't eat, which seemed to include virtually everything apart from what was on her mother's plate. Rowan coaxed her into eating a small slice of tomato. Odette chewed it for a few seconds and promptly spat it out onto the tablecloth.

Sean's eyes were fixed on Alistair across the table with a frown of barely concealed suspicion as if he were waiting for the slightest reason, the slightest provocation, to restart last night's hostilities. But if he was the least bit bothered, Alistair wasn't letting it show as he uncorked a bottle of Faugères and filled nearby glasses.

We need to talk.

Each word was as heavy as lead.

I took a sip of wine, the taste bitter in my mouth.

Plates were filled and emptied in short order, food eaten quickly as if we all wanted this stilted meal together to be over. After ten minutes or so, as if sensing a need to fill the silence, Jennifer tapped a fork against her wineglass with a *ting-ting-ting* and cleared her throat.

"Well, everyone, since we're all here we've got a bit of an announcement, actually."

All eyes turned to her.

"What with one thing and another"—here she looked pointedly at Sean—"we've decided to head back to England a little bit earlier than planned."

There was a stunned silence around the table.

"You're leaving?" All my thoughts of Izzy were momentarily forgotten. "When?"

"That's such a shame," Rowan said. "Aren't you having a nice time, all of you?"

Jennifer ignored her question.

"There's an evening flight tonight. We just need to get packed and sorted out here and then we'll be off."

I put down my fork and pushed my plate away.

"There's no need to go early is there, Jen?" I said. "We've only got a couple of nights left."

Jake sat up straighter in his chair, tuning in to the adult conversation for the first time.

"Hang on, what?"

"We've changed our flights, Jakey. There's one at ten tonight from Béziers."

"Why?"

"Your dad and I thought it was for the best, Jake."

"Best for who?"

Jennifer's blue eyes fell on Sean again.

"Everyone."

"I don't want to go home." Jake's face was flushing red. I'd never seen him blush before. "I want to stay here, all of us together."

"Let's talk after tea, shall we, Jakey?"

Jake stood up.

"This is bullshit."

"Language, Jake."

He pushed his chair back and stormed off into the villa, throwing up a hand.

"Whatever."

Ethan stood up, too, looking at Daniel.

"You coming?"

"I suppose," my son said, looking over at me. "Can I?"

"We're in the middle of tea, love."

"I'm finished."

"You've got a whole piece of pizza to eat."

His cheeks started to redden, too: I was embarrassing him in front of a bigger boy. His friend.

"Please?" he said. "It's our last time to play together on vacation."

"What about the pizza?"

He bit off half the pizza slice and spoke with his mouth full. "Finished now."

I sighed. "Go on then."

He scampered off into the villa after Ethan, following the bigger boy toward the staircase down to the games room.

Odette pushed her chair back and stood up.

"I want to go, too, Mummy."

"You can wait until Mummy and Daddy have finished."

"Not fair!" She stamped her little foot. "All the other children have got down!"

"No, they haven't—look, Lucy is still here."

"She's not a *children*."

Odette ran off to catch up, shouting, "Sardines!" at the top of her lungs.

Jennifer was already on her feet.

"I should talk to the boys. Explain."

"Jen," Alistair said, "just let them go. Let them do what they want to do."

She ignored him, hurrying after her sons.

The rest of us—six adults plus Lucy—sat in silence

for a moment, none of us quite sure what to say next. It was as if a bomb had gone off and we were slowly emerging from the rubble, trying to assess the damage. "Another lovely meal all together," grunted Russ. Rowan jabbed him in the ribs with her elbow.

"Such a shame you're leaving early," she said to Alistair again.

Alistair refilled his wineglass. "Well, I think things here have pretty much run their course, don't you? No point in stringing it out any longer."

"The kids seem to be getting on well, really getting to know each other."

"Perhaps." He threw a glance at Sean. "But I've always maintained that one needs to know when to cut one's losses."

The silence resumed and we continued eating, listening to the voices of the children floating up from the games room below. After a few minutes, Lucy pushed her chair back and walked off toward the garden without saying a word.

Later, as the men wandered off in search of their children and we finished taking all the tea things back through to the kitchen, Izzy caught my eye.

It was time.

60

DANIEL

Daniel trailed after the two bigger boys, the thick green grass tickling his toes in their sandals. He was tired and bored and didn't really know what they were doing down here in the garden. They'd done table tennis and air hockey and pool, and now he was just following them because he didn't know what else to do.

All in all, today had been a rubbish day. The ice cream at lunch had been nice, but that was about it. Then Jake and Ethan's mum had told everyone at dinner that they were going home early, like *tonight,* and that seemed really unfair because it meant that the only children left at the vacation house were him and his sister and Odette, who had told him six times now that she didn't like boys.

Something bad had happened last night but neither of the bigger boys would tell him what it was. From what Daniel had overheard from the grown-ups, Jake had been sick and needed to be carried back to the villa by the dads. And today Jake was cross, especially after his mum had announced that they were going back to England. Everything was *f-this* and *f-that*. He'd always seemed a bit crazy, but today he was acting properly weird, like he didn't care about anything anymore. It made him even more unpredictable than usual. But it was also—in a weird way that Daniel couldn't really explain—more exciting to be part of his gang, to be an insider for once, rather than on the outside.

Jake crouched down suddenly behind a stone bench and hissed at his brother to follow suit. There was a man by the swimming pool, with his back to them. Jake and Ethan's dad.

"Jake?" Alistair called out into the garden. "Ethan? Are you going to come back into the villa now, gents? We need to pack."

"Get down!" Jake hissed under his breath.

The three of them huddled behind the bench so they couldn't be seen.

Alistair stood on the far side of the pool, looking all around, one hand stroking his beard. "Jake?" he called again. "Ethan? Time to go, come on."

With one final look around, he shook his head and began walking back up the staircase into the villa, away from them.

After a minute, Jake rose up to a kneeling position and the other two did the same.

"You still got your lighters?" he said.

"Yeah," Ethan replied, fishing in his pocket and holding out the green plastic Bic lighter.

Daniel nodded, too, blushing, hoping they wouldn't notice. "Yeah."

The truth was, he'd managed to lose the little yellow lighter they'd given him for being a member of their gang. It had been in his bedroom. But he'd gone to look for it yesterday and it had disappeared. He searched under the bed, in his bedside drawer, in his empty suitcase, but it was nowhere to be found. He didn't want to ask Jake and Ethan because they'd think he was stupid for losing it. It must have fallen out of his pocket when they were playing outside.

He wasn't about to tell Jake and Ethan that, though.

Ethan held out his lighter, sparking the flint to make a tall flame.

"Still got loads of fuel left. Might as well have some fun before we have to go home."

Across the garden, Odette wandered alone in her little pink sundress, long red hair held back with a sparkly tiara. Heading away from the villa with no adults in sight. Scanning left and right, she disappeared through the big gate that led down into the vineyard and the woods beyond.

Looking for us, Daniel thought with a twinge of guilt. She looked small and a bit lost, heading down the hill on her own.

Jake turned to him and grinned, putting the lighter back in his pocket.

"I've got an idea," he whispered. "Follow me."

61

Izzy followed me into the dining room and we sat down at the end of the big table. There was a floor-to-ceiling window and I looked out over the landscape as if seeing it for the first time: such a breathtakingly beautiful place for something so ugly to happen. To the south, the clouds were much closer now, ominously close, a wall of gray and black blotting the light from the sky. The villa was quiet. Rowan was making cocktails in the kitchen—apparently to cheer us all up—while everyone else was spread out in the gardens and vineyard below.

"Sorry for the cloak-and-dagger stuff at dinner," Izzy said. "Didn't want to do this in front of everyone."

"Of course," I said tonelessly.

She blew out a breath, blowing her fringe off her forehead.

"This is tough, Kate, but I've given it a lot of thought and I know it's the right thing to do under the circumstances. Since we've been friends for a long time."

"Right."

Not anymore.

Normally I'm good at keeping my emotions in check, but my anger was so hot I could barely bring myself to look at her. I'd been pushing it down, forcing it back down for so long now that I wasn't sure what was going to happen when I finally set it free. And the deceitful cow actually looked as if she felt *sorry* for me, giving me that sad little smile as if to say *this is going to be tough on both of us.* As if on cue, a tight little bubble of fury rose up inside me and it was all I could do to stop myself from reaching across the table and slapping her, really winding up and smacking her across the face as hard as possible.

How could you do this, Izzy?

But I didn't hit her. Instead I clasped my hands together in my lap, fingers laced tight. I knew what was coming, I knew what she was going to tell me. Did that make it any easier? Was it a consolation? It didn't feel like it. It felt as if my life had been in a free fall for the past week and I was finally about to hit the ground. Terrified of the impact, but at the same time ready for it to be over.

"Kate, I don't know how to say this. I've agonized over whether to tell you about—"

I cut her off. She didn't deserve this moment, didn't deserve the satisfaction of being the one to break it to me.

"I know what you're going to say, Izzy."

A ripple of surprise crossed her face.

"Really?"

"Took me a while to work it out, but I got there eventually."

"Oh. I see." There was confusion in her tone. "I was under the impression you didn't know."

"Did Sean tell you that?"

She nodded, slowly.

"Yes."

"He wanted to keep it a secret, did he? I saw you arguing before dinner."

"He, erm . . . he thought it was better to keep it under wraps."

"Of course he did."

She hesitated, as if choosing her words carefully. "How long have you known?"

"I've known the basics since last week. And the rest for a couple of days. Do you remember when Sean sent you a message on Tuesday, asking to meet? It wasn't him that sent that, it was me."

"Tuesday?"

"I unlocked his phone and found your conversation on Messenger. Your secret little trail of messages about what's been going on." I thought about our conversation at the Gorges d'Héric on Monday morning, feeling the anger at her betrayal surge again. "In fact, why didn't you just tell me on Monday? Didn't I at least deserve a bit of honesty? Why wait until today?"

She frowned. "Well, for one thing, because I didn't realize on Monday that —"

The door flew open and Rowan burst into the room, her eyes wide with alarm.

"You two! Oh my God, you have to come! Now!"

Then she was gone, clattering away on her heels toward the back of the villa.

Izzy and I jumped up and followed her out onto the balcony. For the first time since we arrived, the afternoon sun had disappeared behind huge dark clouds that were blanketing the sky. The wind had picked up and it whipped the hair around our faces, the air almost fizzing with the pressure of an impending thunderstorm.

"Guys!" Rowan said breathlessly. "Do you see that?"

We turned to look where she was pointing. Down into the vineyard, where the rows of vines met the tree line on the edge of the woods.

Smoke.

62

Odette

Odette crouched in a nest of leaves, her arms tucked tightly around her knees.

She had to be quiet. Very quiet, because the boys were letting her play their game for the first time. Well, she had *told* the boys she was going to play and she thought they were going to laugh and tell her to go away, but they didn't. They said OK, told her she could play, and didn't even mind when she told them she was going to be the hider instead of the seeker. Except it wasn't hide-and-seek—hide-and-seek was for *babies*—it was a better game called sardines. One person hid and the others had to count to fifty without looking. Then they all had to come and find her, on their own, and the first one to find her hid in her hiding place, too. They hid together, squeezed in tight like baby mice. And then the next and the next, until only one person was still looking and then that person was the loser. But if she could stay hidden until they all gave up, *she* would be the winner.

The boys had told her to go into the woods to hide and then they would try to find her.

And she had *such* a good hiding place that she didn't think they would find her even if they looked for an hour. Even if they looked until it got to bedtime. She was in a little dip, a hollowed-out bit of the ground in the woods where there was a big tree trunk that had fallen over. Because she was small—and quite bendy—she had been able to squeeze up inside a bit of the trunk where it was hollow in the middle and make a little nest for herself among the crunchy leaves and pine needles, like a hamster or something. It was hard to see out because there was a bush in the way, but she could just about make out the little path and the clearing where her mum said she wasn't allowed to go.

She was good at hiding. She could hide all day. She would show them that she was big enough to play their games, that she could join in just like them and be a big girl. That she could even win their games if she wanted to.

The tree trunk had a funny smell, a musty, fusty smell like the wood Daddy stacked in piles by the fire at home. It was dark and there were a few little bugs, too, creepy-crawlies busy going up and down the inside of the bark, but she didn't mind them, not really, because if they got close she would just do what her daddy did when there was a spider or a fly or any sort of little beastie. She would take her shoe off and just whack it with the heel. *Splat.* No more bug. Mummy tried to save them with a glass and a postcard but Daddy never did. He just whacked them.

Odette sat, her chin resting on her knees, and wondered what a sardine was. Daniel said a sardine was a fish but that couldn't be right: fish lived in the sea. Maybe it was like a kind of mouse? Or a hamster? Sardine sounded like a funny name. She wished that Lucy was playing the game with them; Lucy was so pretty, the prettiest girl she'd ever seen. She looked like a princess, or maybe even *more* beautiful than a princess. Sometimes she'd wished on the vacation that Lucy was her big sister so they could play together every day and do each other's hair and all those things that sisters did. But Lucy wasn't there when they started the game, so she couldn't play.

She froze. There was a noise, footsteps on the path. Voices talking, laughing, deep voices. Grown-ups? No. The boys.

She tried to keep herself very still, as still as a statue like when you played that game at a birthday party, holding her breath until the boys passed by. They were talking in low voices. When she peeped through the gap in the tree trunk she could see their feet on the path, see them walking in a line and whacking sticks on each tree as they passed. Her cheeks burned with indignation. They weren't supposed to *be* together, they were supposed to be searching on their *own*. Doing it in a team was cheating, it really wasn't fair. Boys always cheated. That was why she didn't like playing with them.

She felt like crawling out of her hiding place and telling them off, telling them the *proper* rules and how sardines was supposed to be played. Making them do it properly. But then she'd have to give away the secret place she'd found inside the fallen tree trunk.

Their footsteps moved away, farther into the trees. When she was sure they were gone, she shifted position a little bit inside the tree trunk to get more comfortable, resting her back against the smooth curve of the bark. It was actually quite nice in here; she could make a proper little nest with her dolls and have tea parties with—

The boys were back, coming from the other side this time. They were making a lot of noise again, telling one another to shush and then snickering; and close, so close, they must be standing right next to the tree trunk without even realizing she was in there! Odette had to put her hand over her mouth to stifle a giggle. Boys were so *stupid*.

Jake's voice was loud in the quiet of the woods.

"She's not here, lads." More snorting laughter from the other two boys. "It's a proper mystery, I don't know *where* she could have got to. Maybe she's gone down into the gorge."

The sound of them tramping away through the leaves again.

Odette kept watch through her little peephole in case the boys came back. They had been right next to her, without even realizing she was there! She was going to win. It would be so funny when she told them how close they'd been.

It was warm in her secret hiding place. Cozy. And it was so hard to sleep in her vacation bed . . . it was different from her normal bed at home, too hard; but then sometimes it was too soft, and she couldn't usually get comfy without all of her toys. Her nest inside the fallen tree *was* quite comfy, though, even if some of the leaves were a bit scratchy. She actually felt more comfy in here than in her vacation bed.

Her eyes felt heavy.

She let them close.

She woke without even realizing she'd been asleep. Her shoulder ached where she'd leaned on it against the bark, and the light outside was a bit different. But no one had found her. None of the boys had guessed where her hiding place was. She was going to win.

Outside in the woods it was getting noisier.

Voices, shouting the names of all the children.

Shouting *her* name.

"Odette! Where are you?"

Odette knew what they were doing: they were trying to trick her into coming out, show where her hiding place was. They were trying to make her look silly.

She smiled to herself. She was cleverer than them. She would show them. Something smelled bad, though, like when Mum burned her toast and made the alarm go off at home. But Odette wasn't going to fall for that one—she knew what boys were like.

She wasn't going to give up that easily, not when it was her turn to hide.

She wasn't going to come out for those silly boys.

She wasn't going to come out for anyone.

63

For a second, the three of us just stood and stared.

A pall of billowing smoke rolled across the vine-yard, blanketing the hillside in a thick, gray cloud. Orange flames licked up the vines near the woods, creeping from one to the next as we watched. Flames were visible in the woods, too, flaring and dancing in the muggy late afternoon air. Everything down there—everything for miles around—was bone dry after weeks of unbroken summer sunshine. Every-thing was ready to burn.

Rowan moved first.

"Oh my God!" There was panic in her voice. "The kids!"

She ran headlong down the stone steps, taking them two at a time, with Izzy and I following close behind. Running through the wrought-iron gate out into the vineyard we almost bowled into Alistair coming back up the other way. He was red faced and out of breath, cradling his left arm in his right as if protecting an injury.

"Got to get my phone," he said, scrambling sideways. "Call the *pompiers*."

"Are you OK?" Izzy shouted back at him.

He waved a dismissive hand and stumbled on toward the villa.

We rushed through the gate and into the vineyard, Izzy in front, then me, with Rowan at my shoulder. Her panicked voice was right behind me as we pounded down the hill toward the flames.

"Odette!" she shouted. "Odette! I'm coming!"

I couldn't see anyone. Any of the children, or the men, for that matter. All I could see was smoke, thick gray smoke rising up from the bottom of the vineyard and in the woods, too. Something stuck in my head about the sight but there was no time to process it, no space in my head for anything except Daniel and Lucy.

We ran on, tendrils of drifting smoke reaching for us, trying to choke us. My breath rasped loud in my ears and at some point I lost my flip-flops, flying off my feet as we sprinted toward the woods. The stony ground cut into my feet but I barely noticed.

As we approached the tree line, Izzy shouted over her shoulder, "I'll find Jen!"

She veered off left into the woods.

I went right, cutting across the rows of vines toward the path that wound through the trees, shouting as I went.

"Daniel! Lucy!" I waved a hand in front of me, swatting at the sheets of smoke. "Where are you?"

No answer.

Panic started to rise in the back of my throat like bile. The smoke was a hazard and the flames would be dangerous if they spread much farther, but the real danger was what was hiding on the far side of the clearing. A cliff edge and a hundred-foot drop onto the rocks below, just waiting for one misstep, one confused stride in the wrong direction among the smoke and chaos.

"Daniel! Lucy! Can you hear me?"

The heat was strong on my face from the crackle and hiss of flames as they leaped from branch to branch. I pulled in a lungful of acrid smoke and instantly started coughing, trying to call out again before the words were cut short by a retching, choking gag that tore at my throat.

Smoke drifted between the trees, stinging my eyes. It was getting thicker.

There.

A child, shouting. High and terrified.

I felt a fear I had not felt for years, not since he had been born, tiny and silent and blue lipped, slick and motionless in the arms of a maternity nurse, the cord lifted away from his neck. Willing him to breathe, willing to trade my life for his, just to hear him cry. To hear him breathe. A visceral fear that clutched at my heart, squeezing and squeezing until all the blood was gone and I couldn't catch my breath because the terror was so close, so close I could feel its hot breath on the back of my neck, the fear that maybe this was the moment when my world would go dark. Silence. Doctors and nurses working fast, skilled hands desperately trying to tether my baby to life. But silence, still. Only silence. *Please let him cry. Please let him be OK. I will do anything to hear him cry. Anything.* And finally, wonderfully, he had: a fierce gargling cry that pierced me with a shaft of pure love as I lay exhausted in the bed, tears hot on my cheeks. And then he was in my arms, tiny and perfect, his face screwed up and purple and crying hard, the most beautiful sound, his voice strong and high and bursting with life.

He was crying now.

"Mum! Mum!"

I turned toward the sound of my son's voice, leaving the path and plunging blindly into the woods on my right. My eyes streamed with tears from the smoke.

"Daniel! I'm coming!"

"Mum!" he shouted again, his voice taut with panic.

There was movement to my left, people in the smoke near the clearing, but they were adults. They were not my concern, not right now.

Daniel was straight ahead. My son. My boy.

And then he was there, stumbling through the trees toward me, his face dirty and streaked with tears. I grabbed his little hand tightly and we ran, both of us coughing and hacking in the smoke, through the trees and back out into the vineyard.

"Come on!" I shouted, pulling him as he stumbled along by my side. "We have to get higher up!"

Halfway up the hill, well away from the smoke and flames, we stopped to catch our breath.

"Where's your sister?" I said, puffing hard. My throat was raw. "Where's Lucy?"

"I don't know, didn't see her."

"Are you hurt?" I knelt down next to him, checking him over, brushing his hair back off his forehead and checking his head and arms for any obvious injury. "Does anywhere hurt?"

"My throat's a bit sore."

"Anything else?"

"No." He looked at the ground. "We—we left Odette in the fallen tree trunk."

"What?"

"We were playing sardines but Jake said we should do a trick on her, make her hide and then not bother coming to get her." His words were tumbling out, falling over one another. "We knew where she was but pretended we didn't and she was in a tree trunk near the gorge. Is she all right? I haven't—"

Sean burst out of the smoke, bare chested, his T-shirt tied over his mouth and nose.

He was carrying Lucy in his arms, her head resting against his shoulder.

"Sean!" I shouted. "Over here!"

He ran up the hill to us, laying our daughter gently on the ground. One of her sandals had come off. She was conscious, but her mouth was tightly closed against the pain.

"Lucy," I said. "Are you OK?"

"Twisted my ankle."

Sean pulled the T-shirt down off his mouth.

"Did someone call the fire brigade?"

"Alistair."

"How many are still down there?"

"I don't know. But Daniel said Odette's hiding in a fallen tree trunk—have you seen her?"

As if in answer, a woman's voice reached us from within the smoke.

"Odette!" Rowan's scream was raw and desperate in full-fledged panic. "Odette! Where are you?"

Sean stood up.

"I'm going back," he said to me. "Look after our babies."

He pulled the T-shirt back over his nose and plunged downhill into the smoke.

64

I watched my husband disappear into the rolling gray cloud of smoke that enveloped the bottom of the estate. The smoke was getting thicker as the fire spread, long flames licking quickly from branch to branch, fanned by a warm wind coming out of the south.

Be careful, I should have shouted as he ran back into danger, as he put his own safety at risk to search for someone else's child. But I didn't shout that. I don't know why. I didn't shout anything. I just sat and watched him go, fearless, heedless of the consequences, back into the woods where everything was hidden from sight.

I wondered if it would be the last time I saw him.

Please be OK, Sean. Whatever you've done, whatever has happened between us, whoever you've chosen over me, I don't want it to end like this.

From somewhere over toward the village, the wailing two-tone siren of a fire engine reached us.

Hurry up.

The fire danced on, smoke darkening against the blue sky. The wind shifted for a moment, pushing clouds of smoke back toward us, burning throats and making us blink back tears. My head began to pound from breathing it in.

It could only have been a minute, maybe less, before there was movement again at the edge of the smoke, coalescing suddenly into real flesh and blood. A figure. An adult.

Russ stumbled out of the smoke with Odette clutched tight in his arms.

Rowan ran behind him, holding her T-shirt to her mouth and nose, following them up the hill until all three of them collapsed next to us in a heap of panting, crying, coughing relief. Rowan tried to gently loosen Odette's grip on her father to check her over, but Odette was attached to Russ like a limpet, as if her very life depended on it.

Sean was the last to appear, an arm out in front of him against the choking smoke. He staggered up the hill and collapsed, exhausted, next to me, pulling the T-shirt down from his mouth.

"Is everybody out?" he gasped, trying to catch his breath. "Did everyone get out?"

"Think so."

"Good," he said. "You all OK?"

"We are. Just need to get some water for the kids, and Lucy will need to have her ankle looked at."

I turned to look at him properly. His face and torso were smeared with dirt and shiny with sweat, his eyes wild and bloodshot, and both his knees were cut and bleeding. There were small vertical scratches on his chest and high up on his right cheek.

He coughed hard and spat on the ground.

"Sean?" I said more quietly.

Staring hard into the flames, eyes wide, he didn't seem to hear me.

"Sean?" I said again.

His head snapped around to look at me. "What?"

"Are you OK? You're bleeding."

He waved a hand dismissively and I noticed that he was shaking with adrenaline.

"It's nothing. Fell into a bloody bush, couldn't see where I was going. Can barely see your hand in front of your face down there now."

We stared at the fire for a moment, mesmerized by the flames.

"Christ," he said under his breath, "how the hell did it all start, anyhow?"

"Good question." My throat was raw and my head was pounding so hard I could barely think straight. But I remembered now what had struck me when I first saw the flames—I just didn't know what it meant. Not yet.

Jennifer brought a pack of mineral water bottles down from the villa and we sat, sluicing the smoke from our throats, as the fire brigade went to work.

The *sapeurs-pompiers,* in their blue protective suits

and red helmets, played their hoses over the remains of the fire, damping down the smoldering trees and three lines of vines that had been ablaze only minutes before.

Daniel watched with the kind of awed fascination that young boys reserve for firefighters.

"Is there going to be an ambulance, too?"

"These guys can do that as well, Daniel," I said.

"Sick."

The senior fireman, a tall, severe looking *caporal* who introduced himself as Bernard Lepine, brought out a first-aid kit and checked the children over. Rowan, who was the most fluent French speaker, acted as translator while he gave Lucy a heel strap bandage to support her ankle, then applied a dressing to a small burn on Alistair's arm. Sean waved away treatment for his cuts and scratches, insisting he would clean them up himself. Lepine packed up his kit and strode down the hill to inspect his crew's work. The fire was out now, all the woods and surrounding area thoroughly soaked to prevent any lingering sparks from restarting the flames. Crewmen tramped through the woods, checking their work, making sure the seat of the fire was well and truly extinguished. The storm had yet to break and the afternoon heat was still brutal, a furnace of humidity that seemed to press down into the top of your head and push against you from every side.

Lepine returned a few minutes later, talking and gesticulating at Rowan at some length. From the rapidity of his speech, and his grim expression, I guessed that she was being given a talking-to on French fire safety measures.

Eventually, Rowan turned to the rest of us with a rueful smile. "He says not to have barbecues or discard cigarettes anywhere outside. Not to allow open fires, not to discard glass bottles anywhere apart from in the recycling, and to keep children away from matches, lighters, and cigarettes."

"Of course," I said, giving the fireman a nod.

"Oh," Rowan added, "and he's asking if everyone in our party is accounted for."

In all the panic and confusion of the last twenty minutes, I realized that had slipped my mind. I was so wrapped up in making sure my children were OK, the drama of the *sapeurs-pompiers* arriving, and the disorienting effect of breathing in smoke, that it had not occurred to me to check.

I did a quick head count to make sure all twelve of us were present and correct.

Counted once.

That can't be right.

Counted again.

Eleven.

65

I shook my head to clear it.

Only eleven of us. Not twelve. The radio on the breast pocket of Lepine's uniform crackled into life, a young voice, breathless and urgent, calling his name over and over. Lepine answered it and was met with a torrent of French from one of his crew members. He fired two questions back. Two quick answers.

Rowan's hand flew to her mouth.

Lepine gestured to her to come with him, quickly. I stood up, too, icy fingers starting to curl around my heart.

Daniel took my hand, as if to come with me.

Lepine waved a finger and shook his head.

"Non, madame," he said. "Pas avec le garçon."

Not with the boy.

The world felt as if it were falling away beneath my feet.

Daniel looked at me uncertainly. "What did he say?"

"You stay here for now," I said, my voice shaky. "With Daddy." I let go of Daniel's hand and followed Lepine down the hill toward the blackened woods, scorched by flames and soaked with water, the nearest small trees twisted and black. The Frenchman led the way, with Rowan, Alistair, and me following close behind in single file.

My legs were rubbery and weak. With every step over the uneven ground of the vineyard, I thought they would give way and buckle under me. Our footsteps, sandals and flip-flops crunching over dirt and stones and leaves, were the only sound as we made our way into the woods. There were no running men, no more sirens, no beating rotors of an approaching helicopter; no sounds of desperate activity, no lifesaving urgency.

Just the three of us with Lepine walking stolidly ahead, a tarpaulin in a sealed plastic bag under his arm.

Here was the worn dirt path that wound around the big oaks and sycamores, here was the dip, the hollow, then up and around again, past the big rock and the fallen tree where Odette had hidden. The sign stuck lopsidedly into the ground, ATTENTION! in faded red lettering. We reached the clearing and the edge of the bluff, let Lepine lead us down the steps carved into the limestone cliff face, my legs threatening to buckle all the way. I realized, absently, that this was the first time I'd been down into the gorge since we got here.

I didn't know what the fireman had said to Rowan, I didn't know much French, but at the same time I *knew*. Against my will, against every fiber of my being, I knew what we would find. Ahead of me, Rowan was already sobbing softly, her shoulders hitching up and down as she walked, arms crossed tight over her chest. Seeing her, I couldn't hold it in any longer. My tears started when we were halfway down into the gorge, and by the time we reached the bottom I was sobbing, too.

The youngest of the firemen was there, his hat in both hands in front of him. He couldn't have been much more than eighteen, his face ghost pale. He looked close to tears himself.

He cast his eyes down and stepped aside as we approached.

"Madames," he said, his voice choked.

She was there. Arms outstretched against smooth rock, at the foot of the cliff.

Motionless.

Izzy.

66

She lay on her back, her head encircled by a dark halo of blood.

Her eyes were open, staring up at nothing. One leg was tucked under the other, both arms flung out to the side, on one of the flat slabs of rock that formed the bottom of the gorge. Blood dripped slowly from the back of her head, down the edge of the rock and into the stream gurgling below, deep red drops diluting and mixing and disappearing, carried away downstream by the mountain water. A fly buzzed around her, settling next to the blood dripping down her grotesquely bent arm until I waved it angrily away, swatting at more flies circling her head.

Rowan spoke to Lepine in rapid, urgent tones, staccato questions one after the other. But he simply looked at her and shook his head slowly, apologetically. Izzy was gone.

Alistair stood back, his face frozen in shock. Rowan and I approached her body slowly, arm in arm, not wanting to see. To see would make it real. Make it permanent.

Our friend.

"Oh God." My voice sounded weird, disembodied, not my own. "Oh no."

Rowan was shaking in disbelief, a hand over her mouth, deep, racking sobs that echoed off the walls of the gorge. I hugged her and we held on to each other for a few minutes, crying and trying to give comfort even though we both knew there was none to be had. Not anymore.

"How could . . ." Rowan started through her sobs. "How could she have fallen?"

"I don't know. I can't believe she's . . ."

I couldn't finish the sentence. It felt as if I were floating above the scene, not part of it. I'd seen photographs of dead bodies before in the course of my job—it was an occasional but inevitable part of what I did—but never anyone I knew. Never anyone who had meant so much to me, shared so much of my own history, my own past. My own life.

Lepine cleared his throat and spoke quietly in French, Rowan nodding and answering in a voice so low it was almost a whisper. From what I could make out, he was asking her to identify the body. Rowan nodded again and said something else in French, her voice cracking.

Lepine put a hand lightly on her arm, his severe features softening.

"Je suis vraiment désolé, madame," he said.

He unfolded the tarpaulin and laid it gently, carefully, over the body.

I couldn't bear to look at her broken body, but I didn't want her to be covered, either. It seemed so impersonal, so final, that she was beyond us and beyond all hope of help, beyond the bond of friendship that had bound us together for half our lives.

Without thinking, I knelt down and stroked her outstretched hand, the skin waxy but still warm to the touch.

My friend. Little more than an hour ago I had faced her across a table, trying to contain my fury, clenching my hands in my lap to stop myself from lashing out at her.

And now this.

Somehow it seemed as though it was my fault, my responsibility. My suspicion and ill will and anger toward Izzy had sent her over the edge of that cliff.

I'm sorry, Izzy. Truly, I am.

"We need to get in touch with her family," Rowan said, her voice shaking. "Her brother. Ring the Irish consulate."

"I think the police will take care of that."

"Madame?" Lepine said, with an apologetic smile. He was gesturing for me to move away from the body.

"Of course." I stood up. "I'm sorry. *Pardon.*"

"What's the matter?" Rowan asked.

"We're not supposed to touch anything."

"Oh. Of course."

The fireman spoke to her again, Rowan translating for my benefit.

"He's going to put a call into the regional Police nationale office to report what's happened," she said. "One of his men will stay here until the police arrive. Stay with . . . Izzy."

Alistair spoke for the first time, his voice flat.

"Shouldn't we take her up to the villa? We could make a stretcher out of something, perhaps put a couple of the—"

I cut him off, my professional instincts kicking in. "No," I said.

"We can't just leave her down here!"

"They have to preserve all the evidence, and the police will want everything left as it is."

"Evidence?" He sounded confused. "What do you mean?"

I hesitated, not wanting to say it, hating myself because I knew I had to. "This is a potential crime scene."

67

No one could speak.

We sat in horrified, shell-shocked silence in the living room, all of us gathered in one place, trying to absorb the horrifying news we had carried up from the gorge. Some crying, arms around shoulders, others staring at the carpet. Lucy and Daniel sat close together by my side, both in tears, holding hands. They hadn't done that for years.

A pair of officers from the gendarmerie office in Béziers had been notified and would be here within the hour, Lepine had told us. Despite his promise that one of the firemen would stay in the gorge until then, he had pulled his young crewman out at the last minute, insisting he needed his whole team to attend a road accident on the nearby D909. Izzy's body was covered and marked off with red-and-white tape, and Alistair had volunteered to go down and wait, to ensure nothing was disturbed before an officer could get here. We were told—strictly and without exception—that no one was to touch or move the body.

Finally, Russ spoke up. "A crime scene? Really?"

"*Potential* crime scene," I said.

"I suppose I assumed that it was an accident."

Sean nodded grimly, tears on his face. He looked wretched. Broken. "Me too," he said.

I wiped my eyes with a tissue that was already sodden.

"Yes, but the police will have to start from an assumption that all possibilities are open, then work their way back from that. They have to rule out all other options before they declare it an accident. That's what UK police would do."

Jennifer sat with her boys, each hand tightly clutching one of theirs, staring ahead, unseeing. She looked shattered, defeated, devastated. I suppose we all did.

"I can't believe she's gone," she said, almost to herself.

"But what if it wasn't an accident? What if it *was* something else?" Russ asked.

"Like what?" Sean said.

There was more silence, for a long moment. No one wanted to say it. Eventually, I spoke up.

"Foul play," I said quietly.

"But that's crazy," Rowan said, looking around the room. "Isn't it?"

"Yes," Sean said abruptly.

"Of course," Russ said.

"Crazy," Jennifer agreed.

I studied the faces arranged around the living room, ten of us where just an hour ago there had been twelve. Friends and families. Rowan and Russ, Jennifer, Jake and Ethan, Lucy, Daniel, little Odette.

And Sean, sitting next to me with his strong arm around my shoulders.

Even though I knew what it meant, it wasn't until that moment that the enormity of it hit me. It felt as if all eyes in the room were on me.

Izzy had been involved with my husband. She had been about to confess to their affair, about to detonate a bomb under his marriage. About to expose his adultery and lies.

And now she was dead.

I couldn't stop glancing at the scratches high on my husband's right cheek, three small vertical lines of angry red, close together, from his temple to his ear. He'd said he'd fallen, been scratched by a thornbush amidst the smoke and chaos while searching for our children. But they didn't look consistent with that kind of injury to me—they were too regular, too uniform. Too straight.

They looked like fingernail marks.

An ugly, twisted thought came crawling right after it: *Izzy was left handed. A left-handed person would lash out on the right side of an attacker's face . . .*

After the fire started, Sean was in the woods the longest. On his own. He went back in on his own. He came out on his own. I didn't see what he was doing. No one did. So no one saw how he got those injuries.

Perhaps he hadn't been on his own the whole time.

The logical part of my brain laid out a horribly plausible scenario, displaying it like a reel of found footage. No matter how hard I tried, I couldn't get rid of it. Couldn't turn the projector off. Every time I tried, it just came back louder and brighter and more convincing than before: Jake and Ethan, angry that they had to fly home early, messing around with matches in the woods, accidentally starting fires not in one place but in two. *That* was why my first view of the fire had struck me—because it was not just in one spot. Two separate fires, thirty feet apart. Perhaps a competition between teenage brothers, to see who could get flames going the quickest? And then panicking when it spread, running away and leaving it to burn. In among the smoke and chaos, Sean finds Izzy out by the bluff. Or she finds him. A chance meeting, and their lovers' argument is reignited—she wants to get their affair out in the open; he is desperate to keep it a secret. Passions are high and tempers flare, things get out of hand. She had always been feisty, but he is almost a foot taller than her and so much stronger. She makes an ultimatum: perhaps she lashes out and he is just defending himself, perhaps he doesn't realize they're dangerously close to the edge of the cliff and then—

All of a sudden I can't stand him touching me.

The scenario plays on a loop in my head, a grimly credible montage of images that becomes more and more real, the longer I think about it. The hairs on the backs of my arms rise.

What have you done, Sean?

My God, what have you done?

68

"Crazy or not," I said, trying to keep my voice level, "if the police end up going down that road, they'll have an immediate short list of suspects."

"Who?" Rowan said.

"Well, the people in this room."

She was shaking her head. "One of us?"

"Yes."

There was another uncomfortable silence while that sank in.

"In that case," Rowan said finally, "we should probably get our story straight."

"Our *story*?" I said. "What do you mean?"

"Just—you know. What happened."

I wanted to hear Sean's story more than anything. I was tired of suspicion, of guesswork, of only knowing half the facts and trying to work out the other half for myself. It had been five days since discovering the messages on his phone, five days of anguish and lies and heartbreak that had ended in tragedy. So I wanted to hear Sean's truth. I owed it to my friend. But at the same time, I was terrified of what he might say.

"How about the truth?" I said.

"That's what I mean," Rowan said.

"OK. The truth." I turned to look at my husband, my eyes drawn again to the three vertical scratches on the side of his face. "How about we start with you, Sean?"

"Me?"

"Did you see Izzy in the woods?"

He shrugged, shook his head. "Don't think so. I found Lucy well off the path, then, when I went back in, Russ was already on his way back with Odette."

Liar.

But Rowan was nodding. "I saw you heading back down to the clearing as we were coming out."

"Then what?" I said.

"Then I looked around a bit more for anyone else, but the smoke was really thick by that point and I could hardly see anything. I blundered into that thornbush like a proper *eejit* and thought it was time to get the hell out of there."

"You didn't see Izzy?" I asked again.

"Nope." His voice cracked. "I wish I had."

"Did anyone else see her?"

Everyone shook their heads.

"No one saw her fall?"

Silence.

By virtue of my job, I knew something that no one

else in this room did. Pushing someone from a significant height—a tower block window or a rooftop or a cliff edge—was tough for investigators because there were virtually no forensic traces unless there was a struggle beforehand. No murder weapon—just gravity; no blood spatter on the offender's clothing. No defensive wounds. No forensics to link victim and perpetrator. Without a witness, CCTV, or a confession, it was incredibly difficult to prove the victim didn't just fall.

From a forensics point of view, it was pretty much the perfect murder method.

"OK," I continued. "What about the fire?" I turned to Jake and Ethan. "How about you two? Do you know how it started?"

Jennifer jumped straight in before they could respond, an indignant edge to her voice.

"Hold up just a minute! Why should my boys know anything about it?"

I ignored her.

"Did you boys see anything?"

Both teenagers shook their heads, but neither of them would meet my eye.

"Did *anyone* see how the fires started?"

More shaking of heads.

Jennifer said, "It could have been kids from the village, coming up through the gorge."

"All right, did anyone see any local kids down there this afternoon?"

She shrugged. "Can't say I did, no."

"Has anyone seen any local kids down there on *any* day this week?"

There was a muttering of negatives from around the room.

"Maybe we should wait for the police before we start getting into this?" Russ said.

I turned on him, my frustration boiling over.

"We have to pool what we know, work out how it might have happened."

Sean took his arm off my shoulders.

"One of the firemen found Izzy's glasses in the clearing," he said. "Near the edge of the gorge. He had them in one of those plastic evidence bags."

Rowan nodded. "I saw that, too. One of the lenses was shattered."

"She must have lost her glasses in the confusion down there," Sean added, "and been disorientated by the smoke. She might have been running?"

There was a brittle, mechanical edge to his voice that I didn't recognize.

Liar, I thought.

But once again, Rowan was nodding. "There was a lot of smoke blowing around," she said. "Maybe she just didn't see the edge."

It was the third time in as many minutes that Rowan had done it. *Every time Sean says something, she backs him up. Why? What does that mean?*

But even as I asked myself the question, an answer arrived. An answer that was supremely cynical and cruel and unfair in the circumstances, but wasn't that what my life had turned into? This was how my mind worked now.

You don't want a scandal, do you, Rowan? No sordid affairs, no foul play, no criminal investigation. Just a tragic accident. Nothing that might derail your precious business deal—and your multimillion-pound payout.

69

Jennifer seemed to come to her senses, sitting up straighter in her seat.

"OK." She looked pointedly at me. "What else will the detectives want to know?"

"I don't know too much about French police procedure," I said, "but I'd assume they'll want to take statements from all of us, establish some facts, look at the scene, and make a decision from there."

"And what else, Kate?"

"What do you mean?"

Jennifer looked at her sons, slumped on the sofa. "Hey, why don't all the young folk go downstairs to the games room while the grown-ups talk about this? What do you think, guys, get some drinks and put a DVD on or something? Would you do that for me, Jakey?"

Jake shrugged and stood up, followed by his brother. Then Lucy and Daniel were on their feet, Lucy taking her brother by the hand and leading him out to the staircase. Of the five children, only Odette remained, thumb in her mouth and anchored to her mother's lap, head against her chest. Normally a babbling spring of chatter, I had not heard her utter a single word since returning to the villa after the fire, and she didn't speak now—but neither did she move. Rowan stroked her daughter's long red hair, a gesture that said to everyone: *my baby stays with me.*

Jennifer gave Rowan a sympathetic smile and turned back to me.

"Listen, Kate, I know it was an accident, we *all* know it was an accident; I just think there are certain things we don't need to tell the police."

"Such as?"

"Do you really want me to say it?"

With most of the children gone, that left an even half dozen of us: me, Jennifer, Rowan, Odette, Russ, and Sean. And now all eyes were on me, on the blush rising up in my cheeks. But why not? Why not just put it all out there? It didn't matter anymore, none of it mattered, not really. The events of the past week were distant and trivial compared to the tragedy of today.

"If you have to."

"Well, like what we discussed at the café yesterday." She hesitated, then plowed on. "That you thought Izzy was having an affair with Sean."

Russ looked up sharply.

"What?"

Beside me, Sean put his head in his hands. "Jesus H. Christ," he said. "No, no, no."

Russ said, "An affair? What the hell?"

Sean just shook his head.

"I found messages on his phone the day we got here," I told Russ. "Saying he *couldn't stop thinking about her* and *did Kate suspect anything?* But I wanted solid proof, so I got into Sean's phone when he was sleeping, pretended to be him, and asked whoever it was to meet down in the woods. It was Izzy."

"Jesus," Russ said under his breath.

Rowan said, "Is it *true,* Sean?"

He simply shook his head, eyes fixed on the floor.

Please just tell me. No more deception. No more lies.

"Tell me, Sean," I said, pleading with him. "I have to know the truth."

"No." His voice was barely above a whisper.

"I don't believe you. Why can't you even look at me?"

He lifted his head to face me, his eyes bloodshot and brimming with fresh tears. "I said no. It's not true."

I shook my head. Even now he couldn't come clean. I wondered what had happened to the man I married, how long ago it had gone wrong between us.

And look at us now: wronged wife and desperate lover. De facto suspects in the death of our dear friend.

"It doesn't matter if you deny it," I said. "Izzy was about to tell me herself, she asked me for a private talk after dinner tonight. Something personal. She actually started telling me, and then everything went crazy with the fire and—"

"And now here we are," Rowan said quietly.

"I didn't do anything to Izzy," Sean blurted suddenly. "I swear. I would *never* have hurt her."

Jennifer gave him a sympathetic smile. "I know that, Sean, we all know that."

Do we?

"I'm so sorry for bringing it up, Kate," she continued. "I just think it's better if we don't mention any of this to the police. It gives you . . . motive, I guess?"

"*I* never hurt her!"

"I know, but that's exactly what I mean. If we tell the police about all of this, it will send them on some kind of wild-goose chase that none of us wants. We'd all hate for Izzy's family to have her name dragged into that kind of tabloid nonsense."

"Agreed," Rowan said.

I swiped at my tears with the heel of my palm. "I never even saw her down there in the woods when it was all happening."

Jennifer patted my knee. "No one did, Kate. It's not your fault."

Odette, still sitting on Rowan's lap, whispered something to her mother. Rowan frowned.

"Say that again, darling."

Odette shook her head vigorously.

"Come on, darling. It's OK, I promise."

Odette put her mouth close to her mother's ear and

whispered again, louder this time, but not loud enough for the rest of us to hear.

"Are you sure, darling?" Rowan said softly. "Super *super* sure?"

Odette nodded. Just a tiny movement, almost invisible, a dip of her little chin without breaking eye contact with her mother.

"What is it?" I said. "Does she want to go down to the games room with the other children?"

"No," Rowan said, her face darkening. "She said she—she saw something. When she was hiding in the tree trunk, she saw Izzy at the edge of the bluff. With someone."

I flinched as a distant rumble of thunder rolled across the sky.

"Who?" I said. "Who was she with?"

Odette looked at us, all of us, her big hazel-green eyes seeming to see us for the first time. Slowly, tentatively, she raised her hand and pointed.

70

Odette didn't blink. She didn't speak, or cry, or hide her face.

She just pointed.

Her finger shaking, her whole hand shaking, her index finger singled out one person sitting on the sofa opposite.

Jennifer.

Time seemed to slow down as all eyes in the room turned toward her.

"What?" Jennifer said, a confused half-smile on her face.

Finally, Odette found her voice. "They were shouting. Saying mean things to each other. And then the smoke blowed in the way and when it was gone again only Jake and Ethan's mummy was standing there. The other lady was gone."

"That's not true," Jennifer said. "I was nowhere near the cliff edge."

Rowan turned to her daughter again.

"Do you think maybe it was another lady that you saw, Odette? Was it someone else's mummy?"

Odette shook her head but said nothing.

"Maybe it was Lucy's mummy?" She gestured to me.

"Uh-uh," Odette said, shaking her head. "The tall blond lady."

Jennifer said, "Lucy's blond, too."

"Jake and Ethan's mummy!" Odette said indignantly.

"She seems quite sure," Rowan said, "that it was you, Jen."

Jennifer threw her hands up.

"She's five years old, for Christ's sake—not exactly the most reliable witness, is she?"

"She doesn't lie."

"She's an attention seeker!" Jennifer said, her voice rising. "She's been doing it all week, only everyone is too polite to point it out!"

"What?" Rowan's face was flushed with anger. "Where the hell do you get off, having a pop at my—"

"She's acting up again now! Just to get attention!"

"Rather than being model citizens, like your boys?"

"How *dare* you!" Jennifer pointed an accusing finger. "You have *literally* no idea what you're talking about."

"How dare you criticize *my* child when *your* eldest spent last night rolling around in his own vomit!"

Their raised voices began to overlap in a continuous barrage of accusations and counteraccusations, colliding and clashing and bouncing off the walls.

"You have no right to bring my boys into it—"

"You have no right to talk about my daughter—"

"She's a spoiled little—"

Russ joined in, veins standing out in his neck.

"You've got a bloody nerve—"

"*I've* got a nerve! Says the man whose daughter could have drowned while he was—"

"That is absolute bull—"

"And then virtually accused my boys of—"

"For all we know, your boys could have started the fire in the first—"

"For all we know, you could have coached Odette to say she saw—"

"Coached her? Are you out of your—"

Abruptly, Rowan stopped.

Odette had her hands tightly over her ears and was crying, silently, fat tears rolling down her freckled cheeks.

"Shh," Rowan said, stroking her daughter's hair with a shaking hand. "It's OK, baby, I'm sorry, no more shouting. I'm sorry, it's OK."

Silence returned. The shouting had stopped but the tension in the room lingered like a bad smell.

Finally, Jennifer held her hands up. "I'm just trying to help Kate and do the right thing for Izzy, that's all."

"We know," I said. "Everybody's in shock."

"But I have no idea why Odette would think she saw me with Izzy. I was much more worried about getting my boys out of there."

It was true that Odette could not be considered a

particularly reliable witness. If we were all totally honest with one another for once—and as parents, we had all learned long ago never to be totally honest when it came to talking about one another's children—she had been acting up since the day we arrived. It was what she did. The fits of temper, the fussiness with food, the bedtime routine, were all ways of getting attention from parents whose focus was more often on their cell phones.

And yet . . .

And yet she had been sure, she had been *positive,* that she had seen Jennifer at the cliff edge with Izzy. She had been near enough to see, despite the smoke. Near enough to hear the two of them arguing.

It didn't fit. It didn't make sense, didn't mesh with what I knew.

Until a few minutes ago, I had been resigned to the fact that I had discovered the sordid, dirty truth at the heart of my marriage, was resigned to the fact that I would not lie to the police, would not withhold evidence, would not go against everything I believed in. Resigned to the fact that my husband—the father of my children, the man I loved with all my heart, the man I had wanted to grow old with—had betrayed me. Resigned to the fact that betrayal had somehow tumbled into murder.

But Odette's words didn't fit.

And there was something else, something more, just beyond my eyeline. I could sense it was there, but when I tried to look straight at it, it slid out of sight.

What if I had been looking at everything the wrong

way, all this time? A few days ago I had been convinced that Rowan was the guilty party, then Jennifer, and now Izzy. I had been getting it wrong all week. Now my friend was dead—and maybe I was *still* wrong. What if I had let my emotions get the better of me? What if I hadn't parked my *work brain,* as Sean liked to call it, but put it to use here instead?

I remembered one of the case studies I'd analyzed while I was training, soon after joining the police. A burglary at a house, nothing particularly unusual apart from the large volume of jewelry, cash, and electronics taken by burglars who had not left a single forensic trace. No fingerprints, no footprints, no DNA. It had been a scrupulous job. It had also been totally bogus: the homeowner, a *CSI: Miami* fan angling for an insurance payout, exposed months later when his pictures of a "stolen" Rolex were found to have been taken *after* the burglary had supposedly taken place.

The lesson for us trainees had been: *First impressions can be misleading. Look harder. Follow the evidence.* The question hung over me: Was I allowing myself to be misled now?

I thought back to my conversation with Izzy in the dining room, only a couple hours ago. What had she said? What had she *actually* said?

This is tough, Kate, but I've given it a lot of thought and I know it's the right thing to do under the circumstances.

I don't know how to say this. I've agonized over whether to tell you about—

I didn't realize on Monday that—

Didn't realize what? I had assumed at the time that meant she hadn't realized I was on to her, that I already knew Sean had betrayed me. But maybe I had jumped to the wrong conclusion.

Outside, the thunder was getting closer. Something clicked in my head and finally, *finally,* I thought I might be starting to understand.

71

I studied my friends on the sofa opposite. Rowan comforting her daughter, jigging her gently on her knee. Russ, slapping a pack of Marlboros into the palm of his hand, looking as if he'd like to continue the shouting match. Jennifer, close to tears again, spots of color high in her cheeks.

"Jen," I said, "why did you send the kids away?"

"What?"

"Ten minutes ago. You sent the other four kids downstairs to the games room."

She shrugged, distracted.

"I thought there were things they probably shouldn't hear." She threw a pointed look at Rowan. "And I'm mighty glad I did, now."

"Anything else?"

"It's so tough for teenagers to process grief. It's a new experience for them, I didn't want them getting any more upset than they already are. They're devastated, trying to deal with what's happened. And . . ."

She hesitated. "I guess I didn't want to embarrass you."

"I get all that, and I appreciate it." It was my turn to hesitate. "But what was the *other* reason?"

"Other reason for what?"

"Separating the kids from this conversation."

"Not sure I follow you."

"What I mean is, what has all of this got to do with the kids?"

She shrugged.

"Nothing. Apart from them being here this week, with all of us."

Cogs were turning in my brain. My daughter's tears. A conversation on the beach. A tribute page on Facebook. Ethan sprawled in the grass, staring up at the night sky. Jake so drunk he couldn't stand. Izzy bringing him back from the gorge.

Every time we stopped for him to be sick, he wanted to have a chat, she had said.

About what?

All kinds of stuff.

"I was wondering," I said, "what Jake told Izzy last night. When he was drunk?"

"I have no idea."

"Really? No idea at all?"

It was almost imperceptible. Almost invisible, but not quite: a slight twitch of the muscle under her eye.

"You saw how bad he was," she said. "Absolutely blasted, he was almost incoherent most of the time."

"He was 'looking for oblivion,' according to his brother. Why would he be doing that?"

"They're teenage boys. They're testing boundaries, looking for new experiences."

I changed tack.

"Do the boys know someone called Alex Bayley?"

I thought I caught a flash of something crossing her face, just for a split second. Then it was gone. My judgment had been so wide of the mark this week that I almost dismissed it.

"No," she said. "I mean, I don't think so. Did he go to their school?"

Something about that didn't quite ring true, either, but I let it go for now.

"How about the fire?" I continued. "Why today? How did it start?"

She held her hands up in exasperation. "We've been through that already. What is this, twenty questions?"

"Because one fire could conceivably have been an accident. But it looked to me like the fire had been started in *two* different places, and I started out thinking that Jake and Ethan had—"

Jennifer stood up, eyes brimming with tears.

"Enough! How long have we been friends? I can't believe all of you think it's OK to attack my children like this. *Again.* It's just so hurtful and horrible, I can't believe what I'm hearing. We're all devastated and heartbroken about what happened to Izzy, me just as much as you."

I raised my hands in a calming gesture.

"Let me finish, Jen. I *was* thinking that two boys meant two fires. But what if it wasn't that—what if it meant something different?"

"Like what?" Russ asked.

"Two fires to make sure it caught. To make sure it got going, make sure there was lots of smoke. To make sure it couldn't be put out straightaway."

"What would be the point of that?"

"To cause a distraction," I said. "A diversion."

"An actual smoke screen," he said.

"Exactly." I turned to his wife. "Do you remember, Rowan, when we first saw the smoke and the three of us were running down through the vineyard? Me, you, and Izzy?"

"I remember being terrified."

"But do you remember the last thing Izzy said to us, as we ran into the woods?"

Her expression changed, eyes flicking to Jennifer and then back to me.

"She said she was going to find Jen, help her round up the boys."

"Yes. That's what I remember, too."

The silence stretched out for a long moment.

"So?" Jennifer said. "So what?"

"Izzy went looking for you," I said. "To help you. And she *did* find you, because Odette saw you together a few minutes later."

Jennifer was moving toward the door.

"You know what? I don't have to listen to this, it's

ridiculous!" Her voice was shaking with anger. "My friend is dead because of a terrible, horrible accident but all *you* want to do is find someone to blame. Well, how about you look a little closer to home for that, Kate? How about you look at your role in all of this? *You're* the one who stalked your own husband for a week, *you're* the one who figured out he was fucking one of your best friends, *you're* the one who confronted her. Why don't you tell the police all that, see how it goes for you?"

"Yes," I said, a strange calmness coming over me for the first time in days. "That's exactly what I think we should do. I think we should tell the police everything."

She shot me a look of disbelief, mixed with pity.

"Good luck with that, honey."

With that, she stormed off, calling to Jake and Ethan to go to their rooms and start packing.

To my surprise, Sean jumped up and followed her out.

Rowan handed Odette to her husband and came to sit next to me.

"Are you OK, Kate?"

"No. You?"

"Not really." She squeezed my hand. For the first time I could remember, she seemed to struggle to find the right words. "Do you really think she did it?"

I shrugged.

"Honestly? I don't know. But that's for the police to decide, not us."

"But what do we do now?" She lowered her voice to a whisper. "If she's capable of something like that, who knows what she might do next?"

I didn't have an answer for her. We had sailed off the edge of the known world into uncharted waters, and there was no map to take us home. There was only one thing left to do: keep on going.

"We have to sit tight, Rowan, until the police get here. In the meantime, I'm going to talk to Sean. Find some answers."

He was in the kitchen, Jennifer backing him into a corner. The argument died on their lips as I appeared in the doorway.

"I need some air, Sean. Let's go out to the balcony, shall we?"

He nodded. He looked like a man who was on his way to the gallows and knew his soul was already damned.

"Aye," he said softly.

It was time for the truth.

72

The air outside was thick with humidity, the storm to our south casting the land into deep shadow. It was pushing up fast and would be overhead soon. For now, though, the evening sun continued to beat down on the villa with an intense, relentless Mediterranean heat that started to bake my skin as soon as we stepped outside. Sean and I found a couple of chairs and sat down at the far edge of the balcony, the French countryside spread out below us like a watercolor painting in vivid greens and deep, earthy browns.

"Before I say anything else, Sean, I just want to make one thing clear between us."

"OK," he said uncertainly.

"I've never trusted anyone in my life the way I trust you," I said. "Not even my parents or my sister. The things I tell you, the things we share—I trust you completely."

He nodded but said nothing.

"But this week that trust has been tested to the limit,

to the point where I thought things would never be the same again, that we could never go back to the way they were. But I still think there's a chance we can go back. Do you?"

He swallowed hard. "I hope we can."

"Well, the only way that's going to happen is if you trust me. You *have* to trust me. You have to tell me what's going on, right here, right now. I need the truth."

"I know."

"And I swear to God, I swear on my life, if you don't tell me the absolute truth—and I mean *everything*—the first thing I'll do when we get home is file for divorce. It'll kill me, but I will do it."

"Don't," he said quickly. "Don't do that."

"No more secrets, then."

He nodded. "No more secrets."

"Good."

He seemed to buckle in on himself, slumping into his chair as if he had been holding something back for so long that all of his energy was exhausted. When he spoke, his voice was barely above a whisper.

"I didn't do it. I didn't push Izzy over the edge."

I took his big right hand in both of mine. "I know, Sean. I know you didn't."

He looked up, blinking in surprise. "You do?"

"Yes."

"But you thought I . . ."

"I've finally figured some things out." It was nowhere

near the truth, but I needed him to *think* that I knew, to push him into telling me. "I just need you to help me put the pieces together in the right order."

He leaned back in his seat until he was staring straight up at the sky, at the dark clouds gathering overhead.

"Jesus, what a mess. What a fucking mess." He looked down at me again. "It was when you mentioned Alex Bayley that I knew there was no point carrying on. That it was all over."

"Tell me," I said. "All of it."

He rubbed his face in both hands, exhaled heavily, and looked out at the view for a moment, at the dark hills in the distance, before turning his attention back to me.

"It all started a few weeks ago," he said.

"Go on."

He hesitated, then plowed on.

"I was out running, training for that half marathon I was going to do. It was late and I was on those quiet little back roads out by the golf course and I came up behind a car stopped at a junction, just sitting there, lights on, engine running. Just this one car, no one else around. I thought maybe they were lost or something. It was only when I came level with it that I could see the driver was sitting behind the wheel, on his phone, and there was this mountain bike on the road in front of him, all bent out of shape. I looked back at the driver and recognized him."

I remembered yesterday, Daniel finding himself alone in the villa; Jennifer's insistence that her boys would *never* have taken one of the cars out.

"It was Jake, wasn't it?"

"In Jennifer's car. I'm about to knock on his window but then the next thing I know he's slammed the car into gear and he's off, like a bat out of hell. So it's just me and this twisted-up bike, but then I see the cyclist. The impact had thrown him into the hedge on the far side of the road. I was sort of in shock, I think. I checked on the lad and he still had a pulse but he was in a bad way; he wasn't wearing a helmet and his face was covered in blood. I take my phone out to call an ambulance but as I'm dialing, it starts ringing in my hand. It's Jen, in floods of tears, begging me not to say what I just saw, not to give her car's license plate number, to leave Jake out of it. I didn't know what the fuck to do, she was so upset."

I force myself to breathe.

"So you agreed."

"I didn't know what to do! I wanted to do the right thing and Jennifer was distraught. I wanted to help her, so I rang off, called the police and said I'd just found this lad and his bike, and that was it."

"You didn't mention the car, or the driver."

He shook his head, the wind whipping at his hair. "Jen was in such a state, I thought it was the right thing to do."

"You lied to the police?"

"I wish to God I hadn't now."

*One little lie, one little deception to help a friend.
And it had led us all here, shattered by grief, waiting
for the police to arrive again.*

"And that's why you stopped going out running."
I shook my head. "I thought it was because you were
saving your energy for an affair. *God,* I'm such an
idiot."

"We created fake profiles on Messenger to stay in
contact, in case either you or Alistair ever looked at
our phones. We were updating each other, working
out what we should do next if things got dicey. The
cyclist was in intensive care, and everyone was hoping
he'd pull through."

Need to talk to you
　　—Does K suspect anything?
She has no idea. But I can't go on like this
　　—We'll decide when we're in France. Figure
out what to do
Can't keep my mind on anything else

"*She* was CoralGirl—those were the messages I saw on
your phone." I frowned at another memory. "But what
about on Tuesday when I unlocked your phone and sent
an invitation to her? It was Izzy who turned up."

He looked at the ground.

"As soon as you went inside, I checked my phone
and saw what you'd done. I managed to send Jennifer another message, calling her off. I was panicking,
sure you knew what was going on by that point, so I

suggested to her that she send Izzy up instead so she could get started on making tea."

"And Izzy did what she was asked."

His face crumpled, as if he might break down again.

"She was trying to be helpful."

"Sean," I said, "the cyclist was Alex Bayley, wasn't it? From Lucy's school?"

He nodded but said nothing.

"And he died."

"Yesterday."

"His friends put a tribute page up on Facebook. So that's why Jake wanted to get wasted." I had a sudden flash of Izzy trying to prop the teenager up as they struggled up the garden. "Why he was looking for oblivion."

"He'd been holding it together, more or less, while Alex was still alive in hospital and they thought he'd pull through. It must have been after the water polo yesterday evening that they found out he'd died of his injuries."

I thought about Jake's and Ethan's phones bleeping every few seconds while they were in the pool, notifications on social media as the news spread across their peer group like a wildfire.

Another piece fell into place.

"And when Izzy found him in the gorge, he told her what he'd done, didn't he? When he was drunk, he told her he'd killed someone?"

"Izzy confronted Jen about it this afternoon. Jen told me she begged her to keep it secret but Izzy wasn't having any of it because of what happened to her fiancé."

I remembered a packed church, standing room only, Izzy lightning-struck with grief for Mark, the man she had been about to marry. "Killed in a hit-and-run, and they never found the driver. There was absolutely no way she was going to be a party to that happening again, was there?"

"Not in a million years."

"The one crime she was absolutely never, ever going to overlook, no matter who was involved. Because it happened to her." I took a deep breath. "She was about to tell me this afternoon but I was too pigheaded to listen. And that's when the fire started."

"Yes."

A cloud covered the sun, the temperature dropping a few degrees as the wind grew stronger.

"Fires started in more than one place, a distance apart, to ensure the flames take hold and can't quickly be put out—I've seen it in arson cases before." I shook my head. "I *knew* there was something off about it as soon as I saw it."

"I had no idea Jen would go as far as she did," Sean said. "No idea what she was capable of."

"She was determined to keep it from me, at all costs."

"She was."

The picture was becoming clearer, but there was still one crucial point that I didn't understand.

"Jen and Alistair are our friends and we want the

best for their boys, I understand that. But what I don't understand is, why didn't you tell me about this?"

He stared at me as if the answer were obvious.

"Because of who you are, because of what you do. Because of what you're like. *The truth, the whole truth, and nothing but the truth.* If I'd told you, it would have put you in an impossible situation, and we both know what you're like: everything is black and white in your world; you would have marched me down to the police station in five seconds flat to change my statement."

I considered this for a moment.

"You're probably right."

"You know I am."

"They can't stand outside the law. No one can."

"Maybe not. But there's another reason I didn't tell you. A much more important reason."

"What reason could there possibly be for withholding evidence and impeding a police investigation into a serious accident?"

"Because, Kate," he said slowly, "it wasn't an accident. Our daughter asked him to do it."

73

DANIEL

Daniel couldn't remember the last time it had happened: a text from his sister. Maybe never. Back in England, most of the time she barely even noticed he was there, let alone spoke to him. Let alone *texted* him. But out here at the vacation house it was different. He'd given her those sweets last night and they'd had a nice chat, about all sorts of things. Daniel loved proper talks with her. It was true that he enjoyed winding her up, but he also looked up to her and was proud of her in a way that he couldn't quite explain, and when she was nice she was *so* nice, so thoughtful and sweet and kind to him, that he wondered where that nice sister went the rest of the time.

He'd bought more sweets in the village today so maybe they could have another chat, and he really wanted to talk to her now after what had happened at the gorge. There was a funny, hard lump in his throat whenever he thought about Izzy. His eyes got twitchy, like he might cry again. She had fallen into the gorge and banged her head and now she was . . .

He didn't want to think about it on his own anymore.

What he wanted to do was talk to his sister. He clutched his phone, the old iPhone with the cracked screen that he'd begged to inherit when his dad had last upgraded.

And then, like magic, it pinged with a text.

You OK? Got something to cheer you up, little
bro. X

Sitting cross-legged on his bed, Daniel grinned and texted back three smiley face emojis and three kisses. He bounded across the corridor to her room, knocking lightly on the door, but she wasn't there. Her room was empty. He texted her back.

Where are you? x

Lucy's reply dropped in immediately. He read it and frowned, replying as fast as he could type.

Are we allowed? x
  —Of course, little bro x

He smiled again. He couldn't *ever* remember her getting him a present. Maybe when he was small, like a baby or something, but not that he could actually remember. The idea that she had gone out and spent her own money on a treat made him a bit happier just thinking about it.

Something to cheer you up, she'd said.

Daniel wondered what she'd got him. Sweets, hopefully. Maybe an inflatable for the pool, or a Frisbee for the beach. He was good at Frisbee.

He ran to his room, grabbed the bag of Haribo that he'd bought from the village supermarket, and ran down the curving staircase to the ground floor. Mum and Dad were still on the balcony, deep in conversation. Their heads were close together, like they were talking about a top secret thing. Something told him that he shouldn't disturb them so he went back into the villa, down the steps into the games room, and out the side door that led straight out to the pool. There was no one around. The wind was whipping up little waves on the surface of the swimming pool and big gray clouds filled the sky, covering up the sun so it looked more like home than being on vacation. The clouds made it weirdly dark already, like it was almost bedtime.

Daniel made his way down through the garden and out through the big iron gate into the vineyard.

Halfway down the hill, he flinched at a colossal crack of thunder almost directly overhead.

And then the rain came.

Just a few spots at first, *pit-patting* on the vines alongside him, warm drops on his forearms and cheeks, growing faster and faster, every new drop followed by two more until, within a matter of moments, it had turned into a continuous roar as the full fury of the storm broke overhead. For a second, he thought about turning around and going back up to the villa. But Lucy was down in the woods, waiting for him. He didn't want to let her down. *And* she had a present.

He decided to run instead.

A flash of lightning hit across the valley and another furious boom of thunder ripped the sky, so loudly that he hunched his head into his shoulders as he ran. It sounded as though the thunder was right above him, right on top of him.

At the edge of the woods, near a burned patch of grass, he stopped to catch his breath. The rain pounding on the leaves of the trees was a continuous barrage of noise and his T-shirt was already drenched. His hair was plastered to his scalp with rain and his glasses were smeared with raindrops. He took them off and wiped them on his sodden T-shirt, but as soon as he put them on they got smeared again. It was like looking through a car window when the wipers weren't going fast enough. He peered into the woods.

There. A glimpse of his sister's blond hair moving through the trees.

He set off after her.

74

I thought I'd misheard him.

"Lucy did *what*?"

Sean didn't break eye contact.

"Did you know they were in a relationship, her and Alex Bayley?"

"What? No!"

"She was well and truly smitten. He was this good-looking rugby lad, played for one of the big team academies. Saracens, I think. I only found this out from Jen after what happened."

"Why did she never tell us?"

"She thought we wouldn't approve, that he would distract her from her GCSEs. Anyway, they broke up about a month ago and he had—he had a video of her that he was circulating to his mates."

There was a sudden chill at the top of my spine, icy fingers lain across my skin.

"What kind of video?"

"The worst kind."

I remembered our conversation from a few days ago.

A video with you in it, Lucy?

The sort of thing . . . you wouldn't want me to see?

She had told me, she had *tried* to tell me. But I hadn't got the message, too preoccupied with my own problems.

"As soon as I knew it was out there," Sean said, "I did what I could. I got it taken down off a couple of sites, but by then a lot of her classmates had already seen it."

"Christ," I breathed. "Go on."

"Do you remember Russ and Rowan's barbecue, when we all got together to plan for the vacation?"

"I remember Lucy being particularly grumpy and shouty and making us half an hour late because she wouldn't get up and get dressed."

"Jake followed her around like a puppy dog all afternoon, remember? Then she and the boys disappeared for an hour, in that office pod thing that Russ has at the bottom of his garden."

"Daniel teased her about it."

"Yeah." He looked up at the sky, the clouds now hanging ominous and dark above us. The wind was picking up. "Let's go inside, looks like the heavens are about to open."

We went into the dining room and sat down at the end of the long table, right where I had sat with Izzy just a few hours before. My heart was heavy, like a lead weight in my chest, just thinking about her. I felt the tears coming again and blinked them back.

Sean held his hand out to me.

"Have you got your phone?"

I took my phone out of my pocket and unlocked it for him.

"What are you doing?"

He took the phone from me and went to a site called VideoVault, logging in with his own ID.

"Apparently Ethan was in the habit of taking candid pictures of girls, to look at afterward. He took some of Lucy. Little video clips, too, when she didn't realize it."

He found whatever he was looking for and turned the phone sideways, holding it up so we could both see.

"What am I looking at?" I said.

"Just watch."

The video loaded. No titles, no intro, the film jerky like cell phone footage. The angle was looking up toward Lucy, as if it had been filmed from someone's lap, but she was close and clearly identifiable on the left-hand side of the screen. A wooden-paneled wall behind her—presumably the inside of Russ's garden office—and a bottle of his favorite cognac open on a low table in front of her. Our daughter was slumped on a sofa, one strap of her low-cut top loose on her shoulder, angry spots of color in her cheeks.

"Alex fucking Bayley is a piece of shit." There are tears on her face and she is slurring a little, but her words are clear enough. "But he just gets away with it, without any punishment, because he's this big rugby boy that all the girls supposedly fancy. I wish someone would make him feel the way I feel, just once. Just for a day, or an hour. Make him feel used and dirty and worthless, like he wished he was dead. I wish he'd . . ." She waves a hand in the air. Her voice is wobbling. "I wish he'd fall under a bus. Fall off a cliff. Just fucking . . ."

She picks up her glass of cognac and drinks deep before slamming it back down on the table.

"I wish . . . I wish he'd just fucking die!"

She puts her head in her hands and there is silence for a few seconds, a hiss of static on the video. The silence is broken by Jake's voice, loud and close to the camera.

"I'll do it for you."

She snorts, half a laugh, looks up.

"What?"

"Sort him out, if you want. I'll do it." His tone is studiedly casual, full of broken-voiced teenage bravado. "Sounds like he's fucking got it coming anyway."

"Damn right," Ethan said. "He deserves it, bro."

She frowns as if she can't tell whether they're joking. "Seriously?"

Ethan's voice is calm and cool, always pushing his brother a step further. "I've seen him out cycling on his training route. I know where he goes."

"You want him to have an accident?" Jake said.

She leans forward, blinking fast, tongue flicking over her top lip. Takes another drink of cognac, sits back, runs a hand through her blond hair. Crosses one long leg over the other.

"Yeah." Her voice is detached, determined. A cold, hard tone that I've never heard before. *"Yeah, I do."*

The screen went black as the video ended.

I sat for a moment, trying to process what I had seen and what it meant, trying to grasp the full scale of what our daughter had set in motion. Conspiracy to commit murder. Our daughter, our smart, talented, beautiful daughter. If this video ever got out, she could be implicated in a death. Prosecuted. Her bright future would come crashing down in flames.

"Hold on, this video is already out there somewhere on the internet? How many people have seen it?"

"It's set to private view only," Sean said, "which basically means you need a password to access it—a password that only me and Jennifer have. She sent me the link and told me that if it ever comes out that Jake was involved, it would take her thirty seconds to lift the restriction and upload it to YouTube, put the film out there for the whole world to see. To justify why he did it."

"She's been holding that over you all this time?"

"Yes."

I remembered the messages I'd seen on his phone.

Can't stop thinking about what you said x
　—I meant every word

"Does Lucy know Jake was the one who knocked Alex off his bike?"

He shook his head.

"She doesn't even know about the video of her asking him to do it. Only Jennifer, her boys, and I know that footage exists."

"And me."

"And you. So now you know, what do we do? What about Jennifer?" He checked his watch. "The police will be here soon."

I looked at my husband, my brave, kind, protective husband, my heart overflowing.

"You know what we have to do, Sean. You've known all along."

After a long moment, he stood up.

"Yes." He nodded. "I do."

One last thing niggled at me.

"Why did you have the condoms, Sean? I found them in your suitcase."

He looked confused.

"I didn't put any condoms in there. I swear."

"Who used that case before you?"

Even before the question had left my mouth, I knew the answer.

"Lucy," I said. "She took it on the German trip."

"Yeah, you're right," he said slowly.

He looked around. "Where are the kids, anyway?"

"Games room?"

"I'll go and have a look."

He headed for the basement room and I picked up my phone, scrolling to the Find My iPhone app.

I selected Lucy's phone and waited for the location finder to work its magic.

After a few seconds, the map showed Lucy's location on the west side of the property, near the gorge. There was no good reason for her to be down there in the middle of a thunderstorm. I felt a sudden plunge of panic at the thought of her standing at the edge of the cliff, full of self-loathing over how she'd been treated, feeling used and dirty and worthless, wracked with guilt over a drunken prophecy come true. I sent her a quick text and stood up, preparing to head out into the rain.

Sean came back into the room, his face lined with worry.

"The kids aren't in the basement or in their rooms, either of them."

I held my phone up, showing him the icon for Lucy's phone on the map.

"For some reason, Lucy has gone back down to the gorge."

Suddenly, Lucy appeared in the doorway, her eyes red from crying. "Don't suppose anyone has seen my phone?" she said. "I left it charging in the living room and now I can't find it anywhere."

I looked at my phone again, selecting the icon for Daniel's phone, feeling my heart thumping against my ribs as I waited for the app to locate the signal.

It zeroed in on the location of my son's phone, and my heart rose up into my throat.

75

DANIEL

Daniel ran.

The rain was a pounding torrent that made a thick wall of noise as it struck the leaves on the trees around him and the ground at his feet. He was properly soaked now—he may as well have jumped into the pool; there wasn't a bit of him that wasn't totally drenched. Hopefully Lucy would have an umbrella, and they could both go under it and wait for the rain to stop.

He squinted through his rain-smeared glasses. She was up ahead. Near the edge where . . . He didn't want to think about what had happened to Izzy; it was too sad. Why his sister had wanted to come down here again, he couldn't figure out. But she had a present for him, and she'd texted him specially, so he'd come. Remembering the bag of Haribo in his hand, he held it up behind his back so that it would be a surprise.

He slowed his pace as he came into the clearing next to the big fallen tree. She was right on the edge of the cliff, with her back to him, long blond hair plastered to her head. He slowed to a walk, trying to catch his breath. As he watched, she turned around.

He gave her his best smile. Here she was: his sister. Oh. No, she wasn't.

It wasn't Lucy.

It took a moment for that to sink in, for his thoughts to catch up, as he blinked up at her through the downpour. *Not* Lucy. It was Jake and Ethan's mum, Jennifer, her makeup smeared and smudged in the rain, black lines running down from each eye.

She was here, too, that was a bit weird. And she had a phone that looked just like Lucy's. Like, *identical*.

"Hello," he said. "Have you seen my sister?"

Jennifer smiled at him.

"She's on her way." She indicated the hand he held behind his back. "What have you got there, Daniel?"

He brought the bag of sweets out to show her.

"A present for Lucy."

"Aren't you sweet? Guess what—I've got a present for you, too."

"What is it?"

She reached into her pocket.

"A surprise, honey."

Daniel took a step nearer. Her smudgy makeup and her smile reminded him of the clown he'd had at one of his birthday parties once when he was little. The clown had smiled all the time but it was sort of fake, like it was supposed to be nice but was actually just creepy and scary. He'd been scared of clowns ever since.

"How do you know Lucy's on her way?" he said.

"She told me." She beckoned him closer. "Don't you want your surprise?"

"Umm, OK."

She held out her hand, opening her palm to reveal a clear yellow plastic lighter.

"It's yours, isn't it? Not much fuel left now, sorry. Gives a heck of a good flame, though, doesn't it?"

Daniel blinked raindrops out of his eyes, the words coming out before he could stop them.

"Was it you that made the fire?"

She held the lighter closer to him, her smile widening.

"Hope you didn't mind me borrowing it."

As he reached out to take it, Jennifer's other hand shot out and grabbed his arm tight, her grip like steel rods squeezing the bones of his wrist.

She dropped the lighter and dragged him toward the edge of the cliff.

76

I heard him before I saw him, his cries cutting through the roar of the storm on the hillside.

"Ow, you're hurting me! Mum! Dad, help—"

Then nothing.

Rivulets of rainwater poured in streams toward the gorge and I stumbled on as the rain lashed down, catching a glimpse of figures through the trees before losing my footing in the wet and crashing onto all fours. Scrambling back to my feet, mud smeared up my arms and legs, I plunged on until I reached the clearing.

My heart stopped beating.

Jennifer was holding Daniel right at the very edge of the cliff. His feet were half on, half off the rocky promontory, the front of his sandals hanging in thin air above the drop, arms held out for balance. The back of his T-shirt was bunched in her fist, gym-toned muscles standing out on her strong right arm.

One quick shove would send him over the edge.

Daniel turned to look at me over his shoulder, eyes bulging with terror, cheek blazing red from a fresh blow. Next to Jennifer's tall frame he looked tiny and thin and vulnerable.

"Mummy!" he gasped, his voice strangled with panic.

I tried to speak but no words would come, my jaw locked with fright. The terror was rising up inside me, filling my chest, filling my throat, bile rising into my mouth. I felt sick. With my hands held up in a gesture of surrender, I took another step toward them.

"Stay where you are!" Jennifer barked. Her eyes were wild, with a strange intensity that gave a cold, hard edge to my fear. She looked *mad*. As if something inside her had been stretched and stretched over and over again until finally, decisively, it had snapped.

I stopped.

"Jennifer, please, please don't hurt him, I'm begging you." My voice seemed thin and distant. "It's OK, Daniel. It's going to be all right."

Jennifer glared at me.

"He told you, didn't he? Sean told you everything."

"Yes."

"So I need to make you see. Make you understand."

"Please just come away from the edge a little bit."

She shook her head.

"Remember when we first came out here, Kate? When Jake was here, on this spot, right where I'm standing now?"

"Yes, I remember."

"Do you remember what I said to him?"

I searched my memory. It seemed like a hundred years ago.

"I don't know . . . we just wanted him to be safe, for all the children to be safe."

"I told him something important: whatever you do, don't look down. Because if you look down, you fall."

"Yes," I said breathlessly, "I remember now."

"Well, my son is looking down now, Kate. My boy is looking right into the abyss, just like yours. And you're the only one who can save him. How does that feel? To have the power of life and death over someone's child?"

"We can both save him, Jen. I know your boys mean everything to you. Just like Daniel does to me."

"Your son. My son. They mean the same, to us. So I had to find something to make you understand." She gestured toward my terror-stricken son with her free hand. "To persuade you to keep our secret. You'd do the same for your kids, wouldn't you?"

"Believe me, Jennifer, I understand what you—"

"This is what you'll do to my Jake if you tell the police, your *colleagues*." She shook the handful of Daniel's T-shirt that was clutched in her white-knuckled fist, and he wobbled on the edge, arms windmilling crazily to keep his balance. His glasses fell off, spinning end over end into the gorge. "This is what it means. You'll ruin him. He won't be able to cope with it. You'll kill him, just as surely as if you'd done it yourself."

Bile flooded my throat again and I almost gagged. The rain, pounding and incessant, hid my tears.

"Please, Jennifer!"

From the trees on our right, Rowan emerged slowly with a man I didn't recognize at her side. He was young, maybe early twenties, slim and clean shaven, holding a police ID wallet open in front of him so that Jennifer could see it. He said something in French to Jennifer, but she gave him barely a glance before turning her attention back to me.

"Promise me, Kate."

"I promise," I said, my voice cracking. "I'll do anything, *please*."

"Swear it on your son's life."

"I swear on his life. I won't say a word, not to anyone."

Daniel suddenly seemed to wobble on the edge and for a second I thought he would pull her over with him, but she braced herself and pulled him back at the last second.

"Oh God, please just let him go, Jen!"

I would have told her anything, *anything,* to step away from the edge and give my son back to me. She seemed to sense it, too.

The young policeman said something to her in rapid-fire French again.

Rowan said, "The detective says step away from the side, Jennifer."

But Jennifer was staring at me.

"Izzy was going to tell you, she was going to lay it all out for you. I couldn't let that happen, but she wouldn't listen to reason. She just refused to see my side of it, *Jake's* side of it." Her voice took on a hard, unyielding tone. "I didn't mean to . . . what happened wasn't what you think. She just slipped."

"I believe you, Jennifer. I do."

"Do you really?"

"Absolutely. Of course."

She smiled, just for a second, before it faltered and died on her lips. "You know what, Kate? You've always been too honest. Too straitlaced. And you've always been a crappy liar."

"I'm not lying!"

The sky flashed with lightning as another blast of thunder ripped over our heads.

In that instant another figure burst from the trees on our left, a stocky, bearded man in a jacket and jeans, sprinting hard at Jennifer and Daniel with his arms outstretched.

Everything seemed to slide into slow motion.

The bearded man's jacket flew up to reveal a pistol and handcuffs on his belt. He shouted commands in French. Then he was losing his footing on the sodden ground, stumbling forward, lunging with open hands, trying to grab something, anything, to stop the child going over—but he was too slow, too late, the yards between them too far. I started forward, my feet leaden. Jennifer turned toward the bearded man, flinching backward. The other policeman lunged forward, too, hands grabbing at her, grasping her arm and reaching across her chest.

Jennifer released her grip on Daniel's T-shirt. Hands flailed toward him, grabbing at the empty air. But he was already overbalancing, tipping, arms extended, reaching out to grab something, anything. He was dropping too fast, too fast, and we were too slow.

All I could see was my son's face. All I could hear was one word.

"Mummy!"

He turned toward me at the last second, his skinny arms outstretched, hands grasping, eyes wide with terror. Disappearing over the edge. There, and then gone.

My boy.

Falling.

ONE MONTH LATER

77

We shuffled slowly through the churchyard under a slate gray English sky.

Hundreds of black-clad mourners, faces pale with grief, moving in silence, conversation rendered meaningless, pointless on this day, in this place. Friends and family gathered, babies and toddlers, children and teenagers, parents and grandparents, old and young. Too many who were young. Far too many.

Like a blade sliding into my heart, I remembered the last time I had been inside this church.

Daniel's baptism.

The tears came again and I felt Lucy's arm slip through mine, holding me up. We filed in through the arched stone doorway and took our places at the front, soft organ music playing beneath the whispers of shuffling feet. It was impossible, inconceivable that we should be here, having to endure the unendurable. It was not right, not *natural,* that we should be here in grief for one so young. This wasn't the way it was supposed to be. The normal order of things was turned on its head.

And yet, here we were. Ready to say goodbye for the last time.

I had cried every day since it happened, set off by anything and everything. Every morning I woke from restless nightmares, my cheeks wet with tears. I was numb from crying, hollowed out with shock and grief. I couldn't work, couldn't eat, barely slept. Everything I thought I'd known had turned out to be wrong, and nothing would ever be the same.

Rowan appeared at my side and we hugged each other. Her pregnancy—the secret she had been keeping from her husband, from her potential new business partners, from everyone—was just about starting to show. It was her pregnancy test that I'd found at the villa, discarded somewhere she thought Russ wouldn't find it. She handed me a fresh tissue and squeezed my hand before going to a pew with Russ and Odette. I could hear the low voices of people in the row behind, asking one another where Jennifer was, snatches of whispered conversation passed back and forth:

Why isn't she here?

Haven't you heard?

Oh, that's just awful.

Can it be true?

I can't believe it.

And then the abrupt silence as they realized we were sitting right in front of them.

Jennifer was not here. Of course she wasn't. She

was where she had been ever since the day it happened, in jail in Béziers, and she was not expected to get bail while prosecutors argued about the charges she should face. We had agreed on a story, a narrative of what had happened, to ensure that Lucy and Jake were shielded from blame—in exchange for our silence on everything else.

The thought of her made me cold with fury.

Ahead of us, a small coffin covered in white lilies was laid gently on a stand by the altar. Sean stepped back with the other pallbearers as they turned to the cross and bowed, as one. How he found the strength to do this, I will never know.

He returned to me, his face ashen.

Lucy cried quietly beside her father. She had finally opened up to me about Alex Bayley, about what went on between them and what he did to her. For today she has agreed to play the piano, a piece by Debussy, but I wondered if she would be capable when we reached that part of the service. I was certainly in no fit state to do a reading, or a tribute, or anything so private in such a public forum. Sean would speak for us both.

We had talked about what he will say. The words he will choose when he walks to the front of the church and stands at the lectern. There is so much to say, a world of emotion and experience and shared life, and yet words are supremely inadequate. Words are clumsy and blunt, hopelessly crude as a means of expressing our love, our loss, our heartbreak. But words are all we have now.

My mind drifts back to France, and I think of a boy. My brave boy, the day before *that* fateful day. I had found him with cuts and grazes on his hands and arms, mud and blood on his knees, tears on his face. His favorite T-shirt torn. Still shaking with adrenaline but refusing, steadfastly, to tell me what had happened. Only later did I find out about the dare: to jump across the crescent gap at the cliff edge.

An *initiation ceremony* to be part of an older boys' gang. A jump that fell *just* too short.

A moment of pure panic, his hands scrabbling for a lifeline.

A thick looping tree root below the edge, just strong enough to hold a small boy's weight.

It is this fragment of knowledge that saves his life the next day, in a thunderstorm, when I watch him disappear before my eyes at the very same spot. When Jennifer releases her grip and I watch him dropping into the gorge, turning at the last second as he falls, but he's not turning to see me. He's turning to grab onto that tree root, onto life. His scared eyes never leave mine as the two French policemen haul him back to safety.

Not bad for a nerd, Mummy, he'd said through his tears.

No, I'd said through mine, *not bad at all.*

Beside me, Daniel studied the order of service, his little hand tight in mine. The bandages were gone now. I squeezed it gently and he squeezed back, once, twice. Our secret code.

Chris, the new partner Izzy had been so excited about, sat next to him.

Or Christine, to use her full name.

Of course I had *assumed* in France that her new love was a man, but Izzy had never actually said that. I knew now why she had been cagey, not revealing too many details too soon—she had wanted to tell us at her own pace, in her own way. She had been so looking forward to starting that next chapter in her life, so excited to make the most of her second chance.

But that story will never be told. Not now.

The priest stood up.

"Dearly beloved, we meet here today to honor and pay tribute to the life of Isobel Margaret O'Rourke. Or, as most of you knew her, Izzy. Loving daughter, devoted sister, doting auntie, a true and loyal friend."

My throat tightened and I waited for the tears to start again. But this time my eyes stayed dry.

A true and loyal friend.

78

An email arrived the day after the funeral, from an unrecognized address.

The subject line said simply: *Reminder.*

There was no text, just a link to a video. I knew what it was and who had sent it as soon as I saw the link, but I clicked on it anyway. Watched the video again, even though I knew it line for line, word for word. Every second seared into my brain.

You want him to have an accident?

Lucy's voice in response.

Yeah. Yeah I do.

It was still secret, still password protected and private, only five of us now who even knew it existed. Me, Sean, Jennifer, and—of course—Ethan and Jake.

I read the subject line again.

Reminder.

A reminder of my promise, my oath to Jennifer to keep our secret. I had given her my word. And Jennifer knew she could trust me because of who I was, because she knew what I was like: *straight as a die*. Make a deal and stick to it.

But we had all seen what secrets did to people, even to the very best of friends. Even to a friendship that had endured for half a lifetime. The secret that now bound Jennifer and me together had also torn us apart. I had been thinking about that a lot, since returning from France, about secrets, and lies, and taking responsibility for what we've done. About the ghosts that follow us, the damage we leave behind.

About justice.

I thought about that now as I sat in my car, on a suburban street in Ealing.

In one way I was grateful to her for sending me the reminder email, because it helped to make the situation perfectly clear, in case I had been in any doubt: safety for Lucy meant justice denied for Izzy, for Alex Bayley. It meant this one careless comment would be hanging over my daughter forever, with the power to wreck her brilliant future, even though she was not the one who had got behind the wheel of the car.

It meant lying—for the rest of our lives.

Unless I took the initiative.

Jennifer had made her choice. She had been willing to sacrifice anything—even my son's life—to protect her own children. She had shown me the way.

Now it was my turn to make a choice.

A true and loyal friend.

Two people were dead, their lives snuffed out. And if we allowed their deaths to go unpunished, we were all as good as lost. Their loved ones deserved to know why: the truth, the whole truth, and nothing but the truth.

Most of it, anyway.

Izzy's family deserved justice. Alex Bayley's family, too.

And as I now knew, sometimes justice needed a helping hand.

Checking up and down the street one last time, I got out of my car into the morning drizzle. Heart beating wildly in my chest, I opened my umbrella and held it low over my head as I walked up the short drive to the house, through the side gate to the garden and the back door. I carried a clipboard and a shoulder bag, with a lanyard around my neck, in a trouser suit with a white blouse plus clear-lens glasses. To the casual observer I was just another anonymous charity fundraiser knocking on doors and generally making a nuisance of myself. Worse still, a local councillor looking for votes or a Jehovah's Witness giving away copies of *The Watchtower.* All to be avoided, if possible.

The house backed onto a railway line and was not overlooked by the neighbors on either side. From my pocket, I pulled on a pair of disposable latex gloves and plastic covers for my shoes.

No traces. No fingerprints.

From my other pocket I produced the back door key that I'd had for years. With one last quick look back to the street, I eased the door open and let myself in. The cats—Pickle and Maisy—were onto me straightaway, trotting into the kitchen and rubbing around my shins. To them I was just the person who fed them when Alistair and Jennifer were away. My arrival meant food.

"Not today, ladies," I said, shutting the back door behind me. "Sorry."

I went through the house quickly, double-checking all the rooms. I'd watched them all leave this morning but wanted to be sure. The boys were at school and Alistair was at work, none of them due back for hours. I hated myself for what I was about to do, hated the creepiness of skulking around my friends' empty house. But I had to do it, to protect Lucy. To protect my family.

There were two things that needed to be done.

First, the car.

From the hallway, I went through the connecting door into the garage. In the days after Jake's hit-and-run, as they corresponded secretly on Messenger, Sean had counseled Jennifer against taking the car in for immediate repairs because he thought it would look too suspicious. *Better to wait a few weeks until the lad's out of the hospital and everything's calmed down a bit.* I was grateful, now, for his caution. Jennifer's blue Volvo was here in the garage, still with minor damage to the front offside wing and the hood—dents and scratches in the bodywork where the car had hit Alex Bayley. It looked as if someone had tried to wash it down, but no matter: it was virtually impossible to get rid of every small trace of blood. I took my tools from my bag and chipped away some small flecks of paint from one of the damaged areas, sealing them inside a plastic evidence bag. I would make sure they found their way into the collection of physical evidence on the case.

Next, I went up to Jake's bedroom.

Sean had explained it to me. *Every file—every document, every video, every email—leaves a unique footprint, a trail. If you have the right tools, and you know what to look for, you can map out the whole life cycle of a particular file, its whole family tree, including how many copies have been made and where they've been sent or saved.* He had followed the same process after hacking into Alex Bayley's accounts to track down and delete copies of the naked video of our daughter.

But the video of her inciting a crime was far more important, the one Jennifer had uploaded to Video-Vault. Sean's investigations discovered only two additional copies: one on a PC and another on an iPhone. Cell phones were strictly forbidden at school on pain of a week-long confiscation, and I was relieved to find Ethan's phone where I hoped it would be—plugged in to charge in his bedroom. I took out the device that Sean had given me, no bigger than a USB drive, purchased on the dark web. I plugged it into Ethan's phone and watched as it wiped the device completely blank—every file, every photo, every video deleted—and returned it to factory settings.

I unplugged the USB device and did the same to

the PC in the study, deleting every single file in its memory. *One copy of the video left.*

A few years ago, in a flap because she'd let her car insurance lapse while they were abroad, Jennifer had asked me to log into her account from this very same PC and renew her coverage before they made the journey back from Gatwick. She kept all her passwords on a couple sheets of handwritten A4 clipped into a black plastic binder.

I opened the second desk drawer and dug beneath a stack of bank statements, found the black plastic binder. Same place. Same old Jennifer. The username and password for her VideoVault account was the newest addition at the bottom of the list. I took out a cheap pay-as-you-go phone and sent a text to an identical handset—both of which would soon be on their way to a landfill site.

Ten miles away, in central London, my husband went to work at his keyboard. A text pinged on my throwaway phone two minutes later.

It's done x

I took out my regular cell phone, went to the email with the subject line *Reminder,* and clicked on the link to the video for the second time this morning.

Error
File not found

I went back to the email and clicked on it again, just to double-check it was gone.

Error
File not found

No copies left.

Finally I checked the bedroom and the garage again, making sure to leave everything exactly as it was, before making my way back to the kitchen. The cats sat on the countertop, staring at me, still expecting to be fed. I put down a little bit of dry food in their bowls and sent a quick reply to my husband on the pay-as-you-go phone.

Same here x

Outside the back door, I took off the plastic overshoes and latex gloves and put them back into my jacket pocket. Umbrella up, clipboard under my arm, I shut the side gate behind me and walked back to my car. The rain was heavier now, a steady downpour signaling the end of summer and the beginning of a cold, dark autumn.

Turning the keys in the ignition, I drove away.

I knew what she would do when the video evidence of Lucy's involvement in the crime was erased. Jennifer would take the fall for all of it, take all of the blame on herself for the deaths of both Izzy and Alex. Because admitting one would mean admitting the other—and to keep her son out of it, she would have to keep Lucy out of it, too. She would provide a human shield for her son.

But it would be justice for Izzy, at least.

I hoped that would be enough.

79

DS FOSTER

Detective Sergeant Hayley Foster pulled up and parked, squinting into the low September sunshine.

"OK," she said. "What number are we on now?"

Her colleague, a brand-new DC she was babysitting through his first week out of uniform, ran his finger down the page of a file in his lap. The sheet showed a list of names and addresses, most with large ticks added in messy blue pen.

"This is the thirteenth," he said. "Only three more to go after this one."

"You know, Rob, thirteen is my lucky number."

"Really?"

"No." She sighed heavily, unclipping her seat belt. "Come on, let's get it done."

She got out of the car, taking the list from the young DC as they crossed the street and walked up the short drive to the house. It was their second day of driving around, knocking on doors, ticking names off a list. She was starting to suspect that their search area was not large enough. If these addresses were all duds, they'd have to expand to take in the whole of west and north London, and so on, and so on. The Bayley hit-and-run had been kicked up the priority list since the boy's death, with more media attention and more pressure from the powers that be to get a result. Luckily, a closer reexamination of the victim's clothes by forensics earlier this week had revealed microscopic fragments of dark blue paint that had been previously overlooked. Further analysis had matched the paint to a Volvo V40.

The paint fragments had been missed on first examination.

There were a total of sixteen matching cars registered in Ealing, Acton, and Wembley, in the immediate vicinity of the incident and the starting place for renewed police inquiries.

DS Foster consulted the list in her hand and rang the doorbell.

A bearded man opened the door, late forties, unkempt, and red eyed.

"Yes?"

"Alistair Marsh?"

"Yes?"

She held up her police ID in its wallet.

"My name's DS Foster and this"—she indicated her colleague—"is DC McKevitt. Would you mind if we came in for a few minutes?"

"Why?"

"We're carrying out an investigation into a hit-and-run. A teenage boy was knocked off his bike and killed not far from here. You may have read about it, seen it on the news?"

"Indeed." He stood up a little straighter. "What's that got to do with me?"

"Are you the owner of a blue Volvo V40?" She read out the registration.

Alistair crossed his arms. "No."

DS Foster checked her list again. "It's registered at this—"

"It's my wife's car."

"Jennifer Marsh?"

"Correct."

"Is the vehicle here?"

"In the garage."

"We're going to need to look at it."

For a moment she thought he was going to argue, but then he just gave a quick nod. "I see."

"Is your wife here? We'd like to talk to her as well."

"She's . . . no, she's not here. Not at the moment."

"Can you tell us when she's due back?"

Alistair shook his head.

"No," he said, his voice lowering. "Jennifer's . . . in France. It could be some time before she's back."

"A vacation?"

"It was a vacation, at least to begin with. But it's turned into a rather extended stay."

"Really? Why's that, sir?"

Alistair looked from one detective to the other, his shoulders sagging.

"I think you'd better come in, officers."

He ushered the two detectives inside and shut the door softly behind them.

ACKNOWLEDGMENTS

I remember when *The Vacation* started coming together. It was on my birthday, a long lunch with my wife talking about story and characters, plotlines and locations, when all the different elements that had been going around in my head for a while started to fall into place. So, to Sally—thanks, as always. A big shout-out also to her longtime friends Charlotte, Jenni, and Rachel: the fact that you four have been going away for long weekends together for years is a total coincidence (honest).

Thanks as ever to my excellent agent, Camilla Bolton, whose experience, guidance, and enthusiasm were crucial in the creation of this novel. And to her colleagues at Darley Anderson—Sheila, Mary, Kristina, Rosanna, Roya—you are the best.

My brilliant editors at Bonnier Zaffre, Sophie Orme and Margaret Stead, helped to make this story better in every way. Thanks also to Jennie Rothwell, Francesca Russell, and Felice McKeown, for all their hard work behind the scenes on this and my previous novels.

Massive thanks to *you,* for picking up this book in the first place. To everyone who has recommended it to a friend or had kind words to say about this or my previous two books—I really do appreciate it.

Likewise, to all the bloggers who have given time and space to my stories, the wonderful library staff who have asked me to come and talk to readers, the festival organizers who have invited me to speak at their events—sincere thanks. I'm very grateful to Dan Donson of Waterstones Nottingham, for providing a wonderful venue for my book launches and giving me the opportunity to meet one of my very favorite writers, Michael Connelly.

Thanks to Dr. Gill Sare, for advice on medical matters. I'm also indebted to Paul Boyer, French wine-maker extraordinaire, who was very generous with his time talking about all things Languedoc (his organic wines also come highly recommended). Thank you to my fellow author Diane Jeffrey, for help with the French text, and for putting me in touch with Michael Moran who answered my questions on French policing. Anyone who has been to Autignac or the surrounding area will know I've taken a few liberties with the local geography, for story purposes, but it remains an absolutely delightful little village in a beautiful part of southern France.

To my children, Sophie and Tom—thanks for being two of my first readers, and for picking up things that no one else has seen. To my mum and dad, for their continuing support, and to Jenny and Bernard, John and Sue for promoting my books at home and abroad (you really should be on commission).

This book is dedicated to my big brothers, Ralph and Ollie, with whom I shared a lot of holidays when we were growing up—luckily, they were never like Jake and Ethan (although they did bury me in a hole in the garden once). Thanks for your kind words of encouragement, your ideas, and your interest in my writing over the years. The beers are on me.